DARK ANGEL

JOHN SANDFORD

DARK ANGEL

G. P. PUTNAM'S SONS
NEW YORK

PUTNAM
— EST. 1838 —

G. P. PUTNAM'S SONS
Publishers Since 1838
An imprint of Penguin Random House LLC
penguinrandomhouse.com

Copyright © 2023 by John Sandford

Library of Congress Cataloging-in-Publication Data

Names: Sandford, John, 1944 February 23– author.
Title: Dark angel / John Sandford.
Description: New York : G. P. Putnam's Sons, [2023] | Series: Letty
Davenport ; volume 2 |
Identifiers: LCCN 2022059972 (print) | LCCN 2022059973 (ebook) |
ISBN 9780593422410 (hardcover) | ISBN 9780593422427 (ebook)
Subjects: LCGFT: Thrillers (Fiction) | Novels.
Classification: LCC PS3569.A516 D366 2023 (print) | LCC PS3569.A516
(ebook) | DDC 813/.54—dc23/eng/20221213
LC record available at https://lccn.loc.gov/2022059972
LC ebook record available at https://lccn.loc.gov/2022059973

Printed in the United States of America
1st Printing

ONE

In the summer of 2021, the woman flew into Miami International with nothing to declare but the clothes she stood in, a phony passport, an iPhone with a broken screen, and a ballpoint pen. The pen didn't work, but did conceal a two-inch-long razor-sharp blade that could be used to slice open a carotid artery (for example).

She looked more than tired. Exhausted, but fighting it. She had dishwater blond hair that hadn't been washed recently, a mottled tan, turquoise eyes, and a thin white scar that extended from one nostril down across her lips to her chin.

The clothes she stood in were speckled with mud and what the young Customs and Border Patrol officer thought might be dried blood; the clothes reeked of old sweat and something else, like swamp water.

Her ragged tee-shirt—the only clothing above her waist, worn paper thin, he could see her nipples pushing out against it—featured a drawing of a llama with a legend that said "Como Se Llama?" which the young officer understood as a Spanish pun. She had flown in on United, from the Aeropuerto Internacional Jorge Chávez in Lima, Peru. How she'd gotten on the plane, he couldn't even guess.

The CBP officer was giving her his best no-admittance stink-eye as he thumbed through her passport. He asked, "Your name is Angeles Chavez?"

The woman shook her head: "No."

"What?" Hadn't heard that before; he checked her turquoise-green eyes. "Then what is it?"

"I'm not allowed to tell you that."

He was about to call for help when the head of the CBP unit stepped up behind his booth, took the passport from his hand, and said, "Let her in."

Hadn't heard that before, either. He let her in.

A man in a plutonium suit and tie was standing a few feet behind his boss, rolling a wooden matchstick between his lips. When the woman whose name wasn't Angeles Chavez stepped past the CPB booth, the man took the matchstick out of his mouth, grinned, and asked, "How you doin', honey-bun?"

"I think I got a leech up my ass," the woman said.

So THEN LETTY DAVENPORT was sitting on a battered swivel chair in a near-empty room on the second floor of a warehouse off Statesville Road in Charlotte, North Carolina, watching a door on another warehouse across the street.

August was slipping away, but the heat was holding on with

both hands, and the warehouse was only somewhat air-conditioned. When she lifted her arms to look through her binoculars, she could smell her armpits, if only faintly, and her face was . . . moist.

Letty was twenty-five, of average height, dancer-slender and dancer-muscled, with dark hair that fell to the nape of her neck. Crystalline blue eyes. A whiff of Tom Ford's *Fucking Fabulous* perfume mixed with the perspiration. She was an investigator for the inspector general of the Department of Homeland Security, although her real boss was a U.S. senator.

She'd suffered a spasm of fame, or notoriety, after a shoot-out in the Rio Grande town of Pershing, Texas, the year before, in which she'd killed two men. She'd shot to death a third man earlier in the same trip.

All for God and Country; Country, anyway.

Behind her, in the long, wide, near-empty room was a ping-pong table. Three youngish FBI agents were taking turns being bad at ping-pong when they weren't trying to determine her relationship status.

Nothing had come through the door across the street in the two hours that Letty had been watching it, but she wasn't bored. She had a laptop where it was supposed to be—on her lap—and she was riding on a wi-fi signal from the food wholesaler next door.

From Bing, the search app, she'd learned that South Koreans now disliked China more than they disliked Japan, that housing prices might be peaking. She'd also read in the *New York Times* about five fascinating things she could do this weekend, if she lived in New York City, which she didn't, and if she was easily fascinated, which she wasn't.

Without warning, a door popped open behind her.

Letty swiveled and reflexively picked up the Sig 938 from the windowsill as a woman came through the door, saw the pistol, lifted her hands and said, "Don't shoot."

Letty: "Cartwright?"

"That's me." The woman with the turquoise-green eyes had a fresh set of clothing. "I wanted to be here for this."

"I was told you had a leech up your ass."

"All taken care of," Cartwright said. She waved to the three FBI agents, but strolled over to Letty. "Tequila works wonders, when properly applied. You know. By drinking it."

Letty smiled and said, "We were supposed to get a call to say you were on the way up."

Cartwright shrugged. "I dunno. The drop-off guy just dropped me off and said to go to the second floor."

"Sounds about right for government work," Letty said. She looked back across the street. "Bogard and Holsum haven't shown up yet. Dupree walked around the truck and looked inside, an hour ago. That was the last time I saw him. The feds over there"—nodded at the FBI agents—"are all looking for dates, so you might keep that in mind."

"I will." Cartwright looked through the dirt-spotted window at the semi-trailer backed up to the loading dock across the street. Like Letty, she was average height and dancer-slender. Her blond hair was pulled back in a short efficient ponytail. Like Letty, she was wearing jeans, but with a khaki overshirt to hide her pistol. She was seven years older than Letty, but they might have been sisters.

"Got a good spot here; how long does it take to get across the street?"

"From here, standing start, eleven seconds to get across the room, down the fire stairs, to the exit, which is right below us," Letty said. "They'll see us coming."

"You think they could be trouble?"

"Don't know. I interviewed Dupree. You should have gotten a transcript."

"I did. Sounded fake-cooperative," Cartwright said.

"Exactly. But, I got him jumpy, with the urge to move. When I saw him, he wasn't carrying. On the other hand, he's an office worker in a government building. Bogard and Holsum are the reddest of necks and they're freelance. Even if they're not carrying, I'd be surprised if they didn't have a few guns around."

"And this will go off around six o'clock?"

"Yes. Most of the employees get out around four-thirty. I think they'll wait until it's quiet. Give it an hour or so."

The FBI agents had given up on the ping-pong and come over to meet Cartwright. One of them said, "An hour or so if it happens at all."

"It will," Letty said. "They want to move it fast, before I have more time to dig around in there."

Letty had a CI, a confidential informant, inside the FEMA warehouse. The CI said Dupree, Bogard, and Holsum were planning to steal eight forklifts from the FEMA warehouse; the CI also wanted Dupree's job, so there was that.

The three-and-a-half-ton-capacity, rough-terrain, four-wheel-drive forklifts were valued at $12,500 each, making eight of them worth $100,000 if sold in Charlotte.

If sold in Chancay, Peru, to JuFen Industries, a Chinese company working on the construction of a spanking-new Pacific Ocean port, they'd go for twice that price, less the $1,200 apiece that it cost to ship them.

Small potatoes compared to the $1,500,000 they'd gotten for the five hundred FEMA army-style field tents they'd sold to the same Chinese company to shelter the families of its Peruvian workers. Still, two hundred grand is two hundred grand, especially when it was tax-free.

Cartwright had spotted the tents while doing research in Chancay for an Unspecified Agency of the U.S. government. Her research had included cutting serial number labels off several of the tents, which had later been identified as FEMA property. That vandalism, when discovered by a Chinese security officer, had led to a brief chase across the desert and then an unscheduled swim in the Rio Chancay, followed by a hitchhiking trip to Lima in clothing stolen off a clothesline.

After Cartwright arrived in Miami, the Unspecified Agency had dropped a note to the powers that be at the Department of Homeland Security, and Letty had been sent to Charlotte to investigate the status of the tents.

In the warehouse where they should have been, she'd found an empty space. Dupree had explained that the tents had been shipped to Africa to shelter children at a free school, that all the paperwork had been perfect, and he hoped the kids appreciated their new homes.

Nope.

CARTWRIGHT, AS IT HAPPENED, wasn't a great ping-pong player, but she was better than any of the feds. After they'd chatted for a while, to bring her up to the minute on their plan and determine her relationship status, she held the table for six consecutive games, until Letty called, "We got Bogard and Holsum."

DARK ANGEL

The two had just arrived at the parking lot across the street in Holsum's pimped-out red Chevy Camaro, and Holsum was talking on his cell phone as he got out of the driver's side. Letty was watching them through a pair of Leica binoculars. When Bogard got out of the passenger side of the car, he did a hitch-up to his pants and Cartwright asked, "You get that?" and Letty said, "Yeah," and one of the feds asked, "What?" and Letty said, "Bogard's carrying."

Another of the feds said, "Let's gear it up," and the three agents began pulling on armor.

Dupree opened a door, and Bogard and Holsum disappeared inside. Two minutes later, the overhead door at a loading dock rolled up, and Letty said, "Let 'em load, let 'em load."

A minute after that, the first of the forklifts rolled through the loading door, across the dock, and into the semi-trailer, with Holsum driving, Dupree keeping watch, and Bogard sucking on a Tootsie Pop.

"Go," Letty said, and the three feds headed for the stairway fire door at a trot.

Fifteen seconds later, as Letty and Cartwright watched, the three agents were running across the street, guns in hand. Dupree saw them coming, apparently shouted a warning to the others, and turned and ran into the warehouse.

Bogard, who'd been watching from the other side of the semi-trailer, jumped off the dock and began running to the far side of the warehouse. The feds didn't see him because their line of sight was blocked by the truck.

Letty headed for the door, her 938 in her hand.

Cartwright, following: "What?"

7

JOHN SANDFORD

"Bogard can't get out that way. The chain-link fence hooks on to the next warehouse. He'll have to run down an alley at the other end of the building . . . He'll be coming back to us."

Eleven seconds later, they were out the door with Letty leading the way up the street, Cartwright next to her shoulder, both of them running easily. One of the feds saw them running and shouted something at the other two agents and began running after them, but fifty yards back.

The warehouse was a full block long and Bogard wasn't a runner: he was overweight with the red face of a longtime drinker and smoker; but, he was carrying.

As they came up to the alley, Letty split left and Cartwright went right, and when Bogard staggered out from behind the building, Letty screamed, "Stop! Stop or we'll kill you!" Bogard turned toward them, almost fell, saw three guns pointed at him as the fed came up, and put his hands over his head.

"I'm having a heart attack," he said, and to prove it, he toppled over, hitting the ground facedown, like two hundred and fifty pounds of uncooked beef; he half rolled, clutching his chest, and groaned.

The agent said, "Good gosh! I think he really is." He pulled back Bogard's shirt and dug a chrome revolver out of his belt.

Bogard groaned again. "Call an ambulance . . ."

Letty was already on her phone, calling 9-1-1.

"Another beautiful day in the American Southland," Cartwright drawled, looking down at Bogard as Letty finished the 9-1-1 call. She turned to Letty and asked, "What would you have done if he'd pulled?"

"Shot him," Letty said. "I would have tried not to kill him with the first shot."

"Then you're a better woman than I am," Cartwright said. "I would have shot him in the eye."

"You think you could have hit him in the eye from thirty or forty feet, when he was moving?" Letty asked.

"You're looking at the best shot in North Carolina right now," Cartwright said.

Letty slipped her 938 back in her jeans, smiled, showing some teeth, and said, "No, I don't think so."

Cartwright, cocking her head: "Really."

Letty nodded: "Yes. Really."

Bogard belched, loudly, and the fed said, "Maybe it was just gas."

Bogard moaned and cried, "Help me . . ."

Cartwright: "Gotta stay away from that barbeque, man."

Made Letty smile, but she turned her face away so Bogard wouldn't see it.

A WEEK LATER, Letty was sitting in her closet-sized office behind a half-open yellow metal door, in the basement of the Senate Office Building in Washington, DC. She was struggling with the executive summary of the full report she'd just finished writing. She'd learned that if you want your report noticed by a Senate panel, keep the summary under two hundred words. Longer than that, and the senators started getting chapped lips, which they didn't like.

". . . intelligence reports indicate that all five hundred tents were being used in a tent city operated by JuFen Industries, a Chinese construction company working on the new Pacific Ocean port being built by the Chinese in Chancay, Peru. The eight forklifts had been illicitly purchased from FEMA stocks by the same company . . ."

―――――

Cartwright knocked on Letty's door and Letty turned to look at her: "Barbara. Where'd you come from?"

"Across the river. I have an invitation for you." She thrust an ivory-colored, heavy-paper envelope at Letty.

Letty took it. "An invitation? I . . ."

Cartwright was already walking away, turning to say only, "Come or not."

Letty looked at the outside of the envelope. "Letty Davenport" was written in a neat female hand, in blue-black ink from a fountain pen.

Beneath her name was another legend:

Washington Ladies Peace-Maker Society: You're Invited.

"You gotta be kidding me," Letty said aloud. She called her friend Billy Greet. "I got an invitation from the Ladies Peace-Maker Society."

"I thought they were . . . a rumor. What does it say?"

Letty: "I don't know. I haven't opened the envelope."

"Well, open it."

Letty opened the envelope and took out a card and read it into the phone: "You are cordially invited to a reception for Ms. Elaine Shelton at the clubhouse of the Washington Ladies Peace-Maker Society. Respondents only, please."

The date of the reception was September 25, a Saturday, the location on Cemetery Lane near Mount Pleasant, Virginia. The note specified "practical attire" and "personal equipment."

"Who's Ms. Elaine Shelton?" Letty asked. "I never heard of her."

"Look at the medals list from the last Olympics," Greet said.

"Really? Huh. Think I should go?"

"I . . . dunno. There's some odd rumors about them. I don't know much more. Maybe . . . a gun club?"

"That's what I've heard. Do you think when it says 'personal equipment' . . . "

"I guess. What else could it be?"

Practical attire.

After obsessing on the phrase for two weeks, Letty went with jeans, a tee-shirt under a loose nylon long-sleeved Orvis fishing shirt, and lightweight hiking boots. The drive out to the Ladies clubhouse, in her hybrid Highlander, took almost two hours from her apartment in Arlington.

Autumn was breaking out in brilliant, spangled color, making the trip into the Blue Ridge spectacular, all that red, yellow, and orange against the remaining green of the forest, and a flawless robin's-egg sky.

She drove most of the way with the driver's-side window down, so she could smell the dusty, astringent scent of the roadside wild-flowers. The clubhouse, she'd imagined, would be something like a southern mansion, long broad porch, white pillars, a place where George Washington or Robert E. Lee might have stopped to take a leak.

She found Cemetery Lane on the main road out of Mount Pleasant, a place which barely qualified as a hamlet. A few minutes north, a gravel road branched to the west, taking her past a small, unkempt cemetery guarded by a rusting barbed-wire fence strung on rotting wooden posts. The track took her up a hill, and then over a ridge and down into a heavily wooded valley.

The road narrowed as she went along, went from gravel to packed dirt, weeds growing up in the middle of the two-track, all of it spotted with fallen red and yellow maple leaves. The track passed through an open metal gate, and finally ended at what she guessed must have been the "clubhouse"—a row of three green-painted industrial-sized Quonset huts. They were neatly kept with stone steps and zinnia gardens around the foundations. But still . . . Quonsets. No porch with white pillars.

Two of the Quonsets showed open doors toward the parking lot. She could see farm-style equipment in one—two corn-green John Deere Gators, an orange Kubota backhoe, walls hung with what looked like landscaping tools. In the other, she could see a group of women in practical attire, standing, talking.

There were thirty or so cars in the parking lot, with another following her in. Letty parked and sat for a moment. The woman who'd followed her in hopped out of her car, opened the back door, and took out a five-foot-long nylon rifle case, slipped it over her shoulder, twiddled fingers at Letty, and then walked up the stone steps and through the open door of the center Quonset.

All right.

Letty got out, took her equipment case out of the back—black nylon, soft-sided, smaller than a briefcase—and walked up the steps to the Quonset. There were thirty or thirty-five women standing down the length of the building, chatting, some of them drinking from bottles of water, all casually dressed, as Letty was, which immediately took some pressure off.

A fortyish woman caught Letty's eye, smiled, and walked over and said, "Letty! So happy you could join us. Very nice work you did in Pershing."

Letty said, "Thank you, thanks for inviting me." She tried not to crane her neck around, though there really wasn't much to see—a series of what looked like small offices and storage rooms, built with drywall and painted a government tan, a concrete floor. The largest room showed a table with some energy bars and cookies, bottles of water sticking out of a basin filled with ice, and several ranks of folding chairs.

An oversized reproduction of a nineteenth-century newspaper advertisement, four feet long and two feet high, was framed and hung on a wall in the middle of the building. The advertisement showed an exploded view, an engineering drawing, of a Colt Single-Action Army revolver, the M1873, in .45 Colt. The gun was also known "in the trade" as a Peace-Maker, according to the ancient advertisement, though Letty had only seen it spelled as one word, Peacemaker, like the comic book superhero.

Hence, Letty thought, the Washington Ladies Peace-Maker Society, with a nineteenth-century hyphen.

"I see you brought equipment," the woman said.

Letty nodded and held up the case: "I wasn't exactly sure what I could use, but it's a Staccato XC."

"Excellent. What kind of sight?"

A few other women drifted over, to listen: "A Leupold Delta-Point Pro," Letty said. "The gun is pretty much stock. I did replace the grips with checkered cherry."

"We have a couple of members shooting Staccatos," one of the other women said. "Nice gear."

Cartwright threaded her way through the crowd. "You decided to show up."

"Thought I'd give it a try," Letty said. She held up the case. "Brought my good gun."

"Still carrying the 938?"

"Yup. In the Sticky," meaning her pocket holster.

The woman who'd come to meet her said, "Cocked and locked, I hope."

"Of course," Letty said.

The woman grinned and said, "Of course."

THE WOMAN SAID her name was Jane Longstreet. She was black, thin, looked to be in her mid-forties, her trim dark hair touched with strands of gray. She wore an antique African trade-bead necklace, an open-necked man's white dress shirt worn loose, and jeans. The shirt showed a bump on her left hip, a cross-draw holster.

With Cartwright hooked into a different conversation, Longstreet told Letty that the program would consist of three rounds of shooting with evaluations—"It's competitive, but we pass it off as friendly." Then the day's honoree, Elaine Shelton, would give a half-hour talk on .177-caliber Olympic air pistols.

"We serve a modest round of alcohol during the talk. Some of the ladies like their G&Ts and red wine, though we don't want anyone driving their cars off the lane. That happened once and we had a dirty time getting her out of the ditch. We finally had to put a chain on the Kubota and drag her out backwards."

"How do you get to be a member?" Letty asked.

"You're a candidate, if you wish to be. We evaluate candidates by email. If we decide to offer membership, the candidate will get an invitation to our next meeting. If we decide not to, she won't hear from us. Dues are . . . modest."

"Fair enough," Letty said. "Though I'm not terribly social."

"That's not disqualifying," Longstreet said, glancing around. "Some of our members are only social in the sense of being sociopathic. All of them are decent shots, though. Ranging from good to fantastic."

THE SOCIALIZING CONTINUED for a while; several handguns and one rifle were produced by various women to be examined, discussed, and, in a few cases, argued over. Letty found herself being moved from one circle of women to the next, to look at guns, talk about her own, relating what happened in the gunfight at Pershing, Texas. It occurred to her after the first few minutes that she was being interviewed.

AN HOUR AFTER she arrived, the members began drifting out the back of the Quonset, carrying their guns. The shooting itself took place at ranges dug into the valley wall, one for pistols, one for long guns. The pistol range was nothing fancy: cutbank dirt walls as backstops, with targets stretched between wooden racks.

The women were a bit ragtag, Letty thought: some camo here, a boonie hat there, boots and athletic shoes, sunglasses everywhere, and more than a few cargo pants. The oldest was probably in her sixties and Letty was the youngest. Most seemed to be in their thirties or forties. They were friendly, but with edges.

Letty was wearing jeans she'd had modified by a dry cleaner's seamstress. An extra piece of material was sewn into the right-hand pocket, which made the pocket gap slightly. The gap allowed her hand to get in fast; the slick interior of the Sticky holster inside meant the gun would come out clean.

They shot in groups of three and times and scores were recorded. They shot at three distances: three yards, seven yards, and twenty-five meters. Speed was essential for the first, speed and accuracy given equal weight on the second, while precision counted most in the third round.

"You getting tight?" Longstreet asked Letty, as the first group of three moved up to the firing line.

"Not yet. I used to shoot in a police league, including my dad. That's when I'd get tight—when I started beating him. Neither of us liked to lose. At all."

"Your father is a U.S. Marshal."

"You've done some research," Letty said.

"Yes, we have."

THE FIRST TWO ROUNDS were fired from holsters. Letty had brought an appendix carry holster but asked if her pocket holster qualified: "That's the one I work with."

"That's fine," Longstreet said.

Another woman said, "Looks like you had some work done on those jeans."

"A little bit," Letty said. "Didn't want to break a nail going in."

"Yeah, that's nasty," the woman said.

"Isn't it a little slow?" Longstreet asked. "The pocket holster?"

"No," Letty said. "It's not."

Letty was in the last group of three in the first round. She had nerves until she walked to the firing line. When the starter clock beeped, the Sig was up and fast and accurate, but Cartwright, also shooting in the last group, was two-tenths of a second faster and nearly as accurate. In the close-up shooting, as might occur in a street fight, speed counted for more than accuracy.

Longstreet came over and said, "My. You're pushing Barb. If that's her real name, which it might not be. That doesn't happen very often."

"She's fast," Letty said. "And good. We worked together last month and she told me so."

Longstreet leaned toward her and lowered her voice. "Most all the women here work with the military or specialized law enforcement of one kind or another. Often, undercover with agencies like the DEA. Others are . . . consultants. I guess you know that Barb works for what we call the Unspecified Agency, as do two of the other women. That's the CIA, of course."

"Of course."

In the second round of shooting, Letty and Barb exactly tied in time and Letty was barely more accurate.

When the results were announced, a short break began, and the twenty-five-meter targets were set up. Cartwright wandered over to Letty and said, "You aren't that bad. I wasn't sure what to expect. When did you start shooting?"

"When I was five," Letty said. "I didn't shoot targets until I was twelve."

"You were shooting with a .22 single-shot rifle," Cartwright said. "Rabbits and squirrels."

"Cottontails in Minnesota, sometimes. I stopped shooting squirrels the first time I cooked one and the meat turned black. Mostly I used it on racoons when I was running a trapline at the local dump," Letty said.

"That thing down in Pershing," Cartwright said, popping a stick of gum into her mouth. "Pretty fine."

"It was interesting," Letty admitted.

"Who was that big guy?" Cartwright asked. "The guy who picked you up like a football and ran you off the bridge?"

"John Kaiser. Former Delta. He's an investigator with DHS. We work together sometimes, if there's a threat."

"Cool. Listen: good luck in the last round."

"Thanks. You, too."

WHEN CARTWRIGHT HAD GONE to get ready for the slow-fire, twenty-five-meter round, Longstreet slipped back over and asked, "Barb trying to psych you?"

"She wished me luck."

Longstreet smiled. "What did you think about that?"

Letty was loading her Staccato, the one she'd use for the slow-fire round. "Fuck a bunch of luck."

Longstreet laughed and touched Letty on the shoulder, like a mom might; people turned to look.

THE THIRD ROUND was five shots at twenty-five meters in less than ten seconds; time didn't count unless the shooter went longer than ten seconds. Nobody did. Letty took it easy with her big gun and put all five shots in a group the size of a ragged quarter.

Cartwright didn't. She put them in a group that might have been covered by the rim of a teacup. She came over to shake hands and asked, "Okay. You were the best shot in North Carolina. How did you get hooked up with Homeland?"

"I was working for Senator Colles as an aide. He spotted an opening that he thought I might be more interested in," Letty said.

Cartwright nodded. "You went to Stanford. Master's in economics."

"Yup."

"You ever think about moving, give me a call."

"What?" Letty was packing up the Staccato. "You mean, go outside and yell? People here aren't even sure your name is Barbara, so I don't know how I'd call you."

"You'll get a link, and my name really is Barbara," Cartwright said. "Anyway, nice shooting."

THE DAY'S HONOREE, Elaine Shelton, was a willowy redhead who gave an interesting account of using a .177-caliber air pistol to win a silver medal in the Olympics; she was both funny and crisp.

Cartwright, who'd taken a chair next to Letty, leaned over and muttered, "She's poked more holes in paper than a Swingline punch."

"Dissing another member?"

"She's not a member," Cartwright whispered.

When the lecture was over, Letty turned to Cartwright and said, "Listen, unless the Unspecified Agency keeps you penned up in a gopher hole somewhere, and you get the time, we ought to hit a range together. Piss off some goobers. Get a couple of margaritas after."

Cartwright peered at her for a moment, then nodded and said, "That could happen."

As Letty was leaving, Longstreet came over to say good-bye, and Letty asked, "Why isn't Elaine a member?"

Longstreet took Letty by her elbow to walk her to the steps and said, "Being a good shot is not enough. None of us are . . . what you'd conventionally call criminals, sugar, although, mmm . . ." She stopped to gather some words. Her eyes were black as coals. "We're *all* good with guns and we're *all* killers. Elaine is good with guns."

A WEEK LATER, as Letty was getting ready for work, she was buzzed from the lobby of her apartment building by a red-shirted courier-service deliveryman. She buzzed him in, and at the door signed for a heavy, rectangular package wrapped in brown paper.

Inside, she found an envelope and a dark wooden box. The envelope contained an invitation for the November shoot, a key card for the entry gate, and a Yale key for the Quonsets. A note said she was invited to shoot anytime she wished, day or night. If at night, be sure to turn off the range lights when she left. Dues were one thousand dollars a year, payable when convenient.

Inside the wooden box was a new Colt Single-Action Army revolver, in caliber .45 Colt, as well as six cartridges, each in its own slot. She took the gun out and rolled the cylinder, feeling the weight in her hands, the smoothness of the action.

She was a Peace-Maker.

Of the .45-caliber kind.

TWO

Over the next four months, Letty went to the monthly shoots and began to learn about the other members, and she and Cartwright hooked up a half-dozen times in the evenings, to shoot at a local gun range, to talk circumspectly about their jobs and less circumspectly about men—Cartwright, at thirty-two, was twice-divorced, Letty had no ongoing relationship.

Her first marriage didn't count, Cartwright said, as she'd been a teenager and had moved out after three months to join the Army. The second marriage, to a man who also worked at the Unspecified Agency, had lasted a bit more than five years and had ended because of infidelity.

"Mine, not his," Cartwright said, wryly. "How come you're not hooked up with somebody? You're not gay . . ."

Letty tugged at an earlobe for a moment, then said, "I have a lot of first and second dates, but . . . I think I might be too harsh for most guys. My father . . ."

"I looked him up," Cartwright said. "I mean, Jesus Christ . . ."

"He and I are a lot alike. Uh . . . My mom says we both look at the world through untinted glasses. We don't think about what it might be, or should be, or used to be, only what it is. Most guys have a hard time with that. Being seen for exactly what they are."

"I'd say most *people* have a hard time with that," Cartwright amended.

On two occasions, they'd driven together to the clubhouse to work out with rifles. Cartwright was better with a rifle than Letty, especially at longer ranges, with the ability to judge, offhand, bullet-drop and wind drift. Cartwright shot an accurized and scoped Remington Model 700 in .300 Winchester Magnum, and Letty a high-end AR-10.

"Yours is a gun you'll never need," Cartwright said. "It's a rapid-fire combat-style weapon, too big and powerful for self-defense in an urban area, not accurate enough for sniping. Shoot that off in Arlington and it'd go through three apartment buildings and a beer truck."

"You shoot a heavier cartridge . . ."

"Only one at a time and very carefully. If you want to pick off Mr. American Asshole during the International Asshole Pageant, you need a sniper weapon, not something that kills all the innocent bystanders."

In February, on Valentine's night, with a cold, heavy rain falling outside, they were sitting in a dark political bar a few hundred yards from the Capitol. They'd hung their rain jackets on the back of their chairs; whisky and a whiff of illegal cigar smoke were in the air and middle-aged guys in expensive suits were ignoring them. For some people—many in DC—politics was better than sex.

Like Letty, Cartwright had an apartment in Arlington, across the Potomac from the District, and, like Letty, would be taking a train home and walking from the station. They'd traded life histories, which were roughly similar. Letty's father had abandoned her and her mother when she was a toddler. Her mother had been a helpless alcoholic, and Letty had been the adult in the family from the time she was in grade school.

Cartwright's parents, she said, hadn't wanted her. She had been an unplanned baby, the fifth borne by her mother, and been looked upon as one mouth too many.

"My old man was a tree-shade mechanic, had a few acres outside Sulphur Springs. I had an uncle with a shithole ranch and he and my aunt sort of adopted me when I was a year old or so, and I never went back to my real folks," Cartwright said. "My aunt died of cancer when I was twelve, and my uncle hanged himself a couple years later. After that, I was on my own."

"I never go back to my hometown," Letty told her. She'd been born in a particularly bleak stretch of the Red River Valley in Minnesota. "Too many bad memories. I like the people, though, most of them."

Cartwright nodded. "My cousins own the shithole ranch now," she said. "I go back, because I like my cousins."

LETTY HAD GOTTEN LUCKY and had been adopted by the Minnesota cop who'd investigated her mother's murder, during a particularly brutal winter in the Red River Valley. The cop was rich, and she'd lived a privileged life as a teenager, before going to Stanford.

Cartwright had had no such help. She'd managed to get a high school equivalency degree, enlisted in the Army, done well, used her Army benefits to enroll at the University of Texas, returned to the Army as an intelligence officer, and from there migrated to the Unspecified Agency.

"I know of another woman, same kind of Texas background, became a domestic terrorist. I'll kill her sooner or later, if I can find her," Letty said.

"I know who you're talking about—that Jael woman who led the attack on Pershing," Cartwright said. She held out her glass for Letty to clink: "Good hunting."

THEY WERE FINISHING their third margaritas when Letty's phone buzzed in her non-gun pocket. She pulled it out, looked at the screen.

"It's the boss," she told Cartwright. Senator Christopher Colles (R-Fla), was chairman of the Senate Homeland Security and Governmental Affairs Committee.

She answered: "Chris?"

"Letty? How early can you get to my office?"

"Early as you."

"I'll see you at eight o'clock," Colles said. "Jeans and sneakers are fine, no need to get dressed up. Actually, I don't want you dressed up. I want you to look . . . road-weary. A beat-up traveler."

"I can do that," she said. "Am I going out of town?"

"That depends on the people we'll be talking with. They know all about Pershing and they know about your background and they think you might fit their program. Things could get a little rough."

"Did you invite Kaiser?"

"No. He won't be going. We've got a problem that I can't talk about on a radio, which these cell phones are. I'll see you tomorrow. Eight o'clock sharp."

LETTY RANG OFF and Cartwright asked, "Taking your gun with you?"

"I always take it. From the way he was talking, he thinks I might need it." She trailed a fingernail through a wet spot on the table. "The way he was talking . . . you guys don't do stuff inside the U.S., do you?"

Cartwright neither confirmed nor denied that she was with the CIA, and it had become a joke between them. "If I were in the agency you're talking about, no, we'd generally not be allowed to do that, not on our own. If we were officially working in a consulting capacity with another law enforcement agency, like you guys, or the FBI, then we're okay. If I were in that agency."

"Consulting capacity? After quickly checking my federal government guide to dodges, circumventions, and evasions, that means you can do anything you fuckin' well please," Letty said.

"That would be correct. You up for a fourth?"

"I'll be totally loaded, but what the heck," Letty said. "Let's go for it."

"Attagirl," Cartwright said, raising a finger to the waiter. "Nothing quite as exciting as getting drunk on your ass while angry and in possession of a dangerous weapon. Says so right in the Second Amendment, I think."

"I'm not that angry," Letty said.

"Yes, you are. You have been since birth. All us Ladies are angry."

WHEN LETTY'S ALARM went off at six the next morning, it rang in her head like the bells of Notre Dame: five margaritas, not four. She stumbled through the shower, brushed her teeth, and did nothing more to clean up. She forced herself to go for her morning run, splashing along the rain-soaked Arlington streets, before heading across the river to the District.

Senator Colles had an office suite in the old Senate Office Building, a stained lump of what Letty thought looked like an eroded limestone cliff, but with windows. She got to Colles's office five minutes early, a hangover lurking at the back of her skull, and found Colles's brutally efficient executive assistant, Claudia Welp, already at her desk outside the door of Colles's inner office.

Welp was not only a bulldog, she resembled the real thing, especially with her small, suspicious eyes and the slight outward set of her lower teeth. She and Letty didn't like each other, but under Colles's critical eye, they had worked out a relationship that they both could live with.

When Letty walked through the door, Welp said, "Senator Colles is inside with two persons from somewhere secret. I see you took the senator's advice on your appearance."

Letty was wearing black jeans, fuzzy white threads at the heels; a red-and-black plaid flannel shirt, much-washed and untucked; and scuffed black cross-training shoes. Her dark hair was ruffled, unkempt, her eyes hidden behind cheap sunglasses. No makeup. "He said 'road-weary,' and that's what I went for," Letty said. To say nothing of hungover.

"You got there," Welp said. "You're supposed to go in."

Letty pushed through the door into Colles's private office. He was rich, and looked it: tall, tanning-bed toned, wavy gray hair, bright white teeth, as though he'd been designed for television. He'd had the office professionally painted and decorated, in tints of artichoke green and cream, at his own expense, though it still, somehow, looked exactly like a government office.

The senator was talking with two federal officials who looked almost identical to each other—office pallor, upper-level navy suits, glasses with tortoiseshell frames, carefully coifed dark hair at eight o'clock in the morning. Well-buffed black shoes. They would have been hard to tell apart, Letty thought, if one hadn't been female and the other male, and if one pair of shoes hadn't had stacked heels.

Colles pointed at Letty and said, "Sit." She sat in a visitor's chair as the two suits looked her over. Colles said, "These folks are from the National Security Agency. Don't tell anybody."

Letty: "What's up?"

The woman said, distantly, as though Letty weren't sitting six feet from her, "She looks right." And she asked Colles—not Letty—"Does she have any tattoos?"

Colles said, "I haven't looked. If I tried, she might whack me. Whack, like in *The Godfather*."

"I don't have any tattoos," Letty said. "I'm not getting any."

The woman said, to the man, "Jeff Toski."

The man nodded. "Yes. She wouldn't be in long . . ." He looked back at Letty and said, "Fake tattoo. Good for a week to fifteen days, depending on how often you shower and how hard you scrub it. My daughter had one for a while. It was convincing. For a while."

Letty nodded: "I'd go for a fake."

The woman: "You killed three people in Texas, and two more, years ago, in St. Paul. How do you feel about that?"

"If you're asking if I'm suffering from PTSD, the answer is 'No.' If you're asking if I enjoyed it, the answer is 'No,'" Letty said. "I have no urge to kill anyone, but I'm willing to, if pushed into a corner."

Now the woman said, "Huh. Do you think that makes a difference in the world? Killing people?"

"Of course it does. We'd be living in a lot different world if John Kennedy, Robert Kennedy, Martin Luther King hadn't been murdered. On the other side, if you could kill any one hundred people in the United States, right now, think about what the country could be like without them."

The other three stared at her for a moment, then the man said, "You could be a very dangerous woman."

"Fortunately, I'm neither crazy nor a murderer," Letty said. She turned to Colles: "What's going on? You'll have to tell me sooner or later. You might as well tell me now."

"If we tell you, and you talk about it, you'll go to prison," the woman said.

"Probably not," Letty said, looking back at her. "If it's that kind of deal and I talked about it, you'd all be running for cover."

For the first time, the man smiled: "You nailed that. We probably would be."

The woman said to Colles, "She'll do."

COLLES, BEHIND HIS DESK, steepled his fingers, then said, "There's a company in Sunnyvale, California, called Pastek Cybernetics . . ."

"I'm familiar with it," Letty said. "Does machine control software. Not real big. Revenues of, what, a half billion a year?"

The woman asked, "Why would you know about Pastek?"

"I went to Stanford, as I'm sure you know," Letty said. "The place is lousy with computer people. I don't know a lot about Pastek, but I'd heard the name."

The man nodded. "All right."

The woman said, "We're now going to talk about severely clas-

28

sified material. Senator Colles has assured us that you can keep your mouth shut when necessary."

"I can," Letty agreed.

"Three years ago, Pastek was the victim of a ransomware attack. You know about those."

"Of course. A hacker takes over your computer system and locks you out," Letty said. "You no longer have control of what your system does, or the files inside of it."

"You wouldn't think a software company would be vulnerable, but Pastek was, in one particular segment of their business," the woman said. "A Russian hacker group calling itself DarkVenture, one word, capital V, got into their machine control servers and locked Pastek out."

Pastek had become desperate, she said. The company not only provided software, but also maintained it, and upgraded it, and adapted the software to any changes in the machinery for which they provided controls.

The company could not allow the lockout to continue for more than a few days. DarkVenture wanted twenty-five million dollars in a Bitcoin payment and, unlike most ransomware attackers, they wouldn't negotiate. They wanted every penny.

"I assume Pastek paid," Letty said, "since you're here."

"They did. Twenty-five million dollars. Paying it, by the way, was technically a crime," the man said.

DarkVenture, he said, was a well-known hacking combine and there was a widely held assumption that they worked with the tacit approval of the Russian government. But Vernon Pastek, who founded Pastek Cybernetics, was not a pushover. He gritted his teeth, paid the ransom, and then went looking for revenge.

The man leaned forward. "The six principals of DarkVenture

are well known to most intelligence agencies and even some civilian hackers here and in Europe. Pastek isn't a hacker, but he knew how to get in touch with an American hacker group that calls itself Ordinary People. They started out doing political hacks—Donald Trump's IRS files, Republican emails, harmless stuff. Pastek won't admit it, but he came up with a revenge scheme and paid Ordinary People one million dollars, personal money, to carry it out."

The two NSA operatives took turns explaining what happened next.

Russia, they said, has the second largest rail system in the world in terms of tons of freight moved per kilometer, after China. The U.S. is third. Ordinary People got into the Russian rail system and essentially owned it for several months. The Russians could move trains, but they didn't know what was on them. They'd get Mercedes-Benzes in Nizhny Novgorod and tractors in Moscow. A trainload of Army rations in Vladivostok and commercial ocean-fishing gear in Belarus.

Then Ordinary People, operating under another name, DarkVirus, a riff on the DarkVenture name, just to stick the fork in, made a ransomware offer to the Russians: publicly execute the six principals of DarkVenture or put fifty million into a Bitcoin account. The Russians had to think about it for a while, but eventually paid up . . . or DarkVenture did. The NSA wasn't exactly sure of the mechanism of that decision.

"Who got the money?" Letty asked. "Ordinary People, or . . ."

The woman: "Pastek got it. Or, he owned the Bitcoin wallet that held it, initially through a shell company registered in the British Virgin Islands, and from there to a half-dozen other offshore accounts. Where it went from those accounts, we don't know and probably can't find out. That's also illegal, but we're not the IRS.

Ordinary People got their million, up front, nothing more. And that's the problem we're getting to."

"I have to fight the Russians? Or Vernon Pastek?"

The man shook his head. "No. Ordinary People started out as idealists who . . . well, they really had their heads in the sand, money-wise. Eating tuna fish sandwiches for supper. Peanut butter for lunch. Fighting for the right to be progressive. There are probably not more than twenty or thirty of them. They got a million dollars from Vernon Pastek, but after you split that twenty ways, you've earned about what you'd get as an elementary school teacher. We think they've become unhappy with their lifestyle and were impressed by how lucrative a ransomware attack can be. And how easy it is, if you pick the right target. And how anonymous. How safe."

Letty: "So they're going off the rails, so to speak?"

"Yes. We watch critical computer systems in the U.S.—thousands of them, which is neither here nor there, not something you have to worry about," the woman said. "We believe Ordinary People have been nosing around natural gas distribution systems. We have no definitive proof, but we suspect they plan to turn off the natural gas supply for a northern city, or even multiple cities."

"Like the Twin Cities," Letty said. "I used to live there. We had gas heat."

"Yes," the woman said. "So you know what we're talking about. If somebody takes out the natural gas system for a northern city in the next month, it'll be a huge disaster. When natural gas goes down, you can't just turn it back on. It takes days, or if the outage is big enough, weeks, even when you have full control of the system."

"You're the computer geniuses," Letty said. "Why not just grab the gas-system computers before Ordinary People do? Lock *them* out?"

"Because they may already be in there and they'd see us," the woman said. "If they see us, they might pull the plug and we don't even know exactly where they'd pull it. It's a cold winter in Minneapolis, Rochester, Bozeman. So cold the ski trips are down in Jackson and Big Sky. It was twelve below zero at the Butte airport last night."

"Okay. So why not figure out who Ordinary People are and sic the FBI on them?"

The man nodded. "The FBI is not known for its subtlety. They'd start an investigation, and about the time they interviewed their second subject, the word would get out, and OP might very well shut down a city."

NSA had been aware of the group for some time, but OP was not a small, well-organized cell. They were an amorphous group, with hackers coming and going. There were apparently different factions—one wing purely political, another environmental, some were anti-gun, there was a pro-choice faction.

"We could figure out who they all are, separate the factions, if we had the time. Maybe . . . three or four months, or a year?" the woman said. "We might have a week or two . . . The current cold front is clearing out, but there's another one behind it."

"And I can fix that by . . ."

"By doing what you just suggested that we do—figure out who they are. You'll do that by hooking up with one of our computer specialists," the man said. "You're his girlfriend. He drives an old, rehabbed Toyota Tundra, he has tattoos, he's got very strong computer skills, he talks the hacker talk. We put you where we think

Ordinary People might be . . . dangle him like a trout fly . . . and hope that he gets a bite. Hope you two can identify them."

"That sounds like a major fail," Letty said. "I've had a couple courses in JavaScript and Python, but I'm no kind of programmer."

"We don't want you for your computer skills. We want you for your gun skills and your believability as a very young and somewhat cheesy girlfriend. Somebody who couldn't possibly be a federal officer," the man said. "We want you to take care of our guy while he figures out who the Ordinary People are. If Ordinary People are planning to take down a natural gas system, that means they're dangerous folks who are willing to kill for money. Or have become that way. Our boy is a little . . . not to say wimpy, but . . ."

"Wimpy. Despite the macho truck and tattoos, he's a wimp," the woman said. "He's agreed to do this, after some arm-twisting, but he's scared. We need somebody to take care of him."

"I'm not going to sleep with him," Letty said.

The woman winced. "We'd never suggest such a thing."

She said it in a way that made Letty think they actually *had* thought of such a thing. "That's good, because I won't."

Colles: "Understood. If he jumps you, some people will hang for it." His eyes scanned the two suits, who both nodded.

"One last question," Letty said. "If you're so hot to get to Ordinary People, why not go after Pastek? Grind him down. If he was upset by having to pay twenty-five million, how upset would he be if you threatened to put him away for five to ten? And take his company away from him?"

"There are other issues," the woman said. She glanced at Colles. "Having to do with campaign contributions. Pastek's campaign contributions."

Same old story, in certain quarters of America, like the one they were sitting in. Money bites. "Okay."

The man asked, "So. You'll do it?"

"If Senator Colles asks me to," Letty said.

"I'm asking," Colles said.

"Then I'm in," Letty said. She turned to Colles. "I assume I'll get a heavier briefing than this. Where and when do I get that?"

"At Homeland," Colles said, meaning the Department of Homeland Security. "Tomorrow. Time is short. You'll have homework to do when you're on the road. We don't have time to give you everything tomorrow."

The woman said, "I'll be at the briefing with Rod Baxter and some other folks."

"Baxter is . . ."

"Your companion."

"What's your name?" Letty asked.

The woman had to think a moment, then said, "Mary . . . Johnson."

"Who will I be reporting to?"

"Me," Johnson said.

Letty turned to Colles and said, "Great. I'm reporting to somebody who lies about her name."

Colles: "Yeah. That's true."

Letty held his eyes for a moment. "They're lying about something else, too. Are they going to tell me what it is?"

Colles shook his head: "I don't know about that. All I know is what you've heard."

Johnson said, "We're not lying about anything. Cross my heart. We'll be briefing you tomorrow. Today, you need to buy clothes and get ready to fly. Like Senator Colles said, we have no time. No time. We're posing your associate as a rogue programmer-for-hire, down on his luck, on the run from law enforcement after a ransomware attempt went wrong. We haven't finished that cover yet, we're putting the final touches on it. It's not something we usually do. We're talking to some . . . mmm . . . other people about that. But you will be his college-dropout girlfriend and maybe something a little rough . . . like, mmm, a barmaid. Or a scullery maid."

"I don't think they're called that anymore," Letty said.

"Whatever. You need the clothes to fit that image, that background. Get some today, you'll be compensated later," Johnson said. "You'll be flying out of here tomorrow night, to Orlando, Florida."

The man, who'd not yet introduced himself with a fake name, said, "Ordinary People are based in Los Angeles. They might be planning to attack a northern city, but we don't know if they've even bothered to go to any of them. This is all computer stuff— they don't need to go there."

"If they're in LA, why am I flying to Florida?"

"The Orlando stop is part of your developing cover," Johnson said. "We'll know more about that by tomorrow. Your partner, Rod Baxter, went to school at the University of Florida in Gainesville, which is just north of Orlando. He spent three years there, in grad school; he knows it well. You need to give it a look. You'll be driving his truck from Orlando to LA—the truck should arrive in Orlando late tonight or early tomorrow morning; we're having it driven down there. We're hoping you can drive it on to Pasadena, to Caltech, in three days. The drive is part of your cover."

The man added, "We also have a lot of material for you to absorb—your new identity, what information we have on the

Ordinary People, investigative processes, your law enforcement contacts on the West Coast, emergency contacts with us . . . and so on. Your time in the truck will be busy."

"Excuse me for saying this, but it doesn't sound to me like you're even sure Ordinary People is going to attack anyone," Letty said. "It sounds like you're guessing."

The two spooks nodded, and Johnson said, "That's fair. Let me put it this way—we know for sure that they're researching natural gas systems. We know that a couple of years ago, the natural gas system in Aspen was sabotaged and the gas companies had a heck of a time getting it back up. We know for sure that Ordinary People has done at least one spectacular ransomware attack. What do *you* think they might be doing?"

Letty pushed out her lower lip, thought about it, and nodded: "I guess you have to look at it. If that's not the part you're lying about."

The man said, "About the tattoos . . ."

JEFF TOSKI WAS a burly tattoo artist with a full russet neck beard, peering blue eyes, and a nose that might have sniffed too much ale. He lived just east of the Anacostia River in Northwest DC, with a tattoo parlor in the front porch of his house. He put Letty in his chair and said, "I don't fool around, I'm good at this. You're one of the Specials, so you've got some choices."

"Like what?"

He had three ranges of inks, he said: standard tattoo, which was permanent ("Don't believe that Dr. Tattoff bullshit"), an ink for fake tattoos, which essentially sat on the surface of the skin, and Derma-Oil, a new ink made of a natural plant-based pigment that literally got eaten by the wearer's body.

"The fake will look good for up to two weeks, with a daily shower. After that, it doesn't look so good, and with a daily shower, it'll be gone in three weeks. Derma-Oil will look good for six to eight months, depending on your body chemistry, and not so good for another two, and then it's gone. Not a trace. When it's there, it's a real tattoo: you can get in a shower with . . . whoever . . . and they can scrub your tattoo as much as they want, and it will *not* come off. 'Cause it's real."

"I don't want to go permanent," Letty said.

"Then I'd go with the Derma-Oil. I've done a few of these Specials and have an idea of what you guys are up to," Toski said. "Undercover, the fakes would be kinda . . . scary. 'Cause they're not real."

"Then let's do that, the Derma-Oil," Letty said. "Is it going to hurt?"

"A little. Not too bad."

With further consultation, Letty got a pair of raven wings in black ink that covered the entire top of her back; a miniature yellow-and-black tiger swallowtail butterfly inside the point of her hipbone, which might peek out of a pair of low-rise jeans; and a Buddhist saying on the inside of her right forearm: *All Wrongdoing Arises Because of Mind.* That tattoo was in what Toski said was Sanskrit, and as far as Letty—or Toski—knew, it could actually say, *Death to All White-Eyed Devils.* But then, maybe it really did evoke the Buddha.

The tattooing did hurt; it didn't feel like millions of needle pricks, but more as though somebody was scraping her skin with a piece of glass. When each of the tattoos was done, Toski washed them first with a disinfectant and then with an antibiotic. When she told him she'd be doing some flying and driving, he also gave her a package of peel-off plastic sheets that combined a light adhesive with a topical anesthetic.

"The tats will be raw for two or three days, they'll weep some, but the sheets will keep that from soaking into your clothes and keep you from itching too bad," Toski said. "They should be fine after that. They're shallower than standard tattoos, so they're not raw as long."

When she was dressed, Toski said, "A little advice. Come back when you're done with the job, and I'll make the butterfly permanent. That is *awesomely* hot."

ON MOST OF HER WORK for Homeland Security, Letty had been briefed by Billy Greet, a DHS executive, now a friend of hers. Greet and Letty's frequent investigative partner, John Kaiser, had developed an on-again, off-again relationship that would have been deeply frowned upon in the halls of Homeland Security, had anyone other than the three of them known about it.

When Letty left Toski's shop, she found Greet on the street, waiting, hands stuffed in her jeans pockets. She was wearing a fashionable High Plains Drifter pre-dirtied jacket against the February chill, and her aviator sunglasses. Her hair was pulled back in her usual tight bun, with a few strands floating loose; she looked like a harried third grade teacher after a bad day. "I don't like any of this, what I know about it," Greet said. "But if you're doing it, I need to take you shopping for your cover."

"Then you need to take me shopping," Letty said. "'Cause I'm doing it."

GREET DROVE THEM to an Arlington Goodwill store, where they spent an hour picking through, discussing, and choosing her new old clothes. They didn't need a lot, but it had to be right. An old jean jacket, tee-shirts, much-washed bras, skinny jeans worn and holed, boots and socks, a fleece-lined trucker jacket for cool weather. A faded blue trucker hat with "USA" on the front panel.

She bought six pairs of faded different-colored Ralph Lauren men's briefs. The briefs rode a half-inch higher than the jeans in the back; and the jeans rode low enough in the front to allow the butterfly some freedom. They added a pair of silver loop earrings, a ring with a cracked glass emerald and a fake-gold brass setting, which fit nicely on Letty's right index finger, and a battered REI Co-Op duffel in dog-shit yellow to carry the clothes.

"Okay, you're sleazy," Greet said, taking her in. "Let's buy it and get over to your place and sort it out."

At her apartment, Letty changed into the Goodwill clothes and jewelry—Greet insisted on soaking the earrings in a dish of alcohol before Letty snapped them into her ears. "That raven on your back is terrific, but a little goop is bleeding through the dressings," Greet said. Letty was walking around in a pair of red Ralph Lauren shorts and a pinkish bra that may have become pinkish when it was washed with something like the red Ralph Lauren shorts.

Greet helped peel off the plastic anesthetic sheets and apply new ones. "When your back heals, get yourself one of those off-the-shoulder peasant tops. It'll be warm out in California and it'll look cheap. That's you. Let the raven fly."

THAT NIGHT, LETTY told John Kaiser as much as he needed to know to provide cogent advice.

"My advice is this. Undercover guys look like everything from movie executives to street people. And housewives," Kaiser said. He was an ex–Delta operator who'd gone undercover in several different Middle Eastern countries, as well as Sweden and Canada. "It's not like on TV where everybody has permanent three-day beards and dark glasses and foreign noses."

"Foreign noses?"

"Always. On TV. Foreign noses," Kaiser said. "Anyway, what undercover people never are—in my experience—is gimps."

"There's a choice, socially sensitive word," Letty said. "Gimps."

"Okay. They're never differently abled. If you really want to sell yourself, you could be differently abled."

"How would I do that in a non-fake way?" Letty asked.

"I was hoping you'd ask. I'll be right back." Kaiser disappeared into his bedroom and came back with an elastic knee brace and a roll of surgical tape. "Pull your pant leg up."

Letty had learned not to question him on such things, so she pulled her pant leg up. With her leg straight, Kaiser put a marble-sized knot of tape behind her knee, took three wraps of the soft tape around her knee to hold it in place, then had her pull the brace over her foot, and up to, and over, her knee.

"You were hiking, tried to jump across a creek and tore your MCL," Kaiser said. "Pull down your pant leg and walk around."

Letty did; and she limped. Couldn't help herself. "That's really annoying."

"I imagine being a gimp is annoying," Kaiser said. "But it gets you something you need."

"That would be?"

"A cane," Kaiser said. "A nonobvious weapon . . . and non-lethal, if you need it to be nonlethal."

"I'm not that good with a stick yet . . ."

"You're good enough. Way good enough. You won't be stick-fighting somebody like me," Kaiser said. He'd been giving her lessons. "You'll be beating some IT nerd over the head."

"I'll think about it," she said.

"I'll be really disappointed if you don't do it," Kaiser said, settling back on his heels. "Undercover . . . you might not be able to keep your gun. But who's going to take a cane away from a gimp? A girl-gimp?"

"I suppose you've got the perfect stick," Letty said. Then, "Wait: you were hoping I'd ask."

"Exactly." He went back to his bedroom, and Letty could hear him rummaging around. A moment later, he came back with a dark brown wooden cane with knobs along its length and a right-angled steel grip that looked like an ice-climbing pick.

"Blackthorn," he said, running his finger down its bumpy length. "Bought it in London. Hit somebody with the stick hard enough, you'll break his arm or kneecap, crack his skull. Hit him with the grip, either the blunt end or the point, you'll kill him. Heavy as a hammer, with a three-foot handle."

"Killing is easier with a gun," Letty said.

"Sure. If you don't have to drive back to your hotel to get it."

THREE

When Letty limped into the Homeland Security briefing room the morning after the interview at Colles's office, she found Mary Johnson talking with a fiftyish man. He was thin as a pencil, wearing rimless glasses over a dry, narrow face, and a forest-green suit that Robin Hood might have envied; a bystander might have thought him an Ivy League professor of some archaic and useless subject near the top of an ivory tower.

A younger man, thirtysomething and bulky, with dark loops under his eyes, and thick black hair so heavily gelled that it glittered under the overhead lights, was slumped in a plastic chair behind the thin man.

The younger man—Letty hoped he wasn't her new partner but suspected that he was—looked at her with a nearsighted squint. He was in shirtsleeves, the sleeves rolled up to his elbows, showing tattoos on both arms. As she walked by him to an empty chair, she picked up the musky scent of a men's cologne.

Greet sat in a corner with her arms crossed, and when she looked at Letty, her eyes drifted upward in an unspoken "might be bullshit" signal.

Letty nodded at Greet and said "Hello" to Johnson, who was wearing either the same, or a duplicate of, the blue suit she'd been wearing the day before.

Johnson took in the cane and asked, "Letty . . . Oh, God, you didn't hurt yourself?"

"I'm a temporary gimp for undercover purposes," Letty said, and the thin man smiled. Johnson nodded and waved a finger at the two men. "Richard Taylor in the suit, and Rod Baxter, who you'll be working with."

From her corner, Greet said, "If we decide to go ahead with it."

Johnson said, "That's already been decided, Ms. Greet. We have no time to argue about it. No time."

"Letty's never had undercover training," Greet said. "Yet you expect her to spend several days and maybe weeks in close contact with . . ."

"Yes, we do," Johnson snapped. "She has a number of desirable characteristics that are nearly impossible to find in a government employee. For one thing, she looks far too young to be a threat to Ordinary People. And we know she's smart and actually did spend some time undercover at Pershing."

"Yeah, about fifteen minutes," Greet said.

Baxter spoke up. "I'd hoped I'd have a little more cover than a girl with a limp. Like somebody said, Ordinary People could be dangerous."

From the back of the room, Billy Greet muttered, "Makes my face hurt."

Baxter turned his head to look back at Greet. "I'm not being sexist, if that's what you think. She's pretty, but not particularly . . ." He paused, looked at Letty, and continued, "prepossessing. If somebody gave us serious trouble . . ."

Letty slipped her hand in her pocket and brought out her Sig, a chunk of black metal that hit the tabletop with a *clunk*. "Prepossess this," she said.

"Ah, man," Baxter said. "I don't like—"

"For your protection," Greet said. "The woman can shoot the balls off a gnat, you fuckin' turnip."

Baxter got pissed: "These people we're going against are nuts! You got that! Capiche? They're wacko!"

Greet: "That's why you need Letty."

AFTER A PERIOD of awkward silence, Greet asked, "What if somebody runs a facial recognition app against her, and Letty Davenport, heroine of the Pershing Bridge, turns up?"

"They won't find Letty Davenport, heroine of the Pershing Bridge, no matter how deep they go," Taylor, the older man, said. "They'll find a young woman named Charlotte Snow, nicknamed Charlie."

Johnson laid it out:

Letty, as Charlie Snow, had dropped out of the University of Florida after two years, where she and Baxter had met.

The two of them would fly to Orlando that night, then drive to Gainesville in his pickup, which would be delivered to the Orlando airport that afternoon. Baxter would spend a morning showing

Letty around the campus, and his old haunts, before they left for Los Angeles. Ordinary People were believed to have gone to college in the LA basin—UCLA, USC, and Caltech, so they should not be intimately familiar with Gainesville, if any had been there at all.

Letty: "If any of them were at Stanford . . . I was there for six years."

"We don't see that," Johnson said.

"Better not," Greet said. "What kind of cover have you built for her?"

Taylor spoke up. "Ordinary People are undoubtedly adept at all kinds of computer searches, of course. But not as good as we are. We have made changes in several Florida databases to include ID photos for Ms. Davenport, a couple more photos of her participating in the University of Florida Ayn Rand Club—"

"Give me a break," Letty said.

Taylor chuckled and said, "Small tolerance for charlatans, eh? Good for you. In any case, we inserted a number of documents in a variety of databases, including grades for freshman and sophomore classes—you did quite well, Letty, though you faltered in Introduction to Computer Science. We also have a brief story about your arrest for vandalism in the student newspaper, the *Alligator*. It seems that you got caught spray-painting the personal parts of Albert and Alberta, bronze alligator mascots to make them more . . . interesting. The story says you'd probably done it more than once."

Letty: "Okay. My name's Charlie . . ."

"Charlotte Snow," Taylor said. "Charlie. By the way . . . do you play a musical instrument of any kind? I couldn't find it in your résumé."

"I took six years of drum lessons," Letty said. "Sub Focus, 10

Years, bands like that. I played in a jam band in college. I can hold my own. Both play it and talk it."

"Excellent," Taylor said. "We were looking for another possible article for the *Alligator* database. We can slip in a picture of you and your drums."

"I don't have a picture like that," Letty said.

"Don't worry about it, we'll make one," Johnson said. "We'll locate a used electronic drum set, put it in Rod's truck."

"Great stuff," Letty said. "Now, how are we going to find Ordinary People?"

Johnson sighed: "That, we don't know. We believe they hang around Caltech and UCLA. We believe they are politically involved, although they may have curtailed that activity when they started looking at the Russian trains and then the natural gas systems. We know the OP are, or were, basically anti-Trump lefties, so you'll have to do some reading. We'll give you a flash drive with a collection of political articles for you to digest; they'll make you a believable advocate of the left, should anyone question your politics."

"Rod got involved in the research after he volunteered for this project," Taylor said. "He may have more to say about finding the OP."

Everybody turned to Baxter, who heaved himself more upright in his chair.

"When I was poking around after the Ordinary People attack on the Russian rail system, I got a guy at the agency to look at phone and email records from the time Pastek was commissioning the train hack. We found a burner phone that we believe belongs to Vernon Pastek, although we think it's now at the bottom of a Sunnyvale sewer. There were calls from the phone that link with calls received by a Caltech professor named Eugene Harp. He's a computer science professor there and also a political lefty."

"You think he's a member of the group?" Letty asked.

"Don't know," Baxter said. "He's older, mid-forties, so I kinda don't think so. But, he's very likely Pastek's initial connection to Ordinary People. He got divorced two years ago, no children. One of our researchers took a look at the divorce settlement. He and his wife were married in California for eleven years, so under California laws, they split everything fifty-fifty. He bought out her share of the house, paid her one-point-three million for her half, got a mortgage from Wells Fargo to cover it. He might need money. If Ordinary People pull off an attack on, say, the Minneapolis natural gas system, there'll be a very large payday."

"What does he teach?" Letty asked.

"Specializes in machine-control software," Baxter said.

"So . . . you really got him. He's got to be the connection," Letty said.

"I'd be willing to bet on it," Johnson said.

"*Willing to bet on it.* So now we're rolling the dice," Greet said from the back of the room.

WHEN JOHNSON PULLED GREET out of the room for a private come-to-Jesus chat, Baxter grumbled to Taylor, "Volunteered for the job, my fat white ass. If I hadn't, I'd be working in the back of the NSA furnace room for the next thirty years."

Taylor smiled at him and said, "Yes. I believe that is correct. On the other hand, since you did volunteer, promotion is a distinct possibility. We never do this kind of thing. You're sort of the canary in the coal mine."

Baxter to Letty: "These guys could kill us."

"You, maybe," Letty said. "Not me."

Baxter: "I'm putting in for a lot of overtime."

Letty: "You go, girl."

Baxter: "Fuck you."

"No chance of that."

Taylor smiled again in his dry, pencil-thin, rimless-glasses way.

THE BRIEFING CONTINUED when Johnson and Greet came back to the room. Most of it involved possible places they might look for politically involved hackers: bars and diners and hipster hangouts in Pasadena, where Caltech was located. They were given thumb drives containing lists of computer academics who might know members of Ordinary People, even if they didn't know what the OPs were up to.

Letty took notes, Greet mostly kept her mouth shut.

Johnson said, "When you find them, we need names and emails and physical locations, phone numbers if you can get them, the kinds of equipment being used, where they hook into the Net. We need to isolate the leadership, if there is a leadership. From what we've been able to gather, the group's organization may be communal rather than hierarchical. There may be no single leader . . ."

The NSA also had what Johnson called a "valuable resource" should it be necessary to follow someone in the LA area and a few other cities. Johnson explained that the Los Angeles Police Department and the Los Angeles Sheriff's Department had an Automatic License Plate Reading (ALPR) system and could track license plates through the city, in real time, from cameras on patrol cars, traffic signals, and light poles throughout the LA basin.

"The original idea was to pick up on stolen vehicles and to track fleeing vehicles. That was years ago and things have come a long way since," Johnson said. "We, mmm, mmm, have *access* to the system."

"How long does it take to get hooked up to it, if we need it?" Letty asked.

"It's real time," Johnson said. "We'll give you a number to call and an identification code and you can track anyone you want, any time you want, night or day."

Halfway through the briefing, a busy-looking man showed up, carrying a battered leather briefcase stuffed with manuals. He had too-long hair for the government and glasses with steel frames.

When Johnson called on him, he said, "Okay . . . Rod. I've got some stuff for you. The software used by most gas companies. Most of it is standard PLC stuff, from Schneider and OMRON and LySer-gicAD Labs, if you know those guys. We've got some malware code that goes after Codesys that underlies the software . . . We dug this out of an APT actor, and tell you what, it's now a level above Stuxnet or Industroyer . . ."

Baxter understood it all, but Letty didn't. One minute into the tech talk, she was lost. As Baxter and the new man went back and forth, Johnson waved Letty toward the door.

GREET JOINED THEM in the hallway and Johnson said, "As you can see, Rod's a little reluctant, Letty, so you'll have to push him. We need him out there. He'll understand what Ordinary People are up to, if we can get him in place. I can't emphasize enough how fast you've got to make your connections."

"Nobody's said anything about backup," Greet said.

"We're talking with the Los Angeles office of the FBI. They've been read into the problem and we have a contact for Letty," Johnson said. "If she gets in trouble, she can call up anything from a single undercover agent to a SWAT team with automatic weapons."

She put her briefcase on an upraised knee, fished around, and produced a foot-square Ziploc bag that appeared to be full of trash and a cell phone.

"A cheap-looking burner phone, which wasn't cheap, believe me. It has a secret cache with phone numbers and IDs and other information you might need. Instructions are in the bag. There are two credit cards for you, a Visa from a Wells Fargo Bank in Gainesville, and a Target, also from Gainesville, as well as a perfectly good Florida driver's license and some other wallet trash. All well-used. And some grade reports from the university . . . photos of your 'mother.' You were a single-parent family. You're Charlotte Snow. Charlie."

"She needs to take her federal carry permit and senate ID," Greet said. "If she's carrying a gun and gets tangled up with a California cop . . ."

"Yes. Talk to Baxter. I understand he has some hiding places in the truck. He says they're secure against anything but a complete disassembly."

"When are we leaving?" Letty asked.

Johnson glanced at her watch. "A little before seven o'clock tonight. You fly into Orlando. Rod's truck will be in a parking garage there. We'll text you the parking-lot space. On your new-old phone . . ."

"Why are we driving, anyway? We could fly all the way . . ."

"We need you to be on the road, we need you to have legitimate gasoline and motel receipts scattered around the truck, we need you to go through Gainesville, to look at it, we need you to see the highway, I-10, we need you to *drive* into Pasadena. We want you to push it: it'll be something like thirty-six hours on the road, you should be able to make it in three days. You'll be pretty far south, so you shouldn't run into any snow in the mountains . . . if there are mountains. Every time you stop at a McDonald's or wherever, grab the receipts and throw them in the back of the truck."

"Will Rod try to wrestle me into bed?"

"No. But here's a warning for you: don't keep yourself *too* separate," Johnson said. "Rent one motel room, get two beds. Get to know what his underwear looks like. You need to have some degree of intimacy. Not sex, but you need to know him. You need to create a persona that might be sleeping with him."

Letty nodded: "Got it."

"By the way, I love that cane," Johnson said. "You really look helpless."

"That's not the entire point," Greet said.

"What's the entire point?" Johnson asked.

"She's been stick-fighting with a former Delta operator," Greet said. "She could kill you with it."

"As the Delta guy told me, I might not be able to pack a gun," Letty said to Johnson, "but who's gonna take a cane away from a gimp?"

Johnson smiled: "I like that."

WHEN JOHNSON HAD RUN OUT of things to talk about, Letty took Greet aside and asked, quietly, "What do you think of Baxter?"

"He's gonna be a load," Greet said. "I feel for you. But he's nothing you can't handle. I can't promise the same about these hackers. They'll be smart and wary. And probably horny, so keep your knees together. Going deep doesn't mean you have to screw any-body."

Letty nodded: "I'd already figured that out. Screwing: optional."

"Something else," Greet said. "I don't trust the fuckers from the NSA and I don't trust the fuckers from the FBI. You feel like you're getting in a jam, if you even get a hint of that, I'll put Kaiser on a plane and you can have him in six hours, armed to the teeth and off the books. Don't mention it to Johnson."

"Excellent."

"Got both guns?"

"Is a frog's ass watertight?" Letty asked, adding: "Sorry. I hang around cops. I might need help getting the guns on the plane. I don't want to check them."

"Got you covered on that," Greet said. She looked at her watch. "I'll walk you through the back door."

Letty spent the tag end of the afternoon cleaning out her re-frigerator and purse, packing, talking to the apartment manager, paying rent in advance.

GREET PICKED HER UP after dark, drove her to the airport, then lit-erally walked Letty through a back door at Reagan National, a door reserved for security personnel, obviating any problems with the two pistols, the ammo, or the five-inch switchblade in Letty's duffel bag.

Nobody asked about the black camera bag slung over her shoul-der. The bag contained a diminutive Panasonic GX8, equipped with a single zoom lens equivalent to a 24mm–120mm lens on a full-frame camera, and a pair of Leica Ultravid 8x20 binoculars. Letty had learned that decent optics came in handy when sneaking around.

She carried the cane, but wasn't yet hobbling.

"I gotta get Kaiser to train me on the stick-fighting stuff," Greet said.

"Oooh, sexy. Discipline me with the stick and then take me to bed," Letty said, pitching her voice into a plea.

"The shit that comes out of your mouth sometimes . . ." Greet shook her head.

Greet watched them from the gate as Letty and Baxter boarded an American Airlines flight to Orlando, called "Be careful," and raised a hand as Letty disappeared down the jetway. Letty and Baxter sat in separate rows, ignoring each other until they touched down in Orlando two hours later.

They found Baxter's truck in a parking structure, exactly where the NSA spooks said it would be. As they walked out to the truck, Letty made an effort and said, "Warm and damp."

Baxter nodded and said, "That's the main thing about Florida. The heat and humidity. I was born and raised in Belle Glade, and in the summer, it gets so hot and humid you can't breathe. We didn't have air-conditioning until I was twelve, and Mom started getting sick from the heat and the air when they burned the sugarcane fields. My dad didn't believe in it. Air-conditioning. Said it made you weak."

It was the single longest thing he'd ever said to her.

The Toyota Tundra looked rough—gray, ten years old, door dings—and when Letty asked about it, Baxter grunted, "I like old Tundras. I'm a fanboy."

"Will you like old Tundras if we break down in the middle of the Sonoran Desert?"

"Not gonna happen," he said. "The truck is perfect. I maintain it myself. Get in."

The truck had a crew cab with a short bed, and they threw their bags in the backseat. The interior, Letty admitted to herself, was flawless and comfortable, with aftermarket leather bucket seats. A green deodorizer tree hung from the rearview mirror, and a black carbon-fiber clamp-like mechanism extended from the dashboard between the driver's and the passenger's positions.

Baxter took an iPad out of his bag and clipped it into the clamp and said, "It doesn't look new, but it is. Nothing on it but bullshit. It's on a swivel, so either one of us can use it. Hooked into Verizon. Password is 3890@7703. If you forget it, and I'm not around, you can look it up on your phone by searching for the geographic coordinates for Washington, DC. Remember to put the 'at' sign halfway through."

"Got it," she said. And, "We need to talk, since we didn't on the plane or back in Washington. Before we get to the motel."

"I know."

Baxter put on a pair of black-rimmed glasses and wheeled the truck out of its parking spot, then stopped as a metallic rattling noise came from the truck bed. "What the fuck is that? It can't be the truck, unless some asshole ran it into something."

He pulled over, popped the truck bed cover, looked inside, relocked it, got back in the truck, and said, "Drum set. Gotta stop in the morning and get some padding or Bubble Wrap. I'm not gonna listen to that thing rattle all the way to the Pacific Ocean."

THEY DROVE OUT to the freeway in silence, then Baxter said, "I know I'm not supposed to try to hustle you into bed and I won't."

"Good. We need to be clear about that," Letty said.

"I'm clear about it," he said. "I'm too scared to think about sex. Besides, you're not my type. I like robust blondes. You're not one.

And I'm clear about the fact that I don't want to die out there. Did you even listen to what Delores was saying about these guys?"

"Delores?"

"Mary Johnson. Her real name is Delores Nowak. I'm not supposed to tell you that, but fuck 'em, I'm the one whose ass is on the line. If you read even a little between the lines, the Ordinary People are willing to kill off a few hundred people, or maybe more, because that's sure as shit is what's gonna happen if they pull the plug on the heat in the Twin Cities in February."

"You think so?"

"I know so. Remember when the power grid crashed in Texas a few years ago? More than two hundred people died and that only went on for a few days. And it wasn't really that cold. Not like a northern city. The Ordinary People gotta know what they'll be doing. Killing us? We wouldn't even be a pimple on the ass of what they're planning to do."

Letty shrugged: "We can handle it. We don't have to make lifelong friends with these people—we just have to identify them and call the FBI."

"Bullshit. I'm gonna have to talk to them. You will, too. I don't want to die for Delores's little Hail Mary pass," Baxter said. "What they really need to do is send some guys like me up to the possible targets, shut down the gas hardware long enough to clean out the corrupt software, if it really is corrupt, and install new stuff, with better security. This sneaking around in LA is crazy."

"They may be doing that," Letty said.

"What?" Baxter frowned as he glanced over at her.

"I talk to security people all the time, at Homeland. They believe in compartmentalization like the pope believes in Jesus," Letty said. "I wouldn't be surprised if NSA is working on a backup that you don't know about. They didn't tell you because they want you focused on Ordinary People. They want to identify them because they want to stick guns in their ears. Let them know if the Twin Cities or Bozeman or Rochester goes down, they're all getting the needle. No money, just the needle."

"That's harsh, but you could be right," Baxter said.

"One more thing. They're lying about something. *You're* lying about something, since you're NSA, too. You want to tell me what it is?"

Baxter steered around a slow-moving Prius and said, "I don't know what they're lying about. I know they're lying about something. Interesting that you picked up on it, though."

"You're telling me the truth now?"

"I am," Baxter said. He nodded, and she believed him.

LETTY KNEW HER COVER but hadn't gotten the details on Baxter's. She asked about it.

"I got it on a flash drive, I gotta memorize it on the way to LA," Baxter said. "You'll have to take the wheel for a while. We need to be on the road at least twelve hours a day. I'll drive eight, if you can take four in the middle."

"That's fine."

He'd read through the material once, he said, on the plane. According to the legend created by the NSA, perhaps with input from the CIA, Baxter, whose new name would be Paul Jims, had run a ransomware attack on the Confederate Memorial Medical Center in Willow Branch, Georgia.

There had been an actual, real-world attack on the hospital, but the perpetrators hadn't been identified. The attack had taken the ICU offline just long enough for an elderly patient to die, although some news stories about it suggested the patient was about to die, or already had died, when the attack took place. In any case, the hospital's insurance company had paid the attackers five hundred thousand dollars to turn the hospital back on.

One of the now-online news stories, from an actual newspaper, said that a confidential source told the paper that the attack had come out of Florida. The original story hadn't said that, but the original story was now long forgotten in the stream of daily media crap. The new story, as placed by the NSA, was now the ongoing truth.

"That's great, as long as Ordinary People didn't do the hospital," Letty said quietly.

Baxter shook his head. "They didn't. I looked at the Russian attack and the hospital attack. Totally different software writing styles."

"So we're good," Letty said.

"No, we're not," Baxter said. "We're trapped in a bad movie. That's what we're in. A really bad fuckin' movie, poorly written. Especially my part."

THEY GOT TO GAINESVILLE and checked into a Hampton Inn near the university campus, a few minutes after midnight. They agreed they'd get up at seven o'clock, grab a quick sandwich and hit the campus, do a tour of student bars, try to get out of town before noon.

In the room, with two beds, Letty took her pistols out of her duffel bag, checked them, though they were in perfect condition, to make a point about guns and her familiarity with them. Baxter was curious, said he'd gone to a gun range with friends from Houston, where he grew up, and fired rifles, but had never felt the need to own a gun.

Letty let him handle the two weapons, explained the mechanisms, which he picked up on. After dry-firing them a few times, he said, "When this is over, maybe I'll get one. Though I'm more software than hardware. Of course, that's assuming that I'm still alive, which seems unlikely."

Letty put the guns away, and said, "Let's get down to our underwear. I need to know if you've got a hairy back."

"I do."

They undressed to their underwear, checked each other out: Baxter was pale, hairy, and overweight, with full sleeve tattoos—heavy on astrological signs and numbers, like fifty digits of pi—and breasts larger than Letty's. He was unembarrassed. To Letty, he said, "You're got four small moles on your back, under the wings, that look like the handle of the Big Dipper."

She hadn't known. "Remember that. You might be able to use it."

"Yes. I'm not going to push on you because Delores said if I did, she'd ship me to Diego Garcia. But I gotta say, you're not totally unattractive."

"Thanks for the thought," Letty said. "I'm going to need you to pull the dressings off my back and put new ones on."

He did that and was gentle about it. He said, "Wings like a dark angel. No blood. Healing good. Day after tomorrow, it'll look like it's two years old."

"A raven, not an angel," she said. And, "What's Diego Garcia?"

"Island in the middle of the Indian Ocean. Listening post. The closest thing on earth to nowhere."

When the pads were covering the tattoo, Letty fished a tee-shirt out of her bag and pulled it over her head, to sleep in. "I'm setting the phone to get up early."

BAXTER SLEPT SOUNDLY and silently; Letty didn't, half-conscious part of the time, wondering if the bear-sized man was about to drop on her.

At five minutes before six o'clock, five minutes before the alarm was set to go off, and feeling foggy, she rolled out of bed, turned off the alarm, moved quietly to the bathroom, shut the door, showered, brushed her teeth and hair, and dressed. When she left the bathroom, she found Baxter sitting on the edge of the bed, elbows on his knees, looking at the floor between his feet.

"You okay?"

"Yeah, I guess," he said. He was the living definition of *morose*. "Give me thirteen minutes."

Made her smile, a little, because it sounded so nerd-like. "Exactly thirteen minutes."

He looked up and said, seriously, "Yeah. Thirteen. I'll be out in thirteen minutes."

He took his clothes with him and, thirteen minutes later, emerged from the bathroom, showered, shaved, dressed, and reeking of Drakkar Noir. "Let's get breakfast and walk the campus. The buildings will be open pretty soon, if they're not already. I'm not sure—when I was here, I never got up this early."

They left the truck in a parking structure by the student union, walked through the bookstore, which had more orange and blue Gator shirts than books, and into the union, where Letty hit the Wells Fargo ATM for the receipt, and they got bagels and coffee at a Starbucks. With the food and drink in hand, Baxter led the way outside and across a broad lawn to an uncomfortable concrete picnic table under an enormous live oak.

As they ate, he pointed out a variety of classroom buildings: "What we're sitting on is called the Reitz Union lawn, and that . . ." He pointed across the lawn at an undistinguished redbrick building, ". . . is the computer science building. Right next to it is the Marston Science Library. I spent ninety percent of my time here in those two buildings, along with the union. I lived close enough to campus that I could ride my bike in and . . . that was about it."

"You don't strike me as a cyclist," Letty said.

"I wasn't trying out for the Tour de France. I was trying to get my ass from my room to Computer Science without paying for parking. Physics and other engineering shit is over there on the other side of the union . . ." He waved in the general direction of the student union. ". . . and really what you need to remember is 'redbrick.' You remember that, and you mostly can't go wrong."

As they walked around, they passed a pond with a sign that said "Danger—Alligators and Snakes in Area."

"Yeah. We're in Florida," Baxter said.

WHEN THEY'D COVERED most of the campus, they went back to the truck, and Letty threw the ATM receipt on the floor of the backseat. Then they took a trip down Congress Avenue, where Baxter pointed out his two favorite bars and a pizza joint where he said he lived much of his campus life; Letty took photos.

Next, he drove them past his old living quarters, which were in the rear of a house owned by an old lady who, he said, "was a pretty nice old lady. I was there for three years."

"It's like every state university, but with palm trees and Spanish moss in the live oaks," Letty said. "I've seen enough. I couldn't remember much more. What we need to do is talk about your time here. We can do that on the way to California."

"Thirty-six fuckin' hours," Baxter said. "You ready?"

"Yes. After a couple of stops."

They stopped at an Office Depot and bought Bubble Wrap and wrapped the drum set, and from there, went to a Guitar Center, where Letty bought six drumsticks, two sets of brushes, and a practice pad. Before she got back in the truck, she rolled the tips of the drumsticks over a rough concrete curb, to give them a worn look. They made a final stop at a Whole Foods market, where they bought sandwiches and crackers for the trip, along with off-brand cola and ice that they put in the Yeti cooler that sat on the truck's backseat.

"I liked this place all right," Baxter said, as they headed for the I-75 on-ramp. He thought about it for a minute, then said, "Actually, I didn't like it that much. I can't really say that I ever had a good time here. Not one that lasted, anyway."

They left Gainesville behind at ten o'clock in the morning, give or take, ground through the I-75 traffic jam going north, made it to I-10 and took a geographical left. Except for a brief loop around New Orleans, they'd stay on I-10 all the way to Los Angeles.

"Tell me stories about Gainesville," Letty said, as they rolled out of town. "Your main girlfriend there. The time you got drunkest. Getting high on weed and where you bought it. The fight you saw in a bar . . . what music you listened to."

Baxter talked, getting into it, reminiscing, sometimes amusing, and it seemed to Letty that he kept coming back to one particular girlfriend who might have dumped him. Was she his only serious girlfriend? Letty didn't ask.

"I liked weed and I liked micro-dosing on acid. But you know what? I almost never did it, because I couldn't afford it. I mean, I had about two extra dollars a week to live on. I actually worked part-time in a men's clothing store, selling accessories, which was stuff like ties and underwear and socks, minimum wage with a two percent commission. I only got to work in the suit department for a day, where the big commission money was. The buyer over there thought I was . . ."

He hesitated, and Letty filled in: "Unsuitable?"

"I was gonna say that," Baxter said.

"Bull. You never thought of it," Letty replied.

Baxter's amusement didn't extend to Letty's suggestion that they skip a few of the McDonald's restaurants that they passed on the highway.

"You're probably seventy or eighty pounds overweight and you're not using any calories sitting in the truck," she said. "You must have eaten three thousand calories already today and . . ."

"Shut the fuck up."

"You could at least drink Diet Coke. Every one of those . . ."

"Shut the fuck up."

". . . is like a hundred and forty empty calories per can . . ."

"Shut the fuck up . . ."

"Maybe you would have had more girlfriends if you lost weight," Letty said.

"I don't have much trouble that way," Baxter said. "Women are basically simple creatures. Taking them to bed isn't a problem."

"Shut the fuck up."

Baxter laughed as Letty fumed and looked out the passenger window, but finally she couldn't stand it any longer, and said, "Women are *not* simple. Not as simple as men."

"Then how come they're so easy to manipulate?" Baxter asked. "You tell the pretty ones that they're smart, and the smart ones that they're pretty, and badda-bing, you got them in bed."

"That's the most cynical thing I ever heard."

"And you work in the Senate? I don't believe you," Baxter said.

"Okay. It's *one* of the most cynical things I've heard."

"Not even in the top hundred."

Letty had to think about that for a while, finally admitted, "Okay, not in the top hundred. But still cynical."

Baxter laughed again.

Baxter turned out to be a car freak. They were still in North Florida and they were passed by a car doing perhaps a hundred miles an hour and he said, "Whoa! See that?"

"See what?"

"BMW 8 Series convertible. Rare car, at least around here."

"Jesus. I thought you'd run over a snake or something," Letty said. "Or a sharecropper."

Later: "Got a Range Rover coming up behind us."

"So what?"

"Nice car. Clumsy, unreliable, expensive to service, but nice-looking."

"If you like cars like that, why do you drive this piece of shit?"

"This is *not* a piece of shit," Baxter said. "This is a highly tuned, expensively upgraded Q-ship. Fast and agile, for a pickup truck. It can go places that would cause a Range Rover's fenders to fall off. Where not even a cop would follow."

"If you say so."

After a moment, Baxter asked, "What do you drive, anyway? Wait: let me guess. A Mini. Countryman."

"A Highlander hybrid." When Baxter didn't respond, she asked, "What? It's a piece of shit?"

"No, actually, it's a pretty good machine. Makes sense, especially in California. Mountains and high prices for gas."

IN THE EVENING, pushing into the night, Letty got out the practice pad and a pair of drumsticks, pushed the seat back as far as it would go, put the pad on her knees and began drumming, with side trips to the dashboard and the windowsill. Baxter found a classic rock station and she played along and he didn't seem to mind.

The trip across country, Letty would later tell someone, was like a survey of American foliage: going from lush, semitropical palms, into piney woods, into desert, and back into lush, semitropical California.

They spent the first road night at a Days Inn in Houston, Texas. Though it was late, they hauled the electronic drum set into the motel and Letty set it up, to make sure it was working. She'd used electronic drums when she was taking lessons. After working with the drums and the console for a few minutes, she said, "Welp. I suck."

Baxter said, "We should have time for you to practice when we get to LA. I mean, how hard could it be?"

"Hard," she said. "I sound like I'm in junior high band class."

The last half of the second day and most of the third was done through desert of various degrees of hardness, with long intervals between stops; Baxter began getting three Quarter Pounders at the infrequent McDonald's they passed, but turned up his nose at Burger Kings.

They spent the second night in Deming, New Mexico, and the third day threaded their way through the traffic in Tucson and Phoenix and from there across the California line. Letty had driven I-10 from LA to Phoenix and was somewhat familiar with it. Baxter was not.

"Doesn't look like the Sahara, just looks kinda shitty," Baxter said of the desert miles, as they approached Palm Springs. "Except for the car that passed us a minute ago. A fuckin' Bentley convertible, can you believe that? Driver looked like he's about nineteen."

Along the way, they'd collected receipts from fast-food places, bought a chunk of petrified wood at Quartzsite, and a bag of elk jerky, which Letty emptied out the window when Baxter told her it would give him cataclysmic gas. She threw the bag in the backseat, where it infused the truck with jerky molecules, a little nasal music for the possibly curious.

When they passed the wind turbine field on the west edge of Palm Springs, Letty said, "This is where the West Coast starts. Those windmills. That's what I always thought, anyway."

Baxter took the truck to the edge of LA, jogged north to the 210, and then into Pasadena where they found a long-term motel called the La Rouchefort where the spooks had made reservations for them.

"We made good time," Baxter said, as they pulled into the parking lot. The motel was a dump; if there was anything on the front façade that wasn't peeling, Letty couldn't see it. "Not quite dark."

Letty: "Yeah. Let's get a key. You can take thirteen minutes to clean up while I haul the drums inside. Then you can call Delores while I'm cleaning up, and we'll go scout out Caltech and this Professor Harp guy."

"Already? Tonight?"

"We're in a hurry, remember?"

"Yeah." He was suddenly glum again. "Shit just got real, huh?"

65

FOUR

Caltech was a bust.

They walked around the campus, which had tasteful landscaping surrounding boring stuccoed buildings—Baxter referred to it as "a symphony in beige"—and was oddly quiet for a university. There were few people on the interior sidewalks in the evening, or strolling between the buildings, although the buildings were still lit.

"Everybody's studying?"

"More like watching porn," Baxter said. "It's the opiate of the coding class."

The school was adjacent to a residential neighborhood of well-kept homes on its south and east sides, including the home of Professor Eugene Harp.

Harp lived off Arden Road, three blocks south of the campus. They cruised the curving street in the pickup. As they passed Harp's house, Baxter said, "I'll tell you what—if he bought half of that place for one-point-three, he got a crazy deal. Maybe he had something on her."

Harp's house was a sprawling stone-and-board two-story house of no particular architectural style—"California nice"—set above the street in a heavily treed landscape. They could see bright shimmering light coming from the backyard and could hear the thump of soft-rock music. A half-dozen cars were parked in a long circular driveway in front of the house.

"Nothing in the driveway but junk," Baxter said, checking the collection of small Toyotas and Hondas.

As they lingered on the street, a group of four young people, three men and a woman, strolled down the sloping street, up Harp's driveway and around the side of the house to the back. As they walked, they passed a joint between them.

"Party," Letty said.

Baxter: "I don't like the way you said that."

"Let's get back to the motel," Letty said. "I need to change into something more party-like."

"I don't *have* anything party-like," Baxter said.

"That's okay," Letty said. "You're not invited."

"Ah, man . . . this is . . ."

"C'mon, c'mon," Letty said impatiently.

At the motel, Letty changed into a blue cotton sleeveless blouse that showed the tips of the raven's wings on her back, a washed-out denim skirt that fell barely south of criminal and, at the waistband, freed the butterfly tattoo, and plastic flip-flops. Baxter looked at her, shook his head and said, "Not fair."

She didn't ask him what wasn't fair because she had an idea what he meant, and instead asked, "Too much?"

"No. You could lose the bra, but that would be asking for trouble. I dunno. What do I know? The cane and the knee support makes you look weird, with the skirt, but hot-weird."

"That's good," Letty said. "Hot-weird, I'll take that."

She was checking herself in a full-length mirror that was covered with coppery amoeba-shaped corrosion spots. As close as she could tell, through the spots, Baxter's assessment was accurate; she'd keep the bra, which, in any case, wasn't much sturdier than Kleenex.

"Please, please don't do anything that will cause trouble," Baxter said.

"I'm going to a party," Letty said. "What could possibly go wrong?"

Baxter had no more complaints. He dropped her a block from Harp's house, said, "Be careful," and drove away. Letty shoved her NSA phone into the denim skirt's side pocket, adjusted the knee support, and limped around the house, leaning lightly on the blackthorn cane.

Harp's heavily landscaped backyard sloped gently up to a forty-foot swimming pool that glowed aqua-green in the night. Two dozen people were scattered around the patio that surrounded the pool, all with drinks. Nobody was swimming, but several people sat with their bare feet in the pool, drinks by their sides, two peering at their phones. Letty limped to an unattended bar where she found three metal tubs, one holding bottles of Dos Equis, with a sign that said "21+" and the other two holding Coke, Pepsi, Sprite, and Fiji Water.

She grabbed a beer, popped the top with a bottle opener on a chain, and sidled into the party, beginning with a group of four male students who stopped talking as she wandered up. They were dressed in jeans and short-sleeve shirts and leather sandals that sent subtle signals of helpless computer nerdism.

"What happened to your knee?" one of the men asked, a crafty sally.

"Tried to hop a creek," she said. She took a hit on the beer. "Didn't quite make it. Hit a slippery rock and went down."

"Up in the mountains?"

"Florida doesn't have mountains," Letty said. "Florida has swamps."

"Florida, I know it well," a second man said. To the others: "It's that thing that hangs down from the East Coast, like an elderly penis."

That was weak, but she smiled, which the men took as encouragement, and they all simultaneously began chatting her up. As they were doing that, Letty was watching a fortysomething man wearing jeans and a tee-shirt with a picture of Karl Marx wearing sunglasses and the legend "Class Dismissed." He was the oldest man at the party, looked in good shape, thin, Roman nose, receding dark hair. He had a beer in his hand and Letty asked Larry— one of her new posse—"Is that Dr. Harp?"

"Yes, it is," he said. "You don't know him?"

"No, I . . . I'm sort of party-crashing. I'm here checking out your economics department. I was talking to a girl there and she mentioned the party . . . though I haven't seen her."

"Probably Carol. She can't decide between computer science, math, and economics, so she tries to do all three. Doesn't party. Tall, iridescent blue hair . . ."

"Mmm . . ." Neither yes nor no, in case Carol showed up.

ONCE ADOPTED BY her group of males, Letty kept them moving, integrating her original group with others, then peeling away, nursing the beer, watching Harp, and noticing the younger woman hanging behind the professor, who was watching Harp even more closely than Letty was.

The woman was a semi-attractive blonde, who might have been quite attractive if she'd done anything with it: her hair was frizzy, glasses tended to slip down her nose and she'd push them up with a middle finger. A loose shift-like dress concealed her body, which Letty judged was solid, athletic. Every once in a while, the woman would slide up to Harp's side and throw a comment at whoever he was talking to.

The whole party tended to drift clockwise around the pool, and Letty watched the woman. She was young, younger than Letty. Twenty? Twenty-one? Drinking a Coke . . . but maybe she simply didn't like alcohol. At one point, as Harp's group rotated clockwise, the woman stepped slightly in front of him and he put one hand out, on her back, guiding her along the edge of the pool.

A familiar touch, Letty thought. A few minutes later, he did the same thing during the next ambling turn, but this time, his hand was lower, on the top of the woman's butt. She didn't react, which suggested a deeper intimacy.

Made Letty smile; her wolverine smile.

Her posse wanted to know more about the wings they could see at the top of her back, so she let one of them pull up her blouse to check it out, which the posse did, with unanimous praise. Harp was going by and took a look, grinned at her and said, "Ouch. Bet that hurt."

He kept going, the young woman next to him, like a remora.

At eleven o'clock, Letty called Baxter and said, "People are leaving. I might be a while. I'll call."

"What are you doing?"

"I don't know exactly. I'm watching."

"Please, please . . ."

The pool patio was set in a garden, the edges spotted with densely foliated trees that Letty recognized from her Stanford days as fern pines. A groping couple had occupied a niche between two of the pines, and when they departed, Letty slipped into the niche, and then pushed farther back into the dark.

She didn't know exactly why she did that, but it felt right.

Harp's woman friend began walking around the pool area carrying a garbage bag, picking up party scraps. Letty took a video with her phone. The woman carried the bag into the back of the house, but didn't reemerge.

Letty waited for another fifteen minutes in the trees, until Harp had shooed the last of the partygoers away. That done, he carried a Whole Foods bag around the pool, picking up bottles and cans. He emptied the bag into a recycling bin that sat in a corral at the corner of the house, turned off the backyard lights at an exterior switch, took a last look around, and went inside.

Second-floor lights came on a moment later. Letty waited. The second-floor lights dimmed, then went out, replaced by the flickering light of a candle.

Letty moved out of her fern pine hiding place and walked to the house. There was still a lamp turned on in a ground-floor room, casting a bit of light into what appeared, through the back-door window, to be a kitchen. She tried the doorknob, and it turned. The door gave a little raspy grunt when she pushed it open, but then swung in.

She hesitated . . . If she got caught . . .

With her arm hair bristling a bit, she listened, heard nothing. She kicked off her flip-flops and walked barefoot through the kitchen, down a hallway to a stairway going up. Standing quietly, she could hear, from the second floor, the sounds of a couple making love.

In the light from the lamp in a corner, she saw a green leather purse sitting on a couch near the bottom of the stairs. She tiptoed over to it, picked it up, carried it into the kitchen. With the illumination from her telephone, she dug a wallet out of the purse, and extracted a California driver's license and a Caltech student ID.

She put both on the kitchen counter and made two photos with her phone. That done, she put the cards back in the wallet, the wallet back in the purse, and the purse back on the couch. Upstairs, the lovemaking was getting noisier. She tiptoed back through the kitchen, out the door, and put on her flip-flops.

LETTY WALKED AROUND the house, moving slowly in the dark, and then out to the street. Baxter had proven himself to be reliable with communications, and when she called, he picked her up from where she waited behind a thick-trunked coast live oak.

"Do any good?" he asked.

"Depends on your moral position," Letty said.

"Moral position on what?"

"Blackmail," Letty said. "I'll have to go online and check Caltech's attitude on professors having sex with students."

"Uh-oh. Really? He's banging a student?" Baxter asked.

"Not so much banging as making love to, which is why I might feel a little guilty about using it. Her driver's license says she's twenty-one, so she's an adult. She should get to pick who she . . . you know."

"Bangs."

"Has sex with," Letty said. "On the other hand, you have to consider the lopsided power equation . . ."

"Only if she's a student of his. If she's not a student of his, she's bangable. In my opinion," Baxter said. "I'm not a Title IX fanatic."

"I'd suspected that," Letty said. "We'll have to see what Caltech says. Most universities ban that kind of thing. I'm saying, we go talk to him . . ."

"And he freaks out, pulls a gun and kills us."

"You, maybe, not me," Letty said. "After you're dead, he and I discuss what he knows about Ordinary People and I get him to cough up some names. Or, I tell him, I'll call Caltech's HR department, and turn him in."

"Brutal," Baxter said. "If I were naturally mean, I'd tell you I like it. But I'm not that mean."

"You don't have to worry about it, because in this particular scenario, you're dead," Letty said.

ON THE WAY BACK to the La Rouchefort, Letty plugged their iPad into the truck's swivel clip, and Googled "Caltech Sexual Conduct Guidelines." A document popped up immediately and she read down to section 17.3.

17.3 Prohibition on Relationships between Employees and
   Undergraduates

This policy prohibits sexual or romantic relationships between an undergraduate student and a faculty member, post-doctoral scholar, or staff member. Any Responsible Employee who becomes aware of such a relationship is expected to report it immediately to the Title IX Coordinator. The non-undergraduate party in the relationship will be held responsible for prohibited conduct violating this policy, regardless of whether a complaint is filed.

"We got him if we want him," Letty said, shutting down the iPad.

"Makes me a little queasy, but if we're really going to do this, he'd be the place to start," Baxter said. "Better than hanging around in student bars, hoping for the best."

"I'll talk to him tomorrow," Letty said. "I want to keep you out of sight until we've got a better grip on what we're doing."

"Good with me. Say, isn't blackmail against the law?" Baxter asked.

"You got Google," Letty said. "Look it up."

THE LA ROUCHEFORT didn't have bedbugs, Letty thought, only because they'd been eaten by the cockroaches, one of which scuttled into the kitchen sink cabinet when they turned on the lights. The room stank of tobacco and alcohol and cleaning liquid, but did have two beds with clean sheets, along with a compact refrigerator, a coffeepot, and a small sink. An ice bucket sat next to the TV, with a Holiday Inn logo on the lid.

Baxter looked at it, then at Letty: "They steal their fuckin' ice buckets?"

"Trying for a more classy presentation," Letty said.

The wi-fi was acceptable, the bathtub wasn't; the shower was merely annoying, providing a sprinkle rather than a torrent.

Baxter had helped Letty set up the drum set on the first night, and while she was changing into jeans and a tee-shirt, he took charge of setting it up in the room. That done, they both went to their laptops.

The laptops had been supplied by the spooks and both had encrypted mail caches hidden on the hard drives that worked both sending and receiving. Letty had mail from Johnson asking for a report; Baxter had the same thing. They both shut down the mail without replying and Letty moved over to the drum set with a pair of sticks.

"What are we doing tomorrow?" Baxter asked. He'd shed his jeans and shirt and was crawling into bed in his underwear.

"I'm going to find Harp and ask the question."

"You're going to tell him the Big Lie? We're on the run?"

"If it seems . . . appropriate."

"I'd feel bad about blackmailing him, if that's what we do," Baxter said.

"I understand," Letty said. "I'd feel bad about it, too, but I'd feel worse if Ordinary People killed a few hundred people in the Twin Cities because we had qualms about blackmail."

Letty plugged her headphones into the iPad, called up the video of Twenty One Pilots' "Ride" and began drumming along, and followed that with the Preoccupations' "Bunker Buster."

Thinking it out. Considering her qualms.

Getting her rhythm on.

FIVE

Early the next morning, right at daybreak in the Mojave Desert, more or less 160 miles northeast of downtown Los Angeles, California:

An obsidian black Mercedes-Benz G-Class, a *Geländewagen*, rocked and rolled down an arroyo, kicking up wheel-high dust as it went. At the base of a stony bluff, it stopped, and two men got out, while a third man remained in the backseat.

The two men, dressed comfortably in tee-shirts, cargo pants, and cross-training shoes, walked around to the back of the vehicle, popped the hatch, and dragged a living body out.

The body was that of a youngish man or woman, though it was hard to tell exactly what he or she might look like, or even its sex, since the body had long brown hair and the lower part of its face was heavily wrapped in silver duct tape.

The men dragged the tape-wrapped body to the bluff, and propped it in a seated position, its head against the rock.

When the body was in position, the third man got out of the truck. Unlike the two hard men, he wore a pale yellow dress shirt under a linen sport coat, light blue chinos, and tasseled loafers, suitable for lunch at a country club.

He walked to the bluff, picking up his feet, to keep the dust off the shine of his shoes, then squatted to look at the body. The body looked back at him, its face wet with sweat, although the day was not that hot. The man reached out and pulled tape off the mouth of the body.

"We would not be here, Daniel," he said in excellent but accented English, "if you had given me the names back in LA. Now we're going to give you a painful demonstration of what your very short future looks like. No questions, just the demonstration."

He pressed the tape back across Daniel's mouth, and gestured to one of the other men, who went to the SUV and came back with a red two-gallon gas can. The man in the yellow slacks stepped back and the man with the gas can poured a pint of gas on Daniel's lower legs, and asked, "How's that, Mr. Step?"

"That should do it."

He leaned toward Daniel and said, "You should have talked to us last night."

Daniel grunted something and Step pulled the tape off his mouth. "What?"

"Fuck you."

"All right," Step said. He took an antique Zippo lighter from his pocket, clicked open the top, and sparked up a flame. Daniel said, "Please . . ."

Step put the flame next to the gas-soaked legs and the flame leaped across them and Daniel began screaming and screamed for a long time, as the smell of gas fumes and burning pork spread across the desert landscape.

Step gestured to one of the other men, who stepped up with a fire extinguisher and sprayed it on Daniel's legs; Daniel moaned and began to weep.

Step said to the man with the gas can, "Do it."

The man poured the rest of the can over Daniel's entire body, started with his head and hair, then down across his face, chest, and hips.

Step said, "Daniel, give us the names, or I swear to God, I'll kill you. I'll burn you to death. Right now, right here."

"Please . . . don't, please . . ."

The man in the chinos came back, squatted again, the end of a lit cigarette dangerously close to the captive's gas-soaked shirt. He said, "Give me the names, Daniel, or you burn."

Daniel began to cry uncontrollably, his body writhing and shaking, and the man in the chinos waited patiently, said, "Give me . . . the names. If you give me the names, we will walk away from you. We will not take the tape off. If you can't get it off, then you'll die here like a bug in a cocoon. But, we'll give you that chance. On my word. On my honor. If you refuse, then you burn."

Silence, a beat, then, "Loren Barron."

"Spell."

"L-o-r-e-n B-a-r-r-o-n."

"And the woman?"

"Brianna Wolfe."

"Spell."

The body spelled the name.

"And their location?"

"Los Angeles? I don't know the address, I've never been to their house. We always met at the place in Venice. The bar."

"Okay," said the man in the chinos. "I believe you." He patted Daniel on a knee, stood and said to the other two, "Leave him. Let's go."

The three men walked back toward the vehicle, side by side. Ten feet short of the truck, the man in the chinos spun, drew a pistol from beneath the sport coat, and fired a single shot at the taped-up captive.

One of the other men whistled and said, "That's some good shooting, Mr. Step."

"Not that good," Step said. Daniel had been hit just to the left of the bridge of his nose. "I'm out of training. I was shooting for his forehead."

"But a one-shot kill," one of the hard men said.

"Yes, but I fired too quickly. I didn't want him to see it, to fear it, so I tried to move too fast and missed my target. I need some work," Step said in his excellent English. He scratched the side of his face, gestured with his gun toward the body. "Listen, you two. If you want to go into business, you should know that this is bad business, this killing. *Bad* business. Bad *for* business. Sometimes necessary, but not often. Keep that in mind."

He looked at his Rolex, which glittered gold in the sunrise. "Get the shovels. He doesn't have to go deep; nobody will ever find him here. Then let's get back. I promised Victoria I'd come out to the club and watch her 'Old Girlfriends' tennis match."

SIX

As Daniel was being murdered in the Mojave, Letty was getting out of bed, again, five minutes before the alarm went off. She killed it, cleaned up, and dressed. Again, when she left the bathroom, Baxter was sitting on the edge of his bed, elbows on his thighs, peering at the carpet.

Letty said, "Thirteen minutes."

He looked up. "Are we in a hurry?"

"Yes. Harp has a nine o'clock class in Control and Dynamical Systems, whatever that is. He'll be getting up soon and I want to talk to him before he goes to class."

Baxter was out of the bathroom in thirteen minutes, and they were out the door in seventeen. On the way across town to Caltech, Letty said, "Banging."

"What?"

"I'm going to use your crude sexist language on him, to add some weight to his predicament," she said.

"Crude, yes, sexist, no," Baxter said. "Predatory women are known to bang innocent young seminary students for their own animal purposes."

Letty shook her head, watched the landscape go by: after three days in the car, including two days in the desert, it seemed unreal, too lush, too LA, too Disney-like, like one of the Seven Dwarfs might pop out from behind a fire hydrant.

HARP'S HOUSE SHOWED a second-floor light and Letty wondered if the woman—Hannah Baldwin, according to her driver's license and student ID—had stayed overnight. She'd rather not have to deal with that.

She mentioned the problem to Baxter as they did a preliminary cruise past the house, but Baxter said, "Nah, she didn't stay. If you're banging a student, you want her leaving in the middle of the night, not at seven-thirty in the morning. You don't want the sun shining on her illegal ass, and all the going-to-work faculty seeing her."

"Good point." One thing she'd learned about Baxter, Letty thought, was that while he was personally unseemly, tatted-up and hairy, over-gelled and -cologned, looked like he bought his clothes from a tent maker, and was unselfconsciously cowardly, he was also wickedly intelligent. She wouldn't fool him about much.

"You can drop me," she said. "I'll walk up to the corner of California when I'm done; I'll call."

"Whatever you say, my little blueberry muffin."

"You can knock that shit off right now," Letty said.

"I don't think so. I'm tired of being bossed around . . . my little pink desert rose."

"Yeah, fuck you, Baxter . . . No, wait . . ."

They were both laughing, sorta, when he dropped her off with her limp and her cane. She walked up the circular drive and knocked on the door and leaned on the doorbell to make sure she was heard.

Two minutes later, Harp answered the door barefoot, in sweatpants and an orange tee-shirt. He frowned at her and said, "You're the girl with the crow tattoo . . ."

"Raven," Letty said. "We need to talk. Right now. Urgently."

"About what?"

"Your future at Caltech," Letty said.

"What?"

"I'm not crazy. Do you have tea, or coffee? I'm feeling a little cranky," Letty said.

"Why should I . . ."

"Because I need some information from you and I need it bad enough that I'm willing to blackmail you with Hannah Baldwin, the undergraduate student you're banging."

Harp's mouth dropped open, but after a brief hesitation, he stepped back and let her in.

LETTY WALKED THROUGH the entry and living room, to the kitchen. On the way, she paused at the couch and said, "I followed you into your house last night, after the party. While you were upstairs banging young Hannah, I took her student ID and driver's license from her purse, posed them against that great custom backsplash tile in the kitchen, and took a photo that will show time and GPS location in the metadata."

"I should strangle you and dump your body," Harp said, taking a half step toward her.

"No. If you tried, I'd use this cane to beat you to death. Take a look at that point . . ." She twirled it in her hands so he could see both the sharp and hammer-ends of the cane head. "So, you got tea?"

He did.

He had an electric Cuisinart kettle and made them cups of English Breakfast tea; they both took four packets of sugar. Watching him do it, quick and competent, he struck Letty as unconventionally attractive. She could see why Hannah Baldwin was with him, even if he was too old for her. He put the cups on the kitchen table, and they sat across from each other, and he said, "Talk. What do you want?"

She took a sip of the boiling-hot tea, and said, "I'm here from Gainesville, Florida, with a friend, who happens to be a computer genius."

"Those are a dime a dozen around here, if you're bragging," Harp said, crossing his legs and sipping his own tea. "You can't throw a rock without hitting one."

"Yeah. Well, this particular one is mine. We're poor. We tried to fix that a few weeks ago by locking up the computers at the Confederate Memorial Medical Center in Willow Branch, Georgia . . ."

A look of amusement crossed his face. "That was you? There's a rumor that you screwed the pooch."

"Yeah. We did. The feds are all over us. They don't know who we are, but they're still digging and they know where the Bitcoin is. Half million dollars."

"What does this have to do with me?"

"Some time back, a hacker combine called Ordinary People, which rumor says comes out of Caltech, held up the Russian rail system for fifty million dollars. Another Bitcoin deal. We need to get in touch with Ordinary People and we think you can help us with that."

"How could I . . . ?"

Letty noticed that he didn't blurt out something about not knowing who the Ordinary People were. "My computer genius looked at Vernon Pastek's phone records about the time he was extorting the Russians, and then did a search of the phone records of Caltech staff, and guess what? Yours matched up. You're either a member of Ordinary People, or you're close enough to them that you could act as a contact between Pastek and OP. So. We need names, five hundred thousand dollars' worth. If we don't get some from you, I'm going to call the Title IX people."

"C'mon, goddamnit, Hannah and I . . . there's real affection. She's not in any of my classes anymore . . ."

"Affection? Anymore? There you go. You're banging a good-looking chick and when you're done with her, you'll throw her away," Letty said. "You know it, and I know it."

"How do you know it?" Harp asked.

"Because I've been there," Letty said. "At Gainesville. Getting banged by a postdoc."

Harp stared at her for a moment, then said, "I'm begging you, don't call anyone. I don't know Ordinary People, but I've heard of them and I know they're local. I can ask around without anyone getting suspicious. If you give me a number . . ."

"The feds have grabbed a bunch of Bitcoin accounts. They're getting good at it. We need to move fast. You've got twelve hours to call me," Letty said. She took a slip of paper from her hip pocket and pushed it across the table. "I've got a burner. Call me at that number. No point in trying to track it, you'll only get back to Walmart."

"I'm not sure I can—"

"Twelve hours." Letty took a last sip of tea, pushed the cup away, walked out the front door—he made no attempt to catch her—and turned left, up the hill, and down California Boulevard, where Baxter was waiting in the shade of a ginkgo tree.

After confronting Harp, Letty and Baxter spent part of the morning at the motel, where Letty worked out on the drums and Baxter remained glued to his laptop; they spent the other part of the morning prowling around Pasadena in Baxter's truck and walking around the buildings at Caltech.

Baxter slipped into the Caltech computer stream like a long-time native. Letty got curious looks, and with her spaghetti-string blouse, her raven wings got even more.

"How did I get a fake name like Paul Jims?" Baxter asked at one point. "Makes me sound like I should be out shooting woodchucks."

"Probably picked by a computer program," Letty said. The ball of tape behind her knee was intensely annoying. "They fed in six hundred desirable fake name characteristics, and it spit out Paul Jims."

"You think you're joking, but you're probably right," Baxter said.

At one o'clock, they were eating burgers and cherry pie at a place called Pie 'n Burger when Eugene Harp called. "I have an address for you. Not names. Blond man and a redheaded woman. They'll meet you on the outdoor patio of Balls' Café on Colorado."

Letty: "What time?"

"Where are you?" Harp asked.

"A place called Burger 'n Pie."

"Pie 'n Burger," Harp corrected. "They'll be at the café in ten minutes, and they'll wait for ten minutes after that. If you don't show up by then, they're gone. You've got twenty minutes to get there."

"How far away are we?"

"Maybe five minutes, but parking can be a problem," Harp said. "Look at the mapping app on your phone."

He clicked off; Letty took a last bite of cherry pie and said, "Let's go."

On the way to Balls', Letty repeated to Baxter what she'd been told by Harp. "You'll go in by yourself. I'll hang back with the camera. If we're not going to get names, maybe we can get some facial recognition material."

"Ah, boy, this is it. This is it," Baxter moaned. "You're supposed to be there with the gun, to cover me."

"I'll only be a minute or two behind you," Letty said.

"How long does it take to shoot somebody?" Baxter asked. "Lot less than a minute, huh?"

THE CAFÉ, AS it turned out, was on the left side of the street as they drove east; the outdoor patio was a small alcove with a half-dozen tables, only one of them occupied, and that by an aging hipster with a gray man bun. As they drove past, a blond man and a red-headed woman, both wearing sunglasses, were walking down the sidewalk toward the café.

"Gotta be them. Don't look, don't look," Letty said to Baxter. "Go up a couple of blocks and turn around, cruise by again. If they're on the patio, I'll shoot them from the truck, then I can come with you."

Baxter nodded. They made an illegal U-turn two blocks down

Colorado, Letty checking for cops as they did it, then Letty rolled down her window, propped the GX8 against her arm, and looked straight ahead as they passed the café. The camera, in burst mode, fired off a series of frames.

When they were past, Letty checked the camera's screen, and found five frames that caught the pair with good resolution and from slightly different angles.

"Find a parking spot," she said. "We got what we need."

They lucked into a car vacating a space just around the corner from Balls'. Baxter hurriedly parked, and they were out and down the sidewalk, Letty clomping along with the cane and the limp.

"I'll do the talking, you answer the computer questions," she said. "Remember, you're nervous about this."

"I *am* nervous, won't have to fake that," Baxter said. "You got your gun?"

"I do."

"Ah, man, I don't want this. I'm a lover, not a fighter."

"That has been my understanding," Letty said.

As they approached the café, the redheaded woman saw them coming and said something to the blond man, whose back was to them. A waiter had just walked up to the couple, and as Letty and Baxter stepped onto the stone patio, the redhead said, brightly, "Here they are. Could we get a couple more menus?"

The waiter went away, and Letty and Baxter scraped back two of the metal chairs and sat down, and the woman said to them, "I'm Sue, and this is Bob. Who are you?"

Letty: "That's really funny. We're a Bob and Sue, too."

The woman smiled. "That *is* a funny coincidence. Our mutual friend . . ."

"You mean Professor Harp? He's not a friend of ours."

The waiter came with two more menus, and they ordered lemonades and Cokes, and he went away again.

The blond Bob said, "You're not cops? You have to say if you are."

"Well, Bob, that's complete bullshit," Baxter said, to Letty's surprise. She was supposed to do the talking. "You should look it up sometime. There's this thing called Google. They don't have to admit anything. There have been undercover cops who went so deep they had children with their targets. Anyway, we're not cops and we're only here to ask you for advice. How do you get Bitcoin out of a wallet that you have an address for . . . but that somebody else might be interested in? We're told that you would know."

"Couldn't you look that up?" Bob asked.

"We tried, and it all sounded like thirdhand bullshit." Baxter leaned across the table. "If you can help, we'll give you a taste."

"How big?" Sue asked.

"Twenty-five K?"

"No way," Bob said. "I'm not risking federal prison for twenty-five K."

"So don't take anything," Baxter said. "Tell us what to do and we'll go away . . ."

"We'd take half," Sue said.

Now Letty jumped in. "Fuck that." To Baxter: "C'mon, Bob. These nitwits got nothing for us."

She started to stand up when Sue said, "Bet there's a reward out for you. Professor Harp told us about the hospital thing. We could probably get fifty thousand for turning you in."

Letty sat back down and said, "You know what else you could

get, bitch?" She tilted the menu down to cover the move, pulled her hand out of her jeans pocket and pointed the 938 at Sue's chest. "You could get a nine-millimeter right between your tits."

They all sat frozen for a couple of beats, then Bob put up two hands and said, "Hey! Hey!"

Baxter growled at Letty: "Put the piece away, Charlie. They're fuckin' harmless." Letty slipped the gun back in her pocket, and Baxter said to Bob and Sue, "Call Harp and tell him if he resigns today, the university probably couldn't touch him."

Letty and Baxter pushed back in their chairs. Sue said, "Okay. Okay. We can tell you a couple of things."

Letty and Baxter settled again and Letty said, "Like what?"

"You're never going to see that money," Sue said. "The Bitcoin. If I were you, I'd send the address back to the hospital's insurance company and hope if the feds ever do track you down, that'd lighten your sentences. I'm serious about that."

"No help," Letty said.

Sue shrugged: "Nothing to be done about it. If you want to get in the ransomware business, you've got to set up your exit ahead of time. If you don't do that . . ."

"What do we do?" Baxter asked.

"When you get the coin, you move fast," Sue said. "Really fast. You've already set up accounts in every shithole money-laundering country you can find and run the Bitcoin through them as fast as you can. Overnight. Not the whole amount with every jump—you break the take up into smaller pieces, different for every jump, so the transactions aren't immediately obvious. You don't want a million disappearing here and another million immediately popping up somewhere else. And then, after you've run it through all these other places, you take the Bitcoin to El Salvador, where it's legal tender. You've already arranged to sell it to a guy at a discount, maybe twenty percent, but you'll have anonymous cash. All that needs to be set up in advance—the whole sequence."

Bob: "If it's not set up in advance, you're shit outa luck. And you two . . . are shit outa luck."

"Can't be," Letty said. "We can't lose it all."

"You already have," Sue said. "It used to be, Bitcoin was fairly anonymous. Now the feds have gotten good at tracking it. The way to defeat them is to move it so fast that they can't keep up. They'll eventually get to El Salvador and then they'll give up."

"Because they know you've got a box full of nice greasy much-used greenbacks, courtesy of a Mexican drug cartel, and there'll be no way to trace it," Bob said.

Baxter: "Goddamnit." He looked at Letty. "I told you."

"There is one other possibility," Sue said. "But it's kinda nasty."

"I'll listen to anything," Letty said.

"There are some great hacker combines in Russia and North Korea. Do your research, you might be able to hook up with one of them, sell the Bitcoin address. Since they're government-sponsored, they can pull the Bitcoin out and there's nothing the feds or anyone else could do about it. You might get ten percent. You might also get ten years if the FBI finds out."

Baxter shook his head and said to Letty, "We should go."

"We gotta do the North Korea thing," Letty said to him. "Fifty thousand is better than nothing."

"I'll figure out something," Baxter said. "I can take a job, that'll hold us for a while."

"Hold *you* for a while," Letty said. "Not me. You can drop me off at that boat place we saw. Marina Ray. I'll find somebody who needs a cabin girl."

Sue asked Baxter, "What kind of job?"

Baxter shrugged: "I do machine controls. Always jobs there, good money."

"Not five hundred thousand good," Letty said. "Not tax free. We were gonna buy a boat in Cabo."

"Okay, I couldn't get five hundred, but I could get a hundred and fifty, two hundred," Baxter said.

"Yeah, *per year*. Three thousand a week, pay two thousand a month for a shitty apartment and pay all kinds of tax and . . . Fuck it, I'm tired of talking about it," Letty said. "Drop me at the Ray place. Let's go."

"You can take a fuckin' Uber," Baxter said.

"Not gonna get my drums in a fuckin' Uber," Letty said.

"Not gonna get your drums on a fuckin' boat," Baxter said.

"How good are you with the software?" Bob asked Baxter.

Baxter bobbed his head. "Very. Got a PhD from Florida, but school was one thing, industry was something else. Bores the snot outa me."

Sue cross-examined him with technical questions that Letty could barely follow, at best, and she eventually plugged her phone into a hundred-beats-per-minute blues shuffle that she slapped along with, on her thighs.

After a ten-minute quiz, Baxter got tired of the questioning and said, "Okay, you do what you gotta do. You got a job for me? Fine. If you don't, we'll say good-bye right now."

Sue looked at him for a few seconds, then said, "Maybe a job. If you're not cops."

Letty laughed and said to Baxter, "I'm going. You can have the fuckin' drums, I'm going to Marina Ray."

"It's Marina *del* Rey, not Marina Ray. I'll tell you what, sister: a good off-the-books software job pays a hell of a lot more than blowing some fat old sailor dude for a living," Sue said. "Give us a phone number and a few hours. You're likeable folks . . ."

"Nobody ever said that before," Baxter said, rolling his eyes.

". . . and we know off-the-books computer people. We'll ask around, and we'll take a modest fifteen percent commission," Sue concluded. To Letty: "Was that a real gun?"

Letty: "No. I carved it out of a bar of Ivory soap and colored it black with shoe polish."

"It's real," Baxter said. And, almost reluctantly, picking up on a comment by Billy Greet, "She could shoot the balls off a gnat. I've seen her do it. There are ball-less gnats all over North Florida."

The waiter reappeared. "So, are you folks ready to order?"

SEVEN

Letty and Baxter left Bob and Sue with a phone number and the waiter, and walked around the corner to the truck. "What do you think?" Baxter asked, as they walked.

"What I think is something I never thought I'd think," Letty said. "It's kinda . . . weird."

"What was weird?"

"That you could get a job with Homeland as an undercover guy," Letty said, as she looked up at him. "You're really good at this. I never saw *that* coming."

"Well. Thank you, I guess," Baxter said. He glanced back down the street. "When I saw them, I wasn't scared anymore. They looked like every software couple I ever met. Sue was the brains there."

"I think you're right," Letty said. "About all of it. Let's get back to the motel and call Delores, see what they can do with the photos."

They drove around a couple of blocks to get back to Colorado, then Baxter turned right when he should have turned left, and Letty asked, "Where are you going?"

"Looking in the rearview mirror. There's a beige Toyota back there that followed us through a couple of turns, but it's hanging back at corners . . . Always keeps cars between us."

"They're following us? You *are* good at this," Letty said.

"I read thriller novels," Baxter said. "A lot of them."

He took them down Colorado, then around a corner, where they spotted an empty parking spot across from a Blick Art Materials store. "There," Letty said, pointing.

Baxter parked and they walked across the street to the art store, where they browsed for a few moments, and Letty bought a clutch mechanical pencil, a pack of leads for the pencil, and a drawing book. As she paid with the NSA credit card, Baxter muttered, "I didn't know you drew."

"I don't," Letty said. "The only thing I ever drew was a horse's head in fifth grade and the teacher thought it was a chicken. But . . . we gotta buy something."

They walked back across the street and got in the truck. Two blocks down, Baxter asked, "Is that the same Toyota? Can you see it in the wing mirror?"

Letty looked: "I don't know. Head back to the motel . . . see what this one does. Try not to lose him at a traffic light."

The Toyota stayed well back, sometimes behind two cars, or as many as four, but tracked them all the way to the motel. They parked outside their room, and went in.

"What do you think?" Baxter asked.

"I think they'll talk it over and then they'll come here," Letty said. "Maybe . . . make an offer to test us out."

"Maybe." He considered the idea for a moment, then shook his head and said, "In the meantime, give me the memory card from the camera and I'll pass the photos along to Nowak. Tell her what we've done so far."

"Good. I'll whack on the drums and then I'm gonna take a nap."

Letty suggested to Baxter that if there were a knock on the door, he quickly take off his jeans and answer barefoot, in a tee-shirt and underwear: "We don't want to look ready for anything."

"Yes."

Baxter spent the next four hours banging on his laptop while Letty messed with the drums and then took a nap. At six, they walked out to a McDonald's across the street from the back of a Home Depot store. Letty was halfway through her Spicy Crispy Chicken Sandwich, uncomfortably watching Baxter devastate two Double Quarter Pounders with Cheese, when the Toyota cruised by.

"They're still on us," she said. "Don't look out the window until I tell you . . ." The beige Toyota went past, and she said, "Okay, look now."

Baxter looked. "That's probably the single most common vehicle in California, not counting F-150s," he said. "It does look the same, though."

"And how many cars do you see going fourteen miles an hour past here? They were checking us out," Letty said.

"If you say so. You gonna eat those fries?"

Back at the motel, Baxter shut the door and asked, "You think they're coming tonight?"

"Almost for sure. They've got to worry that we'll pull out, lose them, and then call Caltech and rat out Harp."

Bob and Sue showed up a few minutes after seven o'clock. Letty and Baxter both heard a car pull up outside the room. Letty turned to Baxter and said, "Underpants."

She hustled into the bathroom, pulled off her jeans, blouse, and bra, and pulled on a faded rayon chemise that stopped at her navel. She wore a pair of the Ralph Lauren men's briefs, which were fine, and the knee support.

As she walked out of the bathroom, carrying her clothes, there was a light rap at the door. Baxter, in a stained white tee-shirt and baggy Jockey briefs, looked at her, and she nodded and threw her jeans, with the Sig still in the pocket, on one of the beds. Baxter went to the door, opened it, leaving the security chain in place. Through the space in the partly opened door, he asked, "How'd you find us?"

A woman, whose voice Letty recognized as Sue's, said, "We followed you. It wasn't hard. We got a job. Open up."

"I'll get the chain," Baxter said.

When he opened the door all the way, Bob stepped inside, glanced around the room—hung up for a second on Letty's legs and the butterfly—and then Sue followed. Baxter said, "Let me get some pants on."

Baxter went into the bathroom, and Sue said, "This place is a dump. It smells like old cheese farts."

"We didn't want to be in some superficial first-world capitalist place like a Malibu resort hotel," Letty said.

Bob looked at the drum set, and checked out Baxter's laptop, which was sitting on his bed. There were two chairs in the room, and Sue settled in one, and Bob dragged the other around to face the bed, as Letty sat on it. Baxter came out of the bathroom in his jeans and asked, "What's up?"

"We got a gig for you, if you guys are really good with machine controls."

"I am," Baxter said. He tipped his head at Letty and said, "Charlie wouldn't know PLC from a jelly donut."

Sue nodded. "Okay. Here's the deal. You guys confess to that Willow Branch hit. I record it with my phone. If you try to turn us in, we give the recording to the FBI. We walk, you do time."

Letty shook her head. To Baxter, she said, "As your spiritual advisor, I'd tell them to go fuck themselves. You don't need a recording like that anywhere—they'd hold it over our heads forever. We'd be slaves."

To Bob and Sue, Baxter said, "She's right. No way in hell I'll record a confession."

"You already confessed to Harp," Sue said. "What difference does it make if we know about it?"

"We've got Harp between a rock and a hard place," Letty said. "You guys, we don't know where you're coming from. Or even your real names."

Bob spread his hands. "Okay. So we don't record it, but we need to at least hear it from you. We're going to ask you to do something that's illegal. You did take down Willow Branch, right? You're willing to take a couple of risks?"

"Some, but not much," Baxter said. "When we took down Willow Branch, there was no risk at all. The place was wide open, and we walked right in. The problem came when we couldn't cash out."

Sue shook her head: "Tell me how you did Willow Branch. If it fits, we have a job for you."

Baxter gave them the details of the Willow Branch computer attack, claimed that Letty made him do it, if he wanted to continue their relationship.

Bob: "So you're interested in screwing Charlie, and Charlie's interested in screwing money out of hospitals. I didn't see the attraction before now."

Letty: "How'd you know my name is Charlie?"

"Because Bob just used it," Bob said. "He said Charlie wouldn't know a PLC from a jelly donut. He used it at Balls', too."

Letty took a moment to glare at Baxter, who looked flustered, then said, "Okay. What do you want us to do, anyway? Tell us or get out of here."

"There's a big pharmaceutical supply house here in town, called Benillos," Sue said. "It has an alarm system with motion detectors and cameras, hooked into a computer that's hooked into the Internet. The security people can look around the store anytime they want. They do it several times a night. We need you to freeze the cameras for an hour and cut the alarms out. Not that big a deal."

Letty: "What, you're drug dealers?"

Sue said, "We're associated with a church group that distributes prescription drugs to the street people and the elderly poor. We're not opiate dealers or anything like that."

"But you'll take the opiates," Letty suggested.

"We take everything and sort it out later," Sue said. "We can get you as far as the computer, but we're uncertain about how to freeze the cameras and cut the alarms out. We have the guys to do the entry, but so far, we can't get around the alarms and the cameras. If you could do that . . ."

"I can do that," Baxter said. "How much?"

"We can give you five thousand up front and five thousand

later," Sue said. She opened her purse and took out a stack of currency and held it out to Baxter.

Baxter reached for it as Letty, smelling the rat, blurted, "Wait, wait, wait, wait . . ."

But Baxter took it, and Bob said to no one, "He took the cash, he's got the cash."

Letty: "Ah, shit," and flopped back on the bed and waited.

Not for long.

THE DOOR POPPED OPEN, kicked, and three men pushed inside. They were wearing blue nylon jackets with foot-high yellow letters that read "FBI." They all had drawn guns and one of them half-shouted at Letty, "Where's the gun, where's the gun?"

Letty held up her hands. "In my jeans pocket. Under me on the bed." She was furious and made no attempt to hide it. "Dickwad."

The lead agent frowned at her. "What did you call me?" Another one, talking to Baxter: "Give me the cash."

Baxter, dumbfounded, stood up and held out the block of cash, but stumbled. The agent may have thought Baxter was getting aggressive, and punched him in the eye, hard, and Baxter dropped the money and fell back on the bed, one hand to his eye, groaning, "Ow, ow, ow, you asshole!"

"It's the circus," Letty groaned. "The circus just came to town."

"We're definitely not in any circus," Sue said, with a smug smile.

"Not talking about you," Letty said. "You're just a couple of stupid hapless snitches."

The smile drained away: "What?"

The lead agent said to Letty and Baxter, "You're both under arrest. On your feet."

Letty shook her head. "No, we're not. I want to see your ID, before either one of us does a fuckin' thing." She got louder. "Then you and I are going outside, where I'm going to give you some critical information. This is your only chance: if you don't do that, all three of you can bend over and kiss your fuckin' brain-dead careers good-bye."

"What?"

"You heard me, dumbass."

The third agent goggled at her, confused, while the second had pulled the 938 out of Letty's jeans pocket. He showed it to the leader and said, "Nice little pocket piece . . . not a Saturday night job."

"Put it back," Letty said. "And show me some ID. You want to arrest us, that's your call, and we won't fight you. Like I said, you do it, you can kiss your careers good-bye."

Baxter said, "My fuckin' eye." And, "Easy, Charlie."

"What are they talking about?" Bob asked the lead agent.

"I don't know." The agent stared at Letty, then looked at Baxter, who was supine on the bed, still moaning, sputtering. The agent shook his head, turned back to Letty, dipped into his jacket pocket, pulled out an ID case and held it so Letty could look at it. She'd seen a few dozen federal ID packs and this was a good one.

She nodded, stood up, and said, "Outside. Let me put my pants on. You other assholes, you can stay here in case Paul makes a break for it. He could squeeze out the bathroom window and he can really sprint when he puts his mind to it."

They all looked at Baxter, who struggled to sit up and said, "I wanna see about assault charges on this asshole," and nodded at the agent who'd hit him. Then, still holding a hand over his eye, he said to Letty, "You're right about the circus. They all oughta be wearing clown shoes. Maybe we're done. Maybe we can go home and call the whole fuckin' thing off."

The agent who'd found Letty's gun tossed her jeans to her. She caught them, pulled them on, and led the way to the door, barefoot, as the lead agent followed.

Outside, Letty shut the door behind her, turned to the agent and shouted, "Don't you fuckin' feebs coordinate anything? You just busted a Homeland Security and NSA undercover job. We're dealing with a threat of national significance that could kill hundreds of people. Now . . . I don't know what's going to happen. I don't know if we can salvage it. Bob and Sue and that goddamn Harp can broadcast our identities all over the LA basin."

The agent pulled his head back, as if slapped. "Do you have . . ."

"We've got IDs and my federal gun permit in our truck. I also have the name of the agent in your office who is our contact here, and who should have, if you weren't a bunch of *fuckin'* clowns . . ." She was no longer quite shouting, but she was close. ". . . warned you off any kind of computer-based stings in the Caltech area. But didn't, obviously. Let me get you that number, Bozo."

TELEPHONE CALLS ENSUED.

Bob and Sue kept asking what was going on. The FBI's assistant director in charge, for Los Angeles, whose name was Samuels, got involved, and she and Delores Nowak exchanged hissy fits.

While that was going on, one of the feds filled an evidence bag with ice, gave it to Baxter to put on his eye, and almost apologized. Then Letty came up with a solution for handling Bob and Sue, one she'd heard about from her father.

She asked the lead agent, who'd led the way through the motel door, how they'd gotten Bob and Sue to cooperate in the sting. They were hackers, he said, who'd gotten caught.

"They developed software that allowed them to tamper with certain off-brand ATM machines," he said. "The kinds they have in casinos. We don't know how many they'd cracked before we caught up with them, but it ranged between 'several' and 'many.' They own a condo, free and clear. A one-bedroom, but still . . ."

"You already arrested them for that? The hacking?"

"We didn't formally arrest them," the agent said. "An arrest would kick out too many computer-based court files. We wanted to use them undercover, looking at other hackers. Hackers who might be very good cracking those court files."

"If you formally arrested them now, for the ATMs . . . could you hold them for a while before giving them access to an attorney?" Letty asked.

"I see where you're going with this," the agent said. "Let me call Agent Samuels, see what she thinks."

BOB WHINED AND SUE WEPT, but the feds gave Letty her gun back, and as they led the two hackers to their Tahoe, the lead agent said to Letty and Baxter, "You got seventy-two hours. We might do some bureaucratic stuff that'll keep them quiet a little longer, like, if they have a problem with bail, but we can't guarantee it."

Letty: "Seventy-two hours. After that, we're SOL?"

"That *may* be the case," the fed said. "We'll see what else we can figure out."

When the feds had gone, Letty called Delores Nowak. Nowak said, "We're reassessing here."

"We've got seventy-two hours," Letty said. "We're still operating."

"What are you going to do?" Nowak asked.

"You might not want to know that," Letty said.

After a moment's hesitation, Nowak asked, "Who'd you say this is?"

When she'd rung off the call with Nowak, Letty said to Baxter, "Now for that goddamn Harp."

EIGHT

They made it to Harp's house at eleven-thirty, on what almost looked like a Halloween night, dark clouds scudding across a rising moon. Baxter was back to pissing and moaning, until Letty told him to shut up. "I'm not going to kill him. I'm just going to nick him up a little."

"C'mon, Charlie . . ."

"Suck it up, Paul."

"Hey, I'm the fuckin' wounded one," Baxter said. "My eye looks like a goddamn meat loaf."

"Keep the ice on it, and try to start acting, you know, like a *man*."

"Sexist."

"You're pissing me off, Baxter," Letty said.

"So what?"

LETTY, TAPPING ALONG with her cane, led the way to Harp's front door, with Baxter hanging back on the sidewalk. She could see a light in a second-floor window, and one back through the house in the kitchen. He was still awake.

During the stick-fighting lessons, John Kaiser had taught her a reversed hold on the cane. If she held the cane in a conventional grip, she had to lift it before she could hit with it. If she reversed her hold, so her elbow pointed to the front of her hip, she could wind-mill it, striking almost instantly.

She used the metal head of the cane to bang on the door. She paused five seconds, then started banging again. A moment later, looking through the door's security window, she saw Harp drop down the stairs from the second floor to the living room, and then walk to the door. She reversed her grip on the cane.

Harp turned on the porch light, looked at her through the security window, then opened the door and asked, "What . . . ?"

Windmilling the cane, she whacked him hard on the face—not too hard, she didn't want to crack his skull—and he collapsed backward, landing on his butt, looking up at her, one hand covering his face.

Letty stood over him, pointing the cane at the bridge of his nose. "Tell me why I shouldn't beat you to death."

"What, what . . ." Blood was pouring from his nose, and his eyes were unfocused.

Baxter stepped inside and pulled the door closed behind him. Letty said to Harp, "You put the FBI on us, you twat."

"No, no . . ."

"Yes, you did, and you know it." Letty turned to Baxter. "Give me the hotline number. I want him to hear us make the call."

A woman called, from up the stairs, "Gene? What's going on?"

"Stay up there," Harp shouted. "I've got a problem I've got to work out. Stay up there."

The last command was met by silence, and Harp said, "I'm bleeding."

"Tough shit," Letty said.

Behind her, Baxter called out the ten-digit number that went to the Title IX hotline, and Letty began punching it into her phone. Holding his bleeding nose with one hand, Harp rolled over on his stomach and began to push up off the floor. Letty whacked him, again, hard, across the back, and Harp yelped and went flat and the woman upstairs shouted, "Gene! I'm calling 9-1-1."

"No," he shouted. "No, don't do that."

They heard her stepping down the stairs and then the young woman poked her head around the corner of the landing and she asked, "What's going on?"

Letty: "That ain't Hannah Baldwin, Paul, unless she dyed her hair last night." The woman had dark brown hair, not blond.

The woman asked, "Hannah?"

Harp shouted, "Go back upstairs and stay there." He added, "Please."

The woman hesitated, then turned back up the staircase. Letty said to Baxter, "It's not Hannah, but she left her purse the same place Hannah did. Get her wallet, shoot her driver's license and student ID with your phone."

Harp groaned and said, "Give me a chance."

Letty hit his arm with the cane, not hard enough to break it, but hard enough to hurt. Harp yelped again and said, "Please stop, please stop."

"Why? You tried to put us in prison for fifteen years," Letty said. "To be absolutely honest, Paul talked me out of killing you, but he said I could break some bones. Which I plan to do after we call the hotline."

"I got names. I got real names for you," Harp said, his words shaky with pain.

From the dining room table, Baxter said, "Hey—she's even younger than Hannah. Ashley Klein, twenty. Won't be able to buy a beer until April."

"This asshole's creeping me out," Letty said. "Get a photo. Prop the cards up in the kitchen and get some identifiable background."

Baxter went to do that and Letty said to Harp, "Roll over on your back so we can talk. C'mon . . ."

Harp did that, holding his hands over his bloody face. Letty asked, "Did you talk directly to the feds, or did you go to Bob and Sue?"

"Their names aren't Bob and Sue . . ."

"I know that, asshole. They didn't even bother to pretend they were," Letty said. "About those names—how do I know you won't send us right back to the FBI?"

"Bob and Sue are the only informants I knew about," Harp said. "They've been delivering people to the FBI for months. I wanted to get rid of you. Because you were from Florida . . . I figured you wouldn't know."

Baxter had come back from taking the photo of Ashley Klein's IDs. "He is sort of a dumb shit, isn't he? We're not from Caltech, so we couldn't possibly have any resources here."

"Resources . . ."

JOHN SANDFORD

"We've got a couple of online friends in LA," Baxter said. "They warned us about your Bob and Sue. Every hack in LA knows about them now."

Letty smiled down at Harp and tapped the spike of the cane on the wooden floor. "You might not be hearing from them again."

Baxter walked over to Harp and squatted by his neck: "Names," he said. "They better be good."

"If they're not, we'll . . ." She let the comment trail away, then said to Baxter, "Maybe I should go ahead and do him now."

Baxter winced and said, "No, no. Then you'd have to do Ashley. She's seen our faces. She's . . . innocent. She's twenty."

Letty rubbed her nose, as if thinking it over. "Yeah. Good point." To Harp, she said, "Give the names and contacts to Paul."

"I'll have to look at my laptop," Harp said. "I know people for sure who'd know Ordinary People."

"Where's the laptop?" Letty asked.

"In my study . . . on my desk."

"Lay right there while Paul gets it . . ."

BAXTER GOT THE LAPTOP and Letty ordered Harp to remain on the floor while he looked up the names. The first name, he said, was Benjamin Able, a former student who was the organizer of a hacker combine loosely tied to Ordinary People. "I'm pretty sure he's still at the address I have here. The last time I talked to him, he owned the place. It's not cheap to move in California."

He would, Harp said, know the leadership of Ordinary People, because he'd worked with them since the group was formed. "He's not a regular member, but he knows them."

The second man was named Craig Sovern, who Harp described as "Crazy. Great with computers, but whacko. I don't know where he lives—he moves around a lot. Maybe on a boat. Craig is a major mover with Ordinary People, but he doesn't hang out." He had Sovern's phone number.

"Okay, then," Letty said.

From the second floor, Ashley Klein called, "Gene? Are you okay?"

"He's okay, Ashley, but he was banging another woman after his party last night," Letty called back.

"What!"

"Ah, shit," Harp groaned.

Baxter was at the door: "Let's go. We can always come back . . ."

Letty stepped his way, and as she went, she repeated what Baxter had said: "Remember that: we can always come back. We haven't called Title IX . . . yet. If either one of these names calls you, you better back us up. Charlie and Paul."

OUT IN THE TRUCK, Baxter asked, "You hurt him bad?"

"Didn't break anything, but he's bruised, so he's gonna ache, but probably no worse than your black eye," Letty said. "He didn't ask what happened to Bob and Sue, which was a little odd."

"Might have been afraid to," Baxter said. "He thinks they're facedown in a ditch somewhere. I mean, you even scared the shit out of me. I thought you might stick that spike in his head."

"Jesus, Rod. I'm not a murderer."

Baxter shook his head, but kept his mouth shut.

WHEN LETTY TOLD BAXTER to put Benjamin Able's address in his phone navigation app, he frowned. "We're going to West Hollywood tonight? Now?"

"Why not? I thought you criminal hackers stayed up all night hacking. Big Gulps and bags of Cheetos and weed-smoking hippie chicks with thick glasses, D-cups, crossed eyes, and overbites."

"More movie bullshit," Baxter said, as he started the truck. "But then . . . I almost forgot: this isn't real life. I'm in a bad movie. I'm not even the hero. I'm fuckin' Wile E. Coyote."

ON THE WAY across town, Letty called the phone number of Craig Sovern. It rang seven times, then went to a recording, which informed her that his voicemail was full. She hung up.

Baxter asked, tentatively, "Do you ever think of yourself as a criminal?"

"What? No. Sometimes . . . in my kind of job . . . you might have to do something that's technically illegal," Letty said. "Always for a good cause."

"Like beating the shit out of a harmless computer professor?"

"Think about Harp and the two women we know about—I wouldn't say he's harmless."

"Not everyone would agree," Baxter said.

"I'm not everyone. I make up my own mind and go with it."

"I looked you up, you know? When your name was first mentioned, before the NSA changed everything in your file," Baxter said. "You've killed five people. Your father has killed even more. Some people might argue that you're a family of psychopaths . . ."

LONG SILENCE, THEN:

"I have this theory that everyone is a little mentally ill," Letty said. "No such thing as perfectly *normal*. You've got all these branches extending out of some kind of theoretical normalcy. You've got the schizophrenic branch, the paranoid branch, the psychopathic branch, the sociopathic branch, the manic-depressive branch, the clinically depressive branch, the OCD branch, and so on. Nobody is dead center. Everybody is out on one of those branches. Or more than one. If you're too far out, you're nuts. If you're just a little way out, you're fine, but you have a tendency."

"Where are you?"

"A little paranoid, maybe a little manic, a little sociopathic . . ."

"I'm purely paranoid, right?" Baxter asked.

"I don't think you're paranoid at all, Rod. You gotta face it, people *are* out to get you," Letty said. "Not just Ordinary People. Your own bosses forced you to do something you didn't want to do and that could get you hurt, maybe even killed. Harp tried to turn you over to the FBI and send you to prison. Nope, you're not paranoid. You're wary."

"Maybe I'm normal."

"Mmm . . . no. Given the fact that you're grossly overweight, you swill coffee and Coke like it's about to be banned, I'd say you're depressive, maybe with clinical episodes, and trying to self-medicate," Letty said. "And possibly, a bit obsessive-compulsive."

Another long silence. Then, "Yeah. You could be right."

BENJAMIN ABLE LIVED in a long, low, rectangular building in West Hollywood, a relic of the post–World War II construction boom—flaking brown stucco under a flat roof, a line of four evenly spaced windows between two standard entry doors, with a double garage door at one end. "Not a house. Didn't start that way, anyhow. Looks like it was a shop of some kind," Baxter said.

"There's a light in the back," Letty said. "Let's walk around there and look in a window."

"Why don't *you* go look in a window. I'll sit here with the engine running."

Letty thought about it for a second, then said, "Right. I'll call you if I get in."

Letty got out of the truck with her cane, walked up to one of the entry doors on the building, tugged on it. It was locked, but an outside light came on, apparently linked to a motion sensor. When nobody came to the door, she walked around the side of the building to a narrow backyard, which was surrounded on three sides by a chain-link fence and on the fourth by the building. She let herself through an unlocked gate and walked along the back of the house to a lighted window.

She wasn't tall enough to see in. There was enough ambient light in the yard to see a pile of brush on one side, with several small stumps sitting upright beside it. She walked over, picked up a stump, leaned it against the house, climbed on it, and looked in the window.

Inside, a man was playing an electric guitar while watching a Bob Dylan video on YouTube. He was burly, but not like Baxter—more muscle, little fat. Letty rapped on the window. The man stopped playing, looked around, puzzled. Letty could see that he had a modest black beard, a shock of black hair, and round wire-rimmed glasses. She rapped harder.

He put the guitar on a stand and looked around again. Letty rapped once more, and he looked at the window, stood up, and walked over to it. Letty said, loudly, "Open the window."

He did, sliding it sideways. "Go away. You're not getting a nickel."

"We were given your name and address by Eugene Harp. We need to talk," Letty said.

"Are you Sue?"

"No. We met Bob and Sue and they're not very happy about that. You can call Harp and ask. But: we need to talk," Letty said. "If you're Benjamin Able."

"Who's we?" Able asked.

"Me and my friend. He's out front in our truck."

"What do you want to talk about?"

"Job possibilities . . . and Ordinary People, if you know them," Letty said.

Able peered at her for a moment, then said, "Come around to the front. Give me five minutes."

Back at the truck, Baxter asked, "We running?"

"No. He wants five minutes. Probably calling Harp. Or Ordinary People. Damnit, we should have called Delores to see if the NSA could pick up the phone call. We should have known he'd make one."

"Now that we have his name, we should have Delores take a look at *everything* he does . . . and they can do that."

"If they can get the warrants."

Baxter snorted, amused, but didn't say anything.

ABLE DIDN'T TAKE the whole five minutes; a light came on outside one of the doors, and it popped open. Able stepped out and waved them in. They walked over, with Baxter leading the way. He nodded at Able and said, "We're Paul and Charlie."

"I don't know what you did to Gene Harp, but you freaked him out, whatever it was. He told me he didn't want to talk about it, but I should be careful. Especially with Charlie." He looked at Letty and said, "He said you're a psycho with a cane."

"Yeah, and he's a pervert," Letty said.

"I assume you're talking about his harem," Able said. "You gonna turn him in?"

"Only if he messes with us," Baxter said. "You know what he did to us, right?"

Able looked both ways up and down the street, then said, "Come inside and tell me."

They followed him into the building, which had been divided in half lengthwise. The front half, facing the street, was a long rank of metal racks covered with computer and audio gear, some dating back to late '90s Macintosh and Windows computers, along with an even older Commodore 64 and Amiga 1000.

The back half was a long living quarters, everything jammed together except the bedroom, which was walled off with taped but unpainted Sheetrock, the corner of an unmade bed visible through the doorway.

Computer and TV screens occupied much of the middle of the interior—including on top of the washer and dryer—along with a variety of lounge chairs and several Herman Miller office chairs on casters; the floor was a checkerboard of black and white tiles. One end, outside the bedroom, was occupied by a bodybuilding gym, with racks of free weights on the walls. The other end was dedicated to a collection of guitars and amps.

"Great place, man," Baxter said, so genuine that Able simply nodded and said, "Thanks."

And, "So what did Harp do to you?"

"He sent us to Bob and Sue. You know Bob and Sue?"

"No. I've never seen them, but I know about them."

Baxter laid out their story—PhD in computer science from Florida, possessed of a half-million-dollar Bitcoin wallet with no way to get to it that would not get the feds on their back.

With the help of research and some friends back East and in LA, they'd determined that a successful hacker combine called Ordinary People might be able help them retrieve the money. Harp had sent them to Bob and Sue. They'd been warned about the two and recognized them when they saw them sitting at a restaurant table. They'd stopped to talk to them, recognized the CI shuffle, and left them with their choice of soft drinks and hamburgers.

Able cross-examined them about the Bitcoin disaster.

"I know everything there is about machine controls, but I fucked up the whole blockchain thing," Baxter said. "Went into it without thinking about it much because . . ."

He tipped his head toward Letty.

"Hope it was worth it," Able said, giving Letty a long look.

"It sorta was," Baxter said.

"Sorta my ass," Letty said.

"Your ass was my original thought," Baxter said.

Able laughed, which might have been predatory if it hadn't been obviously good-humored. "That's quite the nice tat you've got on your back," he said to Letty. "Bald eagle or . . ."

"Raven," Letty said.

"Pretty obvious, from the right perspective," Baxter said, with a mock leer.

"Oh, shut the fuck up," Letty said. "You make me tired."

"Easy . . . Okay. Can't help you with the Bitcoin," Able said. "I'm not Ordinary People. Assuming you check out, though, I know somebody who could have a reasonably lucrative job for you . . . and could help with OP."

"I've got my CV out in the truck. Charlie doesn't have a CV, so you'd have to do your own research," Baxter said. "Give me a hint of what you want to know about. Don't have to give away anything specific. Just so I can go back to the motel and start digging into background information?"

"We need the money quick," Letty said. "We're down to seven hundred bucks."

Able thought about that for a moment, then asked, "What do you know about natural gas distribution systems?"

Baxter shrugged. "Nothing. But they gotta have machine controls, and I know everything about those."

"Why would you want to know about natural gas?" Letty asked.

Able held up a finger. "What do you think about SlapBack?"

"SlapBack? Another super-greedy, conscienceless, unethical social media platform that makes big bucks stirring up hate," Baxter said. "Just like the rest of them."

"Took the words right outa my mouth," Letty said.

"*Not* like the rest of them. Facebook and Twitter stir up hate as an unintended by-product of what they do. Or so they say. With SlapBack, hate is the main product," Able said. "That's why they were created: to warehouse and distribute hate. They're not that big, yet. After Microsoft and Amazon kicked them out of their clouds, they hooked into an old server farm right here in the Valley. We keep wondering what would happen if somebody killed the natural gas to the electric utilities that power the server farm."

Letty and Baxter looked at each other, and simultaneously shrugged.

Able: "What? You don't like the idea?"

"I like the idea—taking out SlapBack—but that'd be a back-assward way to do it," Baxter said. "You'd do a lot of collateral damage—all the other places that use the gas-powered electric. And the electric companies could probably switch in power from other sources if they had to. Why not go after the electric substations? I've been to server clusters, server farms. They've all got substations, because they use so much power."

"And they all have backup power packs under every rack, and diesel generators that will come on instantly," Able said. "They'll only run for a limited time, but if you take out gas, it'll be out for longer than the backups will run."

"Not if they can get diesel to the backup generators, and that just takes a truck," Baxter said.

"So what would you do?"

"I'd be surprised if a good operator couldn't get inside of the power companies, and from there, take out the substations. A day's work, we could throw a switch and overload the substations, and there you are. No collateral damage. If you take out the gas, you not only get SlapBack, you get hospitals, schools, airports, and the FBI on your asses like flies on shit."

"Like white on rice," Letty added. "Like holy on the pope."

"Good points," Able said. "We were thinking . . ."

"Could we get some cash up front?" Letty asked.

THEY TALKED FOR two hours—some of it computer tech that Letty didn't understand, some of it about their screwup with Bitcoin. "I did, like, five minutes of research and I thought, *There it is, I got it,*" Baxter confessed. "After the Bitcoin came in, we turned the hospital back on, and I saw somebody really good attacking the ISP we were using, and I thought, *Get out of here.* So I got out . . ."

"You still got the computer?"

"No. It was a crappy old MacBook Air and I ditched it. I went out on a different machine to the account and, like, one second later, we were attacked again. I ditched that machine, too, a pretty good Lenovo. Then I did the research I should have done up front."

"He found out we were probably fucked," Letty interjected. She was digging through her purse. "You mind if I spark one up?" She held up a joint.

"Not if you share," Able said. "Though I gotta say, I prefer the edibles. They don't make the furniture stink."

"They last too long," Letty said.

They continued to talk, Baxter reciting the small details of the hospital ransomware attack, passing the joint around, getting high. Letty told Able how she hurt her leg, and about the drum set back at the motel. Able went to his kitchen, opened a cupboard, and produced a Tupperware container with a magic brownie in it. After a while, through a haze of warming vision, Able asked Letty, "You want to sit on my lap?"

"You got twenty bucks?"

They all laughed and Letty passed the last of the brownie to Baxter, got up, and dropped on Able's lap and put her arm around his neck. His shoulder muscles felt like chunks of wood: free weights. Able said, "What's that I feel? Is that a gun in your pocket?"

"Yup. Sig 938."

"Shoot the testicles off a fruit fly," Baxter said, sounding groggy.

"Bullet flies like an arrow; fruit flies like a banana," Able said, and they all laughed immoderately, because it was pretty good dope.

Able asked Letty, "Can I pull up your top? So I can see the wings?"

"Sure."

She turned and let him pull it up, and he popped her bra straps and pulled them sideways, and he said, "Whoa. That's outrageous."

"You want to feel something really stimulating?" Letty asked, as she rehooked the bra and pulled her top down.

"Absolutely."

He was wearing a thin tee-shirt, and she reached out and pinched one of his nipples as hard as she could, using her nails, and he lurched to his feet, spilling her on the floor, shouting, "Ouch, ouch, ouch."

Baxter nearly fell off his chair laughing. "She does that to me about once a week. I never see it coming."

"Goddamnit, that hurt," Able said, rubbing his nipple. "God-damnit . . . it doesn't stop."

In the end, Baxter agreed to do some basic, but specific, re-search on SlapBack's server farm and the electrical inputs through local substations. He'd come up with a proposal to take the power out, and he'd do the research for free. The attack programming would cost.

"If it looks like it would work . . . five grand. If we pull it off . . . another ten," Able said. "Those fuckers ought to be hanged for treason, in my opinion. Knocking them off the air for a couple of days, that's nothing like what they should get."

"If we do it right, we ought to be able to melt the fuckin' substa-tion, and depending on how the power is routed, we might be able to fry the backups, too," Baxter said. "They'll be off for more than a couple of days . . ." His eyes went to Able's ceiling for a moment, then he said, "You know, if we come up with the perfect, really quick attack . . . we could knock them down, disappear, and come back for another bite. Maybe several more bites."

Able slapped him on the back and said, "Call me when you got it."

"That'll be tomorrow," Baxter said. "This ain't shit."

"I'll believe it when I see it," Able said.

They got a number for one of Able's burner phones. As they were going out the door, Able said, "My tit still hurts."

"Try being a woman. Guys all think it's hot to take a bite," Letty said. And she lifted a hand: "Tomorrow."

WHEN THEY WERE in the truck and pointed back to Pasadena, they called Delores Nowak, who picked up the phone and asked, "You know what time it is here?"

Baxter said, "Well, it's four o'clock in the morning here, so I expect it's probably seven o'clock there, unless somebody changed the time zones. We need some help. Programming help. And we have two names for you."

"You sound different," Nowak said.

"I'm driving under the influence," Baxter said.

"What? You're drunk?"

"No. Under the influence of Charlie Snow, along with some really excellent weed. I don't care, because I'm gonna get hurt. I'm pretty sure of that now."

"You won't get hurt," Nowak said, without trying to sound convincing. "Tell me what you've done."

They told her about meeting Able.

"They want to turn off the gas, like you said—but it had nothing to do with any northern cities," Letty told her. "It had to do with shutting down SlapBack. A political thing. When we told them to forget about gas, to concentrate on the electric power, Able was happy enough to look at that. He even agreed it was probably a better plan. Your guys really gotta rethink the whole natural gas thing."

Nowak said, "We were picking up rumors. It's possible that there was some speculation attached, here on our side, that somebody looked at the obvious. Where would you shut off the gas in the middle of winter, for a ransomware attack? Wouldn't be Miami or LA, it'd have to be in the north. So . . ."

"So it's possible it's all bullshit," Baxter said. "Can we come home?"

"Not yet. It sounds like you're close to meeting with the Ordinary People. Stay with it long enough to get some IDs. We'll talk about it later."

"Then we're gonna need some help from you right now," Baxter said. "We're under a lot of time pressure—we could be screwed if the feds let Bob and Sue out of jail. We need to know how to get into Encino Power and turn off the substation that feeds the Slap-Back servers."

He gave her all the information that he'd gotten from Able and she made notes: "I'll get this to the right people and they'll work through it for you."

"I need it in the morning and it can't be wrong," Baxter said.

When they'd hung up, Baxter said, "Yeah, they're lying about something. They're still lying about it. Seriously."

"I know," Letty said. "I don't think they ever really gave a shit about natural gas computers and Minneapolis getting shut down. The question is, what *do* they give a shit about? Why are we out here?"

NINE

They'd been up all night. When they got to Pasadena, they stopped at a 7-Eleven and bought granola and milk for Letty and three Big Bites and two Red Bulls for Baxter.

Back in the truck, Letty said, "Did you get relish on the Big Bites? Onions?"

"Of course. Why wouldn't I? And mustard," Baxter said.

"They smell disgusting," Letty said. "Give me a bite."

"Hey," Baxter sputtered, a hot dog in one hand. "This is my *breakfast*."

"I'm not asking for a whole one; just a bite."

They *were* disgusting; but she was still a little stoned. Baxter gave her half of a Big Bite and on the way to the motel, both of them chewing, Baxter muttered, "Cruising down Colorado Boulevard in my Tundra. Elbow out the window. Palm trees and starlight. Hot dog in one hand, hot chick riding shotgun. Livin' the life, huh?"

"Remember it, 'cause it probably won't happen again," Letty said.

"That's right. Pee on my shoes when I was starting to enjoy myself," Baxter said.

THEY GOT SIX HOURS in bed, Letty sleeping soundly, given the combination of marijuana and an increasing trust in Baxter. When Delores Nowak called at eleven o'clock, they both popped up, and Baxter took the call, putting the phone on speaker.

"We're sending you the information you asked for, about access to Encino Power," Nowak said. "We trust you'll use it wisely, but if you don't, we'll deny everything. You should have it in the next half hour. I'm sure you'll understand it."

"I'm sure I will," Baxter said. "If we get any money out of this thing, do we get to keep it?"

"I believe you could use it for expenses, but you'd have to turn in any excess . . . if there were any excess," Nowak said.

"Got it," Baxter said. He smiled a dishonest smile at Letty.

Letty chipped in. "We need a prescription for Adderall or Ritalin under our cover names, sent to a pharmacy close to the motel. We need it in the next half hour or so. Thirty tabs should be enough."

"For what? Aren't those attention-deficit things? I don't . . ."

"We had seventy-two hours to nail Ordinary People. Seventeen of them are gone. We may need to stay awake for a long time and Adderall and Ritalin are basically speed," Letty said. "We may also need a few pills for demonstration purposes. You know, to show them how far-out we are. Not only hacker-criminals, we're drug abusers."

"You'll have it in an hour," Nowak said.

When they rang off, Baxter said, "The NSA: America's crime family."

━━━━

A LONG, ENCRYPTED TEXT came into Baxter's laptop twenty-five minutes later, accompanied by a short text with the address of a Walgreens pharmacy in Pasadena. While Letty got cleaned up and dressed, Baxter sat in a chair, in his underpants and tee-shirt, paging through the NSA file.

When she emerged from the bathroom, he turned his head and said, "Got it. I'm not sure it's quite right, but I'm sure we can get into Encino Power for a look-around. Got a good map of their transmission system . . . They sent me a map of the actual physical locations of the SlapBack server farm and the attached substation. I need to work through the controls, see what can be done, set up an attack."

Letty was brushing out her hair: "When can we call Able?"

"I'll need a couple hours to make the information mine . . . I have to actually go online and work it, step by step. If I don't, Able will see through it. He's not stupid."

"How about if you do that and I go get us something to eat?"

"Go," Baxter said, his eyes still fixed on the laptop screen.

Letty drove the truck out to the Pasadena Whole Foods and bought premade sandwiches, a ciabatta loaf, oranges, bananas, and four lemon–poppy seed muffins. When she got back to the motel, Baxter was sitting in the same place, still in underpants and tee-shirt, fixated on the computer screen.

He took a muffin without looking away from the screen and said, "Go walk around. Or gas up the truck or something."

"How long will you be?"

"Another hour, maybe."

LETTY GOT GAS, cruised the Caltech neighborhood, took a quick look at Harp's house—nothing moving there—drove a lap around the Rose Bowl, then stopped at a Walgreens, where an amber tube of Adderall was waiting.

When she got back to the motel, Baxter was in the shower. Half of the ciabatta loaf had been eaten, and three of the four muffins. She knocked on the bathroom door and shouted at him, to make sure he knew she'd returned.

When Baxter emerged from the bathroom, he was fully clothed but still with a distracted look in his eyes; his hair was standing up in wet spikes. He glanced at her and mumbled something under his breath, and then, "Why don't you call Able? Tell him I got it."

He told her what to say and she made the call as he was combing gel through his hair, plastering it to his skull. Able said, "Already? That was fast."

"Paul says it was simple enough once you got through the outer security shell," Letty said. "He wants to show you."

"Give me an hour to get a couple more guys here . . . and bring your drums. One of the guys plays bass and if your boy's stuff is right, we'll need to bring in some more guys to look at it. We could jam while we wait."

"I could do that," Letty said.

"They're testing us," Baxter said when she'd hung up. "Hope you got your groove on."

ON THE WAY BACK to West Hollywood, Baxter seemed to come out of his fugue. He ate a banana on the way and said into the silence, "Unless the guys back at the Fort are fuckin' with me, we could shut down SlapBack like we're slamming a door. The question is, should we do it? Or try to fake it? Or maybe suggest that somebody check our work and try to delay an attack until we accumulate more names?"

"We'll figure that out later," Letty said. "For now, we've got to focus on collecting names."

"Probably aren't going to show us their drivers' licenses," Baxter said.

"Gotta try to get some photos of them," Letty said. "If we're close enough, my phone camera should work, except the light in Able's place isn't good enough. Gotta see if we can figure something out."

"Get them outside," Baxter said.

THERE WERE TWO MEN with Able. He introduced one as Jan, the other as Carl, no last names. Jan was of middle height, maybe an inch short of six feet, and thin like a runner. Carl was shorter, fleshier, pink, blond, lazy-eyed.

Able asked, "Bring your drums?"

"In the back of the truck," Letty said.

"Great. Let's get them. You know the Eagles' 'Those Shoes'?" Able asked.

"I've listened to it. Should be able to find the notation online," Letty said. "Can you play the guitar part? Do you have a talk box?"

"I got the guitar, I sing, and Jan does a great talk box imitation."

Jan said, imitating a talk box: "Buttout-Buttout; Buttout."

"Then we're good," Letty said. "The bass part an idiot could do."

Jan said, "Thanks. I'm the bass player."

"Let's get the drums off the truck. I'll set them up while you guys are looking at what Paul did overnight."

"Did it fast," Able said to Baxter.

"Go-fast pills," Baxter said. "Didn't bother to sleep."

THE HACKS WERE IMPRESSED by the degeneracy of it all.

As the four men walked outside to unload the drums, Letty

took out her phone, tapped the camera app and turned on the video. She stuck the camera in her back jeans pocket with the camera protruding an inch or so above the pocket.

At the truck, the men were unloading the drums. Letty spent a lot of time with her back turned, stooped to tie a shoe, led the way to the door to hold it as the men paraded through with the pieces of the drum set. Able cleared away a weight bench to make space, and they spent two minutes putting the drums, amp, and throne more or less where Letty needed them.

"I can take it from here," Letty said. "You guys go do the computer stuff."

Letty hooked up the amp and moved the snare and kick drum around, set the cymbals, adjusted the pedal on the hi-hat, and made musical noises, while the men moved to the other end of Able's studio to look at computer monitors.

That done, she went out to the truck to get her laptop; on the way back to the studio, she saw Able looking out a window, watching her while staying back and to the side. She pretended not to see him, switched the laptop from one hand to the next so he'd be sure to see it. Inside, she set up the laptop, and yelled down the length of the studio: "Hey. What's the wi-fi password?"

With the password, she went online, took a look at notation for "Those Shoes," played through it a few times—a lot of sixteenth notes on the hi-hat—and then brought up the Eagles' version and played along.

With the men hunched over a keyboard and monitor, she sent the phone video to the laptop, moved the video to the encrypted email app, and sent the video to Delores Nowak with a note that said simply, "Faces."

That done, she deleted all of her copies of the video, on both the phone and laptop, called up a notation for Led Zeppelin's "Rock and Roll," which she already knew well, and worked through it. Able walked down to her, watched for a moment, then said, "No fuckin' way."

"Way," she said.

"Come listen to us talk. We got another guy coming to see what we've done. We can jam until he gets here."

"What about our money?" she asked. Of course she did.

"Coming," he said.

BAXTER WAS LOOKING TIRED. He was sitting in front of a video monitor showing lines of software text. When Letty came up, he said, "Pop me a cartwheel." She walked back to the drum set, got her purse, fished out the amber tube of Adderall, took it to Baxter and rattled out a single orange pill. "That's all you get. Next you gotta sleep."

"Yeah, I'm about done here," Baxter said. He popped the pill, swallowed it dry, made a face.

Letty: "Ready to push the button?"

"No. They've still got work to do. When they push it, I want to be in, like, a game show audience with lots of witnesses," Baxter said.

"But it's almost ready to push?"

"Close. I think they got it." Baxter looked at Able. "You got it?"

"If all those switches do what you say they do."

"They do."

Able nodded: "We'll see."

CARL STARTED PLAYING a video game; Baxter continued probing Encino Power. Able, Jan, and Letty moved down to the drum set, plugged in, and began jamming around "Those Shoes" and "Rock and Roll," and later, Tom Petty's "You Don't Know How It Feels," old stuff that everybody knew.

Able had a decent voice and Jan really could imitate a talk box. At one point, as they were working through a guitar passage, Able stopped long enough to say, "If we practice for a couple weeks, we could do the LA cover-band circuit."

"Maybe some bars in San Dimas, but nothing on the Westside, where the money is," Jan said. "That'd take a year."

While they were working on the Petty piece, Letty saw Carl sneak out the door. He was back in five minutes, looking too innocent: he'd been in the truck, she thought, checking them out.

Which was a good thing.

They'd been jamming for forty-five minutes when the man they were waiting for finally showed up, with a girlfriend in tow. Both were wearing ball caps, sunglasses, and covid masks, although covid masks had been dropped by most people in LA.

The masks were not so much to prevent disease, Letty thought, as to defeat cameras. The man was tall, dark-haired with curls to his shoulder blades, four or five inches over six feet, with big athletic hands. His girlfriend was black, also tall and athletic, dark glasses flashing under the brim of a straw hat.

They'd rung the bell at the far end of the studio, and Carl let them in. Letty, Able, and Jan didn't hear the bell, and kept playing until the newcomers walked into the studio. Letty pointed her sticks at them and Jan and Able trailed off, put their instruments on guitar stands, and they all walked down to meet the masked duo.

The first thing the man said, looking at Baxter and Letty, was "No names."

"Gotta call you something," Letty said.

The woman laughed and said, "How about Bob and Sue?"

Letty asked: "Yeah? You cops, too?"

The new Bob said, "Able told us you dodged the Bob and Sue bullet. We'd like to hear about that."

Baxter told them the story about talking to an LA hacker friend and being warned off.

"Are you really Paul and Charlie?" the woman asked.

"Maybe," Baxter said, with a fake-furtive glance at Letty.

"How about Paul Jims and Charlotte Snow, recently of the University of Florida at Gainesville?" the man asked.

Letty threw a hostile stare at him, then said, "Are we done sniffing assholes? We want you to look at Paul's work and give us some money and we'll kiss you good-bye."

"Where are you going?" the new Sue asked.

Baxter shrugged: "Maybe Seattle."

"Rains all the time in Seattle," Sue said.

"I try to work indoors when it's raining," Baxter said. He turned to Letty and asked, "We still got sandwiches?"

"I'll get some. You want a banana?"

LETTY WENT OUT to their truck. She understood that since they couldn't see the faces of the newcomers, Baxter was suggesting she get a picture of their vehicle. She'd already taken photos of the cars driven by Able, Jan, and Carl, but now there was not an unfamiliar car in the lot; Bob and Sue had parked somewhere else and walked to Able's place.

She got food and Cokes from the cooler and carried them inside. Baxter looked at her and she shook her head: no luck.

Bob and Sue focused on a computer monitor as Baxter walked them through the hack. Baxter paused long enough to take a sandwich and a banana. Letty sprawled in a chair and poked at her laptop. She interrupted the computer work to ask Able if he had some headphones she could use. He pointed at a rack down the studio, and she got a pair and sprawled in the chair again, plugged into YouTube music videos.

After an hour or so, the people around the computer broke up and Letty took the headphones off to hear Bob say, "Looks good to me. Needs somebody to pull the trigger, to write the trigger, but it should work. I'd like a copy of Paul's program to see where I could go with it."

Letty said, "Sure. Soon as we see some cash."

Bob looked at Sue and nodded, and Sue asked, "Really?"

"That's why we brought it," Bob said. "The code looks good. Paul is looking good."

Sue said, "Okay, I guess," picked up her purse, dug into it, and handed Baxter an envelope. "Five thousand dollars. There'll be ten more when SlapBack goes down."

"Pleasure doing business with you," Baxter said. He stood up, tucked the envelope in his back pocket and said to Letty, "Let's get the drums back in the truck and get the fuck outa here."

"Leave the drums," Able said. "That was a great jam this afternoon. I'd like to do it again. Maybe a few times. You'll be back to pick up the next payment, anyway. Lots of righteous stuff could get done, if you stick around."

"Like what?" Letty asked.

"I dunno," Able said. "Like getting Donald Trump completely offline, forever?"

"A worthy goal, if you're into charity," Baxter said. "I'd like something with a few more bucks attached." He ran a hand through his gel-slicked hair, wiped the hand on his pants, and looking at Letty, said, "Instead of moving the drums, let's leave them here and go find a better motel. One that doesn't smell like the toilet is broke."

"Not until we get more cash," Letty said. She looked at Bob and Sue and said, "We're trying to get in touch with Ordinary People. We've been told that they moved a lot of money through Bitcoin and didn't get caught doing it. We need some ideas about that. We've got a half-million bucks hung up in a Bitcoin wallet and we think the feds are looking at it."

Bob shook his head. "Can't help you with that."

"Are you Ordinary People?"

"Ordinary People isn't a thing, like a company," Bob said. "It's more like a . . . cloud. We've been in the cloud and we've been out of it. It moves."

"That helps a lot," Baxter said, sounding discouraged.

"Tell us the problem with the wallet," Sue said. "We'll talk to some friends, see if anything might be done. I doubt it, but we'll ask the experts."

Baxter outlined the problem and answered questions. Letty limped down to the music area, got her cane and purse, and when Baxter was done, she said, "Pie 'n Burger and you need some sleep."

"Meet you back here tomorrow, same time," Bob said. "We'll either have your ten thousand or we won't."

Baxter: "We'll keep an eye on SlapBack."

Outside, Baxter said, "Want to try to spot their car?"

"Yes. Let's figure out how . . ."

Baxter drove them to the end of the block, past an alley that ran from the next block east. Letty said, "There: the banana tree."

"That's a banana tree? Looks like an ancient Egyptian fan. Like on hieroglyphs."

"Your mind is like a garbage dump," Letty said. "It's a banana tree. Keep going, in case they're watching us."

Baxter continued north to Melrose Avenue, as they talked about what to do, turned east, took the next turn south, back to the alley. Letty jumped out of the truck, taking the camera bag with her, said, "Stay on your phone," and jogged down the long alley to the street that Able's house was on.

The banana tree grew at the corner of an apartment building. She slipped behind the tree, where she couldn't be easily seen, but could see the front of Able's place.

She didn't have to wait long. Bob and Sue stepped out of Able's building and turned toward her, adjusting masks and sunglasses. They strolled the block and a half to Melrose, taking their time, looking around, passing fifty feet from her hiding place, and turned the corner.

Letty called Baxter: "They're out. They're walking toward you down Melrose."

Baxter, two blocks east, parked outside a CVS pharmacy, said, "I see them. They're crossing the street, they're crossing Melrose. They'll be going the other way. They're getting in a car . . . uh, I think a van. Yeah, a blue van."

Letty stepped out from behind the banana tree and ran to a Starbucks café that had a covered patio on the corner. Standing behind a support pillar, she spotted the blue van pulling out of a parking place on Melrose. She took photos with the GX8 as the van approached and then as it drove past her. When she could no longer see the rear license plate, she called Baxter and said, "Come down the alley and get me."

"On the way."

When Baxter picked her up, Letty chimped through the images on the GX8: she had clear shots of the van's plates.

"So that's two," she said. "Two Ordinary People in the bag."

TEN

Letty took out the burner phone given to her by Delores Nowak, punched through to the secret cache, and called the number for the LAPD tracking cameras. A man answered, asked for her identification code. She'd stored the code with the phone number, a string of twelve letters and numbers. She recited the code and the man asked for the license plate number.

She read the plate off the screen on the back of the camera, and the man said, "Wait one." A minute later said, "We got it. Blue van heading west on Santa Monica Boulevard . . ."

"I need to know where it goes," Letty said. "Where it stops."

"I've got some other things going on right now, but I'll call you back as soon as it stops," the man said. "By the way, the van's legal owner is a Loren Barron, he's thirty-four, six feet five inches tall, a hundred ninety pounds, brown hair, brown eyes. Residence is listed as 1450 Josie Avenue, Long Beach, California. All of that is from his registration and driver's license. I can get more biography if you need it."

"That's our guy," Letty said. "Give us everything you can find or send us links."

"Will do. I'll get back as soon as he stops somewhere. If he's going to Long Beach, that could be a while."

"IF WE'RE GOING to watch him, he'll know the truck," Baxter said.

"You're right. Maybe the NSA has enough clout to get us a Hertz."

She called Delores Nowak, who went away for a few minutes, then called back to say that a Chevy Equinox was waiting at a Hertz agency on Westwood Boulevard. They drove over, parked the truck in the street, and while Letty got the car, Baxter disappeared into the Panda Express next door, emerging ten minutes later with a sack full of Chinese food.

"Eat it out here, outside," Letty told him. "I'm not sitting in a car for six hours if it's stinking of chow mein or whatever it is."

"The only problem with Panda Express is, they don't have donuts," Baxter said, as he stuffed his face with chicken fried rice and orange chicken. "I'm still gonna feel snacky."

"That's not possible. You're stuffing fifteen hundred calories in your face right now," Letty said.

"STFU," Baxter said.

The NSA tracker called back: "They took Santa Monica Boulevard west then southwest, onto Sepulveda. They stopped somewhere on a block on Sepulveda Boulevard—we had them through one camera, but not through the next, and haven't seen them since. They might have gone down a side street, though, but that's the area they're in. Sorry I can't be more help."

Letty wrote down the address, and the man added, "Barron has, or had, a secret clearance from the military. According to the clearance, he's worked for Oracle, for the Democratic Party, and for the U.S. Navy, doing database security work. He has a PhD in computer and mathematical sciences from Caltech and has taught occasional seminars there. We didn't see anything that suggested he had a wife, so we don't know who the woman is who was with him."

When the call ended, Baxter said, "We don't know where he is exactly. Want to go look anyway?"

"Yes. We need to see who he talks to," Letty said. "Especially since they're looking at your SlapBack program. Could be more OPs."

"I wonder if they'll try to hold up SlapBack—use my stuff as ransomware?" Baxter said. "They're supposed to get us another ten thousand if the code works—and it will—but if they know how to handle a Bitcoin transfer, they could get a hell of a lot more than fifteen thousand dollars out of SlapBack."

They left the truck on the street and drove the Equinox to the stretch of Sepulveda Boulevard where the LAPD cameras had lost the blue van. They found the van quickly enough, at a white single-family home with green shutters and no door on the front of the house, where one would normally be. What should have been a front yard was cracked unpainted concrete, with space for three or four cars, though none were parked on it.

A closed, rust-colored metal gate on the left side of the house led to a side yard, where the home's entrance must be. Baxter, who was driving, spotted the van and pointed: "Is that it? Behind the rusty gate?"

"Go by again." They turned around and cruised past the house again. The gate concealed the van from the bottom of the back window down, but it looked the same. "There might be a hundred like it . . . but it's exactly the same color. Wish we could see the plate."

Baxter pointed to a side street. "I could grab a parking spot, or at least drop you off. If you walked down the sidewalk, you could peek over the top of the gate. As long as they didn't come out of the house at exactly the wrong time, you could get away with it."

"Good. Drop me," Letty said.

Baxter dropped her on the side street. There was no parking and he said he'd keep driving around the block until he found her at the street corner. From the drop spot, Letty walked around the corner and down Sepulveda. The houses were old and jammed close together. If she saw somebody before they saw her, she might be able to get behind a neighboring house . . .

But that wasn't necessary. She approached the gate from the extreme left side and peeked over it. "Gotcha," she muttered.

Baxter was coming down the side street as she got to the corner. "That's it," she said when she got in the Equinox. "How lucky was that?"

"Let's find a place to watch," Baxter said. After they circled the block a few times—the van never moved—they lucked into a space on Sepulveda that was being vacated by an elderly Range Rover. After parking, Baxter got out of the driver's seat and climbed into the back, where he could stretch out, but still see the house.

And hundreds of passing LA cars. "It seems like half the cars are Teslas," he said. "Some of them are truly ugly."

"They don't burn gas," Letty said. "Saves the whales."

"Yeah. Virtue signaling. Not only virtue signaling, the Tesla drivers can pretend that they're actually rich enough to drive a Bentley, but they choose not to, because of the whales."

"What's wrong with that?" Letty asked.

"Nothing at all," Baxter conceded. "Just that they're kinda shitty cars. I'm amazed at all the high-end stuff I'm seeing. I know, movie stars, the industry, and all that, but still . . . I've seen cars here that I've never seen in real life, and I'm a car guy. I go to car shows."

Nothing was happening at Loren Barron's house. After a while, Letty said, "You know about black people buying Cadillacs back in the fifties and sixties, right?"

"I don't think I do," Baxter said.

"I got this in an economic history class," Letty said. "Back then, there was a substantial number of black people who had good jobs, making good money—doctors, lawyers—but they weren't allowed to live in white neighborhoods. They were pushed into ghettoes, where the housing was crappy. And cheap. Since they couldn't spend the money on housing, they bought high-end cars, Cadillacs and big Buicks. I think the same thing might be happening here, to everybody, not just black people. Los Angeles housing is so expensive that you have people making a lot of money, but they still can't afford a house. So, they drive around in big expensive cars, and go home to their little houses."

Baxter said, "Huh. Remind me not to move here. Fires, mudslides, earthquakes, high rents, five-dollar gas. Hey, see that black Tesla, right there? That thing's uglier than my ass."

Letty: "Mmm, no."

THEY'D WATCHED FOR AN HOUR before they got movement at Barron's place. A silver Subaru pulled onto the concrete pad and a man got out, walked around to the gate and apparently pushed on a doorbell. A moment later, somebody from the inside let him through.

Fifteen minutes later, a second car arrived, another Subaru, a green one, with a man and a woman. They carried what looked like brown paper grocery sacks, pushed the doorbell, and were let inside.

"We need to get some tag numbers before they leave," Letty said.

"Yup. Punch up SlapBack again."

Letty went to SlapBack on the iPad, and it was online. "Nothing yet."

"Another car," Baxter said. A man got out of the third car, carrying what looked like two six-packs of something, but they couldn't see what. "Looks like a party."

Two hours passed, and nobody else showed up. Baxter had taken the iPad into the backseat, and was playing solitaire, checking every few minutes on SlapBack. And then:

"Whoa. SlapBack is gone," he said.

"What?"

"Yeah, it's gone, man. They took it down."

"Let's get some license plate numbers before the party breaks up," Letty said. Baxter walked around to the driver's seat, Letty got the camera out of the bag, dropped her window, and shot the tags on the three new cars as Baxter rolled them past the house. She chimped the images and the numbers were clear enough, all California plates.

"This was good, we're piling up names," Letty said. "See if we can get back in the same parking space."

Baxter did a U-turn, and then another, pulling into the same spot they'd left. He put the iPad into the dashboard rack and went to SlapBack again, but the site had disappeared.

"Okay, it's down," Baxter said. "I don't think we tell anyone about this."

"Delores Nowak will know," Letty said.

"She'll know, but she won't *know*, and nobody will make the mistake of asking if she knows," Baxter said. "That happens a lot at the NSA."

As he spoke, the couple who'd brought grocery sacks came out through the gate, closed it behind themselves, got into their car, and turned south. Another ten minutes, and the first- and third-arriving men came through the gate, closed it behind themselves, stood talking between their cars for a moment, laughed together, slapped hands, then drove away.

A half hour later, as they were talking about leaving their surveillance spot, a dark blue SUV went past, its brake lights winking on as it approached Barron's house, then continued down the street and turned a corner. Three or four minutes later, it passed them again, and Letty said, "Is that the same SUV? Look at the SUV. It's cruising them."

"Don't know," Baxter said. "If it's the feds, because of SlapBack, they broke through in a hurry."

"Doesn't feel like the feds," Letty said, as the truck turned at the corner again and disappeared.

Five minutes later, it was back. This time, though, the SUV went to the curb twenty or thirty feet short of Barron's driveway. Two men got out of the backseat: they were of average height, wearing ball caps, sunglasses, jeans, and light jackets. They walked like athletes, and had their right hands in their jacket pockets.

"They've got guns," Letty said. The two walked up to the gate, looked both ways, and then one of the men boosted himself up on the gate, dropped over, and apparently opened the gate for the other man, who stepped inside.

"You see that guy?" Letty asked. "He had a gun in his hand, in his jacket, before he climbed the gate."

"I dunno, I don't know what that looks like. Maybe call 9-1-1?" Baxter suggested.

"We don't know what's going on . . ."

"We need to call . . ."

"And tell them what? The cops aren't gonna hurry over because we saw somebody hop a fence. And if they went there to rob or shoot them, they'll be gone before the cops get here," Letty said. "If they're not out in ten minutes, we call 9-1-1, but if they come out in the next minute, we get our guy to track them."

She fished the camera bag out of the backseat and pushed the zoom lens all the way out.

Baxter: "You'd get a better angle from the backseat."

Letty clambered into the backseat, pushed the door open a few inches.

The two men came back through the gate four or five minutes after they crossed through it, one of them carrying what looked like one of the grocery sacks the couple had taken inside. He carried it with both hands, as if it were heavy. Letty ripped off a series of frames, getting both their faces and the SUV's license plate before the SUV pulled away.

"They're in a hurry and they're nervous," Baxter said. "Something happened in there."

Letty called the NSA tracker and read the license number to him. "They should be heading south on Sepulveda . . ."

When that was underway, Baxter said, "I should call Able. I'll ask him to call Barron. If Barron answers, we'll know he's okay. If he doesn't . . . we gotta go in there or call 9-1-1."

"Call him," Letty said.

Baxter called and Able picked up. Before Baxter could ask about Barron, Able asked, "Have you guys looked at SlapBack?"

Baxter: "Yes. It's down. Listen, can you call your friend, the tall guy? Bob? Call him, ask him if everything's okay. We're worried. Charlie thinks somebody might have followed us away from your house. We lost them, but if somebody was tracking them . . ."

"All right. Call you back in a minute."

Letty and Baxter sat looking at the house, but there was no activity. Able called back and said, "I don't get an answer, from either of them. I called his girlfriend, too."

"All right. We gotta be careful. It's possible that the feds picked them up if they were watching you and then saw SlapBack go down."

"What . . ."

"Stay low," Baxter said. "Tell everybody you know to stay away until we can get them on the phone."

"Dude, you really think . . . ?"

"Dunno, but I'm worried," Baxter said, and he hung up.

"Okay. I'm going in," Letty said. "Is your box of covid masks still under the backseat?"

"Yeah . . ."

"I need to cover my hands and face when I go over the gate. I'll open it from the inside and let you in. We don't want to touch anything with our bare hands, we don't want to be recognizable on a camera."

Sepulveda Boulevard was busy, so they'd have to go in with other people watching. No way to avoid it. "Gotta look confident," Letty said, as they came up to the gate. "Confident and quick."

She'd pulled the masks over her hands—"We should have

thought of buying real gloves"—and at the gate, without breaking stride, she put her hands on the top, pulled herself up and flipped over. The gate had a latch lock and she unlatched it and let Baxter in.

"Back door's open. Not good," Baxter said, looking down the side of the house. "Wouldn't be good in anyplace I've ever lived."

Letty led the way to the door, and then called, "Loren? Are you there?"

There was no sound or movement, so she stepped inside.

Loren Barron was facedown in the living room, a bloodstain soaking into the rug beneath his head, a spray of blood droplets on a wall and on the television that hung on the wall, crimson smears on an anchorwoman's face.

His head was misshapen from the passage of a large-caliber bullet from back to front, exiting at one of his eyes. They found his girlfriend near the back door, which she'd apparently tried to escape through, a bigger puddle around her, on the nonabsorbent terrazzo floor, and another spray of blood across a white washer and dryer. The rooms stank of death: fecal matter, urine, the astringent odor of gunpowder.

Baxter said, "I gotta go outside or I'm gonna puke."

"Go," Letty said. "If you gotta throw up, try to do it somewhere the feds won't find it and test it for DNA. Down the street into some weeds would be good."

Baxter went. Letty, fighting nausea herself, did a quick run through the house. No laptops. A tower computer, with three screens, sat on a desk in a home office; two hard drives had been ripped out. She opened the back door, hoping to get some fresh air in the house. Back in the living room, she found Baxter looking in at the side door. "You throw up?"

"No, I think I'm good, but the smell is bad. Laptops?"

"They're gone. Probably what the guy had in that sack. There's a desktop, but the hard drives are gone."

Baxter stuck his head inside and looked at Barron, on the floor, and then stepped inside, crossed the room, and looked at the woman by the back door. "Those assholes didn't ask any questions, they knew what they were here for," Baxter said. "They just shot them."

"I think so," Letty said.

"I've never seen a dead body outside a funeral home, my aunt Janice, died of breast cancer," Baxter said. "These guys kinda look like . . . dead. Like movie dead."

"Nice if we could get those laptops," Letty said.

Baxter: "No serious hacker is going to leave problematic content unencrypted on a laptop. They may have gotten the laptops, but they probably won't get the content. I hate to say it, because of . . . well, what *you* might want to do . . . but there's a stash place somewhere in this house. The good stuff that no crook will find. Not in ten minutes, anyway."

"We need to find it," Letty said.

"I was afraid you'd say that. Okay. Look for something out of place," Baxter said. "Could be anything. I've lived in crappy houses and hidden a lot of stuff, so I know the possibilities . . ."

"Tell me some."

He told her to check edges and corners, anything that looked like a thick board that might actually be a thin drawer. He told her to look at the power outlets, to see if they all matched. If one didn't, it could be a small safe.

Spice and seed jars needed to be checked—"You can stick an empty toilet paper roll down inside them, so from the outside, you see beans in a jar, and nothing else, but there's a hollow space inside that'll take money or flash drives."

Books could be hollowed out; a stack of books could be glued together, with a single space hollowed out in all of them. Drawers might have false bottoms; if a tennis ball is carefully cut, it could be squeezed to open it, but when the pressure was taken off, it would go back to looking like a regular tennis ball . . .

"Those are pretty small spaces," Letty said.

"The most valuable things that people have are jewelry, which usually fits in small spaces, and information. You can stick an entire library on a single flash drive," Baxter said.

They found a box of plastic gloves under the sink in the kitchen, pulled them on. They started with the woman's purse, which turned up no flash drives, but did provide a driver's license with a photo and her name and age. They took a cell phone photo of it, and then replaced it.

They searched the bedroom and bathroom, checking every pocket in every coat and jacket, assuring that every shoe was empty, that every bottle and can contained what it was supposed to contain, even if that was nothing.

All of the electric outlets were identical, which suggested that none of them concealed a hiding spot.

"The outlet safes look good, but they usually don't match whatever your other outlets look like," Baxter said. "They're usually white and most outlets are beige. Don't know why that is."

There were no false bottoms in the drawers they examined, or secret drawers under the kitchen counters, or beneath the windows. Barron's shaving cream cans didn't unscrew to reveal a secret space.

An hour after they began the search, they found Barron's cache in a hallway, behind a ten-by-sixteen-inch photo of a young Barron and an older woman standing in front of the Eiffel Tower. The photo was in a thick wooden frame, with a glued brown paper backing on the reverse side. Nothing seemed unusual until Letty tried to take it off the wall and noticed that it was far too heavy.

Baxter pushed up on the glass that covered the photo and the whole front slid up, including the photo, revealing a line of narrow shelves, almost like a spice cabinet, holding ranks of flash drives, four CDs in sleeves, and three stacks of currency, two of dollars and one of Euros.

"There we go," Baxter said. He took the cash and stuck it in his jacket pocket. "Let's pack it up and get the fuck outa here before the killers come back."

They did that; once in the car, they scanned the photos of the killers and the SUV into the iPad, and Letty called Delores Nowak.

"We were watching that Barron guy when two shooters showed up," she said. "They went inside and murdered Barron and his girl-friend."

"What!"

"Shot them, probably with silenced pistols and subsonics—we weren't far away, I had the car window down and we didn't hear shots. They had to be professionals. The woman's name was Bri-anna Wolfe and she was thirty-one; we'll send you a photo of her driver's license. We also have photos of the two men and their ve-hicle's license plate. Your tracker guy is following their truck. We want to move that all onto you guys and let your big brains sort it out."

"Murdered! My God! Two people?"

"Get over it," Letty said. "Here come the photos . . ."

Baxter: "You need to tell us what to do."

"We'll talk about it here," Nowak said. "Are you safe?"

"For the time being—but I gotta tell you, Delores, there's something going on that Rod and I don't know about," Letty said. "I have the feeling that it doesn't involve gas companies, unless So-CalGas has hit men on the payroll. I have the feeling you may have been telling us a few fibs."

Nowak didn't respond for a moment, then said, "Hang on, I'm calling our tracker to see where the SUV went."

While she was doing that, Letty put her thumb over the microphone and said, "Don't tell her about the CDs or the flash drives. I'd like to see what's on them before we have to ship them off."

"Probably all encrypted," Baxter said.

"So it wouldn't make any difference if she got them right now, or later."

"Probably not," Baxter agreed. "Except she'll be pissed at me."

Nowak came back: "The tracker says the SUV is on the 405 headed toward the Valley."

"Okay. We may head over there," Letty said. "Maybe you could jack up the FBI SWAT squad . . ."

"We'll talk about that and let you know," Nowak said. "I'm going to take this up a level. Whatever Barron was involved in, even if it wasn't attacking a gas line, he drew in killers."

"That's what it looks like," Letty said.

"This is bizarre," Nowak said. "Nobody knows you were in the house?"

"No. And the killers don't know they've been spotted and tracked. A SWAT team could grab them right now."

"We may not want to do that," Nowak said. Pause. "Or, we may. Is there any possibility these men spotted your Hertz?"

"Don't think so," Baxter said. "Our license plates are in the LAPD database; you could have your tracker look at our plates and see if anyone followed us."

"I'll do that," Nowak said. "If you think you're clean, keep the Hertz. You may need more than one vehicle."

Letty: "What about Able and his friends? We don't know how the killers got to Barron's place—if they followed him from Able's, then Able might be in trouble. We need to warn him and his friends."

"Not yet. I'll be back to you within an hour or two. Maybe sooner . . . Maybe with a plan of some sort."

When they rang off, Baxter said, "They're hiding information from us. What is it?"

"Don't know," Letty said.

"Then what do you want to do?"

"Find that SUV."

Baxter pulled at his lower lip for a moment, then smiled and said, "All right."

ELEVEN

The NSA tracker called back: "They stopped somewhere on Ventura Boulevard. We got them through one stoplight, but they didn't go through the next one. They should be somewhere on that block, since you can't get out of it without running past a camera. It's possible they stopped and changed their license plate, but that seems unlikely. There's a Vons supermarket there . . . they could be in the parking lot."

"All right," Letty said. "If they pop up again, let us know right away."

"I will."

They put the address for the supermarket in the iPad's navigation app, followed it on the 405 freeway into the San Fernando Valley and Ventura Boulevard. They rolled through the Vons parking lot; the SUV wasn't there.

"They went through *that* light," Baxter said, pointing, "but they didn't make it through *that* light." He pointed at a traffic signal at the end of the block. "That means they gotta be in this block."

"Keep moving," Letty said. "They could have pulled through the parking lot and gone out sideways on the next street."

"That street looks big, too. It's probably got its own cameras."

They cruised but found no sign of the SUV.

"If they didn't leave the block, they could be in one of those parking lots across the street, or in that garage," Letty said, looking across Ventura. "I'm kinda liking the garage."

Across the street from the Vons, a line of dingy two-story shops sat up like a row of bad teeth, with narrow parking lots between each shop. An auto-repair garage sat in the middle of the block; what had been its advertising sign above the two garage doors had been roughly covered with green paint. When Letty looked at the garage through her binoculars, she saw a "Closed" sign on the front door.

They found a parking spot in the Vons lot that gave them an angular view, between a Ford pickup and a Chevy van, of the front of the garage. They sat watching for half an hour, but nothing moved in or out of the garage. There was some foot traffic past the place, in both directions.

They passed the binoculars back and forth, and then Letty said, "I'm going to take a walk. See what I can see up closer."

"Call me before you do anything extreme," Baxter said. "Leave the binoculars, you won't need them. I'll watch you, so if you get shot, I can inform the police in a timely manner."

"Great. I'll leave the cane. The cane and the limp attract the eye," she said. She peeled off the knee brace and left it on the car floor, checked her Sig to make sure it was cocked and locked, as always, and it was. She got out of the car and walked toward the back of the parking lot, to a bakery, and then turned left across the lot to Reseda Boulevard, across the boulevard to a Coffee Bean, where she went inside and bought a cup of coffee.

Carrying the cup, she crossed Ventura and walked toward the garage, which was located between a Chop Shop hairdresser and a Katz' Kids Deli. The three businesses had narrow parking lots between them, while the front of the shops went almost to the sidewalk.

The garage had four long, shallow windows on its side walls, set just below the roofline, facing the Chop Shop on one side and the deli on the other. Letty walked down the hairdresser's parking lot, then over to the garage wall. She stood for a moment, listening, but heard nothing from inside. She walked down the wall to the back of the building, where she found a steel door and nothing else—no windows, nothing but yellow-painted concrete.

Crossing the parking lot back to the Chop Shop, she turned down the sidewalk and walked past the garage. The two big overhead doors had glass panels, with bars behind the glass. The glass was frosted and grimed with dust. A bulky shape behind the glass on one side might be the back of the SUV, Letty thought.

Nothing moved.

She called Baxter and said, "That SUV isn't in the deli parking lot and it's not in the Chop Shop lot. I'll check the rest of the lots on the block, and then I'll be back."

She'd checked four lots when Baxter called back: "A guy just came out of the garage and I think it's one of the shooters. I'm pretty sure."

"I'm coming. Stay out of sight."

"He's carrying a cloth grocery bag. He's going into Vons . . . He's in the store."

"At least he's environmentally conscious," Letty said.

"Except that he's littered bodies all over the place," Baxter said.

Letty was back at the car two minutes later, and ten minutes after that, the shooter walked out of the store, carrying a bag in one hand that appeared to be full of groceries. He had a donut in his other hand, which he ate as he walked toward the corner to cross Ventura.

"That's one of them," Letty said. "Good eye, Rod."

Letty got on the phone to Delores Nowak, who answered on the first ring: "Something happen?"

"Yes. We spotted the hideout. It's in a closed car-repair garage on Ventura. One of the shooters bought a bag of groceries and is walking back to the garage."

"Good job. What's the address there?"

Letty gave it to her, and Nowak said, "We've had an extended conference here and we've decided with two dead, we need to know who these shooters are. We've got the FBI's SWAT squad ready to roll and they're not far from you. The FBI and the LAPD are on their way to Barron's house. The SWAT squad is maybe twenty minutes from you, a half hour at most."

Letty said, "I need to talk to the SWAT commander. Like, right now."

Nowak didn't argue: "I'll fill him in and have him call." And she hung up.

Letty waited a restless five minutes, long enough for Baxter to ask, "You think they're fuckin' with us?" then took a call from a man who said, simply, "This is Jackson. FBI. You wanted to talk to me?"

"Did Nowak tell you who I am?"

"Yes. Whatcha got?"

"The walls of the garage you're headed for are made of poured concrete, not concrete block. They look like bunker walls. There are two overhead garage doors in front, with frosted, dirty windows that you can't see through and they're barred. One regular door, but the regular door has steel bars behind the glass and is set in a steel frame. I don't know if you could bust it with a handheld ram. The only other door is a steel door on the back wall. There are no windows in back, but there are four windows on each side. The windows are up high—probably fifteen feet off the ground, and they've got a chain-link mesh behind them. I suspect they look out from a loft. There are two cameras on the front of the building, covering the sidewalks. I don't know if they're real or if they're even functioning, but the cameras look clean, like they might be new."

"Okay. Thanks for this. We've got a scout car out ahead of us . . . Is there any place where we can look *down* at the garage?"

"Not close," Letty said. "All the buildings on that side of the street are the same height and kind of old. They look like they were all built at the same time. There's a deli on one side, people are coming and going from that, but there's no line, not a lot of people. There's a hairdresser on the other side, and that's the same thing, a few people coming and going."

"Do you think there might be roof access from inside the garage?"

"Can't tell, but I can probably find out."

"Don't risk your neck to find out—and don't take a chance of tipping them off. We'll be coming."

"I'll get back," Letty said. She hung up and said to Baxter: "I'm going into that deli to see if there is roof access. The SWAT team is still a ways out, there'll be a scout car ahead of the full team. No, I won't get you a ham and cheese, so don't ask."

"You want me to come with you?"

"I would, but somebody's got to stay here and watch the front of the garage," Letty said. "I'll call you from the roof if I make it up there. If somebody comes out of the garage, or the SUV comes out, call the SWAT guy and then call me."

LETTY CROSSED VENTURA AGAIN, at the corner, walked past the front of the garage to the deli and went inside. In the back, at one side of the kitchen, she could see a set of stairs going up. She stepped past a single customer, who had a finger pressed against the glass front of the meat case, about to order, and said to the counterman, "I gotta talk to the manager. Right now."

The counterman frowned at her over the top of his mustard-stained apron and said, "You gotta wait. I'm already serving . . ."

"Right now!" Letty said. She walked around the end of the counter and headed toward the kitchen, where a single cook was leaning against a sink and was picking his teeth with a red-flagged cocktail toothpick. The counterman yelled, "Hey! You can't go back there," and the cook, a knobby-looking Asian man, moved to block her, but she snapped, "Get out of the way."

She took her hand out of her pocket, with the 938 in it. The cook got out of the way. The counterman had picked up his cell phone and she turned and said, "I'm FBI. Lock the doors. In a very few minutes, an FBI SWAT squad will get here. Some heavy shit is about to go down and you don't want to get caught in the middle of it."

The single customer, a florid, heavyset man wearing a yellow shirt, said, "Fuck this," and walked out the door. As Letty watched, he turned away from the garage and disappeared down the sidewalk.

The stairs started halfway through the kitchen. Letty ran up them, and at the top of the stairs, found a landing, and on the other side of the landing, through double doors that appeared to never have been closed, she could see an office-loft, with a wooden desk, computer, and some filing cabinets.

To her right, a short hallway led to a bathroom—she could see a toilet—and to one side of the bathroom door, a ladder. She went that way and looked up. The ladder, made of gray-painted two-by-fours, led to a push-up hatch. She put the 938 back in her jeans pocket and climbed the ladder. The hatch was dogged down with a steel push-bar. She pulled it loose, and when she pushed up on the hatch, years of dust and dirt fell onto her face and hair. She ignored it, and pushed the hatch all the way open, and crawled up onto the roof.

The roof, half the size of a basketball court, was covered with gravel chips embedded in tar, and worn with age and too much sun: cracked, hard, bare tar showed through in a dozen wide spots; she could smell it. There was nothing on the roof, except a variety of chimneys and vents, and an air conditioner housing. The odor of cooking ham came from one of the vents.

The roof over the garage, across the deli parking lot, had a collection of star-shaped concrete planters all pushed into a corner, with nothing in them. In addition to the planters, vents, and air conditioner housing, a hutch-style shelter sat at one side, apparently covering stairs that came up from below. She walked to the end of the deli roof to get a better angle on the hutch, and saw another steel door.

Letty got back on her cell phone and called the SWAT team leader. He said, without preamble, "Ten minutes out, the scout car should about be there. What do you got?"

"I'm on the deli roof, next to the garage," Letty said. "It looks like the garage has stairs that go right up to the roof, with a shelter over them. So, you could have somebody above you, looking down."

"Thanks. Good to know. We could see a square on the satellite view, but we didn't know what it was. Somebody thought it might be a housing for a garage hoist."

"Got a door on it," Letty said. "You know, for people."

"Okay. Ten minutes. You stay safe."

A minute later, a nondescript gray car rolled down the alley at the back of the line of shops. Letty watched it go by, pause by the garage's back door, then go on and turn at the corner. She walked to the front of the roof and saw the gray car roll by the front of the garage. A man in the passenger seat was looking out at the garage.

The scout car? She thought it probably was. The car went to the end of the block, made an illegal U-turn, rolled back to the Vons parking lot, found a space, and parked where the occupants could watch the garage.

A TWO-FOOT-HIGH PARAPET ran around the perimeter of the deli roof, with crenellations sticking up another six inches. When Letty kicked the parapet, it gave back a hollow thump. Plywood covered with tar paper, not highly recommended as cover in a gunfight, though it offered some concealment. She moved close to the parapet and sat down, prickly little stones pressing uncomfortably into her butt.

As she waited, ticking off the minutes on the phone, a man's head popped up through the hatch that led down to the office loft. He was heavy, red-faced, bald. "What the hell are you doing?" he demanded.

"Who are you?" Letty asked.

"I'm the manager. I just got back and they told me some bullshit about you being FBI. You're not even a fuckin' teenager. Come down from there before I drag your ass down."

Letty put her gun hand on the parapet, so he could see the pistol. "Let me tell you something. The FBI SWAT squad will be here in two minutes or less. All you have to do is wait two minutes, or maybe three, and then you will know it's not bullshit. If you come up here and try to drag me away, I'll probably shoot you, and not only will you be shot, if you don't die you'll go to prison for endangering the life of a federal law enforcement officer in the midst of what could turn into a firefight . . . and all that could be avoided if you go away for two minutes. Think about it."

And her phone rang: she looked down at it, hit the speaker icon. Jackson said, "We have three men coming down the alley in back. Wave to them so they know exactly where you are. Do it now."

"Okay." She scrambled to the back parapet, trying to stay low, though she realized in the back of her brain that wasn't yet necessary, and saw three agents in full armor with helmets, carrying assault rifles, jogging down the alley. She stood and waved and the leader waved back. The three continued to the back of the garage, and as she watched, took up a triangular formation, fifteen yards apart and fifteen back from the steel door.

She turned back to the deli manager, who said, "Okay, I heard that. I'll go lock the door." He disappeared down the hatchway. A moment later, he popped back up. "What they'd do? The guys you're after?"

"Murdered two people," Letty said.

"Okay." He was gone again.

Baxter called: "Something's happening. There are some bad-looking trucks at the end of the block . . . coming slow."

"That's them," Letty said, and hung up. Tasted a little salt in her mouth, waiting.

THE SHOW BEGAN with the sound of trucks in front of the garage and idling there. A few horns honked, and then she heard a bull-horn. Letty could hear it, but not make out the words.

She was sitting halfway down the length of the deli roof, and moved forward, hoping to hear better. She still couldn't make out the words, but she did see parts of two large dark square trucks parked on the wrong side of Ventura and men in dark armor behind them.

More honking horns; the commuters were getting pissed.

As she was looking at the trucks, she heard shouting from the back of the building, and turned and went that way, in time to hear a door slam. When she looked down from the roof, she saw the three SWAT members standing in the alley, pointing their guns at the steel door, which had apparently been opened and then slammed shut. The people inside the garage were surrounded and now they knew it.

She started to walk back to the front of the building, where the bullhorn was at work again, when she heard the door rattling on top of the garage roof. Locked from the inside, she thought, and probably stuck shut with rust and dirt. Now it was being opened. She sat down behind the parapet, peeking out from behind a crenellation, and watched as somebody kicked the door, and then pushed through it.

A man came out and looked around, didn't see Letty, who

showed nothing more than one eye between the plywood crenellations. The man was in a hurry, but she didn't know exactly what
he was doing. He had one arm locked across his chest, as if he was
carrying a bunch of bottles, more than he could handle with two
hands. Then he paused, still with one hand locked across his chest,
and started making flinging gestures with the other hand.

And she thought, "Are those . . . ?"

They were. Safety rings on hand grenades.

Letty screamed, "Grenades, he's got grenades! Man on the roof
with grenades!"

She thumbed the safety on the 938 and snapped a shot at the
man who'd started trotting toward the back of the building. She
knew she'd miss as she was pulling the trigger, and she did, but
she had no time for accuracy, she had to stop him from dropping
the grenades on the SWAT team members in back.

"Watch out, watch out, grenades . . ."

The man lurched sideways, nearly stumbled at the sound of
Letty's scream and the nearby shot and he half turned toward her
as he flung his hands away from his chest, heaving the grenades at
the back parapet.

Three of the grenades, the arming levers flying free, went over
the parapet, but a fourth one hit a crenellation and bounced back
toward the man and he turned to run away from it.

Letty, now tracking him, but at the same time distracted by the
grenade that was rolling in circles around the adjacent roof, missed
him with a second shot, but took a half second with the third, and
shot him in the hip and he went down and then immediately began crawling toward the air conditioner housing.

Letty, still screaming "Grenades," and who had only a Hollywood idea of what a grenade might do, dropped below the parapet

and then all four grenades went off one-two-three-four in fast order. The blasts seemed disappointingly small, and a tiny piece of burning-hot metal, the size of an eyelash, landed on her hand. She brushed it off, but it left a white eyelash-sized burn mark.

Seconds later, automatic rifle fire snapped out at the back of the building but didn't seem to involve her. Letty had to pay attention to the man she'd shot on the garage roof, who'd managed to take cover from the fourth grenade behind the air conditioner housing.

When she peeked at him, he was on his back, but had a pistol in his hand and began spraying the rotten parapet on Letty's building with a full seventeen-round magazine, the bullets buzzing past her like bees, splinters of wood and tar paper spraying from the bullet holes.

Somebody at the back was shouting, "Men down, we got men . . ." but Letty was scrambling as best she could to get behind her own air conditioner housing. She was almost there when a nine-millimeter slug hit the heel of her shoe with the impact of a hammer, twisting her ankle.

As she made it behind the air conditioner, breathing hard, there was another small explosion at the front of the building—another grenade?—but then Letty heard more shouting from the front and thought that the SWATs may have blown open the door at the front of the building.

Then everything went quiet, just for a moment, and Letty screamed, "Armed man on the roof. Armed man on the roof." She screamed twice, then remembered her phone, and called Jackson, who picked up on the second ring, and she shouted, "Armed man on the roof, he's got a pistol."

Jackson said, "Thanks," and hung up.

Twenty seconds passed, then a helmeted head popped out from

behind the stairway housing on the roof of the garage, and Letty shouted, "He's behind the air conditioner on the garage roof . . . He's wounded. I can see him. Should I shoot him again?"

"Can you?"

"Yes, he's right there."

The wounded man was looking in her direction and heard the exchange, and he shouted, "Fuck you, fuck."

Then another helmeted man stuck his head up through the hatchway from the deli and called, "Can he see me?"

"Not if you stay low," Letty called back, "but the parapets are rotten and the slugs pop right through."

The man, dressed in black combat fatigues and armor, slid over the edge of the hatchway and low-crawled toward her, a black rifle riding on his arms. He was good-looking in the swaggering, square-jawed SWAT way. She pointed in the direction of the man on the garage roof, and the new arrival peeked between two crenellations, then got on a radio and said, "I can take him if you give me the green light."

Jackson, on the other end of the call, said, "We're gonna talk to him."

"Let me know." The new arrival turned to Letty and asked, "He's wounded?"

"I shot him in the hip," she said. "I thought we might want to interrogate him."

"Good call."

"What happened out back?" Letty asked.

"One of our guys was wounded, not bad, mostly small cuts, he might need stitches. Two of theirs are dead. They were waiting for the grenades to go off, they were hoping to get all three of ours, but after you screamed at them, our guys got behind enough cover and far enough away that they got through it. Then their two guys came crashing out thinking that maybe all of ours were dead or hurt, and they got cut down before they could do more damage."

"Just the three guys so far?" Letty asked.

"Yeah, just the three, as far as I know."

They both peeked between crenellations and saw the wounded man still behind the air conditioner housing, lying in a spreading puddle of blood. Somebody was talking to him from the stairwell, but they couldn't make out what was being said.

The man with Letty rolled over on his side, keeping the barrel of his M4 pointing between crenellations, and said, "Pretty nice day, huh?"

"Cooler than I thought California would be," Letty said. They were self-consciously laconic, like in the movies.

"Well, it *is* February," the fed said.

"True. I could be freezing my ass off in Washington."

"Talk about a tragedy," the man said.

Made her smile. "There it is. You get a girl hiding behind a parapet and the first thing you do, you try to take advantage."

"I do it every time I get a girl behind a parapet, whatever a parapet is," the man said. He got on the radio: "What's up, boss?"

"We're talking. He's gonna quit."

And after a while, he did.

DELORES NOWAK HAD BEEN TRACKING the conflict in Los Angeles, and when the man on the garage roof gave himself up to the FBI, she was on the phone to Letty within a minute, while Letty was still on the deli roof.

"I'm on my way to National. Senator Colles will meet me there. We've got a flight out to LAX, but we're probably seven or eight hours away. We need to meet."

"Okay."

"Here's the problem," Nowak said. "We still need you on the ground there, undercover, working on Ordinary People. But you shot a man in the leg, as I understand it. You will have to go to FBI headquarters for interviews and to make statements and they will want to take your weapon as evidence . . ."

"Ah, jeez . . ."

"That's not a problem. They will need *that* particular weapon, a Sig 938, I'm told, but you'll get an identical one, new, at the FBI headquarters. I've been told that it will have been fired for accuracy."

"Not the same . . ."

"I know, but it's unavoidable. One of the downsides of living in a democracy with a functioning legal system," Nowak said. "Also, should you wish for a different weapon, that would be provided, at no cost to you. Your own gun will be returned to you at some point in the future, but when, it's difficult to say."

"But I . . ."

"We don't want you riding with the FBI or talking with FBI agents at the scene. I've talked to Jackson about this and Baxter will pick you up at the back door of the delicatessen. He will drive you to FBI headquarters, which is not far away, in the Hertz car. Once there, you'll be handled as a confidential informant. You'll not have contact with any more than the minimum of agents. We hope to have you out of there in a couple of hours."

"I was . . ."

"There are no options. Get off the roof and meet Baxter. He's behind the deli."

"How'd you know I was still on the roof?" Letty asked. "How do you know Baxter is behind the deli?"

"Move," Nowak said.

"One more thing: how much should I tell the feds?"

After a moment of silence, Nowak said, "You can tell them that you met with Barron and Wolfe at a location you can't disclose and if they have a problem with that, they should call me. You should not disclose what you and Baxter were doing. Start with tracking Barron through the Los Angeles cameras, seeing the killers arrive, your discovery of the bodies, and tracking the killers to the garage. You can give them all the details for that, but don't give them any information on your cover IDs or the continuing operation. Tell them that information is classified as top secret and compartmented. Remember the *compartmented*."

"But they know from when they tried to bust us . . ."

"Yes, they know that, but they don't know what we're doing now, or who we've been talking to. Don't tell them. Now go."

Letty went. Down the ladder, down the stairs, and out the back, where Baxter was waiting in the Equinox. Fifty feet away, FBI agents in tactical gear were looking at two bodies. Letty walked up to the driver's side of the Equinox and said to Baxter, "Delores told me not to do it, but I gotta see what happened here."

"Fine with me. I'm kinda curious myself," Baxter said. "What the hell did you do?"

"Tell you about it later."

Letty walked down to the group around the bodies. As she came up, the oldest of the agents, a tall, weathered man with traces of gray in his otherwise dark hair, said, "I'm Jackson. You'd be Letty?"

"Yeah. I want to look at the dead guys, see if they're the shooters we saw at Barron's place."

"Good. Take a look."

Both men had been rolled onto their backs, to see if they needed ambulances. Neither one did. Letty said, "I have to go back to the car for a minute . . ."

She walked back to the car and got the camera. Baxter said, "If you're gonna be a while, I might hit the deli."

"Go for it," she said. "Get me a chicken sandwich with something spicy on it, and a root beer if they have it. We're gonna be stuck at FBI headquarters for a while."

She walked back to the bodies with the camera, called up the photos on the view screen, and with Jackson and another agent looking over her shoulder, said, "One of them is right. The other one isn't and the guy on the roof wasn't, either. So one of the shooters wasn't here."

"We'll talk to the guy we got, but I kinda think this might be the low end of whatever organization they're with," Jackson said. "The garage is set up as a barracks. There's beds and a small kitchen and a bathroom on the second floor, the loft. Space for six. They've all got California ID, but I'll kiss Arnold Schwarzenegger's ass in Saks' front window if they aren't Russians. Or Ukrainians. Or Serbians. Someplace in there."

"Russians? You talked to our NSA contact, right? She filled you in?"

"Some."

"There could be Russian involvement in a really big ransomware hack and counter-hack that the NSA knows all about and that

Barron and his girlfriend might have been involved in," Letty said. "You should talk to her about why you think these guys are Russians."

"I'll do that. You're going over to our headquarters . . ."

"Yeah. Soon as my guy gets a couple sandwiches from the deli."

"Listen, we appreciate your shout-out about the grenades," Jackson said. "Our men could have gotten dinged up pretty bad. As it was, it's all cuts and bruises. But we, you know, appreciate it. Thank you."

"You're welcome. About the guy I shot up there . . ."

"He's a mess, but he won't die. One of the ambulance EMTs said it looks like you hit the ball joint, so he'll probably need a hip replacement. He won't be running anywhere soon."

"Shouldn't throw grenades at people. I was kinda surprised that the grenades didn't do more damage than they did."

One of the agents listening to their conversation said, "Grenades are heavy. You have to throw them, so they can't be too powerful, or they'd kill the thrower. They're lethal out to five meters or so, maybe twenty feet, and maybe thirty feet if you're standing there in a tee-shirt looking at it, but once you're outside of that, especially if you can get down or behind something, or you can tuck into your armor, you'll probably be okay."

"Scared the heck out of me," Jackson said. "When I heard them go off, I thought, oh boy, here we go . . ."

"Good to know about grenades, though," Letty said. "Interesting."

"Long as you're pitching and not receiving," Jackson said. And, "You best take off. The NSA lady said she wanted to keep your face out of sight, so . . ."

"I'm gone," Letty said.

TWELVE

Letty had to wait in the car for five minutes, until Baxter came out of the deli with a sack of sandwiches and a root beer. Hers was a grilled chicken on a ciabatta roll, with green pepper sauce that set her mouth on fire. "This is fuckin' great," she said, chewing as they drove out to the 405 freeway. "I may hire you as my culinary advisor."

"I'd be happy to do it, and ask only a modest compensation," Baxter said.

On the road, Letty told Baxter about her conversation with Nowak, and the restrictions on what they were allowed to disclose.

"That's guaranteed to piss off somebody," Baxter said. "The good thing is, the urination will be way above our pay grade."

Baxter told Letty that while sitting in the car, waiting for something to happen, he'd checked the CDs and flash drives they'd taken from Barron's house, and they were all encrypted. "I doubt that anyone could crack them, but we might as well send them to Delores now, instead of later. Maybe they could do something with them back at the Fort."

"We won't have to send them to her—she'll be here in a few hours, along with Colles."

"Ah, crap. The arrival of the suits is not a good sign. For anything."

THE TRAFFIC ON THE 405 wasn't bad enough to slow them, and the FBI headquarters building on Wilshire Boulevard was basically right off the freeway. They were directed to a surface parking lot and escorted to a conference room where three functionaries waited, and as Letty and Baxter sat down, a court stenographer arrived with her tape recorder and a stenotype machine.

One of the bureaucrats opened with "We understand that you both are working with the Department of Homeland Security and the National Security Agency. We nevertheless need a detailed recounting of exactly how you encountered Loren Barron and Brianna Wolfe, and how you discovered they'd been murdered . . ."

"Are you on that scene?" Letty asked. "Barron's house?"

"Yes. We are, along with LAPD Special Operations. Now, let's start with how you met Loren Barron and Brianna Wolfe . . ."

"We can't tell you everything," Letty began, and she recited the restrictions imposed by Delores Nowak. The FBI bureaucrats said those restrictions were not acceptable and if necessary, they would get a subpoena to require the disclosure.

"That's between people way above all of our pay grades," Baxter said, repeating himself. "Why don't you ask us about the obviously relevant stuff, like how we began following Barron and then what happened? We can tell you everything right up to when you guys killed a couple of people and we didn't."

"And if you're gonna take my gun, give me a new one," Letty added.

The FBI bureaucrats—some of them experienced counteres-pionage agents—were stubbornly insistent about getting more information than Letty or Baxter were willing to give up.

"*We* are the agency tracking Russians in the U.S., not Home-land or the NSA," one of them said, angrily. "We need to know what the hell is going on here . . ."

Baxter: "We appreciate that, but I appreciate my job more and I'll get my ass fired if I tell you more than I'm authorized to. It's top secret and compartmented. I get you're all cleared to top secret but *not* to the compartmented information."

When they looked at Letty, she added, "What Rod said. The people you need to talk to will be here in a few hours, and I'll tell you—what we know won't help you in a few hours. Without break-ing out any secrets, I can tell you that we're pretty much at the end of the line of what we know."

After a moment, she added, "Where's my replacement gun?"

THE QUESTIONS AND ARGUMENTS went on for two hours, but toward the end, the lead interrogator was called out of the meeting twice, and after the second time, came back to say they could go.

"It's been fun," Baxter said, as they walked out, Letty slipping the new gun into her Sticky holster.

The new gun was probably identical to her own, right down to the molecule, but it felt wrong in her hand. She slipped it in and out of the holster as they walked to the car, but it never felt quite right.

DELORES NOWAK SAID the jet carrying her and Colles would be seven or eight hours on the way, but it turned out to be nine before they arrived at the LAX SkyPort hotel, in a black limo, looking beat: "It's three o'clock in the morning in Washington," Colles complained. "But we gotta talk this out now."

Food was waiting in the suite: a basket of a dozen toasted but cold everything bagels, containers of chive cream cheese, plastic knives, a refrigerator stocked with Diet Cokes and Dos Equis beer.

"We've discussed your situation with the top counterespionage people at the FBI and they've agreed to intervene here, keeping you clear of the Los Angeles inquiry into the Russians at the auto garage, and the deaths of Loren Barron and Brianna Wolfe. The sensitivity of the situation has been deeply impressed on the people here. Deeply impressed," Colles told them.

"Why?" Letty asked. "Rod and I have been talking. We think Barron was probably the center of the Ordinary People attack on the Russian train system, and that they were interested in gas systems but weren't interested in attacking a municipal gas system. Now that he's dead, I mean . . . what's left to do?"

"Mmm, it has to do with Loren Barron's birth name," Nowak said. "He's an immigrant. His parents Americanized their names when they immigrated here. Loren Barron was originally Leonyd Baranov."

Baxter: "He's a Russian?"

Nowak: "No. His family is Ukrainian. Most of the family, other than his parents and sister, still live in Ukraine."

Letty: "Oh-oh. CNN says Russia might invade Ukraine."

Colles: "CNN is correct. The Ukraine leadership still doesn't completely believe it. They've got some good sources in Moscow, but we've got better. We've got satellites and a whole selection of them are watching every move that Putin makes and recording most of what he says. He's going to invade, he's made the decision. Probably in the next couple of weeks."

"Oh, boy. We've got a Russian gang killing a Ukrainian who had the Russian train system in his pocket for weeks," Letty said. "A preemptive strike . . ."

"On American soil, by a gang we had no idea existed," Colles said. "Unfortunately, the part of the gang we took down consisted of the lowest-ranking members. They were living in a dormitory and eating out of a supermarket. But they had lots of guns—AR-15s altered to be fully automatic, among others—and even some grenades, as you found out. The question is, who is running this operation? Are they aimed at Ukrainians here in the States? If so, which ones? If we put together arms packages for the Ukrainians, will they try to interfere? We need to know who these people are. You two guys have got hold of one end of that thread . . ."

"Very slim thread," Baxter said. "I didn't sign up to go mano a mano with *spetsnaz* killers."

"These guys we took down weren't *spetsnaz*," Colles said, as though he'd been there in body armor. "They were gangsters. That's bad enough, but they weren't exactly the sharpest knives in the dishwasher."

"What do you want us to do?" Letty asked.

"What you *were* doing," Nowak said. "We think the Russians aren't finished with the train gang. The Russians are heavily dependent on trains getting supplies close to the front. All the fronts. Ukraine uses the same rail specs as Russia, so the Russian supply trains could roll right through the country, behind the invading forces. It's part of the way they do things. If we have assets here in the U.S. who can hinder Russian supply lines, in case of a Ukraine invasion, we don't want them killed. We do want to know who they are."

"All right," Baxter said. He looked at Letty. "You up for this?"

"For a while," she said. "I wouldn't mind having another shooter backing us up."

Colles: "John Kaiser?"

"I was thinking about a friend of mine. Barbara Cartwright with the CIA. We've talked, and I know she's not supposed to work in the U.S., unless it's as intelligence support with another agency. That would be us—Homeland and the NSA."

"Why not John?" Colles asked. "You're friends, you work well together . . ."

"He's sort of a billboard that says 'Delta shooter.' Barb's another *girl*. She's like my older sister. Nobody would ever look at her and think 'shooter.' If we can get her . . ."

Colles said, "If she's willing, and her supervisors are, we can get her here tomorrow."

"That's what I'm talking about," Baxter said. "Another murderous broad."

Nowak: "Excuse me?"

Baxter hastily brought up the subject of the flash drives and CDs they'd taken from Barron's place and that they hadn't told the FBI about. "We figured you'd have the best chance at decrypting them, but I gotta say, it's not much of a chance," Baxter told them.

"We'll take a look; maybe something can be done," Nowak said. "You were right not to mention them to the FBI."

THE MEETING BROKE UP at two in the morning.

Letty and Baxter didn't go back to the motel but stayed in the

SkyPort, in separate rooms for the first time in a week. Letty took a long, soapy, luxurious shower, washed her hair and checked the tattoo on her back, which, she admitted to herself, was awesome.

Baxter called at eight o'clock the next morning: "I'm worried about my truck. We can't leave it on the street, it'll get towed and God knows when we'd get it back. I need you to drive me over there."

She was already up and moving: "We'll stash the car somewhere and take the truck over to Able's place. We need to cook up a story for him."

"We can do that on the way. I'll see you at the car. Five minutes."

They'd left the car in the underground parking structure. Letty walked through the structure once, looking for a likely car to victimize. She spotted a dusty possibility that she thought probably belonged to someone who'd left the car at the hotel and had then flown out of LAX.

Checking for cameras, she slipped around to the front of the car and used a dime to unscrew the license plate. She carried the plate to the truck, where Baxter was waiting impatiently.

"What's that?" he asked when she flashed the plate at him.

"I stole it. Two minutes ago. If we stick it on the front of the truck, Delores Nowak's video goons can't follow us. I don't trust you NSA fuckers anymore."

"Good. I don't trust us myself."

"HERE'S WHAT WE TELL ABLE," Baxter said, as they drove out to the truck. "We almost had a problem with the FBI, when that fuckin' Harp sent us to Bob and Sue. So we're suspicious, about him and this unidentified couple who were paying us money to take down SlapBack."

"So we followed Barron to his house . . ."

"Yes. We didn't know his name, of course, but that's what we did. While we were there, we saw a dark blue SUV circle the place, and then two guys jump the gate—and we could see that one had a gun in his hand. We called 9-1-1 on our burner phone, and told the cops about it, and gave them the license plate on the car. Before the cops got there, the two men came out, carrying a package, and drove away. We were too scared to follow them, so we sat. Then, before the LAPD could get there, a bunch of FBI showed up, wearing those blue jackets, like they knew where they were going. They went in the house and then the LAPD showed up. By that time, we knew something really bad had happened."

"And then . . ."

"We changed hotels, in case somebody might have followed us or gotten our license plate number, and this morning we saw on television that a Loren Barron and his girlfriend had been murdered. We could see from the television clip that the house where the murders happened was the house we followed Barron to."

"Is that true? About the TV news?" Letty asked.

"Yes. I saw it on a couple channels."

Letty rubbed her nose for a few seconds, then said, "I can't think of anything better. When we get to Able's, we tell him we want my drums and then we're out of here. We let him talk us out of leaving."

"What if he doesn't try? What if he wants us gone?" Baxter asked.

"Then we'll have to talk *ourselves* out of it, while he listens . . . We can work all that out on the way to the motel."

WHEN THEY GOT BACK to the truck, they left the car on the street, put the stolen plate on the front of the Tundra, drove to Pasadena, and checked out of the La Rouchefort. On the way to Able's, Letty put on her knee brace and got the cane out of the backseat. She'd be limping again. They got to Able's at eleven o'clock and found him in a tee-shirt and Jockey shorts, just out of bed.

Able was astonished and appalled. "They're dead? They were murdered? Loren and Brianna both?"

"Yes. The morning news on Channel 5 says the killers were Russians," Letty said. "Their reporter said the FBI was all over these guys, they caught them in a garage on Ventura Boulevard. How they tracked them, I don't know. It's possible the killers were waiting for Loren and Brianna to come home, but it's also possible that they were watching this place and they followed them to their house. We're gonna get the drum set and get the fuck out of here and maybe you ought to do the same thing . . ."

"We're not totally agreed on that," Baxter told Able, following the script that he and Letty had worked out while driving to West Hollywood. "I'm kinda thinking, if we have to hide, we're gonna need money. We might want to give SlapBack a call, see if they'd pay for the software that took them down."

"Ah, boy . . . they're still down, there's all kinds of stuff on the Net about it," Able said, running his hands through his thick hair. "The problem with getting money is always the same—how do you do it without the feds crawling all over you?"

Able didn't think the SlapBack attack could have anything to do with the murders, because, he said, he *knew* why Barron and Wolfe had been killed.

He told them about Ordinary People's attack on the Russian train system, and the ransom paid by the Russians to the organizer of the attack.

"I don't know who financed it, but I know that Ordinary People got a good chunk of cash. Six or seven people did the heavy lifting, and Brianna and Loren were the coordinators. Rumors are that they each got more than a hundred K, maybe way more," Able said.

Baxter looked at Letty, who raised her eyebrows, and he turned to Able and asked, "Are those people . . . Can you warn them? Do you know them?"

Able seemed to take a step back: "Look: I mean, you guys just showed up here . . ."

"And took down SlapBack," Baxter snapped. "If we were FBI, would we take down a whole fuckin' company? I don't think so." He jabbed a finger at Letty: "Does that look like an FBI agent to you?"

"How do I know you're not *Russian*?" Able asked. "That raven tattoo looks sorta Russian."

"Ah fuck it, let's load up the drums," Letty said to Baxter. And to Able: "Better watch yourself, man. Those guys at Barron's place weren't fuckin' around. They went in there and capped their asses, cool as you please. Never broke a sweat. We were right up the street and never heard a shot, neither. Had to be professionals, the way they did it."

"So what do I do?" Able demanded. He looked around. "This is my place. It doesn't look like much, but I could get six, seven hundred thousand for it. I can't jump in my car and drive away and never come back."

"I don't know," Letty said. "We're not like private eyes. Are we being watched? Are *you* being watched? The feds were all over the shooters and pretty damn quick, too. I don't know how they did that."

"If we hang around, and we're really careful, and we spot these guys, Russians, we could use a burner and call the FBI and turn them in," Baxter said.

"What if we're wrong?" Letty asked.

Baxter shrugged: "What if we are? Some innocent guy gets hassled, and we're not dead. That's better than some guilty guy doesn't get hassled and we get murdered."

Letty nodded: "When Paul's right, he's right. I'm afraid the Russians might already have me and Paul. We were here for a long time, at the same time as Barron and what's-her-name . . ."

"Brianna Wolfe . . ."

"So they might be onto us, too."

"You know what we could do?" Baxter suggested. "We could go right to the FBI. Tell them that we knew Loren and Brianna, and we didn't know what they were up to, but we heard rumors . . ."

"I can't talk to the feds," Able said. "Neither can you unless you're out of your minds. You did take down that hospital in Georgia. When they start looking at your background, tracking you, and where you're from . . . They might be a little light on brains, but not that light. They'd figure you out."

"Get the drums and go to Seattle," Letty said to Baxter.

Baxter was literally walking in circles. "I dunno, I dunno . . . They were fuckin' assassinated. Loren and Brianna. This isn't a fuckin' shooter game, they don't get to come back from *game over*. They're dead! The problem is, if the Russians did it, the Russians have the money and the people to get you wherever you go. And if Loren really did fuck with the Russian train systems . . ."

"TV says the Russians are going to invade Ukraine," Letty said. "They maybe don't want somebody fuckin' with their trains again."

"Jesus. We gotta . . . I gotta call some people," Able said.

———

ABLE CALLED PEOPLE while Letty and Baxter disassembled the drum kit and loaded it into the pickup, packed in Bubble Wrap. When they back came inside, ostensibly to say good-bye, Able said, "You gotta hang around. Gonna be a serious meet-up."

Letty said, "If they're following even one person to a meeting, they'll get to see all of us. Not a good idea."

Able shook his head. "It'll be okay. It's a bar. There's always a lot of people there, no way to know who's talking to who. And everybody there knows everybody else, so any strangers will stand out."

"Where?" Letty asked. "And when?"

"Venice Beach. A place called Poggers. There's a public parking structure near there, you can walk to the bar," Able said. He looked at his Apple Watch. "It's an hour from here and we're gonna meet in an hour. We gotta roll."

"Sounds pretty hurried . . ." Baxter said.

"It is. People are panicking, they've heard about Loren and Brianna. Nobody wants to talk on telephones."

Letty: "Poggers."

"In an hour."

THIRTEEN

The sun was out and bouncing harsh off the ocean when they got to Venice. They put the truck in the parking structure and walked two blocks down the beach, past the low pastel buildings where aging stoners, pushing their use-by dates, sold crap to tourists, past a pile of weather-beaten tents and caves made of plastic tarps, homeless people sprawled passed out on sandy blankets, their dogs passively watching the passersby, little hope in their canine eyes.

Skaters and bladers wove through the thin winter crowds as they got up to Poggers, a nondescript salmon-colored cube with a bar on the sidewalk. Able had parked on the street and was waiting when they walked up. "This way."

A narrow entrance opened into a dim room housing a few tables and a dozen old electronic arcade games, all being used as they passed through. The place smelled like popcorn, beer, hot dogs, and sweat. Eminem was rapping "Stan" from wall-top speakers.

Able led them through the bar, past the arcade games, nobody paying attention. A tight cluster of men, mostly in their thirties and forties, were gathered around an ancient *Marvel vs. Capcom: Clash of Super Heroes* machine, watching the play. One of them nodded at Able as he led Letty and Baxter between the men, who, Letty thought, might not have been inclined to move for strangers.

Behind them, a door opened onto a wooden stairway. They followed Able up the stairs to a party room, twelve or fifteen men and a half-dozen women, twenties and thirties and one very tattooed and tee-shirted senior citizen. Jan, the bass player, was there, and nodded at Letty. The others acknowledged Able and, cautiously, Letty and Baxter, as one man asked, "Who are they?"

Able asked him, "Have you been on SlapBack today?"

The man said, "Really?" and a cluster formed around the newcomers and somebody asked Letty a question she didn't understand and she said, "I don't do computers." She tipped her head at Baxter and said, "Paul does . . . Anyone got a beer?"

Baxter got into the computer talk and fifteen minutes later, Able asked, "Everybody good?"

Most were, a few weren't—and Able said, "C'mon. You all know about Loren and Brianna. What's this about Danny Delph?"

Somebody said, "He's gone. We can't find him."

"Who is he?" Letty asked. She was limping around the room with her cane.

"A friend of Loren's, he was on the train raid," Able said. "Did he take off, or . . ."

A blond woman, thin, wearing a man's cowboy shirt with pearl snaps and ripped jeans, said, "He didn't take off. Either he or Annie would have told me. He's gone and I don't know where, and neither does Annie."

Letty: "Did he say anything about Russians?"

The blonde shrugged and said, "Not that I heard. But I think we should be scared. My William is in the LAPD files and he looked at the reports on Loren and Brianna and they say they were both executed. *Executed.* Then the FBI landed on those Russians in the Valley and they had hand grenades and machine guns. The Russians did."

Letty asked, "Did you go into Delph's place?"

"No, we don't have any way to get in."

"House or apartment?"

"Apartment. Up the street in Santa Monica . . . sorta. Maybe not quite Santa Monica, but up there . . . in that direction."

"Gimme the address," Letty said. "Paul and I'll check. You could come along if you like."

The blonde was reluctant, but eventually coughed up the address; she didn't want to come along. Baxter was deeply involved in a discussion of the SlapBack hack and Letty asked the blonde if she knew anything about a Russian railroad attack.

"I've heard about it from my William . . ."

"Your friend . . ."

"Yes. When the news said the killers might be Russian, he started packing up. He thinks we ought to head for Vegas. Lay low."

"Not a bad idea," Letty said. "Is your William here?"

She turned and looked toward the party bar, which lacked a bartender or any drinks, and said, "The guy in the blue shirt."

The man in the blue shirt didn't want to talk and tried to turn away as Letty limped up, but Letty said, "Look at me," and he turned back and asked, "Why?"

"I've got some things to ask you and some things to tell you," Letty said. "You don't have to answer the questions, but you better listen to me."

She told him the story about driving west to find Ordinary People, hoping for help in getting money out of a Bitcoin wallet. And then Able had told them about the Russian train hack.

"From what I can tell, the Russians are here and they're pissed. They're not only pissed, they're worried you might fuck with their trains again, right when they need them, if they invade Ukraine," Letty said. "I'm afraid you've contaminated me and Paul—Loren and Brianna were killed right after we talked to them, and it's possible that the Russians trailed them from Able's house. If they did that, they've got my name and Paul's and our truck tags and the same thing for a bunch of Able's friends."

"I know what I'm going to do. I'm going to disappear," William said. "As soon as we're done here."

"That's not a long-term solution. If the Russian intelligence people are here, with guns, they'll find you. The long-term solution is to spot these guys and give them to the FBI," Letty said. "You're all smart—you oughta be able to do that."

"*You* spot them. My Melody and I are gonna take off."

"You think Danny Delph took off?"

"Danny . . . he always considered himself a tough guy. He wasn't gonna take off," William said. "But, maybe he did. He's one of those guys who's always around . . . Nobody's seen him in almost a week."

"What about his girlfriend, this Annie?"

"Able would know about her. She's a sound engineer and she sings and plays the keyboards and so on. She's in a band . . ."

She gave William the number of her burner, turned away and caught Able's eye, and when she had him separated from the crowd, asked, "This Delph guy has a girlfriend who sings and does sound. What's her name?"

"Annie Bell . . . though I think her last name was shortened from something else . . . nothing Russian," Able said. "I don't know what her real last name is, on her driver's license."

"You have a number for her?"

"No. I barely know her . . . You think the Russians got Danny? That they're coming after all of us?"

"Read the papers, then put yourselves in the Russians' shoes," Letty said. "You don't have to abandon your house, but I think you should go pack up, and hide. Your friend William may go to Vegas. Maybe you could share a space."

"I dunno . . . this is fuckin' crazy."

"Or worse," Letty said, as she turned to limp away. "I think you crazy hacker fuckers managed to stick your dicks into the beginning of a war."

She milled around for a few more minutes, listening in, memorizing faces, realized nobody really knew anything about the murders or the disappearance of Delph—but all were involved with Ordinary People in some way. She grabbed Baxter, who was deep in a nonrelevant discussion with some other coders, and dragged him away, saying, "Let's go to Seattle."

They didn't do that.

Letty led him back to the truck, where she ditched the cane and leg brace, changed into a different outfit, and rolled her hair up under a wide-brimmed white Tilley hat. She fished the camera out of the backseat, told Baxter to find something to eat, if he really thought he needed to, and then waited across the beach from the bar. The wait began to get long, then several people left within a few minutes. They walked off in different directions, to their cars, and she followed as many as she could, no limp, no cane, and shot their license tags.

She saw William and Melody leave with Able and another man, got William and Melody's plate, then jogged the opposite direction to catch up with the unknown man they'd come out with, and got that plate.

That was the end of it. She called Baxter and said, "Come back. We need to find this Delph guy."

While she waited for Baxter, she called Nowak. "I've got a whole batch of license tags from Ordinary People. I don't know if that's all of them, but it's a bunch. Most of the people involved in the train hack, I think. They all knew about it."

She told Nowak about the meeting at Poggers. "What do you want us to do now? We could check on this Delph guy, see if he's really missing . . ."

"Do that," Nowak said. "I'll talk to people here and see what they think. Any additional information on the Russians would be extremely useful."

When Baxter got back to the car, they used the Google mapping app to find Delph's apartment, in an area called Ocean Park. The long, low gray building was five blocks back from the ocean, with a glass door, flanked by matching glass windows, all with decorative black steel bars behind the glass. Delph lived in Apartment 360, which Letty assumed was on the third floor.

She put on the Tilley hat with a covid mask, left the knee brace and cane in the car, and walked down to the building to take a close look at the glass and the door lock. The building's mailboxes were on the outside, along with push buttons for individual occupants. Letty stood at the door, digging in her purse, as though looking for her keys, while she studied the problem.

One problem was immediately obvious: at one side of the lobby was an open door, and a shaft of light was coming from the opening. A sign to the side said "Manager."

Letty called Baxter: "Gonna have to do some social engineering. Better come down now."

"One minute."

When Baxter walked up, Letty leaned on the doorbell that said "Building manager." An older woman, gray hair, heavy, lined face, stuck her head out of the manager's office, then walked down to the door and opened it.

"What can I do for you?" she asked.

"We're friends with one of your tenants—Danny Delph in 360. He's missed several appointments with a music group and nobody can get in touch with him. We checked his phone and it's in his apartment, but nobody answered. This has been like a week. We'd like to look in his apartment and make sure, you know, he's okay."

"I can't let you in . . ."

"That's why we checked with you—we want you to look with us. If he's okay, or if he's just gone somewhere, that's fine. But . . . we're worried. He's had some serious depression problems and, you know . . ."

"I'll get the key," the manager said, now looking worried herself.

She got a key and they took the elevator to the third floor. The manager led them to Delph's door, pushed the doorbell. They heard a faint chiming from inside. The manager pushed the doorbell again, held it. No answer.

"We better look," she said, anxiously. She opened the door with a key.

The apartment was a shambles, with an overturned easy chair and coffee table, a thick skein of paper scattered like snowflakes, maybe thrown at someone, and a palm-sized blood spot on the beige carpet.

"Look at this," Letty said, pointing at the blood.

"Oh, my God," the manager said. "I gotta call the police."

"We'll wait here," Letty said. "We won't touch anything."

The manager opened her mouth to say something, thought better of it, and half-jogged down the hall. Letty picked up the edge of the carpet: the blood had barely soaked through. Whoever had been hurt, she told Baxter, had lain on the floor for a short time, but hadn't been terribly wounded: "Looks like a bad bloody nose."

"So maybe he's still alive."

"We can hope, but . . ." She didn't have to say it.

Delph's wallet was on a bedstand, with twenty dollars inside, and Baxter spotted the edge of what turned out to be a cell phone, poking out from under a pillow. Other than the speakers from what apparently had been a desktop computer, there were no other electronics: Baxter said that whoever had the desktop must also have gotten at least one laptop, because everybody had at least one laptop. "It's the Russians, they got him."

"No point in searching the place," Letty said, looking around. "We don't have the time and if Delph was like Barron, we probably won't find anything that's not encrypted."

"I agree. Let's get out of here before the cops come," Baxter said. "We need to call Nowak and have her get the FBI over here to check for DNA and fingerprints. Looks like there was a fight."

"And we need to find his girlfriend; I think that might be her," Letty said, nodding at a commercial double-portrait photo of a young man and a young woman, nicely framed, sitting on a couch table; it looked like a gift.

Baxter said, "Uh . . . wait a minute. What kind of phone was that in there?"

"I don't know . . . is it important?"

"Maybe . . ." Baxter retrieved the phone: "Samsung . . . Android."

He clicked the phone to bring it up, hurriedly stripped the glass out of the picture frame and positioned the phone in front of the photo of the young man. The phone opened up. He said, "Shazam. Shitty Android face recognition. iPhones are way harder to fool."

"Keep it open," Letty said. "Take the photo. And let's go . . ."

As they were walking down toward the elevator, they heard it start up: "Gotta be the manager," Letty said. "Take the stairs."

They took the stairs and got out clean. In the truck, Letty called Nowak again: "We've got a missing guy who probably was kidnapped . . . You need to get the FBI to his apartment to process it. LAPD is probably on the way. Looks like there was a fight, so they may find some biologics."

"I'll get the FBI over there. You two are okay?"

"So far," Baxter said. "We think we're about done."

"Not quite yet," Nowak said. "You've tripped over a situation that has created intense interest here—the Russian involvement. We want you to be careful but keep poking around. See what you turn up."

"We can do that . . . carefully," Letty said.

LETTY GAVE DELPH'S ADDRESS to Nowak, asked her to hold on for a moment while they ran quickly through Delph's phone, where they found a phone number, but no address, for "Annie."

They gave Nowak the number and she said, "I'll get back in a minute."

They waited in the truck for ten minutes, then Nowak called with the billing address for Annie's phone number—another apartment, not far away. Letty called and the phone went to an answering app. "Turned it off. Let's check the apartment."

"You think they took her, too?"

"Don't know. We need to find her."

ANNIE BELL'S APARTMENT had an outer lobby with mailboxes and doorbells in the lobby, but with another set of doors that kept them from getting inside. They found "Bellado" scrawled on a sticky-tab on one of the mailboxes, for an apartment on the second floor, and pushed the doorbell. Seconds later, a woman asked, "Who is it? Danny?"

Letty looked at Baxter and shrugged: "My name's Charlie Snow. I'm a friend of Able's and William's and Melody's and we're trying to find Daniel Delph. Can you let us in?"

"How do I know . . . ?"

"Call one of them. We just came from the meeting at Poggers and we're worried. You know about Loren and Brianna . . ."

"Oh, my God . . ." The woman's voice was a wail, and the inner door buzzed. They climbed the interior stairs to the second floor and stepped into a hallway, where a woman stood by an open apartment door looking down at them. Letty recognized her from the photo in Delph's apartment.

"I didn't know what to do," Bellado said when they were inside her apartment. She was a tall woman, blond and solid, peaches-and-cream complexion, wearing a tee-shirt and blue shorts. An expensive street bike and two pairs of Rollerblades were stacked against one wall.

Letty told her about the meeting at Poggers, and that people said Delph had been gone for a week.

"Daniel did work with Loren and Craig Sovern on the Russian train hack. He was proud of it, but then Loren called and said there were rumors that Russians were looking for them. Some Russian guys were going around asking questions. He was worried but . . . he wouldn't hide. He said, 'Fuck 'em,' they deserved what they got."

"Which would sorta not be the point when you're dealing with Russian gangsters," Baxter said to her, a less-than-diplomatic comment that made Letty wince.

Bellado didn't seem to notice. "I know, I know. When he disappeared—he hasn't been gone a week, he's been gone five days, but he wasn't talking to anyone but me, so maybe they thought he'd been gone longer. Anyway, he'd started doing some research and a couple of days before . . . he got lost . . . he emailed me pictures of cars, but I didn't know what to do with them."

"Could we see them?" Letty asked.

"Who are you guys?" she asked.

Letty nodded at Baxter and said, "He's a hacker. I'm his bodyguard."

"I don't . . ."

"That's the truth," Baxter interrupted. "If you push her, she'll show you her gun. Anyway, we need to see those photos. We've got a guy who can get into LAPD files . . ."

"William?"

"Yeah, William," Letty said. "We need to see the photos, so we can figure out what Daniel was looking at."

"Well . . ."

She showed them the photos, taken with a decent camera, sent in emails to her desktop Dell. Three of the photos showed the blue SUV identical to the one the killers had driven to Loren Barron's house. Three more showed a black Mercedes G-Class SUV, and a dozen more images showed a miscellany of other cars.

Letty tapped the blue SUV and said, "We know these guys. They're Russians."

Baxter asked, "Mind if we copy the pictures?" He took the truck keys from his pocket. The ring included a rubbery pink plastic human thumb as a key fob, which Letty had thought was odd, but then, Baxter was Baxter. He pulled the thumb apart, revealing a USB plug. He said, "Thumb drive."

Letty rolled her eyes and said to Bellado, "Nerd."

"Go ahead and copy them," Bellado said. "If you think it'll do any good."

"He thought he was being followed, so maybe we can find out who those people were," Baxter said, as he sat in front of the computer, plugged in the thumb, and began dragging one photo after the other to the flash drive.

Letty, looking over his shoulder, said, "Look at the backgrounds. He got shots of the SUV and the G-Wagen in different places. Maybe he *was* followed."

"But he was taking pictures of the cars, not their license plates," Baxter said.

"You think the Russians got him?" Bellado asked, fear in her voice.

Letty thought she knew the answer, but said, "We don't know that yet."

FOURTEEN

Baxter sent the photos of the blue SUV and the G-Wagen to Nowak. They said good-bye to Bellado, told her that they'd call when they found Daniel Delph. Back in the truck, Letty called Nowak and asked what the FBI was doing.

"They're putting pressure on the man they've got, but he's not giving up anything—not yet, anyway," Nowak said. "Might be too scared to talk. There are worse places than American prisons."

"So they're not focused on a person or location?" Baxter asked.

"Not at this point."

"We need to know where the G-Class Benz is registered—the owner and the address," Letty said. "We don't have a license, so it may be impossible."

"We're working on it," Nowak said, "though we'll come up with probabilities rather than certainties."

"That could be good enough. Did you hear anything from Barbara Cartwright?"

"She was visiting her cousins on their ranch outside San Antonio. She's already in the air, should be landing at LAX within the hour. We've filled her in as much as we could with nonencrypted messaging, so you'll have to brief her when you get together."

"Got it," Letty said.

They were still talking about the identification of Ordinary People at the Poggers meeting when Nowak broke away for a moment, then came back and said, "The G-Wagen is likely leased to the Mammuthus Corp . . . that's based on its year of manufacture, color, location there in LA, that it has optional armor, and the fact that we don't find its license plates anywhere on LA freeways or streets. That means it's not wearing its legal plates, or possibly the plates have a reflective covering or spray that shields them from cameras."

"Why would the LA cops allow . . ."

"The LA cops don't have that information. We do."

Mammuthus had an address in Long Beach, not far from the port, Nowak said. There was almost no information available on the business, which was registered in Delaware. Satellite and street view available to the NSA suggested that its headquarters were a single-story warehouse-style building that gave no clue as to what might be inside.

"I'm looking up Mammuthus . . ." Nowak said. Then: "A Mammuthus is a woolly mammoth. That's all I have on that."

"Whatever. We're gonna head down there," Letty said. "Give Barb my burner number, tell her we'll pick her up at the airport."

"Don't forget you've got the FBI SWAT team available. They could be anywhere in the LA area in a couple hours," Nowak said.

"Not really something I'd forget," Letty said. To Baxter: "Let's go. Airport."

OF ALL THE BELLYACHING Baxter had done between Washington and Los Angeles, which had amounted to a small mountain of complaints, protests, cavils, groans, whines, and remonstrations, along with his routine bitching and moaning, he reached his peak as he tried to get his truck through the traffic scrum at LAX.

"What's wrong with these fuckin' people? You see that guy? You see that guy? How did he get sideways? Here, he wants to go sideways? The Avis van is gonna . . . Get your gun out, get your gun out . . . Shoot the guy in the Tesla . . . C'mon, shoot him . . ."

CARTWRIGHT WAS STANDING outside the American terminal with two bags at her feet; one was soft and obviously clothing. The other one was hard-sided and had locks that would have protected a bank. She wore a battered straw cowboy hat, a raggedy tee-shirt that said "Born Again Christian Dior" under a tan cotton jacket, black jeans with unfashionable worn spots and tears in the legs, and cross-training shoes. Her sunglasses were as dark as obsidian.

"Shoulda been there when I checked the case at San Antonio," Cartwright said as she climbed into the backseat. "I was told *none* of my mags were legal in California. Not a problem in Texas, of course."

"How you been?" Letty asked.

"My cousin Ray told me my time was running out if I want to have a family," she said. "He told me the baby alarm would go off at any minute and I better have another guy picked out."

"Ah, jeez."

"Yeah, no shit," she said, looking at the back of Baxter's head. "Who's the large guy?"

Letty introduced Baxter, who told Cartwright that Letty had refused to kill anyone in the LAX traffic jam, and Letty told him to shut up and quit whining, because they had a lot to talk about before they got to Long Beach.

"Bet you haven't even shot anybody yet," Cartwright said with a grin.

Baxter jumped in again: "You'd be wrong about that. She shot a Russian killer, which means Russian killers are going to be annoyed with us. Then the FBI took her gun away, and they gave her another gun, exactly the same as the one they took away. She had to sign for it so they can get theirs back, when they return the exactly-the-same gun they took away, cutting down an entire Canadian forest for the paperwork in the identical trade. You gotta love the FBI."

Cartwright looked at Letty, as if judging whether Baxter was joking. She decided he wasn't. "Tell me everything," Cartwright said.

Letty told her everything, including the compartmented top secrets, as they headed south down nearly featureless freeways to the port of Long Beach.

On the way, Baxter said, "Holy guacamole—see the yellow one? The yellow one?" He meant a car. "That's a fuckin' McLaren. I've never seen one on the street. Hell, I've never seen one, period, except in magazines."

Farther down the freeway: "Rolls. Good one, I like that black-and-gray look."

"You're calming down a little," Letty said. "You sound bored by the Rolls."

"I'm kind of overwhelmed. That fuckin' McLaren we saw, after that lime green Lambo this morning . . . I mean, it's like something broke."

Cartwright: "Broke? You mean, in *you*?"

"Yeah, that's what I mean."

Letty and Cartwright looked at each other, and Letty said, "He's weird."

THE NAVIGATION APP took them to an area north of the port, streets lined with parked semi-trailers, fenced-in warehouses with acres of parking lots, power lines strung from a forest of wooden poles.

The Mammuthus building, if it was the Mammuthus building, was a low white cracker box with few windows, and those were covered with something that might have been raw cardboard. The parking lot had a single pickup in it, nosed into the front of the building. Two loading docks punctured the back, but no trucks were loading or unloading. The front side featured a glass door and two uncovered windows, looking out at the parking lot.

Cartwright said, "Cameras."

"Lots of cameras," Letty said. "Four on each side . . ."

"Makes me wonder what needs the protection," Cartwright said. "Or who."

"If you're like, CIA . . . don't you get jump training, parachute training?" Baxter asked.

"Well, some CIA people do, as I understand it, not saying I'm one," Cartwright said. "And I've jumped out of airplanes, but not on the job, just recreationally."

"Could you jump onto the roof?" Baxter asked.

"Maybe, but then what would I do?" Cartwright asked. "I'd have to get off the roof and there are still cameras looking at me. I might as well walk up."

"Right. Sorry about the brain fart."

"Look over there. At the container yard," Letty said, pointing.

Down the block from the front of the warehouse, a sprawling lot was stacked with shipping containers, rust-red, yellow, a few blue, most with Chinese names on them. "Nothing keeping us out of there," Letty said. "We could sneak in with granola bars and some water bottles and watch Mammuthus. See who comes and goes."

"That could work, if you've got the patience for it," Cartwright said.

"What else have we got? I don't see that G-Wagen anywhere . . . And I'd like to get a photo of the plates on that pickup."

"Let's get that and then get those snacks," Cartwright said. "Rod could pick us up after dark . . . Maybe we'll see a way in."

BAXTER ROLLED THEM past the front of the building and Letty got a photo of the plates on the Dodge Ram. She sent them to Nowak, who identified the owner as Dale Weston of the City of Industry. Weston had three arrest records for theft, and one for public drunkenness and fighting with cops, so was unlikely to be either a criminal genius or a Russian spy.

They got snacks and water at a Sunshine Market, which Letty put in her yellow REI bag, along with jackets for both of them should it get cool, and Baxter dropped them off on a side of the container yard not visible from Mammuthus. They walked between stacks of containers until they got to a spot facing the target, found an old wooden cable reel to sit on, rolled it inside an open container, and settled in to watch.

They'd been there for an hour, talking about personalities in their jobs, about growing up with guns, fathers, the stinky-sock smell that seemed to be coming from a patch of small pink flowers, divorce, and etcetera, when a man came out of the Mammuthus building and walked to the pickup, dug around in the backseat for a moment, and came away with a sack that might have had his dinner in it.

He was shaggy: hair on his shoulders, jeans, cowboy boots, a muscle shirt. Earring. He looked up and down the street, unselfconsciously dug in his pants to scratch his balls.

"He's got a gun on his hip," Letty said.

"Saw that," Cartwright said. "Hope he washes his hands before he eats his lunch."

THEY WATCHED AS the man went back inside the building and noticed that he'd left it unlocked as he walked to the truck, so either there were more people inside or he wasn't especially security-conscious.

Baxter called: "You guys want pizza?"

"We're okay."

"I figured out how to get in the building."

"How?" Letty asked.

"There are all these eighteen-wheelers sitting around with nobody in them. Barb's probably been trained how to steal cars and trucks. She could steal one and we could run it right through the front of the building. Probably get five minutes inside, at least, before the cops got there."

"I'll take that under advisement," Cartwright said. "It's a step up from parachuting onto the roof, though."

When Baxter was gone, Letty said, "How about this? Soon as we see him, Dale Weston, we hook our arms up, laugh a little, like we're drunk, yell at him. He's gonna see a couple girls coming up on him and from the looks of him, he'll talk to us. We stick a gun in his ear and walk him inside."

"I like it," Cartwright said. "Simple, yet with a potential for out-of-control mayhem."

THE WAIT GOT LONG and some streetlights came on. No sign of the G-Wagen. The western sky turned red and as the phone-pole shadows got longer than the phone poles, Dale Weston walked back out to his truck.

"We're on," Cartwright snapped, and she and Letty more or less bolted out to the street, linked arms, and Letty sang out the first three lines of Elton John's "Tiny Dancer" and they saw Dale Weston step back from his truck to look at them.

Cartwright laughed and then pulled Letty to a stop and pointed at Weston and said, quietly, "Make it look like we're talking about him. Take a quick peek at him."

Letty did it, and then they walked farther up the street as Dale Weston stepped to the back of the pickup and watched them coming. They slowed as they got close, and Cartwright turned her face to Letty's ear and said, "More whispered confidences about what a stud he must be."

"Makes my heart flutter thinking about it," Letty whispered back.

Cartwright laughed again, a low sexy sound that Letty immediately envied.

Dale Weston had leaned back against the pickup and called, "What're you girls doing out here at night?"

"Ain't night yet, cowboy," Letty called.

Cartwright, leaning hard on a Texas accent: "We're going down to the store to buy some more PBR. We are flat run out."

Letty to Cartwright, loud: "We shouldn't be run out, you almost drunk a whole goddamn case all by yourself."

"And I gotta pee like a Russian racehorse," Cartwright said, looking around. "You see a bush?"

Dale Weston laughed and ambled toward them, asked, "How long you been drinking?"

"Can't remember," Letty said. "I sold my watch. You got a watch?"

Dale Weston was three feet away and Letty identified his pistol as a Smith & Wesson .357, buried in an old leather holster with a retention strap. She said to Cartwright, "Retention strap."

"Yeah, I see," Cartwright said.

Dale Weston: "Wut?"

Cartwright pointed her Walther PPQ subcompact at Weston's left eye and said, "Let's go inside, Dale."

Letty had her 938 pointed at his navel. "It's very unlikely, but you might live through jumping one of us, but the other one would kill you. Do you want one of us to kill you, Dale?"

"Dale? Who the fuck is Dale?"

"That would be you," Letty said.

"I'm George. Hewitt. You girls got the wrong guy," the cowboy said.

"We got the right guy, just the wrong truck plates," Letty said. "What'd you do, George, steal them?"

Hewitt shrugged. "Maybe an MVD mistake?"

"Right. Let's go inside," Cartwright said. "We go inside, we won't have to kill you."

"You wouldn't kill me anyway," Hewitt said.

Cartwright giggled and Letty felt the hair go up on the back of her neck and suspected that it also went up on the back of Hewitt's. Cartwright said, after the giggle, "George, I'd be happy to kill you.

Happy. To kill. You. Got it? Don't even think about that piece of shit on your belt."

Hewitt, if that was his name, got it, and led them inside the building. The front of the place had a counter that something might once have been sold over, and a door that went into the back. The only thing on the counter was a mostly used roll of 3M packaging tape.

They disarmed Hewitt, and Letty said, "You are going to turn around and put your hands behind your back and I'm going to tape them together. Think about that. If we wanted to kill you, we could, and though my friend would really like to do that, I won't let her—as long as you cooperate. So put your hands back, and let me tape them . . ."

It took two minutes and the rest of the roll of tape, but Letty eventually got both his hands and feet taped up, along with a few wraps around his knees and a few more that pinned his arms to his side. When it was done, Letty turned to Cartwright and asked, "Where'd you get that giggle?"

Cartwright said, "With a lot of practice. Sounds exactly insane, doesn't it? Scares the shit out of everybody."

Letty nodded. "Scared me," she said. "Let's find out what's in here."

They opened the door into the pitch-dark back room, though Hewitt said, "You girls don't want to go there, nothing you can use."

They found a light switch and turned on the banks of fluorescent lights. The room, probably forty feet by forty feet, showed an island of cardboard boxes in the middle of the floor: ordinary large-sized moving boxes, sealed with transparent tape. An ill-used kitchen table sat to one side, with a pile of transparent 3M packaging tape on red spools, a couple of box cutters.

"Let's see what we don't want to do," Letty said. She picked up a box cutter, wrestled one of the boxes off the nearest stack—it wasn't especially heavy—and cut the taped top. The box was tightly packed with more, smaller boxes, also ordinary cardboard.

"What the hell?" Cartwright said.

Letty opened one of the smaller boxes and inside found even more boxes, dark blue plastic. "It's like one of those nested Russian doll things." She pulled one of the plastic boxes out and turned it over in her hands.

"Computer chips." She looked at printing on the package. "Intel computer chips, it says . . . 5.5GHz i9-12900KS, whatever that means."

"Think . . . Paul . . . would know?"

Letty shrugged. "I'll call him. Find out."

She did that and Baxter did know: "Holy shit. You say there's a lot of them?"

"Yeah. If all the boxes are like the one I opened . . . maybe . . . thousands?"

"Wow. I mean, wow! Grab a few boxes. I'll come get you."

"What are they?"

"They're Intel's fastest chip. Right now, anyway. Maybe for the next year. I don't think you can export them . . . I think, I don't know, that the Russians wouldn't be allowed to have them at all. Not yet, anyway."

"You think they might be smuggling them?"

"Nowak might know the answer to that," Baxter said. "I'd bet they were stolen, somehow. Look, you say there are thousands of them?"

"At least," Letty said, looking around. "Really, there could be a million."

"They're worth six or seven hundred dollars each, more overseas. If there's a million of them . . . that would be more than half a billion dollars on the open market."

"Okay, probably not a million," Letty said. "Give us five minutes, then come and get us."

"Five minutes," Baxter confirmed. "Bring some boxes."

When Baxter had rung off, Cartwright asked: "What?"

"We gotta talk to Nowak," Letty said. "I do want to take some of these boxes."

From the floor, where the taped-up Hewitt was listening, he said, "You girls really don't know what you're messin' with here."

Letty said, "Yes, we do. Do you know what *you're* messin' with?"

"Some pretty mean guys . . ."

"Russian spies. They are going to cut your head off if you tell them that we were here, that we got past you," Letty said. "They might cut it off just to keep your mouth shut, even if you don't tell them."

"You just gonna leave me on the floor?" Hewitt asked.

"No. Here's what we're gonna do, George," Letty said. "We're gonna take a few of these boxes with us. Then I'm going to cut one of your hands free, but not your feet or arms or legs. I'll leave you the box cutter so you can cut yourself loose. That'll give us time to get out of here. Then you better lock the door, get in that truck and get your ass out of California, as fast as you can. The guys you're working with have killed a lot of people and you'd be nothing to them. They'd cut your head off for looking at them wrong. You got all that?"

Hewitt's oversized Adam's apple bobbed a few times, and he said, eventually, "Yeah. Yeah. Make sure you get my hand free. I'll get the fuck out. I kinda knew . . . I'm just a security guard . . ."

Cartwright had stepped over to a gray metal box hung on a

sidewall. It was locked, but she took a skeletal Leatherman out of her pocket, selected a tool, and broke the lock open. Inside was a mass of wires and a hard drive. On the inside of the cover was an instruction list on restarting the drive, and the name, address, and phone number for the security company.

Letty called Nowak and asked if she could kill the cameras and wipe the video, and Nowak said she could, but it might take a while.

"That's fine. We won't be out of here for ten or fifteen minutes."

When Letty finished with Nowak, Cartwright was looking at the stacks of boxes. "How do you want to do this?"

"Take a few boxes at random, trying to keep the stacks looking about the same," Letty said. "There must be a couple hundred boxes here. Maybe they won't notice right away. And maybe they won't all be the same chip, so we should take boxes from different areas . . ."

They could get six boxes in the short-bed pickup, under the cover, even with the drum set inside. They moved the boxes to the front door, and waited for Baxter, who showed up in exactly five minutes. While Baxter and Cartwright loaded the boxes, Letty cut one of Hewitt's hands loose and put the box cutter on the floor twenty feet away, where he could roll over to it.

"George, I was serious about what I said," Letty told him. "They're gonna kill you. You gotta get out and hide from these fuckers."

Hewitt nodded and said, "I'll go." And as Letty headed for the front door, he said, "You girls be careful. You're too young for this shit."

Letty got in the front passenger seat of the truck, and told Baxter, "Get as far away as you can, where we can still see the front door. I want to see if George actually gets out of here."

They waited fifteen minutes, then Hewitt came out the door. Satisfied that he was alone, he loaded a half-dozen of the chip boxes into his truck, locked the warehouse door, jumped in the truck and took off.

Letty called their traffic-tracking number at the NSA and gave the man who answered the license plate number on the back of the truck, and its location. A minute later, the man said, "We got it."

"Stay with it," Letty said. "We want to know if he gets out of LA."

FIFTEEN

Arseny Stepashin was sitting in his TV room watching a Golden State Warriors basketball game while his wife lay on a yoga mat behind the couch, doing crunches, grunting with each one.

When his cell phone rang, he couldn't find it for a moment, then fished it out from the crack between seat cushions, looked at the caller's name, and said, *"Da?"*

"Mr. Step—we maybe got a problem at the warehouse." The caller was an American named Alan Greens; he knew very little Russian, but was reliable, because Step knew where Greens's bodies were buried, the bodies being literal.

Step sighed and asked, "What's the problem?"

"Well, when me'n Richard got here, George was gone. Door was locked, but his truck was gone and he was gone. We went inside and everything looked kinda okay except there was a bunch of

3M tape on the warehouse floor. I mean, like it was pulled off somebody. Like, there was arm hairs stuck in some of the tape."

"What about the shipment?"

"I dunno. It don't look right, but maybe . . . I dunno, maybe it's okay," Greens said. "There's lots of boxes, Richard is counting them, but I don't know how many there was supposed to be."

"Let me go look," Step said. "Hold on."

Step lived in Beverly Hills—not in the Hills themselves, but down in the Flats—in a Spanish Revival house. The house was nice but wasn't ostentatious by Beverly Hills standards and did have that 90210 zip code, which carried some weight back in Moscow.

He walked down a Mexican-tiled hallway to his home office, lit up his laptop, went to an encrypted file, typed in a fifteen-place password, and ran a finger down a spreadsheet. One hundred and eighty.

There should be one hundred and eighty boxes of advanced Intel chips stacked in the warehouse, ready to go on a South Korean ship that was actually a North Korean ship, but that was registered in Panama and legally owned by a Nigerian business family through a Cayman Islands front. Like the house, the ship was rented.

Step shut down the computer and walked back to the TV room, where his wife was frozen in a plank and was counting breaths, a breath equaling three seconds. She had fifteen percent body fat, which would be good for a gymnast, and she could hold a plank for five minutes. He picked up his phone and said, "Al? One hundred and eighty, exactly."

He heard Greens say to Richard, "You sure? You better be sure. Okay, I'll tell him." Then, "Richard says one hundred and sixty-eight. Exactly. He counted twice."

Step scratched his neck, looked at the ceiling, then asked, "You got enough space on your truck to load them up?"

"No. We took the small box truck and it's full. We were dropping off, not picking up."

"Okay. Call Yvgeny and tell him to get another truck over there, right now. Tell him *right now*. I want those boxes loaded and out of there in two hours. Tell him to put the truck somewhere secure, but leave the boxes on the truck. We'll move them to the port tomorrow. Do not touch that 3M tape. Leave it right where it is, I want to look at it. We still got those bottles of Mr. Clean?"

"Sure, and a box of them paper rags. You want us to start wiping the place down?"

"Yes. Anything anyone might have touched."

"You coming down here?"

"I'll be there in an hour." Step hung up and dialed a new number. When a man answered, he said, "This is me. I need you to get some of your people down to Long Beach. I need to know if anyone is watching the place. Be careful . . . Yeah, right now."

Victoria Stepashin dropped out of her plank and asked, "Somebody fuck something up?"

"Somebody's always fucking something up," Step said. One hand went to his mouth and squeezed. "The security guard is gone and so are twelve boxes of those new Intel chips, the five-point-fives. There's a question of whether he took off or was taken off."

"Twelve boxes, that's . . . one million, nine hundred and twenty thousand dollars delivered in Chongjin," Victoria said, doing the math in her head. "If he took off with twelve boxes, you're gonna have to cut his nuts off."

"I will, if he took off. The way Alan's talking . . . It might be something else."

"Alan's a moron."

"Not about this," Step said. "Not about counting boxes."

"How many boxes are left?" Victoria asked.

"Richard says one hundred and sixty-eight."

"Think the FBI might have grabbed them?"

Step shook his head. "Doesn't seem like it. Why would the FBI take twelve boxes? They'd take them all and have a press conference."

"They were all over us at Ventura . . ."

"Yeah. Something's happening and we don't know what it is."

"Better find out," Victoria said. "If there's one hundred and sixty-eight boxes left, that's still . . ." It took her five seconds . . . "twenty-six million, eight hundred and eighty thousand dollars."

"I'm on it," Step said. "I hope it's not about the other thing."

"Something to worry about," Victoria agreed. "You start mixing political shit with money shit, there's a good chance you're gonna get dropped in the shit."

The *other thing* was the train-hacker problem. They'd promised people in Moscow that they'd handle it. The people they'd promised tended to get cranky if promises were broken. They were the kind of people whose unhappiness tended to become *your* unhappiness, to say nothing of your screaming agony.

Step went out to the garage and rolled Victoria's silver Mercedes SL550 down the driveway. Forty-five minutes later, he took a call. The man, whose name was Tom Boyadjian, said, "This is me. There's nobody watching the place, not right now, unless they're using a satellite. No drones in the area. But: somebody was down in that container yard and not long ago. They ate some cookies inside a container and dribbled some crumbs around. If the crumbs had been there more than a couple of hours, the mice would have eaten them. So, it was a surveillance stand. The container had a perfect view of the front of the warehouse."

"What's on the cameras?"

"Nothing. The cameras were wiped," Boyadjian said.

"You're shitting me," Step said. "Even the cloud?"

"Even the cloud."

"That tells us something," Step said. "Who could erase the cloud video and be interested in stealing high-end chips?"

"Yeah. Hackers. The train nerds," Boyadjian said.

"Which means the train nerds know who we are. That's a problem."

Boyadjian said, "One good thing about that."

"What's that?"

Boyadjian laughed. "It's your problem, Step, not mine. I'll send you a bill for tonight. You'll get the frequent-flier discount."

STEP TOOK ONE MORE CALL, a few minutes later, five minutes out of Long Beach. He didn't recognize the number, but given the ongoing hassle, he decided to answer it.

"Yeah?"

"Mr. Step? This is George Hewitt."

"Where the hell are you?" Step asked.

"On my way out of town. I'm going back to Montana," Hewitt said. "I figure when you find out what happened tonight, you'd cut my nuts off."

"Count on it," Step said.

"How about if I tell you exactly what happened? Maybe you wouldn't do that, if we ever meet up again."

After some quiet consideration, to let Hewitt sweat, Step said,

"All right. If it's any value to me and you're not to blame, I'll let it go. You got my word. On my honor."

Hewitt told him exactly what happened, with only one distinct lie. Two women, young, good-looking, both armed, faked him out when he went to his truck for a pack of cigarettes. They were not armored up, like law enforcement might be.

"They were professionals, Mr. Step," he said. "One of them wanted to kill me, but the other one wouldn't let her. The first one scared the shit out of me. They taped me all up with that packaging tape you had there and took some boxes. Twelve, I think. I could hear them talking and they decided to take twelve so they'd know if it was all one chip, or if there were different chips. I'm so sorry . . . I figured it'd be healthier for me to get out of town, but I still wanted to fill you in."

"You did the right thing, George," Step said, then telling his own distinct lie. "You're good with us. I'd still hire you, if you decided to come back. We can use guys like you."

"Well, I thank you very much, but, I think I'll keep going," Hewitt said. "Oh, and I don't know if this would help, but they were talking about a guy named Paul, like maybe he was their boss."

"A guy named Paul."

"Yeah, Paul. That's all I got. I'm gonna hang up now and throw this phone out the window."

He was gone. He'd keep going, Step thought, as he clicked his phone off, but not to Montana. He almost certainly was headed back to Oklahoma, where he came from. Though Step was pissed, he'd let it go, unless Hewitt was actually stupid enough to come back to Long Beach.

So: two women. Actually, sounded like they might be GRU. The GRU would have the resources to wipe the cloud if they wanted to. While the FBI certainly had women agents, they didn't send out two women, without backup, to steal computer chips. The GRU might . . .

Was Moscow involved? Or was it the train nerds? But where would the train nerds get two female hitters? That wouldn't be a problem for the GRU.

A puzzle that needed to be solved. After he made sure the remaining chips were secure, he'd get back home and talk it over with Victoria.

AT THE WAREHOUSE, he found Al, Richard, and Yvgeny loading the chip boxes into a large box truck, with a smaller box truck sitting off to one side. Inside the building, he took a look at the 3M tape that had been used to tape up Hewitt; Al pointed out what looked like arm hair in a ring of tape. Hewitt had apparently been telling the truth.

Step helped carry boxes himself and when they were all loaded in the second truck, took a look at the alarm console, which operated the cameras. It had been broken open. He thought about it for a moment, then told Yvgeny to call the security company to report the break-in, but to tell them that nothing had been taken because the warehouse had been empty. Probably, he was to say, street people looking for anything they could steal—no point involving the police, because they wouldn't do anything about a theft-free break-in with no damage and no obvious clues. That should also keep the security service shut up.

On the way back to Beverly Hills, he called Boyadjian, the man who'd checked for surveillance at the warehouse and had found the container site with bread crumbs. Boyadjian came up on the second ring: "Yeah?"

"Another job for you. We took that Delph guy, and the couple, but we never did do anything about the crazy guy. Sovern? The sailboat guy? We need to find him and nail his feet to a floor and ask him some serious questions."

"Tonight? You want us to find him tonight?"

"Yeah, tonight. Right now. We took a two-million-dollar hit tonight," Step said. "You told me he might be up in Oxnard, some-where. How many sailboats can there be in Oxnard?"

"Lots. Hundreds. Gotta be a dozen marinas up there, maybe more."

"Get off your computer and do some walking around," Step said. "Knock on doors. You're looking for a crazy nerd computer genius who lives on a sailboat. How many can there be?"

"Many. And we can do that, but it'll cost you," Boyadjian said. "Three thousand a day. No guarantees with a three thousand min-imum, pay me later. I'll send my best team."

"That's fine. Start now. Don't screw me, but don't worry if it goes a few days."

"All right. We'll be up there in a couple hours. Barry might have to find a babysitter. I think this is girls' night out for his wife . . ."

Back at home, Step sat at the kitchen table and told Victoria all about it, as she drank a glass of green juice the consistency of snot; watching her do it made him shudder.

When he'd finished telling the story, she said, "Not the GRU. If they wanted the chips, they would have shown up and taken them. All of them. At noon. And they would have shaken your hand on the way out. But it really doesn't sound like the train nerds. What it sounds like is some kind of semiprofessional hijack team. Might not even have known what they were stealing. People like that work the port. That's where the whole 'It fell off a truck' joke comes from."

"That could be," Step agreed. "But . . . we did Delph, and then we did that couple who engineered the train hack and then the boys over at Ventura got hit, almost instantly, and now somebody's fuckin' with the port . . . To me, it feels like there's a string there. Should we pull it?"

"As long as you keep a plane on the runway at Santa Monica."

"Yeah. Yeah, there's that. I'd hate to go back to Moscow, after this." He waved his arms, meaning the house, the pool, the town, and the United States of America. "Doesn't get better than this."

"Could get a lot worse, though, even here in the USA," Victoria said. "Way worse, like, dead."

SIXTEEN

Letty called Able, identified herself and asked, "You gone?"

"No, I'm home. I gotta do some things here. Then I might take off," Able said.

"We're coming over," Letty said. "We need to show you some computer things."

"Computer things . . . like what?"

"If we knew that, we wouldn't have to show you," Letty said. "Paul thinks they could be a big deal, but he's software, not hardware."

"You sure nobody's tracking you?" Able asked.

"Maybe ninety percent sure . . . no way to be a hundred percent," Letty said.

"Do some countersurveillance stuff," Able said. "You can look it up on Google under countersurveillance technique for cars."

"Okay," Letty said. She was looking at Cartwright, who rolled her eyes. "We'll do that."

When she got off the phone, Cartwright said, "Google, my ass. Why don't I drive? I do countersurveillance and it might not be a bad idea."

"Okay with me, as long as you don't wreck my truck," Baxter said. Baxter had known all about the Intel chips, but Letty had lied to Able about it, because they needed to talk to Able again.

They worked their way to the 405, curling up and down side streets on the way. Once on the freeway, Cartwright put the pedal to the metal, pushing the truck to a hundred miles an hour, weaving through the evening traffic. "What are we doing here?" Baxter asked, lifting his feet to place them on the dashboard.

"Bracing yourself won't help, if we hit somebody," Cartwright said. "The airbag will blow your feet up over your ears and dislocate your hip joints. Anyway, we're not being followed, but we might as well make sure we don't have a drone above us. A drone with a video transmitter won't make more than fifty or sixty miles an hour, and if one was up there, it won't be able to reacquire us after we've lost it."

Baxter took his feet down. "So we're clean?"

"Unless somebody stuck location transmitters under the truck when you weren't looking," Cartwright said.

"Seriously unlikely," Letty said.

"I agree. The biggest problem will come at this Able guy's place," Cartwright said. "I'll want to get out a few blocks away, and have you guys wait until I'm in place, to see if anything moves when you show up."

"There's a handy alley and banana tree . . ." Letty said. She told Cartwright about watching Able's house from behind the tree.

"Sounds good," Cartwright said. "That's what we'll do. We'll run more countersurveillance on the way over . . ."

On the way to West Hollywood, Baxter said he was becoming reluctant to further expose Ordinary People to possible attacks by the Russians. The hackers, he said, were basically his people and if he hadn't been picked up by the NSA, he might have been doing what they were doing.

"Probably too late to back out," Cartwright said. "Listen, from what you've told me, you were originally sent out here to find out if Ordinary People were going to take out a municipal gas system?"

Letty: "Right."

"I've been around the intelligence community six years, and I can tell you, there's something else going on. I think we all know what it is," Cartwright said.

"You're right: we do know," Baxter said.

"Let me say it," Letty said. "They knew about the gas thing and sold it to Senator Colles and Baxter and me, but their main interest was the train hack. The gas thing was a way to get at Ordinary People and get Baxter to go along. He might not have done that if they'd told him he had to fight the Russians. What they really want is a bunch of hackers who already know how to mess with the Russian rail system but have no connection to the government. Ordinary People are not only deniable, but even arrestable if they complain too much."

"Got it in one," Cartwright said. "I'd be amazed if that's not what your Ms. Nowak has been up to the whole time. We represent a small investment for what could be a huge return. A small investment for *them*, not us."

"We could tell them we're bailing," Letty said. "Just not give them a choice."

"And I could kiss my career good-bye," Baxter said.

"So could I," Cartwright said.

"Wouldn't do me any good, either," Letty said.

They sat in silence for a moment, then Baxter said, "So we keep on keepin' on, though I'll probably get killed."

"I don't see that we have much choice," Letty said. To Baxter: "We'll miss you when you're gone."

They dropped Cartwright at the CVS pharmacy on Melrose, with directions to the banana tree that Letty had used to hide from Barron and Wolfe. They gave her ten minutes to get settled, then headed for Able's.

"I'm surprised the guy's still here. He seemed determined to get out, when I talked to him at Poggers," Baxter said.

At Able's, Letty forgot the cane and knee brace, and after knocking on the door, and identifying herself, she walked inside with Baxter, and Able looked at her and frowned and asked, "What happened with your knee?"

Letty looked down and all she could come up with was an old Monty Python line, "Got better," and, a beat later, "Hurts bad either way. I left the cane and brace in the car, to take a break."

Baxter was carrying one of the boxes they'd stolen from the warehouse. He said, "I think I know what these are, but I wanted an expert to look at them."

He put the box on top of Able's washing machine and Able cut it open with a kitchen knife. Letty fished out one of the smaller boxes, and shook out one of the smallest and handed it to Able, who opened it and said, "Wait! The whole box is full of these?"

"We've got six boxes full of these," Letty said.

"If they're all the same . . ." He rummaged through the box.

"There are twenty-four chip boxes in each one of the small boxes, and there are ten small boxes in the big box. Man, I could sell a big box for ninety or a hundred K, maybe more," Able said. "I even know the guy who'd take them. He could come up with the cash in an hour. Where'd you get them?"

"Stole them from an illegal warehouse, probably getting packed to be shipped to Russia or someplace that would pay a lot for them," Baxter said, picking up one of the chip boxes, peering at the chip through the transparent panel on top. "There were probably a couple hundred boxes of these things."

"How did you . . ."

"We saw a guy watching Annie Bellado's place and followed him. He took us to the warehouse, and we watched that, and when they got down to one guy inside, we . . . borrowed the boxes from him," Letty lied.

"Is the guy still alive?" Able asked.

There was a knock at the door. Letty said, "That'd be Barb." She went to the door, peeked out, and opened it.

Cartwright stepped in, looked around, and said, "Cool," and she looked at Letty and said, "Nothin'." And to Able: "Nobody followed us."

"Where are you from?" Able asked Cartwright.

She said, "Texas. Old girlfriend of Charlie's. Don't know nothin' about computers."

Able nodded, shook his head. "To get back to the original question . . . the guy you stole these from, is he still alive?"

"He is," Cartwright said. "We're not killers. I mean, we are, but we didn't kill anybody. Today. Well, in the last couple of hours."

Able chuckled, but insincerely: "Very funny."

Letty said, "Back when we were dealing with Harp, he said there was a guy at the center of Ordinary People. Said he was nuts . . . Craig Sovern?"

"Craig . . . He's a little off-center, I guess. Yeah, and he's a savant. Got OCD, pretty bad. He's a good guy, though."

"Here's the thing," Letty told Able. "We talked to Annie Bellado, and we didn't tell her this, but we think her friend Daniel . . . He's missing and we went to his apartment, did some social work on the manager, and got inside. There was blood on the floor. We think the Russians got him and he's probably dead. We think they're taking down Ordinary People because of the train ransomware. It's not only revenge—they want to take down anyone who might go after the trains again, right when they're about to invade Ukraine. We need to warn this Sovern guy."

"Ah, Jesus, I gotta get out of here," Able said, looking around the place, as if the Russian army might be coming through the doors.

"Your friends William and Melody are heading for Las Vegas, last we heard," Letty said. "Maybe you could call them, see what they've got set up."

Able bobbed his head, looked around his house. "Vegas sounds . . . okay, I guess. Better than anything I've thought of."

"I dunno. If you can't hide in LA, you can't hide," Cartwright said. "You could probably hide six blocks away, as long as you didn't come back here. These guys aren't the FBI or the NSA, they're crooks."

Baxter: "Russian intelligence must be involved somehow, if they're going after the train people. Why would gangsters care about that, if all they were, were gangsters?"

"You've got a point," Cartwright conceded.

"Anyway, could you call somebody about this Craig Sovern

guy, find out where he is?" Letty asked. "He doesn't answer his phone. If he was big in Ordinary People, he'll be a target."

"Yeah, yeah . . . This can't go on too long. I got six grand in the bank," Able said. "Vegas will eat that up in three weeks, even staying in a dump."

Baxter shrugged, waved a hand at the box of Intel chips. "Take the box. We got more where that came from."

Able brightened: "Seriously? That'll make a difference. I can hide out for six months on that."

Able called his friend Jan, the bass player, who Letty and Baxter knew from the meeting at Able's and had seen again at Poggers. On the phone, Able said "uh-huh" a couple of times, made some notes on a yellow legal pad, agreed with Jan that they should both get out of sight. When he rang off, he handed the legal pad to Letty.

"He lives in Oxnard. On a boat called the *Green Flash*, in a private marina at the Motel California."

"Get me online for a minute, we want to look at Google Earth," Baxter said. Able lit up one of his desktop computers and they found the Motel California on the north side of Oxnard. The harbor on the ocean side of the motel had two dozen slips, all of them with sailboats. They looked at a street view of the front of the place—long low motel with an orange vacancy sign and twenty doors facing a parking lot—and shut down the computer.

"We're going," Letty told Able. "And you should get lost."

"I'll call you when I get to Vegas," Able said. "When I unload these chips, I'll call everyone who knows about Ordinary People and get some hideout money to them."

"Great," Letty said. "Give us a little credit for it."

They left the box of chips with Able, followed a navigation app to the 101 freeway and took it north and west.

"Boat seems like a strange place for a guy with OCD," Baxter said. "It'd always be moving around, stuff would get jumbled up."

"Actually, a sailboat would be the perfect place," Cartwright said. "You gotta be a little OCD just to sail. The best sailors are really OCD—nothing can be too well adjusted for them. Everything is tied down. Always with appropriate knots. It's the fussiest hobby in the world."

"You sail?" Letty asked.

"I have, yeah. I've got some friends down in Annapolis, they've got a sailboat. You ought to come along sometime," Cartwright said.

"Not me," Baxter said. "Worst environment in the world for computers."

"That might be true for computers in general, but I'll tell you, on new boats, it's one marine computer after another, front to back. It's all fly-by-wire now."

THEY TALKED FOR a few minutes, locked into the scarlet stream of weaving taillights getting out of LA, then Cartwright, in the backseat, said she was going to take a nap. Letty yawned and said, "Good idea."

"Go ahead," Baxter said. "I'm fine."

Letty dozed in the passenger seat, with the usual jerky half-waking dreams people have when they sleep in a truck, waking again when they came down to city streets and a stoplight. Cartwright woke at the same time, yawned, cracked her knuckles, and asked, "Are we there?"

"We're in Oxnard, a few more miles to the motel," Baxter said. "You guys were down for almost an hour."

"I needed it," Letty said. "Thanks."

Oxnard, the part they saw of it, was a low town of blacktopped streets, small houses with tiny lawns, fences everywhere, strip malls and auto stores, and, unusually for California, it didn't get much better as they got closer to the Pacific.

The Motel California had vacancy and Letty used the NSA credit card to rent two rooms for the night. The clerk was an unsightly man, wearing a white dress shirt sweat-stained at the collar, and a thin brown nylon necktie. A room at the motel came with the right to walk out the back door and down to the boat slips, he told Letty, when she asked. As the clerk was giving her the keys, and warning her that the two rooms were both nonsmoking, she asked, "Does Craig still keep his boat here? *Green Flash?*"

"Yup. He's in A1. You a friend of his?"

"More like an acquaintance," Letty said. "We thought we'd drop by to see if he's in."

"He was here a couple hours ago, barefoot, hitting the candy machine," the clerk said. "He didn't look like he was going anywhere."

Letty thanked him. Outside, they moved the luggage from the truck into one of the rooms and put the five remaining boxes of computer chips in the other. That done, they walked back to the office and the pass-through glass door that took them down a flight of steps to the boat slips. The night was quiet, almost silent, so any noise at all jumped out like a dog's bark.

A couple were walking up the dock toward the motel, towing an aluminum wagon full of garbage bags. They nodded at Baxter, who was leading, and he asked, "Where's Craig's boat?"

The man pointed down the dock and said, "The Pacific Seacraft, the slip on the end, left side. He's got some shirts hanging from the boom."

Baxter thanked him and as they continued down the dock, Letty asked, "What's a boom? I mean, I've heard of them . . ."

"You don't know what a boom is?"

"I'm from Minnesota," Letty said.

"It's the thing the shirts are hanging from," Cartwright said.

"Ah." As they got to the end of the dock, they saw a long canoe-shaped sailboat with three shirts hanging from the boom, a surfboard neatly tied along the deck, and lights in the cabin; they could hear Everlast doing "Smokin & Drinkin," the guitar trickling up from below.

The boat had been backed into the slip, so they could see into the small cockpit and down into the cabin. The extra lengths of the lines from the boat to the cleats on the finger docks were carefully curled in perfect spirals, lying flat on the docks. Up and down the dock, stainless steel hardware was clinking against metal masts, a constant tinkle in the light ocean breeze.

Letty called, "Craig? You in there?"

The music muted, and a moment later a long-haired man, wearing only cargo shorts, came to the cabin hatch and asked, "Who's there?"

"Some friends of Ben Able. We need to talk to you," Letty said.

"Let me get my flip-flops. I'll be right up."

They heard some shuffling around and then Sovern appeared, climbing out of the cabin and into the cockpit. He was a tall, tanned, broad-shouldered man, with an oval face and shoulder-length, slightly curly blond hair.

Cartwright said, "If you had a puka necklace, you'd be perfect."

"If I had a puka necklace, I'd have to shoot myself," Sovern said. "What's up?"

"We need to talk . . . privately," Letty said, looking up and down the dock. "The boat looks like it'd be a little tight for all of us."

"We could probably walk out, if it's important . . ."

"It's important and we have two motel rooms here," Baxter said. "We also have, like, a half million dollars' worth of advanced computer chips we don't know what to do with."

"Maybe I can help with that," Sovern said. "Let's go . . . How's Ben?"

"He's on the run," Letty said. "The train thing. We think there are three of you guys dead. Two for sure."

Sovern stopped. "Three dead? Nobody called me. Or maybe they did, but I didn't answer."

"Loren Barron and Brianna Wolfe were both murdered at their house," Letty said. "Dan Delph is missing and we think he's probably dead as well. They were killed by Russians."

"No . . ."

"Yes. Let's get inside."

Baxter and Sovern led the way back to the motel; Cartwright leaned over to Letty and said, "Christ, he's good-looking. He's like a movie star."

"Not exactly your mental image of a computer nerd," Letty agreed. "On the other hand, neither is Able. That guy has muscles on his muscles."

As they walked up the steps to the motel, Letty asked Sovern, "Why wouldn't a computer guy know about Loren Barron and Brianna? It's been all over the TV."

"I don't have a TV," Sovern said. "I'm not out on the Net very much because it's all bullshit now. I'm not a gamer. I prefer to read."

"It gets better and better," Cartwright muttered to Letty. Sovern overheard that and turned to smile at her.

In the room with the boxes, Sovern took a look at the chips and said, "If all these boxes are full of those chips, they'd be worth killing for. So, what's going on?"

They told him about their move to LA, sticking to their cover story, and how they'd tripped over the train hack, the murders of Loren Barron and Brianna Wolfe, and about the chip robbery at the warehouse. When they were done, Sovern said, "Well, that sounds like a load of horseshit. You mean you drove to LA because you couldn't make a phone call from Florida? Don't they have phones there? And I don't know any Russians, or about any Russians. I was writing software."

"We needed to get out of town," Letty said; it sounded like a lie in her own ears. She added, "When we looked in the phone book, Ordinary People didn't have a cell phone number."

"All of which is totally not the point," Baxter said. "There *are* Russians. And the Russians may be looking for you. Speaking of a load of horseshit, everybody who knows about the Russian train hack say you're the brains behind it."

"Name some names."

Letty waved him off. "We're not ratting out anyone. But think about it—if we're not telling the truth, how'd we get here, to you? We're trying to figure out who the Russians are."

"That's why we went down to the warehouse. We talked to the security guard there, but he wouldn't give us anything, and what were we going to do, torture him?" Baxter said. "We need to get the cops on the Russians without the cops knowing who we are, because if the cops knew who we are, they might decide they'd rather arrest us than some Russians. That fuckin' hospital ransom-ware fuck-up is following us around like a . . ."

He couldn't think of what it was following them around like, so Sovern suggested, "Fuckin' albatross?" As he said it, he moved four chip boxes into a perfect cube and spent a few seconds getting the edges exactly straight, then stacked the fifth one precisely over the junction of the four beneath it, forming a short step pyramid.

"Yeah, exactly," Baxter said. He nudged one of the boxes out of line.

"So . . . a little while ago, maybe two hours ago, before you came, there was this couple here looking at boats," Sovern said, as he made a minute readjustment to the boxes. "Americans, friendly, the guy wanted to shake hands, but I told him I didn't like people touching me. I got this weird feeling about them, like they were too interested in me. Like they came to look at me."

Cartwright: "Uh-oh. Sure they were Americans?"

"If they weren't, they lived here for a long time. I spotted them as being from LA, soon as they opened their mouths. But they were too . . . chatty. Made me nervous. I wanted them to go away," Sovern said. "The other thing was, they weren't staying at the mo-tel, so . . . what were they doing out here? You can't even see the marina from the street."

Letty said to Cartwright: "They found him."

"Sounds like it." Cartwright turned back to Sovern and asked, "How long does it take to crank up the boat and get out of here?"

"Couple hours, normally. I usually go to Ralphs and stock up on food, but I didn't fuel up the last time I came in, either. I'm not empty, but I'm close, and the fuel dock doesn't open until tomor-row morning."

"Maybe you could take it out and just float around? Or, you got a car?"

"I do Uber," Sovern said.

"So take off in the boat," Letty said. "Float away."

"You think it's that serious?" He looked doubtful.

"Three dead," Letty said. "Look it up on the Net. Or call one of your Ordinary People. They know."

"Okay. I'll take the boat out," Sovern said. "Can you guys stay while I get ready to go? That'll take maybe a half hour . . ."

"We'll stay," Letty said.

SEVENTEEN

As Sovern moved around the *Green Flash*, getting ready to go, there was no place for Letty, Cartwright, and Baxter to sit, so they sat on two dock boxes at 2A, one down from Sovern's slip.

The marina smelled of the usual seaweed and dead fish, with a hint of garbage and charcoal lighter fluid, and they could hear a faint mix of music from a bar along the shore, maybe Jimmy Buffett. A woman laughed from outside the marina somewhere, a half scream, half laugh as though somebody had just dropped a squid down her blouse.

Baxter began giving Cartwright a hard time about refusing to admit she was with the Unspecified Agency, and Cartwright offered to shoot him if he kept giving her a hard time, and Baxter asked, "What is it with you two and guns? I'm thirty-four years old and I've gone my entire life without a gun and I've lived in some harsh places. I've never needed one. Never. Never even thought about it."

Cartwright and Letty exchanged glances, and Letty nodded at Cartwright, who said, "In my part of Texas, everyone had guns. We needed them on the ranch. I learned how to shoot when I was five or six. Nobody in Texas is amazed when a woman is good with guns, but maybe they were a little amazed that I got so good, so quick. I shot my first deer when I was seven, with a .30-06. One shot. Never said a thing about the recoil; hardly felt it, I was so excited. But small girls have no power, and they feel it. You get to be ten or twelve, you can feel the ranch hands looking at your ass. So you get a gun in your hand and you know a guy's looking at your ass and you let the gun kinda swing across his gut, and he's like, 'Hey, never point a gun at someone unless you plan to kill them.' That's like one of the Ten Commandments in Texas. And I say, 'I never do,' and the guy thinks about that and is like, 'Whoa . . .'"

Baxter tipped his head back, looking at her, as though he were examining a bug. Then she said, "You know what that surge of power feels like? When you're ten? It's like an ocean breeze blowing through your soul."

Baxter looked at Letty, who said, "My life has been saved by guns a half-dozen times. If it weren't for guns, I'd never made it out of middle school. I'd be dead. I dunno, maybe I go looking for it— like my job now. I could have gotten a PhD, been an econ professor somewhere, never picked up a gun again, and probably would have been okay. That's not what I did. I've shot more people than I've killed, but I've killed five. None of them were mistakes."

Baxter said, "Jesus. When I was a kid, I thought I was being fucked over when I didn't have a Pentium with a one-gig hard drive."

Cartwright: "I don't know what that means."

As she said that, Sovern cried out, "Ah! Ah! Ah, goddamnit!"

They all stood up as Sovern stumbled into the cockpit of the *Green Flash*, and Letty asked, "Are you okay?"

"No. Ah, motherfucker. I was trying to hurry and caught my little toe under the floor mat . . . I think I dislocated it." He bent to look at his foot in the cockpit light. "It's bruising, man, it's already blue."

"RICE," Baxter said. "Rest, Ice, Compression, Elevation."

"What?" Sovern asked, annoyed. "If I'm getting out of here, how am I going to do that? Goddamnit, that hurts." He stumbled to a seat on one side of the cockpit, and he asked, "Could somebody go down to the fridge and get me a blue ice? It's in the freezer."

Cartwright dropped into the cockpit, ducked down into the cabin, and emerged a moment later with a blue ice packet and said, "Lean back."

He leaned back and she wrapped the blue ice around his smaller toes, then wrapped his foot in a dish towel to hold the ice in place. Cartwright asked, "You've got this OCD pretty bad, huh?"

"Yeah. Nothing I can do about it."

To Letty and Baxter, Cartwright said, "You oughta see his refrigerator. Everything is lined up. Perfectly. The ketchup, the mustard, the olives, like little soldiers. Never seen anything like that."

"I like things neat," Sovern said. "Damnit, this toe, how does this shit happen?"

"Want me to kiss it and make it better?" Cartwright asked.

Sovern looked up: "Let me think about that."

Letty: "Once you're out on the water, how do we get in touch?"

"I'll give you my phone number. I don't always have my phone turned on, but I will for the next couple of days. Be careful with it—not a lot of people have my number. Don't give it to the cops . . . I'm almost ready to go."

"Not soon enough," Baxter said, quietly. "Look."

THEY ALL TURNED toward the motel. The lobby that led down to the marina had a glass door and two men were standing in the lobby light, looking down at them.

Letty said to Baxter, "The guy on the right."

Baxter: "Yeah. He's the other shooter. The one the FBI didn't kill."

Cartwright turned to Letty, grinned and said, "Showtime." She turned to Sovern and asked, "Do you have any sort of louder music? White Stripes? Something with drums?"

Sovern said, looking at the men behind the glass, "That's a little . . ." He paused, turned back to the boat and said, "I can stream 'Seven Nation Army.'"

"That'll work," Cartwright said.

He dropped down into the cabin, limping on the bad toe and blue-ice wrap. They could hear him rattling the keys on a computer, and a moment later, after the opening bass riff, Megan Martha White began pounding on her drums.

Cartwright said, "Turn it up a little more," and as Sovern did that, she turned toward Letty to cover her move, took her compact Ruger pistol out of a belt holster, dipped into a pocket, brought out a suppressor and began threading it onto the gun barrel.

"You'll still hear it, if you use it," Letty said, trying to keep her voice conversational.

"Yeah, but it'll be just another pop on top of those drums," Cartwright said. "It's a hundred to one that anyone would recognize it as a gunshot."

"You shooting subsonic?" Letty asked.

"No, I want the punch," Cartwright said. She tightened the suppressor, looked up from the gun barrel and saw that Letty had the 938 in her hand. "Is that the FBI gun?"

"Yeah, it's okay. I wouldn't want to shoot it at more than five yards, though. God only knows where it shoots longer than that."

Sovern poked his head out of the cabin, then stepped into the cockpit, said to Cartwright, "A silencer? Who are you guys?"

"They're crazy," Baxter said. "Excuse me while I dive off the dock."

"Relax, everything is under control," Cartwright said.

Baxter: "Yeah, bullshit," and, "Here they come."

They all looked toward the motel and the two men ambled down a set of steps and along the walkway that led to the dock.

Cartwright said to Sovern, quietly, "Was your father in the movies by any chance?"

"Not exactly. He was a TV weather guy in San Diego. Why?"

"Because you're really, really good-looking."

Sovern: "Oh, yeah. I go to music concerts and my looks get me laid. The next morning, the woman finds out I'm a computer nerd and have OCD and she leaves, for good. Also, I might be a little cranky in the mornings. I don't like to talk before noon . . . These guys don't look anything like that couple that was here before."

"The first ones were scouts," Letty said. "They were locating you for the killers. They're probably watching us right now, from somewhere else."

"They would be, if I were running this op," Cartwright said. To Baxter: "The guy on the right was the shooter at Loren Barron's house?"

"Don't know who did the shooting, but he was there," Baxter said.

"My fuckin' toe is busted, I think," Sovern said. "What are you going to do?"

"We're gonna ask these guys who their boss is," Letty said.

Baxter: "Like they're gonna tell you."

"They're gonna tell us," Cartwright said.

THE TWO MEN came down the dock. Both average height but muscular, dark hair with short haircuts, both were dressed like Cartwright with overshirts over tee-shirts, but with a hint of the tactical about them: the overshirts were dark green and dark gray, the tee-shirts were black. Like Cartwright, they both wore black jeans.

As they came up, Cartwright told Sovern, "Duck back into the cabin. Go on. We want them looking at you, not at us."

Sovern did that, and as he did, one of the men, looking at the three sitting on dock boxes, asked, "How you doin'?"

The words were American, but they didn't sound American; there was an accent in it.

"We're doing fine," Baxter said. "How you doin'?"

"We're doin' fine, too," the man said. "We need to talk to Mr. Sovern, private-like, so if you'd move along, we'd appreciate it."

"Can't do that," Letty said. "We're his bodyguards."

The two men looked at each other, and then the talker said, "You're bodyguards? Two girls and a fat man are his bodyguards?"

"That's right," Cartwright said.

"Then this might be your unlucky night, because . . ." The man moved his hand to the left side of his overshirt, and Cartwright said, "Wait!"

"What?" His hand stopped moving.

"Waiting for the bass drum," she said.

It came: "Boom!" And . . . *BAP.*

Despite the suppressor, the shot was loud, much louder than the drums.

Letty jumped: Cartwright had shot the man in the stomach. His eyes opened wide with shock and he sat down, hard, on the dock, then flopped flat on his back. Letty was on her feet with the 938 up and pointing at the other man's head.

"Your friend might survive a stomach wound, but a head wound, you know, not so much," Letty said. "Want to find out?"

The man, looking first at the nine-millimeter hole at the end of Letty's pistol, and then down at his partner said, "Greg? Greg?"

Cartwright told Letty, "Take him down to the end of the dock . . ." The wounded man was groping for the gunshot wound with his hand, which came away scarlet with blood, and moaned, a rough sound that could be a prelude to death. ". . . and ask him his boss's name. Tell him to whisper it. I'll ask Greg what the boss's name is, and if they don't match, we'll shoot them both. Get Sovern to put them on his boat, take the bodies out to sea."

"That's a plan," Letty said. She waggled her gun at the un-wounded man and said, "End of the dock."

The man moved, reluctantly, toward the end of the dock, Letty keeping a careful six-foot distance away. At the steps down from the motel, the man said, "If I tell you, they'll kill me."

"But you'll make up a story, with Greg, about how we opened fire and he got hit and we ran off and you don't know nothin' and never had a chance to talk to us . . ."

He shook his head and seemed to tense, as though about to jump her, and she said, "I can shoot you three times before you get to me and then you'll be dead for sure. And I'll do that. Then we'll kill Greg, to keep things neat and clean. Dump you both in the ocean."

The man gnawed at his bottom lip for a moment, then whispered, "Mr. Step."

"Step? What's his real name?"

Another hesitation, and a look down the dock, where his partner lay pumping blood on the plastic boards. "Arseny Stepashin."

Letty said, "I'm gonna back away from you, down the dock. You follow. You try to run, I'll shoot you. I'm a very good shot and I'd be happy to do it." They stepped carefully down the dock, and once there, Cartwright looked up and Letty said, "How about, Arseny Stepashin?"

"That's the name I got," Cartwright said. She pointed her suppressed pistol at the standing man and said, "You've got a gun. Drop it on the dock. Take it out with two fingers. You make a move, we'll kill you."

The man took a black suppressed Glock from a shoulder holster and dropped it on the dock. Cartwright turned to Sovern: "You ready?"

"I can go now . . . I need to cast off."

"Then go. I want you on the way before we call 9-1-1 and get this shot asshole put in an ambulance."

Sovern still took five minutes before his boat slowly eased out of the slip and made the turn into the boat channel. He called out once, the fading drums of the White Stripes behind him, "Good-bye. I'd like to see you again, Barbara. You can get my email from Ben."

Letty waved, then looked at Cartwright: "FBI and then 9-1-1."

Baxter: "About time. I think we're all done here. With this whole job."

Cartwright, looking out to the boat channel: "I'd like to see him again, too."

Letty: "Ah, Jesus."

LETTY CALLED her FBI contact first, told him where they were and what had happened, asked him to call the Oxnard police and fill them in on their identities.

"I'll do that and get some of our people on the way," the fed said. "They'll be coming from here in LA, so it could be a while. You want me to call 9-1-1 and get an ambulance moving?"

"If you would," Letty said, looking down at the shooter's body. "The guy seems pretty uncomfortable and he's bleeding bad."

That done, she called Delores Nowak, who was still in Los Angeles.

"Apparently the guy who's running this is named Arseny Stepashin, a Russian gang guy," Letty told her, after telling her what had happened. Nowak didn't seem flustered, as she had been after the call about the Loren Barron murders.

Nowak said, "Wait one." A moment later, "All right, Stepashin's on the FBI's radar, but not prominent, there're no current investigations."

"They should start one. He's the guy behind these killings," Letty said.

As she said that, Cartwright touched her arm: "Cops are coming."

Letty took the phone away from her ear, heard the sirens, more than one, and she said to Nowak, "The police are on the way here."

"What about this Sovern person?" Nowak asked.

"He's gone out to sea," Letty said. "I don't know how you track somebody on a sailboat. He told us that he doesn't have a lot of food or fuel on board, so he'll have to come back somewhere, to stock up, probably tomorrow. His boat's called *Green Flash*, and it has a windmill-like thing hanging on the back."

"Okay. We'll get the Coast Guard to spot him. Try to be nice to the police."

THE UNIFORMED COPS arrived cautiously, coming around both ends of the motel and down the lobby, guns drawn. Letty said to the uninjured Russian, "Walk down to the end of the dock. Put your hands up or they might get antsy and shoot you."

The Russian did that, and Letty said to Cartwright and Baxter, "Hands up."

When they all had their hands up, the cops crept around the motel and down the dock and Letty shouted, "That's the Russian, close to you."

The cops ordered the Russian to lie down, cuffed him, then called, "You the FBI guys?"

"Homeland Security," Letty called back. "FBI's coming. We need an ambulance."

"On the way . . ."

The ambulance arrived along with two detectives, who disarmed the wounded man and sent him to a medical center, impounded the guns from both Russians, placing them in plastic evidence bags, decided the shell from Cartwright's gun was probably in the water, briefly interviewed them on the dock, sent the unwounded Russian to jail.

Cartwright told the lead detective about the surveillance team that had spotted Sovern for the killers, suggested that the team might still be watching, and pointed to a couple of places where they'd be, a man and a woman.

The cop was skeptical but sent a couple of uniforms to look; the uniforms came back shaking their heads, and one of them said, "There was a couple kind of floating around a while ago, but they're gone now."

A crime scene crew arrived, and Letty and Cartwright led them through the sequence of events and they went to work. That done, the cops invited Letty, Baxter, and Cartwright to come to police headquarters for a longer interview and to wait for the FBI.

They went.

Police headquarters looked like a two-story cake with thick vanilla frosting on top. The cops took them to a conference room, where they all spread around a table.

Cartwright didn't want to cooperate at all, but Letty suggested that everything would go more quickly if she did. During the preliminary interview, before the feds arrived, Cartwright told the Oxnard detectives that she was a consultant with the DHS, and never mentioned the Unspecified Agency.

Letty outlined what had happened, including the killings in Los Angeles and the SWAT-team shootout in the Valley and asked that the interview end there, at least until the FBI arrived. The cops knew a developing multiple-agency food fight when they saw one, and agreed to wait, offering soft drinks and packs of cheese and peanut butter crackers while they waited.

Cartwright told Letty and Baxter, "Always eat, drink, and pee when you can," and she and Baxter began devouring the crackers.

Letty, Baxter, and Cartwright had made it from LA to Oxnard

in an hour, but the FBI took two, as they needed to bring a super-vising agent with them, and finding one took a while.

The conference was almost exactly the same as the one that took place at FBI headquarters after Letty shot the man during the SWAT action. One difference was that Nowak took part, via a Zoom call. Letty again related the story from the time they learned of Sovern's identity, to Sovern's departure from the marina and the arrival of the cops.

The FBI wanted Cartwright's pistol, and, to Letty's surprise, she gave it up without complaint.

The bureaucracy took two hours and when it was done, they were allowed to leave. Nowak's last comment was "I'll be calling. Wait for it."

BACK IN THE TRUCK, two o'clock in the morning, leaving Oxnard, Letty took the call from Nowak, who said, "Good. Now we've got something. We had the local Coast Guard admiral jack up his com-mand and we should have located Sovern by tomorrow morning. The FBI will be all over this Stepashin guy, so we don't have to worry about him. I would like a report with all the names and identifying data on the Ordinary People you've spotted . . ."

"Sovern's pretty smart," Letty said. "If he doesn't want to talk to you, it might not be so easy."

"We'll see. I'll look forward to the report, and now I'm going back to bed," she said, and she hung up.

ON THE WAY BACK to Los Angeles, Letty, Baxter, and Cartwright talked sporadically about what had happened on the dock and at the police station.

Letty said to Cartwright, "You gave up your pistol pretty easily."

She shrugged. "I got another one just like it, in my bag. Remind me to get it out."

And Cartwright told Letty, "You know, I got all the reports about what happened in Pershing, the three guys you shot. You have a tendency to walk the edge. You try to be fair. The guy I shot was about to pull a gun. You never let a guy pull a gun. *Never.* There's nothing you can do with a gun except shoot it. Or maybe, if you're building a house, you could use it to drive nails, but basically . . . If a guy's about to pull a gun, shoot him."

"If he's just going to threaten you . . ."

"Bullshit. You don't know that unless you're clairvoyant. If he goes for a gun, you shoot him," Cartwright said. "Once a gun's pointed at your heart, the options get really narrow."

"You think I messed up?"

"Not exactly. There's a learning process. Remember that gun fights aren't fair . . . or shouldn't be. Asshole tries to pull a gun, shoot his ass, right now. Like a cop would."

Baxter: "Remind me not to annoy you."

"I'm easily annoyed," Cartwright said.

Baxter: "Really? Who woulda thought?"

EIGHTEEN

Leigh Lawrence had one defining talent: when she was working, she was invisible. One example: when she was working and second in line at Starbucks, the barista would serve the first person, then go to the third. Another: she'd been on dates, when she was working, and the waiter had asked her date, "Will anyone be joining you?"

If someone looked at her closely, that someone might conclude that she was pretty, but not in a distinctive way, with a slight olive complexion, dark hair and eyes, rounded shoulders. When she was wearing her working clothes, which tended to browns and middle grays, she simply faded away.

On this night, she and her partner, Barry Martin, who was nearly as invisible as she was, were standing at the back corner of the Wanderer, a nice-enough waterfront lounge in Oxnard, looking toward the marina behind the Motel California.

Lawrence and Martin were licensed private detectives, but didn't think of themselves that way. They didn't carry guns, crack wise, hang out with mugs, get rousted by cops, or drink too much. They considered themselves researchers, who researched all kinds of things. Good with computers, good with public files, good with surveillance, good with conversation, they worked for Boyadjian Surveys.

Tom Boyadjian, their boss, operated in the intersection of cops, lawyers, crooks, political consultants, fixers, and others who made their livings by dealing favors. Both Lawrence and Martin had witnessed serious crimes, which they were skilled at forgetting.

"Where are they?" Martin muttered. They'd seen two harsh-looking men get out of a car in front of the motel.

"Could be talking to the clerk," Lawrence said.

"Who will remember their faces," Martin said.

"Not that clerk."

"Mmm."

From their vantage point, they could see the fat man and the two girls sitting on dock boxes, talking, while the target, Sovern, was doing something in his boat.

"How are they going to get rid of the witnesses?" Lawrence wondered. "This could get ugly. Do we really want to see it?"

"Nothing to do with us. We're bystanders." That wasn't exactly true, as they were the ones who'd found Sovern. Sovern had made the mistake of having both phone and Internet bills sent to his boat through the motel, and the further mistake of having his photo on a California driver's license.

Then the glass back door on the motel opened, and Martin said, "Here they come."

They watched the whole drama unfold: the two men walking

down the dock as rock music began banging out of Sovern's boat, disturbing the night.

Step's men stopped to talk to the two young women and the fat man who were sitting on the dock boxes. The conversation was short and then one of Step's men unexpectedly dropped onto his butt, and then fell flat on the dock. One of the women had gotten to her feet, moving fast, her hand pointed at the head of the second thug.

"They shot him. Did you see that?" Martin said. "We gotta get out of here."

He took a step away, but Lawrence caught his arm. "Not yet. Wait. There's something funny going on."

"I'm not laughing . . ."

He stayed where he was, watching with Lawrence, as one of the young women marched the unwounded thug to the end of the dock, and then back. Minutes later, Sovern's boat slipped away into the night. They could see the running lights for a while, and then they, too, disappeared.

And as that was happening, they heard the first of the sirens.

"Now you see what's funny?" Lawrence asked.

"Yeah. The shooters aren't running."

"No. They're waiting," Lawrence said.

"They don't look like cops."

"No, they don't. We need to call Tom and we need to figure out who those women are. And the fat guy."

"If they're not on a boat, they've probably got a car at the motel," Martin said.

"Let's see how they deal with the cops . . ."

AN HOUR AND A HALF LATER, Tom Boyadjian called Step, who picked up on the first ring and said, "Da."

"There's going to be a . . . what would you call it . . . a mandatory combat zone bonus in addition to the three thousand a day. I gotta cover my boys." He said "boys," even though one of his boys was a woman, because that's the way they all talked.

"Tell me," Step said. "Wait, I want to put it on speaker."

Victoria came over and stood next to him, as Boyadjian relayed the details of the clash at the motel. "If those were your men, you got one shot and maybe bad, and one arrested. They took the shot guy to St. John's Medical Center. There was a call from an EMT to the hospital and they used the name Artyom for the victim, no last name. Don't know his condition. The other one is at Oxnard police headquarters . . ."

"You say there were two women and a fat man?" Victoria asked.

"Hi, Vickie. Yes. My researchers say one of the women did the shooting, but both women had guns and looked competent. They went with the cops to police headquarters. They were driving a Toyota truck, a Tundra," Boyadjian said. "The cops let them drive separately. My people think they knew they were being watched, because some Oxnard cops came snooping around the waterfront, looking for anyone who might be watching. The fat guy and the girls took the truck into a fenced lot behind the Oxnard police headquarters, so we can't get at it, at least not yet."

"If they leave the lot, can you track them?" Step asked.

"Maybe, if we're in some traffic," Boyadjian said.

"Do that. Whatever it costs," Step said.

"Hang on a minute, I've got a call coming in from my people . . ."

After a full minute of silence, Boyadjian came back on the line: "Okay, this isn't good. The FBI has arrived at police headquarters. We're thinking it's possible that the two women are undercover FBI agents. You're a good friend, but I'm not going to deal with that. Not on a shooting."

"I have reasons to think that they're *not* FBI," Step said. "I don't know who they are, but I don't think they're feds."

"Then who?" Boyadjian asked.

"That's what we're trying to figure out, what we'd like *you* to figure out."

"We can watch from a distance, but I'll tell my people to break away if there's any risk at all," Boyadjian said. "Your garage over on Ventura Boulevard got hit by an FBI SWAT team and we don't know how they were located so quickly. We know *you* were clean, last time we looked, but apparently, they weren't. Anyway, I can't afford to get in the middle of a war. I don't want to be on anybody's side."

"I understand," Step said, and he did. "You have your business to protect. Watch what you can. Don't take chances, but any information will be appreciated. I mean, big-bonus appreciated."

"We'll do what we can," Boyadjian said.

WHEN STEP HUNG UP, Victoria said, "Those are the two women who took out the security guard at the warehouse and stole the Intel chips. Now they're cooperating with the cops—they didn't even try to run after they shot Artyom. What are they? Not FBI . . ."

"Maybe FBI counterintel?" Step suggested. "Maybe they took the chips just to see what they were?"

"Doesn't feel like the FBI to me. Two women on their own, with a fat man? Who were talking to Sovern and they let him sneak away, when they obviously know who he is?"

Step nodded. "All right. Now what?"

"You need to call Volkov in Washington," Victoria said.

"Then we *could* have a war."

"We've got a war now," Victoria said. "We gotta hope Artyom and Kirill keep their mouths shut."

"They will," Step said. "I don't know, honey. Calling Washington. Gonna have to break out a backup burner and call from downtown. And then . . . what happens?"

"I don't know what happens—but I know what could happen if we don't make the call," Victoria said. "I'm going to look at the accounts, figure out what we can move, and where, like right now."

"Good. I'll call Volkov," Step said. "Goddamnit. The guy skizzes me out."

"He skizzes everybody out," Victoria said.

"Was that the right word? In English?" Step asked. "Skizzes? I heard Tom Boyadjian use it."

"Yeah, that's the right word. Skizzes. It means exactly what it sounds like."

Step took Sunset back toward downtown, pulled into a parking lot, and called Volkov at a number Volkov answered any time of day or night. The discussion was brief and Volkov said, "I'm coming out there. This is a critical moment."

"I understand," Step said. "I'll be waiting."

"We'll need cars; we'll bring money."

"I'll fix it," Step said.

When they'd signed off, Step called Victoria: "Done."

"We should move to the guesthouse."

"In the middle of the night?"

"Yes. Call Boyadjian and have him watch this place. If nobody shows up, that's good. If anybody does . . . we don't want to be here. I've packed jewelry and cash and the Warhol boxes. Anything else, we can fake."

NINETEEN

Letty and Baxter had checked out of the SkyPort and hadn't yet found another place to stay. Back in LA, with Cartwright, they wound up in a Holiday Inn Express not far off the 405. Cartwright wrangled with the night clerk and got them two rooms on the second floor—"Safer than the first floor, plus it's possible to go out the window if you really need to do that," she told Letty and Baxter.

"If I jumped out a second-story window, I'd hit the ground like a fuckin' comet," Baxter said.

"The idea would be to slide down a blanket or sheet," Cartwright said.

"Like a fuckin' asteroid," Baxter answered, enlarging on the theme.

"We've already worked through scenarios where you wind up dead, so this wouldn't be a big change," Letty said.

"I appreciate the effort to cheer me up," Baxter said morosely.

They got two rooms, connecting, Cartwright and Letty sharing one, Baxter taking the other. Cartwright broke a second pistol out of her equipment bag. The bag also contained an M4 rifle with an extended magazine, which allowed the user to select semiauto or full-auto fire.

She put both weapons on the floor next to her bed. "I get a really bad vibe from Russians," she said. "If your lady says we're done here, maybe we can get back to Washington tomorrow."

"She gets cranky when we wake her up," Letty said. "I'll call her in the morning."

"Let's try not to call before noon," Cartwright said. Baxter seconded the motion, and they went to bed.

Leigh Lawrence and Barry Martin caught the Tundra as it left the police parking lot. They stayed well back, as much as a half mile at times, following it down the 110 to LA, Martin driving, Lawrence watching the truck's taillights with a pair of image-stabilized binoculars. If they could spot the truck when it was parked and empty, they could stick a GPS tracker on it, and follow it to South America if they had to.

They closed in as traffic thickened into LA and were only half a block away when the Tundra pulled into a Holiday Inn Express in Santa Monica.

They waited a half hour, then checked in themselves, mostly so they could park their car next to the truck. In the room, they lay on the beds for another half hour, then slipped down the stairs to the parking garage. They rummaged around in the back of their Nissan Pathfinder, while checking out the garage, then Martin used one of the keys on his extensive set of backup car keys to open the truck door.

The Tundra wasn't quite empty. There was trash in the back, receipts, and Lawrence used a penlight to read some of them: "It looks like they're from Florida. Or were in Florida. Looks like they took the 10 from Florida all the way here, and not long ago . . ."

There was nothing of interest in the glove box and Lawrence found what seemed to be drumsticks on the backseat, as well as a set of brushes, but she didn't know what the brushes were and asked Martin, who said, "Some kind of drum thing, I think. Let's open the bed. Push your door shut."

LETTY AND CARTWRIGHT had been asleep for an hour when Baxter burst in and half shouted, "Up! Up! Somebody's messing with the truck."

Letty and Cartwright rolled out of bed, both dazed, and Baxter, looking at his iPhone, said, "They're inside. They're inside the fuckin' truck!"

Letty and Cartwright pulled on pants and shoes, Baxter calling, "C'mon, c'mon . . ."

He went out the door, scooping up Letty's cane as he went, and was standing in the hallway when they got out of the room, both carrying guns, and he pointed with the cane, like a magic wand: "Stairs."

The cars were in the first level of the parking structure and they ran down the stairs to the garage door and peeked, couldn't see the truck, eased out into the garage itself to a corner, where they could see the truck nosed into a wall. They couldn't see anyone at the truck, but after a few seconds, they heard something rattle.

Letty whispered, "Okay."

Cartwright whispered back: "Be ready to jump behind an engine block, and keep your legs behind the tires, if you can."

Letty nodded and they both led off, Cartwright quickly crossing to the other side of the driving lane. As they came up to the truck, they heard a woman's voice, almost a whisper, saying, "I dunno. What are these things?"

A man's voice: "Some kind of drum thing, I think. Let's open the bed. Push your door shut."

The truck door made a *chunk* as it closed. Letty had moved up behind a Mazda roadster, across the driving lane from the truck, and Cartwright was one car away when a woman and a man, both in dark clothing, stepped out of the space between the truck and a gray Nissan SUV and Cartwright said, quietly but distinctly, "If either one of you motherfuckers twitch, I'll kill you."

The couple froze, then both lifted their hands shoulder high and turned their heads to look at her, saw the gun, and saw Letty with her gun, up and pointing at their heads, and Baxter coming up behind them.

The woman blurted, "They're the ones . . ." and then stopped talking.

Letty: "Yeah. We're the ones from the marina, dipshits."

Cartwright: "What do you want to do?"

"If we kill them, we can make it back up the stairs before anybody can react and they'll be out of our hair," Letty said, never taking her eyes off the gun sight. "Nobody would connect it to us—they'd look like victims of a street robbery."

The man said, "Don't do that, don't . . ."

Baxter came up and said, "You fucked with my truck."

Martin said, "Look, we were paid to check you out. That's all we do. We don't have guns or anything."

Letty: "Bullshit. You fingered Craig Sovern for the Russians and they were there to kill him. That makes you the friends of the

Russians and they've killed three people we know of. Sovern would have been four. You probably spotted all of them."

She looked at Cartwright: "What do you think? Kill them?"

Cartwright asked Martin, "Where's your car?"

"We parked it out on the street . . ."

"No, you didn't. There's no place on the street to park."

"Well, I meant around the corner in the parking lot," Martin said.

Baxter: "Empty your pockets. Everything. C'mon. If we find you've left a fuckin' toothpick in your pockets, we kill you."

"Who are you?" Lawrence asked.

Letty: "Shut up. Empty the pockets."

They emptied their pockets, putting the contents on the Tundra's bed cover: wallets, Lawrence's purse, two motel keys, car keys, two small multi-tools, penlights, no weapons. Baxter told them to step away from the truck, picked up one of the two sets of car keys and pressed the button on the remote. The lights flashed on the Nissan they were standing next to and the doors clicked open.

Baxter said, "Around the corner in the parking lot, huh?"

Cartwright: "Get back between the trucks, between your truck and ours, right against the wall."

"Don't shoot us," Lawrence said. "We'll tell you whatever . . ."

"Yeah, you will," Cartwright said. She wagged the barrel of her weapon: "Back against the wall."

Letty said to Baxter, "Clean out their truck. Take everything loose, put it in the back of ours. Wallets, car keys, everything."

As Baxter did that, Letty and Cartwright questioned the couple: They worked for a research agency, they said, and admitted that they'd located Sovern for the agency, run by a man named Tom Boyadjian. They didn't know who the clients were, but believed they were Russians. As they stood against the wall, Letty used her phone to take close-up photos of their faces.

When Letty and Cartwright ran out of questions, Cartwright ordered the two into the back of the Nissan and told them to sit on the floor of the backseat, facing away from each other. "Don't shoot us . . ."

They were clearly terrified, which meant they'd probably witnessed the shooting on the dock. The woman began to cry and Letty asked, "Did you spot all of the people the Russians murdered?"

"We don't know about any murders . . ."

"More bullshit," Baxter said. "The only way you could have followed us here was if you saw us in the marina, and then getting into the truck. You knew what the Russians were there for: they were going to kill Craig Sovern. You were gonna watch them do it."

Lawrence, "No, no . . ."

Cartwright said, "You move, you try to get up, you die."

She pushed the SUV door mostly shut, then said quietly to Letty and Baxter, "We gotta get our stuff out of the room and down to the truck. We'll leave them here without keys. We've got their IDs, their faces, their phones, their license plate, we ought to check their room to see if they left anything there . . ."

"You watch them, we'll get the stuff down. See you in ten minutes," Letty said.

More like fifteen. They jammed everything they had into their bags, quickly checked the couple's motel room—nothing there except two wrinkled pink bedspreads.

Back in the parking garage, they loaded everything into the truck, left the two researchers sitting on the floor of the Nissan. They drove a half mile to a surface parking lot, and Baxter and

Cartwright crawled under and through the truck, with a flashlight, looking for a GPS tracker, while Letty kept watch.

They found nothing, but Cartwright wasn't satisfied. "Lots of cities now have license plate trackers . . . even tollways have them."

"We've been using one here," Baxter said. "And about that— Letty stole a plate off a car where we were last night before we picked you up. We put it on the front of the truck. We didn't want the NSA tracking us, because, you know, one of us might do something technically illegal."

"Let's get it off and put your regular plate back on," Cartwright said. "We're gonna need to talk to your Delores Nowak. If Nowak tracks us to the meeting, that's not a problem. We can steal another plate afterward."

"I hate to do it, but we've got to ditch those iPhones from Martin and Lawrence," Letty said. "They've probably got good information on them, but they're also gonna have a 'find my phone' tracker."

"That's a thought," Cartwright said, bobbing her head. "When we leave here, we'll drop them in the street."

"I've got a better idea," Baxter said. "My car safe . . . my vault . . . is a perfect Faraday cage. We keep the phones until we give them to the FBI or the NSA."

Letty: "Good—if you're sure the box will shield them."

"Absolutely: part of the design," Baxter said.

When they left the parking lot, with Letty driving and Baxter in the backseat, going through what they'd taken from Lawrence and Martin, Baxter said, "Hey: two GPS trackers. Still in the boxes. Good ones. Four hundred bucks each, still got the price tags from the Spy Store, whatever that is. You know, we could make quite a tidy profit from this whole enterprise. We've still got five boxes of chips in the back, maybe we could give SlapBack a call, offer to help out . . ."

Cartwright: "That big set of keys . . . I think they're for opening car doors. I could use those."

"I got dibs on those," Letty said. "I'll let you make copies, if you can. But I could use them, too."

"They're both licensed private detectives," Baxter said. "Martin and Lawrence . . ."

Letty rolled her window down and let one hand trail through the warming early morning air as Baxter and Cartwright rattled on . . .

TOM BOYADJIAN CALLED STEP at seven o'clock in the morning with the additional bad news. His two operators had been jumped by the three unknowns, who now had everything that had been in the operators' SUV, along with their wallets, the registration documents for the SUV, photos of both of them.

They were not, Lawrence and Martin had told him, agents of the FBI.

"Did your boys give up my name?" Step asked.

"No, because they don't know your name," Boyadjian said. "These guys, these girls, do think they're up against Russians— they referred to Russians several times and they know that Barron and Wolfe were killed by your guys."

"They gotta be the train hackers," Step said. "Gotta be."

"I lean in that direction, but how do they shoot somebody, go to the police station, talk with the FBI, and walk away? The only thing I can think of—and even this isn't a great fit—is that they're CIs, confidential informants, for the feds. Maybe . . . we've heard rumors that there are these two CIs named Bob and Sue, not their real names, of course, who've been working FBI stings on local hacker groups."

"Can you get me anything on them?" Step asked. "I'd like to talk with them."

"We can try. If the information is out there, we'll get it off our computers, and it shouldn't take too long," Boyadjian said.

"Then do that," Step said. "These people are really screwing with my business. The stuff they stole really makes it look like it's hackers who are doing it."

"Okay."

"And I got another job for you. Easy and safe. No complications."

"What's that?"

"I want you to watch my house . . ."

COLLES HAD GONE BACK to Washington, but Nowak was still at the SkyPort. She was awake, and they told her what had happened at the Holiday Inn, and Letty asked about Sovern.

"Ah, no. I just got off the phone with the Coast Guard," Nowak said. "He seems to have eluded them for the time being."

"I was thinking—what if he didn't go out to sea? What if he went around the corner, parked his boat somewhere else, and caught a cab? He could be anywhere."

"That had occurred to me, when I was told that the ocean is apparently empty," Nowak said. "It's also possible that he changed the name on the back of the boat and took down the windmill thing."

"There's bad stuff going on. The Russians may be going after the hackers. The hacks could use information fed to them by people they somewhat trust," Letty said. "Like us. That could make them more likely to cooperate."

"That makes sense. I'll make some calls," Nowak said. "How soon can you get here?"

"Not long," Letty said. "We're on the 405 headed your way. We've got some stuff to drop off with you."

"All right. I've got a plane at ten o'clock. I've got to go back to Washington. The sooner you get here, the better."

On the way to the SkyPort, Baxter spotted an open mini-mart, and asked Letty to pull in.

"Food?"

"No. Aluminum foil. And maybe a snack."

They all went inside, found a box of aluminum foil, and bought soft drinks and chips. Back in the truck, Baxter took the two iPhones out of the truck's safe and wrapped them in the aluminum foil, taking a half-dozen wraps on each, carefully sealing the ends.

"Done," he said. "Nowak can take them back to the Fort and our guys can tear them down."

"The FBI has had all kinds of trouble cracking iPhones," Cartwright said.

"Yeah, they do," Baxter agreed, smiling at her.

"You're telling me that you guys . . ."

"Yeah, we can," Baxter said.

Letty: "You know, if the different branches of the government would cooperate with each other . . ."

Baxter made a farting sound with his lips: "Like that's gonna happen."

NOWAK WAS UP, showered, and dressed when they got to her room. She was happy to get the phones, and happier to get the names of the two Tom Boyadjian operators. She got information on Boyadjian from an NSA database and said, "We'll have the FBI go over and chat with him. If you're right, his company has been instrumental in both murder and espionage. He'll cooperate."

"What about this Stepashin guy?"

"Nothing on him, yet, except that the FBI has heard the name."

"Are we all headed back to Washington?" Cartwright asked.

"I need you to hang on for a day or two—I've reserved rooms for you here. You've got a lot of information in your heads about who is doing what to whom," Nowak said. "We may want you to see if Ordinary People would be willing to go after the Russian rail system again."

Letty to Cartwright and Baxter: "There. She finally said it."

"Said what?" Nowak asked.

Cartwright: "Said what we're really doing out here."

"And if they're not interested in going after the trains?" Letty asked.

"We could show them a picture of a cell at ADX Florence," Nowak said. "The federal supermax. That should have an encouraging effect. I mean, they're criminals."

Letty: "Do that, and we'd have to tell them who we really are."

"That may be necessary, although . . . you wouldn't have to tell them exactly which agency," Nowak said.

Baxter: "They'd be my friends if I weren't at NSA. I really don't want to put them away."

"Then you'll have to convince them to go after the Russians," Nowak said.

They sat and looked at each other, then Nowak said, "Listen, people. The United States is not about to go to war with Russia. Neither is NATO. Russia's got nukes and quite possibly an unbalanced dictator running the place. When Russia invades Ukraine, we'll send the Ukrainians some weapons, maybe, but we won't be dogfighting with Russian jets, or putting A-10s on their supply lines. Everything we do will be by remote control. That means slowing down resupply by trains. If an illegal consortium of hackers chooses to go after the Russian rail system, well, that's not the United States of America doing it. The Russians won't have a lot of room to complain, given what their hackers do to us."

"You need to be deniable," Cartwright said.

"That's exactly the right word," Nowak said. "We'll deny, deny, deny, but we won't be unhappy to see Ordinary People back at work."

Baxter looked at Letty: "Sovern would be the key. From what I get from Able, he's the genius behind the train hack, while Loren and Brianna coordinated it."

"If we can find him," Letty said. Her eyes clicked over to Baxter, who dropped his eyelids.

"Gotta hope the Coast Guard can find him," Cartwright said, now catching Letty's eyes. "As far as we know, he could be on his way to Hawaii. But if they can spot him, we'll talk to him."

"Whatever we do, we'll want to keep Ordinary People out of the bureaucracy, away from the FBI," Nowak said. "We don't want any reports written about this."

"The FBI is already pissed at us—and at you," Letty said.

"Yes. They are. I'll deal with that when I get back to Washington—and believe me, I can deal with it. Some people very, very close to the President and the joint chiefs are trying to figure out how we can help the Ukrainians, without kicking the hornet's nest."

Cartwright's eyebrows went up. "So we're cleared to do what we fuckin' well please, to get the job done."

"Try not to blow up any buildings. Not large buildings, anyway," Nowak said. She stood up and wheeled her suitcase toward the door. "We've been told in no uncertain terms to get this done, to stop the trains, whatever it takes."

TWENTY

Raoul, the well-dressed attorney, dark pinstripe suit, French shoes, silk Hermès necktie, pointed the couple known as Bob and Sue at the black Chrysler 300 and said, "There's your ride."

"I gotta tell you," Bob said, as he dragged his soles reluctantly across the sidewalk, Raoul's ham-sized hand on his arm—Bob's real name was Wesley Bunne, pronounced *boon*—"this whole thing scares me. Why would anyone put up that much money to get us out?"

He looked down at the limo, parked in the sunshine outside the Metropolitan Detention Center.

"Because the guy in the limo needs to talk to you about some hacking activities that he believes you're aware of. Nothing to be scared of," Raoul said. "Besides, he expects to get all the money back when you show up for your court date."

"Would you say that we have any alternative to getting in the limo?" Sue asked. Her real named was Sharon Pecker, she'd grown up in Rib Lake, Wisconsin, and had an inborn suspicion of big-city limos, especially black ones.

"You have nothing to worry about. Honest," Raoul said, though he wasn't entirely sure of that. "We are looking to you for information, if you have it. If you don't have it, we drop you off at a bus stop. If you do have it, we send you anywhere you want to go in the limo, with five hundred dollars to buy your lunch."

"Probably want to go to Ocean Park," Wesley said.

"That's great," Raoul said. "The man in the car lives over in that direction. He can run you right over there."

Wesley and Sharon looked at each other, and then Wesley said, "What the hell. Let's take the ride."

As they walked up to the car, Raoul gave them his card. "The FBI is unlikely to press charges. If they do, I'll demand discovery on every computer sting they've done in the last ten years, and the CIs they've used, to discover the extent to which they've covered for criminal activity. The federal attorney will give us some bullshit, but they won't file."

"That would be wonderful," Sharon said.

Step was sitting in the backseat, wearing his beige chinos over cordovan shoes, with a yellow silk shirt, an outfit that you wouldn't want to get blood on. The limo had a window between the front seat and the back and it was rolled up. Sharon got in the rear-facing seating, looking at Step, who smiled at her, and Wesley got in beside Step.

"Where we going?" Step asked. Tom Boyadjian, in looking for the train hackers, had found Bob and Sue. He had determined that they weren't the hackers they were looking for, but had also learned that they probably knew about Ordinary People. He'd called Step with the information, and Step had called the well-dressed attorney.

Wesley gave Step an address and Step took a cell phone from his pocket and called the driver, who sat five feet away, behind the window. Step repeated the address and the limo pulled away from the curb.

"What exactly did you want?" Sharon asked.

Step seemed to think about the question, then said, "You two . . . let's face it, you're criminals."

Sharon opened her mouth to object, but Step put a finger up.

"That's okay. So am I. Like you, I do something that doesn't hurt anyone, but it's technically illegal. I understand you were ripping off casino ATMs, while the casinos were ripping off anyone stupid enough to walk through their doors. Am I right?"

"You're right," Wesley said. "What kind of criminal are you?"

"To put it simply, the United States bans the export of certain computer components to certain countries that really need the parts. I mean, it's ridiculous. Computer components are basically fungible . . . You know what fungible means?"

Sharon said, "Yes. It means one thing can be replaced by another, all commonly available. Oil is fungible. Wheat is fungible. Most hardware is fungible."

Step smiled: "Yes. Anyway, I acquire computer parts here in the U.S. and export them to . . . mmm . . . countries that want them. The way computer chips work, those countries will get all they want in two or three years, or five years, so why not now? Makes no sense. But, it's a business opportunity."

"What does that have to do with us?" Wesley asked. "We're software, not hardware."

"I have been troubled lately by software programmers. We

thought you may be associated with them, but my researchers now say you are not. That you were involved in other activities, the ATM attacks, were caught by the FBI, and were turned as confidential informants. My researchers say that as FBI informants, you may be aware, or have encountered at one time or another, a group of three, two women and a man. The women, I'm told, are thin, attractive, carry guns and are willing to use them. The man is very large—tall and fat, dark hair and black-rimmed glasses . . ."

Wesley sat forward: "*Those motherfuckers!* Those motherfuckers have something to do with the FBI. There weren't two women, that we know of, there was only one. Named Charlie. The fat guy is named Paul. I don't know what they have to do with the FBI, because they're not FBI, but they're something . . ."

Paul: that confirmed George Hewitt's comment about a man named Paul. "Charlie and Paul. Charlie's a man's name . . ." Step said.

"Also a nickname for Charlotte," Sharon said.

"Ah."

They told the story of the abortive sting, about the apparent argument between the FBI agents and people higher up the law enforcement pole, the release of Charlie and Paul, and their own eventual arrest and three-day isolation. They told the story that Charlie and Paul told, the hospital ransomware attack, the Bitcoin problem, and the University of Florida.

"So they're criminals, too?" Step asked. He'd been listening attentively, thumb and middle finger under his chin, index finger along his nose.

"Yeah, but they have *something* that the FBI wants," Sharon said. "We just don't know what that is. I'll tell you, though, if you run into them, watch that chick. Charlie. We were sitting at a café table and she pulled a gun and threatened to shoot me between the tits. That's her words. She was serious. She's a fuckin' psycho."

"I have reason to believe that," Step said.

By then, they were heading west on the 10, toward Ocean Park, and Wesley and Sharon were feeling more confident about their destination being somewhere other than a ditch.

Step asked more questions about Charlie and Paul, and about Ordinary People, and who might be associated with the group. Wesley and Sharon were aware of Ordinary People, as was the FBI. They gave Step some names, including those of Loren Barron, William Orleans, and Michele Obermath.

With the Barron name, Step decided that their information was at least somewhat reliable. He'd never heard of William Orleans or Michele Obermath, but the surnames were unusual enough that they could probably be found. He made notes in an alligator-leather-covered notepad the size of a checkbook.

"What'd they do to you?" Wesley asked.

"They're fuckin' with me and I don't know why," Step said. "They stole part of a shipment of computer chips I had stored in a warehouse. One of those psycho chicks, probably this Charlie, shot one of my men and when the cops and FBI showed up, they let them go."

"That's what we really don't get," Sharon said. "They're criminals, but nobody seems to care. Or they've got influence somewhere."

Step nodded and bobbed his head: "Yes. A mystery. I really don't like mysteries. They tend to bite you when you're not looking."

The ride from MDC to Ocean Park took fifteen minutes and Step dropped them a block from their apartment. At the curb, Step leaned toward Sharon with a thin fold of cash, and said, "Five hundred dollars. For lunch. And give me your phone numbers. I could use a couple like you. Computer people. Be a lot safer than what you used to do, more . . . invisible. Good money, too, and we will get you legal help for your current problems."

They gave him phone numbers and he wrote them in the elegant notepad.

Sharon said, "I know you're a lot bigger than we are, but can I give you something to think about?"

"Sure," Step said, giving her his number-three smile.

"You're selling one chip at a time. You might manage to get hold of a lot of chips, but each one is a separate sale. That's because you're selling hardware. And you have to find and pay the people who . . . acquire . . . the chips for you and organize trucks and ships and airplanes and warehouses, and you have to hide from the cops and pay bribes and legal fees and so on, and then you have to find customers and collect your money. Overall, after acquiring and shipping and paying employees and lawyers, how much do you keep? What's your personal margin? Ten percent? Fifteen?"

"That's not too far off," Step admitted. "Of course, there's no taxes."

"But you're risking prison," Sharon said.

Step nodded: "True."

"The thing about software is that it's usually written by one person or a small team. You pay them once," Sharon said. "When it's done, you can ship the software anywhere in the world. *From* anywhere in the world. Anonymously. For free. If it's the right piece of software, you can sell it over and over and over. You can sell it a hundred times, or a thousand, without lifting a finger or doing any more work. No other employees to deal with. And it's very serious stuff. The U.S. government and the Israelis fucked up an entire top-secret Iranian nuclear processing plant with a virus called Stuxnet."

"Huh. And you know about this sales concept because . . ."

"Because it's done all the time in other businesses," Wesley said. "Stephen King writes one book and the publishing company, not him, prints and sells a million copies. But Stephen King only does that one thing—writes one book."

"So?"

"Wes and I have some ideas for a computer security company that would be able to isolate and destroy the most vicious kinds of viruses and malware," Sharon said. "Do that one thing: destroy them quickly and cleanly and get paid *very* well for doing it. Above-board. Good tax-paying citizens. We would like to find a . . . sophisticated . . . venture capitalist to finance the start-up. We think we could launch for as little as a million dollars."

"Why would anybody hire you in particular?" Step asked. "As opposed to some big security company?"

"Because we'd be so quick and efficient. We'd spot the virus first, we'd spot all the infected businesses—there could be dozens of them, or even hundreds—and one program would kill them. We'd be out there while everybody else is still sucking on their thumbs," Sharon said. "We couldn't be quicker or more efficient with the fix than if we'd created the viruses ourselves, if we'd done that one thing."

She smiled.

"Ah. Now *that* is something to consider," Step said. His eyebrows went up, creating a bank of wrinkles across his forehead.

"If you think you could get serious about it, we've written a detailed prospectus, entirely encrypted, of course. I'm sure you'd find it interesting."

"I will call you when the current problem is dealt with," Step promised.

As they were getting out of the car, Sharon said, "Haven't seen a nice little notepad like that in a while. Alligator hide. Everything goes in cell phones now."

Step said, "Yeah, well . . . You ever try to chew up and swallow an iPhone?"

ON THE WAY BACK to the Flats, Step's phone dinged with an incoming message. The message, from Victoria, was simple enough: "V+ 3." By the time it came in, she would have erased the outgoing message from her phone.

So: Volkov had arrived from Washington and there were three others with him. Step was aware of a Russian intelligence operation based in San Diego, after the spies had been chased out of the consulate in San Francisco. He'd been asked a half-dozen times to provide minor services to agents going through the LA area— cash, anonymous car rides, on one occasion a pistol, and on another, referral to a doctor who wouldn't ask too many questions and would take payment in cash.

The medical problem had been serious but basically routine— nothing like a wound—but Americans were insured up to their necks, and most doctors didn't deal in cash. But a few did, and Step knew two of them.

THE LIMO DROPPED STEP outside a parking structure in Santa Monica, where he'd left his car, and he drove back to his guesthouse from there. The guesthouse was also in the Beverly Hills Flats, a half mile from the main house.

Volkov always made him anxious. But he could, in the end,

handle Volkov, he thought, and if he couldn't, Victoria certainly could. He was more worried about the mystery of the two crazy chicks and the fat guy.

Though Volkov was bad, it was him and three other men. He, Step, had more men than that and if they weren't exactly GRU quality, they were good enough. With the mystery group, he didn't know what he was dealing with. Getting the entire FBI on his ass, or some other unknown American agency with shooters, would be a problem of a completely different order, because he didn't have more men than the FBI.

He wondered, briefly, what would happen if he got a couple of boys, and they walked through the front door of the guesthouse and killed Volkov and the other three, right there, bam-bam-bam, and then denied ever seeing him? He thought about it, decided it probably wouldn't work. Wouldn't for sure if Volkov had already made a call from the house. But the concept was attractive. Maybe some other time, some other place, after he built an ironclad alibi. Talk first.

VOLKOV WAS A modern-day remnant of the old Soviet Union, a hulking, round-shouldered thug with a bullet head and heavy black eyebrows, and a mouth that naturally turned down in a scowl. He was sitting in the diminutive living room with a glass of iced tea. He wore a dark suit over a black tee-shirt, with poorly polished, blunt-tipped black shoes that looked like weapons, de-signed to kick someone to death. None of his three companions looked like him, but they had a GRU family resemblance, a built-in bull-necked glower, that any Russian civilian would have recog-nized and carefully walked around. Two of them had the kind of dark, well-trimmed beards that looked almost like velvet, or fur. One of them had a glass of iced tea, two had glasses of water.

"Ah, Arseny Denisevich, my old friend," Volkov said when Step walked through the kitchen and into the living room. "You have problems."

"Maybe I have problems," Step said, speaking in Russian. "And maybe you have problems. The newspapers here say you're about to invade Ukraine. I believe you might want to use trains to move your men and material to the front."

"That would be classified as secret," Volkov said. "But, as speculation, I would speculate that you might be correct. You were supposed to handle that potential problem."

Step sank into an easy chair and Victoria handed him a glass of tea, heavy with sugar. "We're merchants. We have to take protective steps to ensure the safety of our merchandise, so we have—we *did* have—the capabilities necessary to do that. We were happy to help the motherland if we could," he said piously. "But in the last few days . . ."

He told the visitors about the elimination of three of the train ransomware creators. He added that the FBI had been all over the men who had done the job and had killed two of them and arrested the third, and that when he sent two more men to take out a fourth train hacker, one of his men had been shot, and the other was in the federal lockup.

Volkov's forehead wrinkled: "How reliable are the men held by the Americans?"

"Very. They know we will get them out as soon as we can. Two were shot and are hospitalized and we are looking at removing them from the hospitals when they are recovered enough to travel, but before they are taken to a prison. We can do that. The other is in a federal lockup, but he did nothing aggressive and we think he will be allowed bail. If he is, we will remove him from the U.S. and return him to Serbia, where he won't be found."

"Why is this happening now?" Volkov asked. "Because of Ukraine?"

"I don't know. There's something going on that we don't know about and that we've never experienced before. I think there's an intelligence operation underway, because these people know cops, but they're not cops, they're shooters."

"CIA," Volkov said. "Maybe DIA. They both have shooters and the FBI wouldn't touch them."

"They don't act like CIA. One of the girls looks and acts like a teenager, all tattooed and seemingly not too intelligent. I've been told that she's a psycho. Threatened to kill another woman while they were sitting at a café table; flashed a pocket gun. They claim to have run a ransomware attack on a hospital in Georgia, and that has checked out. They actually stole computer components from one of my warehouses."

"Mmm."

"So . . . my operation may be infected," Step said. "I'm clean, so far, nobody's come at me. This house is clean, I'm not so sure about the main house. I'm shutting down my export operation for now, until I can find out what is going on. What can I do to help you?"

"You can tell us everything you know. We may still need your help, but we will direct the operations against these people. The train hacking can't happen again, not now. He himself . . ." He pointed at the ceiling, meaning Vladimir Putin, "is watching."

"I understand," Step said. "And you must understand my capabilities have been reduced. But I will do what I can. On my honor."

TWENTY-ONE

Nowak was gone.

Big decisions were being made in Washington and she wanted to be there, both to contribute and to be seen. She ignored a perfectly good shuttle and was picked up by a limo at the front door and disappeared toward LAX. All the way down to the ground floor, in the elevator, she had urged them to gather what they could of Ordinary People and get them working on a train hack.

Before leaving, Nowak had made calls to somebody in Washington, who had made calls to the SkyPort, and the hotel provided them with two suites to be used as communal workrooms, and a block of ten additional rooms that would become available during the day, all on the same floor, no questions asked.

"We're gonna need space," Baxter said. "If we can get these guys in here . . . I hope Able hasn't gone to Vegas . . ."

"Vegas is what, five, six hours from here by car?" Cartwright said. "Shouldn't be a problem. But what do we tell them?"

Baxter looked at Letty, then back at Cartwright. "I'm thinking . . . we really can't tell them the truth. Because of the SlapBack hack. Hackers are basically about moving information, and any information they have will get out. If SlapBack found out the NSA was behind their hack, there'd be a shitstorm."

Letty: "You're right. But: these people are big brains. We'll probably not fool them forever, but as long as they don't know where we're located in the government . . ."

"They could tell us to fuck off," Baxter said.

Letty: "We have those chips. Able knows somebody who'll buy them. We could pay them. Pay them quite a bit, and they'd be doing a good thing that fits with their politics and gets back for Loren Barron and Wolfe and Delph."

Cartwright had crossed her arms, usually a sign of resistance, and was wandering around the room, stopping to look out the windows. They had a clear view of jets taking off and landing at LAX, and they'd all spent time watching.

Letty and Baxter waited for her to say something, and she turned and said, "Another possibility: we're working for a Ukrainian lobby group in DC. We tell them that we got picked up by the feds after the shooting on the dock. They know it was self-defense, but they've got a rope around our necks if they need to yank on it. On the other hand, the feds have agreed to look the other way on the shooting if Ordinary People help us pull down the Russian trains."

Letty: "*And* we pay them. The hackers. We offer to do both things."

Cartwright: "You know what? It's your call, Letty. I'm the consultant, not the boss of us."

Cartwright and Baxter stared at her, waiting, and finally Letty said, "I'll call Sovern. See if he can get here. We'll lay it out for him, like you said, Barb. We got picked up by the cops after the shooting on the dock. We tell them that we don't know what government agency is involved, but it's got a lot of clout. Maybe the Defense Department, maybe the CIA or DHS. Anyway, that agency got us cut loose. The FBI would prefer to put all of us in jail, including him and all the other train hackers, and let the Ukrainians deal with their own problems."

"That's a plan," Cartwright said. "Don't know if it'll work."

"Have to refine it a little . . . but it'll still sound like bullshit," Baxter said.

SOVERN HAD DONE what Letty had half-suspected he might do: he'd left the marina that he was in, and had immediately motored to another, owned by a friend, where he'd gone bow-first into a slip so the name of the boat couldn't be read from the dock. He'd also taken down the wind turbine on the stern, which was distinctive. Of course, the boat itself was distinctive, but only to the knowledgeable; a survey of docks by street cops shouldn't pinpoint it.

Then he settled in to wait for news, monitoring incoming emails from other members of Ordinary People, but not replying to any of them. The other members had all been linked to reports of the death of Loren Barron and Brianna Wolfe, as well as the suspected death of Daniel Delph. They were frightened. There was some talk of fighting back, but against what? And who?

He was cleaning the vanes on the wind turbine, in preparation for storing it out of sight, when Letty called.

"We need to meet with you," she said. "Seriously. About something we haven't talked about. Are you on the water? Can we pick you up somewhere?"

Sovern considered the question, then said, "You can't pick me up, but I could come to you."

To get to the SkyPort, he said, would take two hours. "I have an Uber driver I can call and pay in cash, so there's no credit card record. How bad is it?"

"Talk about it when you get here," Letty said. "We've got the FBI flying around and they're pissed off. With this kind of stuff, I hate to talk on cell phones."

"That's wise. Two hours," Sovern said.

BAXTER WENT TO HIS LAPTOP. Letty and Cartwright walked around the hotel. The place was built for travelers, not vacationers; some would have their own cars, but most would be laying over between flights at LAX. Many of them were airplane crew. The place smelled of swift passages and fast food. The walls were covered with beige vinyl wallpaper, the kind easily cleaned; the carpet was deep red, also an easily cleaned synthetic.

Letty and Cartwright looked at the stairways, calculated the time it took for an elevator to arrive, and then, outside, walked the surrounding blocks, checking for cover, concealment, escape and approach routes. The hotel itself was an undistinguished chunk of concrete and glass, but it was big, and by its very bigness provided some cover. Cars were parked in a three-floor garage at the base of the hotel.

Letty hadn't done that kind of reconnaissance before, not with Cartwright's thoroughness.

On the street, Cartwright said, "Always make sure you check up high, even higher than you think is necessary. Everybody has hands-free cell phones, and a spotter up high can kill you if he's talking to somebody on the ground. Nowadays, you're not fighting in two dimensions; in the cities, you're fighting in three."

World War I pilots, in open planes, she said, wore silk scarves as a kind of anti-chafing lubrication because they were trained to constantly turn their heads, looking for enemy aircraft in all directions, back, forward, above, and below. "In a serious threat situation, you sorta have to do that, without being too obvious about it."

"Got it," Letty said. She later realized that she kept forgetting to do it; the difference between understanding the theory and putting it into practice.

SOVERN SHOWED UP at the hotel three hours after the phone call, an hour later than he'd predicted, because his Uber contact had been busy. Letty, Cartwright, and Baxter were all impatient for the talk and the wait had them snapping at each other. Sovern called Letty from the lobby, asking for the room number, and when he stepped off the elevator, Letty waved him down the hall.

He was dressed in a green tee-shirt under a nylon rain jacket, with neat olive-drab nylon cargo pants and boat shoes with non-marking white soles. Inside the suite, he looked around, then said, "You don't look like the types who'd pay for suites."

"We're not," Letty said. "A government's paying."

"You're feds?"

Letty shook her head and began unloading the story they'd been working on. "Barbara and I work for a security company in Washington. The company does work for a lobbying firm. And the lobbying firm has Ukraine as one of its clients . . . They've been in the news a little, you could look them up."

"Uh-oh," Sovern said.

"Yeah. Ukraine is paying," Letty said hastily. "We rounded up Paul here; he works as a freelance programmer in the DC area, and we were sent out to find you guys. Ordinary People. Ukraine would like you to mess with the Russian trains again, if you can."

Sovern nodded: "I thought it might be something like that. Especially after I looked at her, down at the marina." He nodded at Cartwright. "Though I thought she might be a fed."

Letty: "You don't think Paul and I look like feds?"

"You look like you get carded everywhere you go, and Paul doesn't exactly fit my image of a combat-ready law enforcement officer," Sovern said.

"I'm not," Baxter said. "I do have that PhD from Florida. I kill on machine control software, but I don't jump out of airplanes."

"I *know* about the Russian train hack, but from what I've heard, everything was done by remote control," Sovern said, not ready to admit anything. "No fingerprints on anything. The hackers were very, very careful. Anyway, that's all water under the bridge. The question now is, what do you want? Will it get any more of us killed? The dead people were my best friends."

"Everybody needs to sit down," Letty said. They all sat. She said, "Here's the truth: the FBI wants to arrest us, and you, and your friends, if they could find a way to do it . . ."

She went on to spin the story about a powerful agency in Washington interfering with the FBI; about being held by the Oxnard cops, about her security agency getting in touch with the powers in Washington, about the FBI showing up to interrogate them, and about being kicked free with the implicit deal that they all go after the trains.

"If we do that, we're good. You're good. Nobody will come after us. The FBI will be told to shut up and sit down, because we'd all have a story to tell, about how the feds let us go specifically so we could mess with Russia. The feds don't want anyone saying that. Especially not, like, in a courtroom, with our attorneys subpoenaing Washington power brokers."

Cartwright: "Bottom line, what they want is to stop the trains in Russia when Russia invades Ukraine."

"Is Russia going to do that? For sure?"

"Yes. Sometime very soon," Cartwright said. "I thought it might be today, but it's already evening in Ukraine and nobody's moved."

"Somebody here in the U.S., we're told, probably the CIA or the NSA, has been looking down Putin's chimney and he's made the call," Baxter said. "They're going in and Ukraine will fight back. Best estimates are that Kyiv goes down in a week. One U.S. general thinks it might take the Russians a month to swamp the whole country."

They laid out everything that Nowak had told them, along with a few suppositions. Letty concluded with "Your friend Loren Barron was from Ukraine and that may be why they killed him. They killed Brianna Wolfe because she was with him and a witness. The Russians were worried that even after they'd paid, Loren would go back after the train system again, because he was Ukrainian."

Sovern, sitting on a bed, was nodding. "Going after the trains will be complicated. After the big hack, they probably reworked their whole control system . . ."

"They couldn't," Baxter said. "Too much legacy hardware is involved. They would have had to pay billions to upgrade it and Ukraine sees no sign that they've done that. What they would have done is put more security controls on the software you hacked. Might be hell getting through that, but still—with that legacy hardware, there are limits to what they could do."

Sovern looked at Baxter: "Right. You're machine controls." He rubbed his face, popped his knuckles, then asked, "What are you proposing?"

"That you get the train-hacking people together again, here in this hotel, and you hack the Russian trains in a way that doesn't look like it came from an official U.S. source. Maybe make it the 'Loren Barron Memorial Hack.' Make it look like it's revenge for killing Barron."

"The people are scared," Sovern said.

"That's why Barb and I are here," Letty told him. "You saw that on the dock."

"You shoot people," Sovern said.

Cartwright: "We can. We've got two suites up here as a workspace, and a bunch of rooms and good wi-fi. You bring in the team that did the trains. Go in for another look, see what can be done."

"I'd want a room of my own," Sovern said. "Computer people can be messy and I have a hard time with that."

"Done," Letty said.

"I'll start making calls," Sovern said. "I need seven people. I'm not sure all of them will be willing to go along, but I need them. I need Paul to work with us. One of the women I need is fluent in Russian and a decent coder, too. If I can't get her, we'll have to find another Russian speaker."

"I'll call my agency," Letty said. "With our Ukraine contacts, shouldn't be a problem."

Sovern slapped his thighs, stood up. "Nothing will happen before tomorrow or the next day, when we get the people here with their computers and we talk ourselves through the approach and start fiddling around with the Russian systems."

"Sooner the better," Letty said. "We're running out of time."

"Do it as fast as I can, but we won't know how fast that will be, until we get the people here," Sovern said. He looked over at Cartwright: "In the meantime, when I've done what I can today . . . Barb, you want to go out for a drink or two tonight? You know, before the trouble starts?"

Letty: "Hey, wait a minute . . ."

Cartwright: "Yeah, I could do that."

THEY SHOWED SOVERN his room and gave him a key; Letty kept one key for herself without mentioning it. He set up his laptop, opened a file, and began making phone calls. They left him to it.

Baxter wanted to go back to his laptop and left for his own room. Letty said to Cartwright, "So you got a date tonight. You're what, taking care of him? Making sure he's not up to something?"

Cartwright said, "I'm pretty sure he's up to something, but it doesn't have anything to do with computers or the Russians. In the meantime, I gotta run out. I'd like at least one outfit that's, you know, datable."

"Ah, God. Barbara . . ."

"You know how long it's been since I've been out with somebody who's really good-looking and smart and who wasn't carrying three guns and a switchblade? I'm gonna have a good time. You think he dances?"

"He's a computer nerd, so probably not," Letty said. "But you'll take three guns and a knife with you?"

"Well, yeah."

DELORES NOWAK ARRIVED in Washington and called Letty from the airport: "Progress report?"

"We have Sovern here in the hotel. He wants to bring in seven people in addition to Rod, to do the work."

"Stay in touch," Nowak said.

Cartwright talked Baxter into giving her a ride to where they'd left the Hertz rental. He did that, and she drove away to find something that didn't come in camo or khaki, and shoes not made for running. Baxter returned to his laptop.

Letty spent the time worrying, then found out she could stream the old *Justified* series on the room television and sank into a chair and vegged until Sovern knocked on the door.

"I got all seven. I had to sell them a little, but we've got our Russian speaker and six more criminals willing to help." He smiled. "Makes me happy, working together again. We can do this."

And he looked around the room: "Where's Barb?"

"She went to find something she called a 'datable outfit,' and isn't back yet."

"Great. Hope she dances," Sovern said.

"She hopes *you* dance," Letty said. "It's kinda disgusting."

"Dancing, or dating?"

"Both, while I sit here and watch old TV shows," Letty said.

"Well, you could come along," he said. "We could all dance and then come back to the hotel and make a Sovern sandwich."

"That's disturbing," Letty said. "Go back to your room. I don't want to look at you."

Sovern left. He really was disconcertingly good-looking, Letty thought.

As Cartwright was shopping, Baxter browsing the Internet, and Letty vegging on streamed TV shows, Tom Boyadjian was working on his putting stroke on an eight-foot-long practice green/rug at the back of his office in Century City.

Boyadjian was fully aware that a half-dozen of his best clients were criminals, Eastern European or Balkan. Another thirty or so were legitimate corporate accounts, where his operators looked into a variety of corporate-based mis-, mal-, and nonfeasance. He referred more complicated problems, like international corporate espionage, to a larger firm, for a modest kickback on the eventual fee.

When the FBI came through the door, late in the afternoon, and in unnecessary numbers, he was ready. The receptionist, to whom he was married, though she kept her maiden name, hit six keys and Enter on her computer as soon as she saw them at the locked glass doors, and was slow to open them.

As soon as the alarm came in, Boyadjian, whose office was at the back of a deliberate rat's maze of smaller offices and rooms, went to his computer, called up an executable file, and executed it. Encrypted warnings were automatically sent out to clients who would not be calling him again unless he called them first, and their contact information was erased. The file then erased all connections to a specific subscription to the Microsoft cloud, which backed up everything in the computer.

By the time the feds reached his office, all signs of the executable file were gone and Boyadjian was back at the putting green. He didn't have to worry about being trapped by forensic accountants, because his deals with the six off-the-book clients were cash-based. When the lead fed came through his office door, he looked up, surprised, and asked, "Who the hell are you?" and when he was told, he asked, "What do you want?"

They wanted his computers. They gave him a warrant and took them.

They were also looking for Lawrence and Martin, who, Boyadjian told them, had decided to take long-delayed trekking vacations and probably wouldn't be back for weeks. They had, he told the feds, gone to Nunavut, where they hoped to spy the rock ptarmigan to add to their life lists as dedicated birders.

The feds didn't believe him, and they were right not to.

ARSENY STEPASHIN GOT the warning and called Volkov, who was staying at the Peninsula Hotel, not far from Step's guesthouse. "We've lost our surveillance asset at least temporarily," he said, in Russian. "The FBI is raiding him right now."

"More evidence that the Americans are doing something . . . complicated, cooperating with these hackers," Volkov said. "Will they jump from your asset to you?"

"No. I warned him not to keep records of our relationship and I believe he complied, for both our sakes. His difficulty, though, becomes our difficulty, since I have no other way to gather the intelligence we need to spot the hacking group."

"Then I'll give you some intelligence," Volkov said. "This just came in from upstairs, after I requested help. The day that Loren Barron was killed, he made a number of calls to a Benjamin Able. Able also made a call to Barron just a few minutes after he was killed. The Able person, I'm told, is a computer hacker. We need to find him. We are also looking for this Craig Sovern."

"With my asset gone . . ."

"We have other assets. One of them is the license plate reader system used by the Los Angeles Police Department. We are inside it and we are watching for Able's license plates."

Step did a quick calculation—always good to hold back information that can be used later, when needed, and he'd done that—and said, "That license plate thing . . . I have two more names for you: Michele Obermath and William Orleans." He spelled the names. "I'm not one hundred percent sure of the connection, but they may be involved."

"This is good. As soon as we start tracking them, you need to be ready to move."

"You prefer using my men?"

"For now. For reconnaissance. They're familiar with Los Angeles. Mine have more limited uses, after we find the people we're looking for."

TWENTY-TWO

Cartwright came back with a shopping bag of datable clothing—nothing spectacular, a short green dress that picked up on her eyes and showed off her legs, a light linen jacket to conceal her gun, linen shoes that went with the jacket, a leather clutch purse just big enough for her ID, her federal carry permit, her phone, and a credit card.

"I am going to have a good time and I haven't had a good time in a long time," she told Letty and Baxter. "Don't wait up for me."

Letty went back to season 4, episode 9, of *Justified*. That was about as much as she could take, and she clicked over to CNN, where she found the full set of talking heads jumping up and down: the Russians had invaded Ukraine.

And she said, "Ohhh . . . no."

Letty watched for the rest of the evening, although relevant information was sparse—not that the sparseness made much difference to the talking heads, who interviewed a selection of retired generals and retired intelligence bureaucrats, who knew almost nothing but were willing to speculate endlessly.

Still, it felt like a historic moment. When Cartwright hadn't shown up by one o'clock in the morning and the information from Ukraine didn't seem to be improving in quality, she went to bed. When she got up at eight, Cartwright's bed was still empty. Cartwright finally showed up at nine o'clock, looking wrung out. She said, "I feel like a chippy."

"There's a word I haven't heard since, oh, about the nineteenth century," Letty said.

"Well, it was worth it," Cartwright said.

"Really?"

"Oh, yeah. I don't have to worry about sex for at least six months. Maybe eight."

"Where's Sovern? Is he still alive?" Letty asked.

"He's fine, but he doesn't talk in the morning," Cartwright said. "He says he'll be over when the first people start coming in."

"What do you think about Ukraine?"

"What about Ukraine?"

Letty, open-mouthed: "Jesus, Barb . . ."

"Don't tell me I missed it," Cartwright said, fists on her hips. "I haven't seen a television since yesterday afternoon . . ."

Letty picked up a remote and turned on the TV. "Watch," she said. "Europe's got a full-scale ground war."

THE CODERS BEGAN ARRIVING before noon, dragging duffels and roller bags and bulging computer packs. Everybody was talking about the war, and cranked up every television they had access to, to watch the Russians turn apartment houses into smoking ruins. Prime-time war; almost as good as *Iron Man*.

And most were fascinated by the jets taking off and landing down below their windows.

William, who Letty had met at Poggers, brought his girlfriend, Melody. Sovern came over to greet them, bumped knuckles with William, without enthusiasm on either side. When William and Melody went to settle in, Letty asked, "You guys aren't great friends?"

"Not really, but he's a good coder. Clean and fast," Sovern said.

"What's the problem?" Baxter asked, looking up from the floor, where he was poking on a laptop.

"I had a little thing with Melody once," Sovern said.

"Were Melody and William together at the time?" Letty asked.

"Yes."

"It's not a hacker combine, it's a fucking soap opera, with an emphasis on the fucking, except for me, of course," Baxter said. To Cartwright: "You ought to sleep with William. Or Melody. To round out the drama."

"Shut the fuck up," Cartwright said.

"Just sayin'," Baxter said. He went back to his laptop.

DURING THE AFTERNOON, coders named Justin and Jared, Michele and Catrin, showed up, moving into rooms reserved by Nowak. Justin brought his wife and young daughter, Catrin brought her rescue dog, Spot. Benjamin Able came in, bringing a Stratocaster and a travel amp, with Jan, the bass player. "We need to get your drums out of the truck and into my room," Able told Letty. "Gonna be a lot of stress to work through."

Before the coders showed up, Letty had a clichéd idea of what the group would look like, but they didn't look like that: they looked like graduate students or junior faculty, casually dressed, hair longer than corporate but shorter than musician, and Jared and Catrin were obvious jocks who had both run marathons.

The hotel's eighth floor quickly turned into something that resembled an out-of-town trip by a high school sports team. Justin's daughter got loose in a hallway and had to be chased down before she got in the elevator. And she screamed, purposefully and apparently experimentally, seeing how high-pitched, and how loud, a scream she could produce. Justin's wife kept apologizing, and everybody told her it was just a kid, no need to apologize, but as the screams continued through the afternoon, the coders stopped telling her that.

Catrin's German shepherd got loose more than once, romping up and down the hallway, her barks as loud and cheerful as the young girl's screams. She was in and out of all the rooms, including the room of a guest not related to the hacking group; at one point, two of the hackers got down on their knees and began howling like wolves. The dog looked at them with interest, and eventually joined in, until others in the room began shouting at them to stop.

In between chases and screams and dog-howling, and the general milling around, the group moved chairs and tables from other suites to the working rooms and set up computers.

When they were satisfied, Sovern got them together and said, "Everybody, this is Charlie and Paul. They need to tell you some things that I already knew but didn't mention when I called you."

Able: "Is this gonna be bad?"

"Depends on your perspective, but basically, I'd say no," Sovern said. "In fact, it could turn out to be an opportunity for people willing to work it."

Letty stood up and began, "We're avoiding the FBI. That's key fact number one. If any of you are informants, please hold up your hand."

There was a little laughter, but not much. Letty then told them the story they'd told to Sovern. One of them, Michele, asked, "How do we know you're not the CIA?"

Letty smiled: "There's no straight answer to that. I mean, we could be, I guess. But I'm not, anyway. We need all of you to stay, because we need your brains and talents, but if somebody wants to walk away, we won't try to stop you."

Sovern stepped in to talk about the shooting in the marina: "There's some risk, but Charlie and Barbara can handle that, I believe. You can walk away, but if the Russians have your names, then your risk is greater than if you stay, because you won't have Charlie and Barbara protecting you. If it weren't for them, I'd be dead now."

Benjamin Able said, "These guys found, got, stole, I dunno, six boxes of 5.5-gig Intel chips. Carl the Dealer gave me a hundred thousand for the box I got, and Charlie and Paul have five more . . ."

"Which you all can have, if you stay," Baxter said.

"If Carl the Dealer buys them from you, and if Ben chips in the cash he already got, that's six hundred K to divide up . . . if you stay," Letty said.

"Carl wants them," Able said. "He'll pay cash."

"This whole program is off the books," Cartwright said. "You get cash, and you can take it anywhere you want. We don't want the Russians to pinpoint where this problem comes from, who's involved, or where they are."

"Don't they already know?" Jared asked.

"They know some stuff, but we don't know how much. If they

attempt to interfere with this group, they will be warned off," Letty said. "Somebody higher up in government will pretend to know nothin' about nothin' about Ordinary People, except that Russian spies aren't allowed to attack loyal Americans on their own soil."

When Letty, Baxter, and Cartwright were done, Sovern asked them to leave the suite so the coders could discuss what they wanted to do. The three of them went to Letty and Cartwright's room and sat around until Sovern came in and said, simply, "Done deal. They're all staying. They want the cash."

Baxter: "I'm gonna get hurt. I'm gonna get hurt, aren't I?"

Letty: "You keep asking, but we already know the answer to that. I just hope I'm not, you know, what do you call it?" She looked at Cartwright.

"Collateral damage?"

"Yeah, that's what you call it."

Sovern said, "When you're done with the repartee, we need three heavy-duty office-quality printers, preferably Canon, but we'll take HP. Plus two ten-ream cartons of printer paper, and three cartons wouldn't be a bad idea. We'll need backup ink for all the printers, because the starter cartridges last for about fifteen seconds. We need it all now."

Cartwright to Letty: "At least one of us has to stay. Be better if both of us stayed."

Letty: "Paul has a credit card and a truck."

Sovern said to Baxter, "You might need a dolly to move it all if the hotel doesn't have one. That's heavy stuff. Don't be fussy or cheap, though. Buy good quality. I've got a seven-hundred-and-fifty-page document that I need to print immediately and I'll need at least eight copies, one for everybody."

"I'm on it," Baxter said. Turning to Letty, he said, "Let's get Able and haul your drums and the chip boxes out of the truck. I'll need the space. Able can come along to help carry the heavy stuff."

When the drums and chips were in Able's room, and Baxter and Able were on their way to an office supply store, Letty went back to the work suites, where the hackers and their friends had gathered.

The coders were both articulate and argumentative, and sitting around the suites, waiting for direction, didn't restrict themselves to talk about an attack on the Russian rail system. They talked about the morality of the attack, who would win the British football championship, about Windows vs. Mac vs. Linux vs. Chrome, about abortion rights, about zero-day attacks, about whether Antifa actually existed, about computer kids exploiting phony TikTok links to get nude photos of other kids in their schools.

A middle-aged woman named Emilija—Emmy—a longtime friend of Sovern's and a native of Lithuania, not only spoke perfect Russian, but was expert at both the social engineering of Russian males and spear phishing. She had worked closely with Loren Barron on the original attack on the Russian train system.

Ordinary phishing—"This is to alert you that your Wells Fargo bank account has been suspended as a security measure. You should *immediately* sign on to your account at the link below, using your current username and password, and change your password. The new password should contain at least nine letters, numbers, and symbols . . ."—involved sending out thousands of fake emails in the hopes that certain numbers of people would sign on to what they thought was their Wells Fargo account but was actually delivering their name and password to a hacker.

Spear phishing, on the other hand, usually involved a single victim, or a very small group of victims, carefully chosen and researched, in an effort to get specific bites of information. Emilija would be spear phishing members of the Russian rail bureaucracy, looking for entries into the computer system.

"Getting information was easy the first time. I don't think it will be so easy this time, with the war," Emilija said. "Fucking Russians."

"Then what are you thinking of?" Sovern asked Emilija.

She shrugged. "Many of these trainmen . . . they have bad work shifts. Lonely. In the dark, by themselves. Nothing but a *Penthouse* magazine. They might be interested in talking with attractive young women. Especially if they're naked."

"Could they be that naïve?" Letty asked.

Emilija rolled her eyes. "These might be men working in switching stations. This is not a job for geniuses. What harm can there be in talking to a naked young woman who only wants your friendship? Not even your money?"

"Where do we get a naked woman?" Letty asked.

"There are several possibilities in the group here," Emilija said. "Including you. I could talk in the background . . ."

"No. Nope. Not even to stop the war," Letty said.

Emilija shrugged. "Another possibility, we could phish for a Ukrainian working with the trains—there are many of them. You would need a Ukrainian speaker. I'm not one. Russian and Ukrainian are similar, but not the same."

Sovern turned to Letty: "Call up your lobbyist and tell him to get a Ukrainian out here."

"I can try," Letty said.

"A Ukrainian con woman," Emilija said. "Naked would be good."

Letty called Nowak, who said she'd see what she could do, but thought it would be best if they limited their contacts over the next few days. "We all know where we're at, but a minimal back-trail would be good. People are a back-trail, including your unlikely naked Ukrainian."

Cartwright, who'd listened to the conversation, said, after Nowak had rung off, "They're starting to worry about what will happen if somebody has a problem with all this—the hacking. It's the denial thing again, with a twist. They want to be able to deny knowledge of what we're doing out here, if they have to."

Letty tried to call Senator Colles about it, but his executive assistant, Claudia Welp, said Colles was on an airplane and was out of touch for a while.

"We're on our own," Cartwright said. She looked around the suite, where the hacks were poking at laptops, arguing with each other, eating salads that somebody had gone out for. "Don't tell anyone."

When Baxter and Able got back, the male coders trooped down to the lobby to help unload and haul the boxed printers, paper, ink sets, and loose packages of USB cords, report covers, Post-its, three-ring hole punchers, ink-gel pens, and a microwave oven.

Baxter also bought three Lenovo laptops in case they needed to do either work or browsing from anonymous machines that later would be disposable. Letty tipped the bellhop a hundred dollars and when everybody was back inside the linked suites, they began unboxing the printers and tearing open the clamshell packages of other gear.

When they had the printers operating, with USB cords striping the carpet between laptops and printers, Sovern gathered the group and held up an orange flash drive and said, "This is a record and a kind of manual on our hack of the Russian trains. A lot will have changed, but it'll be something of a map. I'm going to start printing these things out and you'll all have your own copy to look at and thumb through and mark up. I'm thinking we'll do that the rest of the day, and tomorrow we'll start looking at the Russians, seeing what's been changed, and what still works."

Emilija, the social engineer, said, "I need help locating targets. Can I subcontract this to my friends in Vilnius? Or is that out-of-bounds?"

Letty: "I don't know about computers. If Sovern and Paul say it's okay, then do it."

Baxter and Sovern agreed that it was okay, but she'd use one of Baxter's virgin laptops for all her contacts, and they'd buy a VPN, charging it to the company Visa card, to anonymize the source.

"We're rolling," Sovern reported to Letty. "You think you guys could rip up all the boxes and packing and get it out of here? Looking at the trash is driving me crazy."

MUCH OF THE TIME that afternoon and evening was taken up by the printing and binding of Sovern's road map for the hack. The bound volumes were distributed as they came out of the printers, each more than seven hundred pages of heavily commented programming text.

At eight o'clock that night, Cartwright said to Letty, "Why don't you take the first shift? From now until three o'clock. I'll come on at three. We need to wander the halls. We need to find a Coke machine, a candy machine, anything that will give us an excuse to be walking around out there, and riding the elevators."

"What are you going to do?" Letty asked.

"I'm gonna make sure that Craig is relaxed and ready to focus tomorrow," she said.

"I can't even get a fuckin' date and you're relaxing the best-looking guy in Los Angeles," Letty said.

"And you *need* a date, sister," Cartwright said. "I'll see you at three."

Letty walked the hallways, carrying an untapped bottle of Diet Coke, trying to look like she was on her way somewhere else. She heard faint laughter from a couple of rooms, neither of them housing Ordinary People. Somebody dropped what sounded like a metal bowl in another room, the clatter followed by what was probably muffled curses. Then Colles called.

"I thought you were stepping away," Letty said. "I got the feeling that Delores was cutting us loose."

"Everybody's stepping back to reduce governmental visibility," Colles said. "Nobody knows I'm talking to you, by the way, not even Welp. I bought a prepaid burner from a valet here in Miami, but it's only got twelve minutes of talk time left. Call if you need to; I'll keep the phone in my pocket. If some kind of shit hits the fan, I'll back you guys up. Try not to let too much shit hit the fan. This isn't the Pershing Bridge and you won't be going on television."

"All right. Well, we're working here, and we're lying to everybody," Letty said. "I don't know if we can pull it off, but . . . we're working on it."

"Good. I've sent you a gift I extorted from DHS. You should get it in the morning. I can tell you this much, Letty: the national security advisor says 'hello.' He talks to the President on an hourly basis. I hope you appreciate that."

"Are *you* going to run for president?"

Colles laughed. "Now I've got ten minutes left. Call me if you need me. And . . . who knows? Maybe. I've got the hair and teeth for it."

TWENTY-THREE

Cartwright showed up at three in the morning, right on time. Letty hadn't seen anything even vaguely suspicious. "You awake?" she asked Cartwright.

"Yup. I'm fine. I got five hours," Cartwright said. "Don't mess around, get in bed. You probably ought to set your alarm for nine. Tomorrow's gonna be busy."

Tired from the day, and from the stress of the night before, Letty was asleep within a couple of minutes of dropping in bed. She slept through until nine o'clock, hurriedly showered and dressed, and walked down the hall to the work suite.

Most of the coders were there, jeans and tee-shirts, both men and women, either reading the red-bound road map volumes, marking them up as they went, adding Post-its, or poking at computers. The television, muted, was on MSNBC, which was wall-to-wall

Ukraine. Baxter was there and working, and when he saw Letty, he said, "FedEx for you over on the windowsill."

The return address on the box said "Colles," and when she opened it, she found four handset two-way radios, smaller than iPhones, boxed, with instructions for use, and a handwritten note that said "Much better and faster than cell phones. Try them out."

When she showed them to Cartwright, the other woman said, "You guys get the *best* stuff. I got to try them in training and they're great, but we never got any in the field. I was told they were good for a mile. Fully scrambled."

Baxter had ordered up food. Letty got a strawberry yogurt and then she and Cartwright worked out a patrol plan that covered both the hallways around the work suites and the exterior around the hotel. They tried the radios from Colles, which worked well, and were fast.

"One thing you oughta know," Cartwright said. "If these Russians are a bunch of gangsters, okay, that's not a problem. The guys we took on the dock probably bought their weapons here, across the counter. Or somebody bought the guns for them. If we run into guys from the GRU or the FSB . . . they tend to like Israeli Mini Uzis. Import them in their diplomatic pouches. They will send twenty rounds downrange in one second. Literally: one second. I mean, they will light you up."

"How do you deal with that?"

"You gotta see them coming," Cartwright said. "Don't see them coming, you're toast."

Letty unconsciously slipped her 938 from her jeans pocket and clicked the safety on and off, until Cartwright, looking at the gun, asked, "Do you know what you're doing there?"

"I'm willing to patrol, but you know what?" Letty asked, slip-ping the gun back into her pocket. "You and I aren't enough. We need more people."

"Talk to Delores Nowak. Get that Kaiser guy out here."

"Kaiser would work as the last-ditch guy, inside the hotel, but not so much on patrol—he's too visible," Letty said. "He looks like a soldier. Can't help it. He's the first guy they'd try to ambush."

"Might have some deterrent effect," Cartwright said.

"I don't want to sound stupid, but . . . do you think a couple of the Ladies might help out?"

Cartwright looked away, raked her lower lip with her teeth: "Could, not a bad idea," she said, after a minute. "With women . . . the Russians wouldn't see them coming. If we could get Jane Long-street. And Patty Bunker. Jane is a federal employee, Patty does contract security work, you'd have to pay her."

Letty shrugged, thought about the cash they'd taken out of Loren Barron's behind-the-photo hideout and the boxes of chips taken from the warehouse. "We can pay her. We're gonna sell those chips. Is Longstreet in the Unspecified Agency?"

Cartwright shook her head. "No. She's ATF. I bet if your sena-tor asked for her in just the right way, the ATF would send her out here."

"I'm gonna ask them," Letty said. "You patrol, I'm gonna make some calls."

LETTY CALLED COLLES, asked that Kaiser and Jane Longstreet be briefed and sent to LA. "Longstreet's an investigator with the ATF, but it's actually Alcohol, Tobacco, Firearms and *Explosives*, and since we had hand grenades used out here, we think they might agree to send her. We're asking for her by name. Kaiser, of course . . ."

"I'll get you Kaiser for sure and ask for this Longstreet," Colles said. "Should have them by tonight."

Patty Bunker wasn't working that day. When Letty explained the situation, she said she would catch a plane to LAX. Letty didn't know her well but remembered her as a chubby dark-haired woman with a tendency toward overbright red lipstick and over-sized plastic handbags, in which she kept large-frame revolvers. Though armed, she specialized in surveillance and surveillance technology.

With the arrangements made, Letty asked Baxter about the cash from Loren Barron's house, and he grumbled something about how he'd hoped nobody would remember it. He agreed to give it up to pay Bunker.

"Nineteen grand and change. Seems like a lot."

"You wouldn't have any use for it anyway, since you're gonna get killed," Letty said.

"You got me there," Baxter said. "Now go away. I'm reading."

He was reading a jumble of text, numbers, and symbols that shouldn't make sense to anyone, but apparently did to him. "By the way," he said, as she turned away, "SlapBack is up again. They claim they were taken down by Antifa."

"They were," Letty said. "You and me are about as anti-fascist as they come."

He nodded: "Yeah, when you think about it."

Kaiser called: "I'm loading up. What do you want me to bring? I'm thinking M4, the 870, maybe a couple of flash-bangs . . ."

"Body armor . . ."

After talking to Kaiser, Letty found Able in the next suite and asked him about the sale of the computer chips. "We're gonna need the cash and we'll need to take a little off the top, to pay for protection," she told him. "Not much; just a little."

"I talked to Carl, he'll need a couple of days' notice to take them all—time to gather up cash. He'll be brokering sales to other people around the country."

"Pretty much a straightforward criminal, then, a fence," Letty said.

"He's not the only criminal around here," Able said. "I'm looking at you, Charlie, or whatever the fuck your real name is."

"Get the cash," Letty said.

VICTORIA AND STEP were also talking about money.

They kept their savings in investment funds, under corporate names; not enough in any one of them to be noticeable, but then, they were invested in seventeen separate funds. Victoria was busy transferring them to similar funds in Switzerland, while Step and his employees were bundling hardware—chips, computer workstations, high-speed printers—and packing it as carefully as they could into shipping containers.

Step rented four warehouses under four separate corporate names but was now afraid to use any of them. Instead, he had moved all of his current merchandise into semi-trailers, which he kept moving until it was time to transfer the merchandise into containers.

Simple enough to command, tougher to actually get done. The equipment, all electronic, was delicate and moisture sensitive and so had to be packed carefully. He was working in the Port of Long

Beach when Volkov called: "I have spoken to the manager, and he says he has a location for the packages we are missing. They're all at the same place."

Translated: GRU computer specialists had been into the LAPD's license plate tracking computer and had followed the known rail hackers to a single location.

"Where are you now?" Step asked.

"I'm visiting with Vickie. We're having tea. Whenever you can get here, we'll be waiting."

"On the way," Step said.

VOLKOV WAS VISIBLY PLEASED with himself. After Step's implied incompetence in getting two men killed, two shot, and one arrested while eliminating only two rail hackers—Brianna Wolfe wasn't actually a programmer—he and his Moscow associates had located the hacker combine in less than a full day.

"Now, we need specifics. They are at the SkyPort hotel, at the airport," Volkov said. "We rely on you to determine exactly where—which rooms. We have penetrated the reservation system, but the coding within the system is crazy. So: we need to know about access, opposition, parking, how many there are. When we know that, in detail, my men will attend to them."

"Good, good," Step said. "However, you know that they have shooters as well. It may not be so easy to get at them."

"We can handle it—we have the tools to hit hard and then get out," Volkov said. "If we have to scramble some eggs, we can do that."

"We will start looking . . . very carefully and perhaps a little slowly," Step told him. "If we've actually located this nest, we don't want to push them into flight."

"Not too slowly," Volkov said. "We don't need the trains confused again. The army is moving swiftly to Kyiv, but as the trail grows longer, the logistical support must move closer."

"How long before it's over?"

"A week, perhaps, they are saying now. I think perhaps . . . two weeks? The exact time depends on some weather conditions . . . A storm is organizing in the north. We're not yet able to predict its exact path and impact."

"Then it will be cold and the fighting will be difficult," Step said. "I know this weather."

"The weather will mostly affect the air arm," Volkov said. "When it clears, the cold won't matter—we'll crush the Ukrainians. The worst of the storm will be over in three to five days, no more. There won't be much exposure."

"God bless the army; I wish them every success," Step said.

WHEN VOLKOV HAD GONE, but before Step had decided how to conduct the reconnaissance at the SkyPort, Victoria asked, "Do you think he's right about the army? A week?"

Step shook his head. "I was a draftee, so I saw it from the bottom. I thought I knew corruption, but in the army, it was a different dimension. Nothing worked. Anything of quality was stolen. Including food and clothing. Weapons. Trucks. Anything. From my base, we couldn't drive into town in a week. It would be faster to walk. In my opinion, there is a very good chance that the army will have its Russian ass handed to it. Except . . ."

"Except?"

"The Ukraine army is possibly as corrupt as the Russian, hard as that is to believe. Maybe they will both have their asses handed to themselves."

"You need to get some people over to the SkyPort," Victoria said. "Who will you send?"

"Still thinking about that. My boys are truck loaders or muscle, not spies," Step said. "We need Tom Boyadjian now. I don't know . . . I can call him, but he might not answer. Did the FBI get his burners? I don't know."

"Well, don't call from here," Victoria said. "While you do that, I'll move the Vanguard account to Zurich."

WHEN STEP CALLED Tom Boyadjian's burner, Boyadjian said four words: "Door whore in one," and he hung up.

The bar-restaurant was called the Morning Glory, but the hostess at the front desk, whose name was Millie, had once referred to herself, while waiting on Step and Boyadjian, as "just another door whore."

By "one," Step assumed that Boyadjian would be there in an hour. Boyadjian lived in an area called Hancock Park and the Morning Glory was about halfway between there and the Flats. They would both have time to check for surveillance before they met.

Step drove back to the guesthouse, took twenty thousand dollars in fifty-dollar bills from a hatbox under the bed, thought about it, added another five, kissed Victoria, who was out of Vanguard and was now closing out a Fidelity account, and headed for the bar.

Boyadjian was waiting, a tall, thick man, balding, heavily tanned from golf, wearing a Polo shirt and a gold Rolex. He was morosely stirring a Bloody Mary with a celery stalk.

Step asked, "You're clean?"

"I'm clean; it's my business to be clean. If I still have a business."

A waiter came over and Step pointed at Boyadjian's Bloody Mary and said, "One of those. Bring some salt and pepper."

When the waiter had gone, Boyadjian said, "Your job has me seriously screwed up. I got the FBI like fleas, they're looking for the boys who were watching those shooter girls."

"I'm moving my business," Step said. "I don't know when I'll be back."

"Too bad," Boyadjian said. "This whole railroad thing turned out to be a killer."

They talked about business damage and the possibilities for recovery, then the waiter returned with the Bloody Mary and packets of salt and pepper, which Step sprinkled in the drink. That done, the waiter gone, Step took the envelope out of his jacket pocket and pushed it across the table. "Twenty-five thousand, cash. That will pay all of my bills, with ten thousand extra."

Boyadjian nodded, put the money in his own jacket. "You're a good man, Arseny. I hate to see you go away."

"I'll be back. New name, new company, same Victoria," Step said. "But . . . I know that some of your employees are not carried on your books. I was wondering if you still connect to them. If they might be interested in a good-paying surveillance job."

"What have you got?"

"We're hunting the same people. We know where they're at, the hotel, but not the rooms, not how many, we don't know about protection or movement, where they might go, what they're doing."

Boyadjian leaned back, took a sip of the Bloody Mary, licked his lower lip, said, "Something might be done. We'd have to be very careful. Be expensive."

"Paid in cash, you know I'm good for it," Step said.

Boyadjian took another sip, said, "I know a woman who does real estate in Dallas. Used to be a cop. I could bring her out on a business trip, check her into the hotel . . ."

"Have to be soon," Step said.

"Probably get her here tonight," Boyadjian said.

Step held up his hands: "Do what you need. I will drop you the cash."

They nodded, sipped their Bloody Marys, looked at their Rolexes.

LETTY AND CARTWRIGHT PATROLLED. They saw nothing. The coders were getting antsy, didn't want to spend all day cooped up in the hotel, but Baxter and Sovern talked them down. The television continued to show videos of destroyed apartment buildings in Ukraine.

Letty asked for a brief, English-language description of what the hacks were doing and Sovern tried to explain.

Russian boxcars, he said, all had individual identifying numbers. The numbers were contained in transponders on the side of each car. Destination rail yards, and switching yards, had trackside readers, which read the numbers from the transponders as each car passed the reader. The numbers were then sent electronically to a central switchyard computer.

The boxcar numbers were matched with computer records of what each car contained, and its destination. The incoming boxcars were then made up into new trains that would take them to another intermediate or final destination.

The original hack had gotten into dozens of the trackside readers and had reprogrammed them to add a single random digit in the car designation. The railroad managers no longer knew what was inside any given car, or where it was supposed to be going.

"We looked at attacking the central computers last year, and we could have, but they could be taken offline and replaced fairly quickly. Then, they'd start getting good numbers again from the trackside readers," Sovern said. "That's why we went after the readers. When we reprogrammed a reader, numbers were wrong from the start, from those readers. But some of the readers still gave good numbers, and it was really hard to figure out which was which, and there were thousands of readers. But, we didn't know what was on the cars either, or where they were going. It was as big a mystery to us as it was to the Russians.

"Now we're looking at the central computers again, because we want to pick out specific groups of cars that are coming from Russian logistics centers and heading for terminals near the Ukraine border. We want to slow those down, turn them around if we can, scatter them. Unlike the deal last time, this time we need to know what's in the cars."

"Didn't you say that the Russians could take the bad computers offline and . . ."

"We're working on that," Sovern said.

IN ANOTHER DEVELOPMENT, their Lithuanian social engineer, Emilija, had downloaded Russian railroad employee payroll lists, looking for spear-phishing targets. She had discovered that employees with names spelled in the Ukrainian style had apparently been furloughed or sent on vacation.

"The common name Ivanoff in Russian is spelled with a Y instead of an I in Ukrainian. Y-v-a-n-o-f-f, instead of I-v-a-n-o-f-f," Sovern told Letty. "If you've got a Y in your name, apparently, you're sent home. At least temporarily."

"Damnit. Some direct contacts, friendly contacts, people on the railroads, they could be valuable," Letty said. "If not right now, sometime later."

"Yes. She's still looking for lonely Russian trackmen who might be willing to talk about how complicated their jobs are, working with all that mysterious computer gear, that maybe she could help with," Sovern said. "We'll see what comes of that."

THE CODERS WERE DISTRIBUTED through the two suites, working at laptops, talking with each other, reading the red book of last year's hack, watching YouTube videos.

One man lay flat on the floor with his lower legs on an arm-chair, eyes closed, his laptop on his chest, wearing earphones, apparently blissed out on a Shostakovich concert. As Letty checked back from time to time, she never saw him move; Sovern explained that "Jack works best at night."

Cartwright was working the streets, staying in touch with one of the handsets.

As the sun sank below the horizon, and lights came on, the man who'd been lying on the floor got up and began circulating, updating himself on who was doing what, ate a microwave burrito, and eventually got to work.

At eight o'clock, Kaiser and Longstreet checked in, Kaiser carrying a fifty-pound equipment bag; an hour later, Patty Bunker arrived.

And Catherine Shofly arrived from Dallas, Texas. She called Tom Boyadjian on a burner number: "I'm on site, checked in and looking around. I'll get back."

TWENTY-FOUR

Longstreet, Bunker, Kaiser, Cartwright, and Letty gathered in Letty's room.

"I really don't know what the heck I'm doing here—we've never had a Ladies action before," Longstreet said. She was dressed in what Letty had come to recognize as female combat clothing, a dark green blouse worn loose, to accommodate a sidearm, with black Lululemon yoga pants and running shoes. "Somebody tell me what I'm doing—what all of you are doing."

Letty explained: trying to keep a group of hackers alive to attack Russian trains, off the government books, but with secret government support.

"Any reason to believe that they're going to be attacked?" Longstreet asked.

"There are already three dead, murdered . . . two for sure, one probable, another narrowly avoided," Letty told her.

"Where's the FBI?" Longstreet asked.

"Too bureaucratic—we can call them if we get desperate, but if we do, the word will get out."

Bunker, a round intense woman with thick dark hair, said, "I'm good for all of that, as long as I get paid. I've been in one awful gunfight in my life and killed two people. That got me in the Ladies, but I'm not really a gunfighter like you people. My specialty is tech. I have more in common with these hackers than I do with you combat dudettes." She looked at Kaiser. "And dudes."

She had brought with her, in addition to her handguns, a sack full of miniature cameras the size of quarters, supposedly adopted from the wide-angle lenses on iPhones. They came with sticky backs and could be mounted unobtrusively in the hallway outside the workrooms.

"They look like spy stuff, like they came out of the CIA's basement, but you can get gear like it on Amazon," she said. "They call it home security equipment, if you ever need it."

Bunker had already walked the hallway and found she could mount the cameras on fire alarms. They looked, she said, like part of the alarm tech. They would ping her on her iPhone when there was motion in the hallway, and she could see on the phone who was creating the ping.

Kaiser had been roaming restlessly around the room, looking out the windows, listening to the women talk. He stopped at one point, as Bunker was talking, and said, "That is really useful, those cameras are," and he asked Longstreet about her weapons.

"Two Beretta 92s, one on my belt and a backup," Longstreet said. She produced one as if by magic, Kaiser nodded, and it disappeared like magic, beneath the green blouse.

Kaiser: "I gotta tell you, I hate the fuckin' Russians. I ran into them in Syria on my last tour. They were responsible for killing some of us, though they blamed the Syrian government. Everybody knew it was bullshit, but we let it go. I'm wondering if you guys have the same motivation to get into this . . . because if we're fighting GRU operators, they're gonna be tough, and some of us could get killed."

They all looked at him for a moment, then Longstreet said, "Okay. Now you've made it sound interesting," and all four Ladies laughed.

Then they got into it. Kaiser, they agreed, should stay close to the work suites, as a kind of last-gasp defense if a Russian shooter should break through. He'd brought an automatic weapon, an M4, as well as a twelve-gauge shotgun, and body armor in his equipment bag.

Longstreet also had body armor.

Kaiser would carry one of the diminutive radios supplied by Colles, Bunker another one, and the street patrollers the others.

Kaiser: "Right now, as far as you know, the level of opposition is these Russian gangsters . . ."

"For now," Letty said. "But we are messing with their army, so we could run into the GRU . . ."

"Then it gets serious," Kaiser said.

"Then it gets serious," Letty agreed, "except that we have no reason to think they know where we are. Ordinary People were scattered all over the LA basin, and some of them were hiding in Las Vegas and San Diego. They might want to shoot us up, but first, they've got to find us."

"If you've got a bunch of people poking holes in Russian software, and they spot it, can they determine your location by backtracking?" Kaiser asked. "I really don't know much about this stuff."

They all looked at Letty, who shrugged. "Something to ask Sovern or Baxter."

They did that, and Sovern said if the Russians managed to backtrack them, it would take time—maybe quite a bit of time. "More time than they have, to stop us," he said.

LETTY AND CARTWRIGHT would patrol from roughly dusk to dawn, when they thought it most likely that an attack would occur, and Longstreet would take the daylight hours. Kaiser and Bunker would doze when they had to, but in place—if the Russians got past the people on the perimeter, they would be ready to defend the hallway.

Letty pointed out that schedule would cut into the time Cartwright might need to keep Sovern relaxed, but Cartwright said that wouldn't be a problem. "Staying alive is more important than being relaxed."

"What are you talking about?" Longstreet asked them, looking from Cartwright to Letty.

"You gotta see Sovern to understand it," Letty told her. "Barb's taken advantage of the poor boy."

"Ah."

CATHERINE SHOFLY HAD A ROOM on the fourth floor; after she checked in, she'd cruised her own floor, found it quiet, then went down to the first-floor restaurant and ordered a drink. She was looking for a particular employee, one who was too busy to be careful.

The best she could do was a frizzy-haired desk clerk who seemed to have trouble checking people in, who was exasperated by demands for service. Shofly stepped behind a man who was visibly annoyed by the slow speed of the check-in. When he left, barely suppressing a sneer, she stepped up to the desk with a Realtor's friendly smile. "I checked in a few minutes ago and I thought my friends were on Four, but they're not. A bunch of computer people working together?"

"Eight," the frizzy-haired woman said, and looked at the next person in line.

Shofly said, "Thanks," and went to check out Eight.

Patty Bunker was watching TV, eating corn chips, and monitoring her iPhone, all at once. She didn't miss much: every time the phone chirped, she was on it. All of the chirps had been routine: people leaving their rooms and walking to the elevator, and vice-versa.

Until Shofly turned up.

Shofly, a square-shouldered, well-groomed woman, with stripey blond hair and Texas clothes, stepped off the elevator, looked both ways. She had a key card in her hand, but something about her attitude ticked Bunker's bullshit meter. She watched as Shofly walked slowly along the hallway in one direction, all the way to the end, looking at doors, then turned and walked in the other direction, all the way to the far end, still looking at doors, pausing at some of them, apparently listening, never using her card.

She got on her radio and called Kaiser: "We might have a live one. Out in the hall. Woman with streaky blond hair, a white blouse, fashion jeans, turquoise necklace. Got a big purse; doesn't look like she's carrying on her body . . ."

Cartwright was on the street and heard the call, said, "I'm

coming up." Kaiser went into the other suite, where Letty was reading a Joseph Kanon novel, and called, "Letty: Patty's calling. Woman in the hallway . . ."

Letty put the book on a side table and headed for the door. Before going out, she used Kaiser's radio to call Bunker: "Is she outside the suites?"

"No, she's down toward the other end of the hall."

Letty called Cartwright, told her to hang in the lobby where she could see the elevators, and gave the radio back to Kaiser. Slipping her hand into her 938 pocket, she stepped into the hallway, closed the door, and started walking toward the elevator. The woman at the far end of the hall had turned and was walking toward her; they met at the elevator.

Letty reached out and punched the down button and the woman asked, "Are you with the computer people?"

"No-o-o . . . What computer people?"

"I've just seen people coming and going with laptops and stuff," Shofly said. "I don't know what they're doing . . ."

Letty shrugged. "Haven't seen anything like that, but I'm not around much. I'm here for an economics conference at UCLA."

"Mmm. Doesn't sound like much fun. The economists I've known have been grumpy old men."

"There is that," Letty said, nodding and smiling. "But, if you want to get ahead . . . at least at Minnesota . . . you put up with it. I probably wouldn't have come, if it wasn't February in Minneapolis."

They were in the elevator and Shofly pushed the lobby button and Letty went with it.

"Do not let the grumpy old men get you down," Shofly advised, as the elevator doors closed. "Believe me, I had enough of that.

That's what I like about being a Realtor. I'm pretty much on my own and we've got more women in my office than men. We won't take any guff from them, and they know it."

"Right on," Letty said, with a grin. A moment later, in the lobby, she found Cartwright and said, "We have a problem."

KAISER, LETTY, AND CARTWRIGHT were in the suites, talking quickly, heads together, guns in evidence. The hackers were concerned, wanted to know what was going on.

Letty told them, "We're not sure. We had an odd person up here, a woman, says she's a real estate agent. She's nosy, and we're not taking any chances."

Able asked, "Should we be worried?"

"Yeah, you should be worried, but not *too*," Letty said. "We really do have you covered."

"Would we be better off splitting up?" one of the coders asked.

"Have you ever even *watched* a horror movie?" Cartwright asked, a little nerd-flavored sarcasm in her voice. "What happens when people split up?"

Letty jumped back in: "If you split up and try to run, we can't cover all of you. We're not sure this woman is even a scout. She was just odd. Out of place. If she was working with the Russians, then they had some way to track us, or some of us. We don't know who. Could be any of you. And like I said . . . we can't cover you all."

Sovern: "Let's sit tight. Go back to work, everybody."

The work would continue through the afternoon, into the night.

"We got it going," Sovern said, as they ate a room-service dinner later that day. "We'll get into some of the central computers tonight or tomorrow morning."

SHOFLY CALLED TOM BOYADJIAN. "They're on the eighth floor. I ran into one of the women you were talking about . . . young, early twenties, too young to be a fed, I think. On the other hand, I think she was carrying. I'm not sure, but she kept touching a pocket. Actually . . . I'm sorta sure."

"What rooms?"

"I haven't nailed that down, yet. I will."

She didn't mention the quarter-sized cameras, because she hadn't seen them.

She did give Boyadjian a detailed description of Letty. When Boyadjian checked with Leigh Lawrence, who wasn't in Nunavut but in Lake Arrowhead, and who was standing on a road, looking down at the smog that concealed San Bernardino, and who didn't give a rat's ass about ptarmigans of any kind, Lawrence said, "I remember those blue eyes. That's one of them, for sure."

After talking to Boyadjian, Shofly went to the restaurant and ordered and paid for six large pizzas with everything, "For my computer friends up on Eight."

She wasn't sure of the room number, she told the woman who took the order, and suggested that the kitchen could get that from the front desk; she didn't have time, she was on her way to a blow-dry and was running late.

A half hour later, she saw a room service waiter push a cart with a stack of pizza boxes out of the kitchen and she squeezed into the elevator with him. He pushed a button for Eight.

"Are these for 804?" she asked. "I think that's too many . . ."

The bellhop shook his head, glanced at a slip of paper: "822."

When he got off at Eight, she stepped into the corridor and

watched him wheel the cart down to the left, then got back in the elevator and pushed the button for the lobby.

AFTER TALKING TO THE HACKS, Letty, Cartwright, Longstreet, Kaiser, and Bunker met again to talk about what to do. Working out their options, they decided that Letty would have to talk to Delores Nowak, even if Nowak was reluctant.

Letty called Nowak, who really *didn't* want to talk. "I've got to tell you what we're thinking," Letty insisted.

They had three options, Letty said. The first was to move the hackers to a new location, which would take some time—a couple of hours, just to get packed up and out of the hotel. They weren't even sure that they had to do that, weren't absolutely sure that the woman was working with the Russians. The second option was to let whatever was going to happen, happen—but to call the FBI in, with a SWAT team set up behind the suite doors, to deal with the Russians, if they actually showed up. The third option was to stay put, with the people they had, and if the Russians showed up, to fight them.

Nowak said, "Let me call you back."

As they waited, Bunker got pinged on her phone. She looked at the iPhone and said, "Uh-oh, we've got a guy who looks like he's from room service, he's pushing a cart toward us. Anybody order room service? And wait, our spy just stepped out of the elevator, behind him. She's watching where he goes."

Letty went to the door between the two suites and shouted, "Anybody order room service? Anybody?"

Nobody had.

Kaiser: "If he comes to our door, I'll meet him. Everybody stay close—Letty, Barbara, you go to whatever suite he doesn't, and get ready to step into the hall as soon as he knocks. Jane, you stay behind me off to the door-opening side, you don't want to be behind it in case I go down, you'll have a shooting lane. Letty and Barbara, you'll be at the other door, the one he doesn't knock on, and you'll step out before I open my door, scream if you see he has a gun and then jump back inside . . ."

Bunker: "He's stopped at 822."

Letty and Cartwright hurried to the door at 824 when they heard the knock at 822. Kaiser called, "Everybody ready?"

Whoever was in the hall knocked again, and Letty and Cartwright, guns in their hands, behind their hips, stepped out the door of 824 and looked down toward the waiter, who shook his head. Not you. With no scream, Kaiser opened his door and asked, "What?"

"Pizzas."

"We didn't order pizzas." He half-turned to look around the suite. "Anyone order pizzas from room service?"

With the chorus of "Nos" he looked back at the waiter, who said, "Well, somebody paid."

"Not us," Kaiser said. "Better check again with the kitchen."

He shut the door, the waiter trundled back toward the elevator, and Letty and Cartwright stepped back inside 824.

Cartwright: "She was nailing down the room number."

Bunker: "Yes. I believe they'll be coming. We should get ready."

"We should get ready to move, is what we should do," Letty said. "How in the heck did they find us so fast?"

"GRU can be good," Cartwright said. "Especially on the operational level, and with computerized stuff. If they had some names, and got into the reservation system . . ."

"The names aren't in the reservation system . . ."

"Something is," Cartwright said. "If they looked at hotels where blocks of rooms were all reserved at the same time, on very short notice, and then looked at who made the reservations, and it turned out to be some bland corporate name with nothing behind it . . . then they send in a woman to check it out . . . People in this hotel know there are a bunch of computer freaks up here."

WHEN NOWAK CALLED BACK, Letty told her what had happened, that the Russians would be coming, and they'd be moving if the FBI couldn't come in with SWAT.

"Sovern wants to make a big move—out of town, up to the Santa Ynez Valley. He says there's a motel there that'll be mostly empty, they've got good wi-fi, and it's easy to protect," Letty told Nowak.

"Maybe you won't have to do that," Nowak said. "We talked about the other options. We don't want the FBI to become officially involved, because then it's the U.S. government protecting the train hack. We don't want a big gunfight inside the hotel, because then the LAPD *and* the FBI will be involved."

"So we move? You're good with that?" Letty asked.

"I'd suggest another option, if you're sure they've located you," Nowak said. "You have a phone number for Tom Boyadjian that you got from Martin and Lawrence. Call him. The FBI seized his computers and his personal iPhone, but the phones you took from Martin and Lawrence have four numbers for him. He may still answer one of them. You simply tell him to stay away. Tell him if the Russians show up there, you'll kill them, that you've got the weapons to do it."

"He'll never admit . . ."

"You don't need him to admit anything. You need him to keep the Russians out of your hair."

Letty looked at Kaiser and Cartwright, who looked at each other and back at Letty and simultaneously shrugged.

"Maybe . . . worth a try," Letty said.

"Try it," Nowak said, and she hung up.

KAISER: "IT MAY BE WORTH A TRY, but we should keep packing up anyway. I took a look at satellite images of the motel Sovern is talking about, up at Santa Ynez. It's a fort, if we need a fort. A lot better and simpler than this place."

"Okay. I'll call," Letty said.

"If he asks who we are, tell him Celeres Services," Cartwright said. "That's what I'm going to call my security company when I quit the government job. Might as well start piling up some cred."

"Celeres Services . . ."

Letty had stored Boyadjian's phone numbers in the "Notes" section of the NSA's burner phone. The first number she called rang for a while and was neither answered nor switched to a voicemail. The second one did the same thing. The third one rang twice, then a man answered with "Yes?"

"Tom Boyadjian?"

"Who is this?"

Letty took that as a "yes."

"We're with Celeres Services. We've been hired to protect a group of people at a Los Angeles hotel. We think you are aware of this location. We want to tell you that if you try to interfere with us, if your clients try to interfere with this, there'll be a bloodbath. We're heavily armed, we have fully automatic weapons, registered with the ATF. We're authorized to possess them, and we know how to use them. Stay away."

"I have no idea what you're talking about," the man said.

"Then maybe you should repeat what I just said to Martin and Lawrence, who gave up this number for Tom Boyadjian. They could relay to Mr. Boyadjian what we're telling you. Stay away."

"I'm looking for Celeres Services, C-e-l-e-r-e-s, on the Internet, on my computer, and I'm not finding anything," the man said.

"You won't, at your level," Letty said. "Final warning: Stay away."

She hung up and Kaiser laughed: "That was nice. *'You won't, at your level.'* He thinks we're some black ops group working for the CIA."

Cartwright nodded. "When they talk to this scout, she'll tell them that they've got a bad problem: moving down a narrow hallway either from the elevator or the fire stairs. If we see them, they're dead. There's a good chance they'll stay away."

"I hope," Letty said, shaking her head. It was all too . . . tentative. "But let's get out of here anyway. I like John's idea of a fort."

BOYADJIAN DROVE A MILE from his home before he called Step and told him about the call from Letty. "If she's telling the truth, your guys are gonna get shot to pieces. There's a chance we're talking about the CIA's special activities group. Shofly says any attack at the hotel will be tough. The attackers would have to run down a long hall from either stairwell, if they come up that way. The elevator's a lot closer—turn left coming out of the elevator—but they're still in that hallway."

Boyadjian gave Step a few more details, and Step passed them on to Volkov.

"What we know is that there is a girl with a pistol guarding the rooms, and that she would also have to step into the hallway to repel an attack. Is that correct?" Volkov asked.

"That's what we know, but we don't know exactly who is inside the rooms. This Celeres Services—we don't know them. Boyadjian said the only reference he can find is to a personal guard of Romulus, the founder of Rome."

"Typical overblown name choice for a private security service. Nothing to worry about," Volkov said. He thought for a moment, flicked fingers at Step. "I have three good, experienced men. One will stay with the car, two will attack the room. They kick the door, throw a flash-bang, go in, burn out these pests, go down the stairs. One minute, no more, from entry to attack, another minute for the attack, one more on the stairs, to the car. Three minutes and gone."

"And if it doesn't work so well?"

Volkov shrugged. "I will get more men. Lots more where they come from."

Step stared at him for a moment: *Lots more where they come from.* That was true, but even a GRU agent wouldn't say it out loud, not if he was really in control. Something was going on with Volkov.

"How is the war?" he asked.

"There are apparently some . . . difficulties, which will soon be resolved," Volkov said. "Don't believe the American television. We are on schedule, but we—you and me—are being pressed on the trains. Pressed hard."

"If you do this, be sure you remove this girl," Step said. "These two girls and the fat man. They've been thorns in my side. They have forced me to close my business for now and they are attacking our trains. You have to take them."

"We will," Volkov said, his face gone grim. "The removal of these people will be a benefit for you. Perhaps you will send me a small gift when it is done."

"A bottle of fine single malt Scotch," Step suggested.

Volkov: "I was thinking one hundred thousand American dollars: no hundreds, nothing larger than fifties. In currency. No need to mention it to the apparat; I will use the money to protect the motherland."

Step felt the pain, but smiled, best he could, and said, "Of course you will."

If they didn't stop the attack on the trains, Step thought, Volkov might be taking up residence someplace warm and obscure. A hundred thousand would top off what he'd undoubtedly already stolen.

TWENTY-FIVE

Letty could feel the stress building with the coders as night came on: the coders were all smart and knew something was up with the people who carried guns. On top of that, they were now probing the Russian computers, trying to figure out what was going on there. In its own way, that was as intense as the talk about a possible Russian attack in the hotel.

Letty told her gun people, "We have to move fast. If the Russians come at us, there'll be bodies and cops and we can't let the cops start jacking up the coders. They've got work to do. If the Russians don't come right at us, they'll still try to find some way to mess with us."

They all agreed and called Sovern down to Letty's room and told him what had happened. "We're going up to your motel in Santa Ynez. Fast as we can."

"We got to take at least one of the printers, be best if we could take all of them," Sovern said. "We need to print a lot of stuff. I'll get people packing up."

"Don't worry about leaving stuff, we'll get it back later. But don't leave any paper," Cartwright said. "Quick, quick, quick."

Longstreet: "Don't panic them."

"They're already nervous," Sovern said. "They look at Kaiser and they think, 'This guy's a starship trooper. Why's he here if we're not in a war?' That's what they're thinking."

"Remind them that somebody already followed them here," Letty said.

Longstreet said, "Give me one of the radios. I'll go watch the garage. Seems like that's a likely place for them to stage. And our people will have to go in and out of there."

Letty: "Good. Go. Both of you."

As Longstreet and Sovern hurried out of the room, Kaiser asked, "Where do you want me?"

"Right next to Patty, looking at her telephone. If they come in, you gotta knock them down. Barb and I will do escort down to the garage and the cars."

"You think they're coming," Kaiser said.

"I think they have to, if they know what we're doing," Letty said, and Cartwright nodded.

The hackers didn't quite panic, but packed up in a rush, a near-frenzy, red books and laptops and clothes and notebooks bundled into anything handy—suitcases, shopping bags, pillowcases.

"We want everybody to leave at once," Letty shouted at them. She'd scooped up her cane, and was using it like a music conductor, directing traffic. "Make as many trips as you have to, but we want everybody back up here after you've packed your cars. We need to go as a caravan so we can cover everybody. Sovern will lead us out."

That caused some noisy complaints, but Sovern backed Letty, and so did some of the others, and as the first people started down the hallway, they'd all agreed to come back up.

At the end, with all the hacks and their friends in the two suites, checking couches and beds for random paper and flash drives, cleaning the place out, four of the men picked up two of the printers and carried them down the hallway to the fire stairs.

Able could handle one by himself, and was carrying it down the hall, back in the original box, heavy and awkward. "Left a goddamn half ream of paper in it, shoulda . . ."

He continued toward the stairwell. Down the hall in the other direction, the elevator dinged, and the Russian scout stepped out and looked toward them. Cartwright looked at Letty: "What?"

"Gotta . . ." Letty started down the hall, Cartwright a step behind her. The woman saw them coming and stepped casually back into the elevator as though she'd gotten off at the wrong floor. Letty shouted, "Hold that," but the woman didn't, the doors were closing, and Cartwright stuck her foot between them and they rebounded and the woman said, "I was just . . ."

Letty had reversed her hold on her cane and now she swatted the woman on the face, as she had with Harp, and just like Harp, the woman went down, bouncing off the back of the elevator car, then going flat on the floor.

Cartwright held the door and said, "Help me," and she started dragging the woman out of the elevator by her streaky blond hair. The woman struggled and fought and Letty got her by the collar of her blouse and lifted her upright and said, "Move-move-move," and Cartwright had her pistol out and pointed at the woman's head and they pushed and shoved her down the hall and into the suite.

Inside, they kicked her to the carpet and Cartwright took her purse, which the woman still had looped around her body, and emptied it on the floor. First out was a pistol, a compact Ruger, followed by an iPhone. Letty picked up the pistol, pulled the magazine and jacked the shell out of the chamber, and put the gun in her belt and the magazine in a pocket. Then she picked up the cell phone.

"Who are you working for?" Cartwright asked.

"I'm a Realtor," the woman groaned. She was bleeding from one eyebrow and her nose and a split lip.

Letty: "What's the phone code?"

"I'm not going to give you . . ."

Letty lifted the cane. "I'll break your arm. If you still won't give it to me, I'll break your other arm. If you still don't, it's a leg . . ."

Baxter was there, pulled in by the noise. He crouched, looking at the woman's face: "Maybe you weren't told, but we already shot and killed two of your guys and shot and wounded two more. If you don't want to get hurt really bad, like dead-bad, you better listen . . ."

The woman looked from Baxter to Letty and said, "9-2-2-3-3."

Letty punched in the code and scrolled down the list of contacts until she got to Tom Boyadjian.

"Tom Boyadjian," she said, showing the screen to Cartwright, who was digging through the woman's wallet, pulling out a driver's license and a variety of wallet trash.

"We kind of knew that," Cartwright said. "Her name is Catherine Shofly . . . Looks like she really is a Realtor. Former Dallas cop."

Letty looked down at Shofly: "You know you're working for the Russians? That they've murdered at least three people? That you're an accomplice now? We expect that some of their shooters could be showing up here and there'll be a mass shooting. Feds still have the death penalty for you spies . . ."

"I'm not a spy," Shofly sputtered.

"Yes, you are. Maybe you can cop a plea, but that's about your best hope," Letty said. "Otherwise, you're going to prison forever."

Able ran into the suite: "Gotta go, gotta go . . . They're yelling at us, we're loaded, everybody's lined up behind Sovern, we gotta go . . ."

Cartwright nodded at Shofly: "What about her?"

"She's gonna call Boyadjian, she's heard us . . ."

Letty lifted her cane, as though to hit Shofly in the face again, and when Shofly lifted an arm to fend her off, Letty hit her forearm, hard, breaking it, and Shofly screamed and Letty bent over her and said, "It's broken. Get the hotel to call the hospital for you."

Able, shocked: "Jesus, that was cold."

"Taking her out of it . . . or as you guys would say, taking her offline," Letty said.

Baxter: "Forget her, she's down. We gotta move, let's move . . ."

He followed Able out into the hallway as they heard the elevator ding again, and a moment later Patty Bunker, in the next suite, shouted through the connecting door, "They're here. Two of them, they've got Minis, they've got suppressed Minis . . ."

Kaiser shouted, "Everybody stay put" as Letty yelled, "Baxter and Able are out there."

Kaiser yanked the charging handle on the M4, let it snap back, lifted the barrel to neck height, popped into the hallway and instantly fired a burst down the hall. Then he popped back and said, "They're down, hope to God they weren't cops."

Cartwright pushed past him into the hall, followed by Letty.

Able and Baxter were twenty feet down the hall toward the stair-well, frozen in place, backs to the walls.

Cartwright and Letty trotted down to the bodies. The two men wore body armor and had been carrying Mini Uzis; Kaiser had shot them at the neckline, above the heavy armored plates that protected the midsection, shredding the softer armor above the plates and also hitting their unprotected throats.

At that moment, Longstreet called on her radio: "I'm in the garage, there's a car pulled up to the side exit where the stairs come down, a black Buick, I think it could be a getaway car . . ."

Letty took the radio from Bunker and called back, "Got it. Stay out of sight."

Cartwright picked up one of the unfired Uzis and handed it to Letty, took one for herself, stripped an armload of magazines from the two bodies and looked up at Letty, who said, "If that's their guy in the car, he could follow us. Let's see if we can slow it down."

"Gotta be quick, the cops will be coming fast."

They both hurried toward the stairwell, Letty shouting to Kaiser as they went, "Cover the rest of our people . . ."

Able and Baxter followed them, Kaiser came last, walking backward, covering the hall with his M4, Bunker at his back. Letty and Cartwright left them behind as they ran down the stairs, and around, one fast flight after another, to the bottom.

Halfway down, Cartwright said, "That Kaiser is a treasure."

"Yeah. Don't tell him that, though. He gets a big head."

At the bottom, they stopped and looked out the six-inch-square window on the fire door. A car was immediately outside, idling, and the driver had an ethnic similarity to the two bodies on Eight. He was looking at the door expectantly.

"That's him," Cartwright said.

"Tires first. If he shows a gun . . ."

"Right. You kick the door open, I'll take the tires . . . On three."

She counted one-two-three and Letty kicked the door and Cartwright was out and the man in the car hit the gas and Cartwright shredded his left front and left rear tires with two quick bursts from the Uzi, and he kept going, made the mistake of turning right, and Cartwright shredded the right rear.

The car continued grinding on, running the rims, slowly, but out of sight. "He won't follow us on the freeway. Let's get everybody out of the garage . . ."

Able ducked out of the stairwell, asked, "What was that?" and Letty said, "Never mind, get in your car, go, go," and Baxter came out next, followed by Bunker and Kaiser, and they ran together toward the parking structure, as Sovern, riding with William and Melody, led the way out in William's Subaru, five other cars trailing behind.

Baxter headed for the driver's seat. "Everybody ready?"

"Wait for Kaiser . . . we'll bring up the rear," Cartwright said.

Baxter: "Barbara, you and Kaiser get in the back. I'm going to drop the back window in case you need, you know . . . to discourage someone."

Kaiser came up, piled into the truck next to Cartwright, and Bunker ran on and got in with Able. Able pulled around them and down the ramp to the street.

"I don't think there's anybody to chase us . . . or anything to chase us with. We took out their car," Cartwright said. "Let's go, let's go, don't lose the caravan."

SHOFLY HAD PARKED on the third floor of the parking ramp. Letty had taken her gun and regular iPhone, and Cartwright her wallet, but they hadn't dug out her car keys. Bleeding from the face, her broken arm screaming at her, she staggered into the bathroom, picked up a box of facial tissue, then walked unsteadily down to the elevator, pushed the button for Three, spitting on a tissue, wiping her face, made it to the exit door for the ramp.

As she pushed the door open, she heard two bursts from an automatic weapon, and a few seconds later, a third. She got in her car, started it, and rolled down the ramp to the second floor, and around again until she was pointing to the first floor.

She got there in time to see a gray Toyota Tundra, which Boyadjian had described to her, rolling out of the ramp and into the alley that led to the street. She gave it a second, then followed.

On the street, with Baxter's truck a half block away, she got straight, driving one-handed, then used the elbow on her broken arm to steady the steering wheel. She used her good arm and dug in a hip pocket for the burner phone she used to call Boyadjian. There was only one number in it, and she poked it, still steering with her elbow. When Boyadjian came up, she told him what had happened, and then, "We're going up to the freeway, hold on."

She dropped the phone in her lap and used her good hand to steer onto the freeway, staying well back. Once in the slow lane, she told Boyadjian where she was, and that she didn't know where she was going, or how long she could keep going with the broken arm.

"Hang in there, Catherine. I'm in my car, up by Westwood. I'll try to get up behind you myself. If they keep going north, I should hook up by the time you get to the Getty and you can bail."

"I don't know where the fuck the Getty is, but I can hang on for a while. That bitch that broke my arm, I'm gonna shoot her."

"Hang on, hang on . . ."

BOYADJIAN HEADED FOR the 405 and used his Step burner to call Step on his Tom Boyadjian burner.

When Step answered, Boyadjian said, "You've got at least two dead, maybe three if they got your car that was waiting for the pickup. They're all together running up the 405, I've got my operator following them, but she's got a broken arm. I'm close, I'm going to follow if I can."

"We'll take care of you, man," Step said. "We'll take care of you."

"These fuckers have hurt my people bad enough," Boyadjian said. "I'll put you right on top of the motherfuckers, if I can."

Boyadjian called Shofly back, monitored the exits as she passed them, and, as he predicted, was able to move up behind her in his BMW as they approached the Getty Museum. He gave her directions to the Sherman Oaks Hospital emergency room. When they got to the Ventura Freeway, she went east and he went west, with the gray Toyota Tundra a half mile ahead, twenty cars between them.

SOVERN LED THE PARADE through the night past Oxnard, where he kept his boat, and up the coast past richie-rich Santa Barbara, through some hills with moderately scary drop-offs, and down into the Santa Ynez Valley.

"Great road for a Porsche," Letty said. "My dad would love this."

"Sure, if you don't mind killing yourself," Baxter said. "Which you would, eventually."

As they reached the high point of the road, before dropping into the valley, Kaiser said to Cartwright, "Those headlights."

She said, "Yeah."

Letty: "What?"

"We've had a set of those super-white European car headlights behind us since the 405," Kaiser said. "Sometimes way back, sometimes closer, and there are a lot of other super-whites, but . . ."

"They're not all the same," Cartwright said. "And these looked sorta the same, all the way up here."

Baxter: "Fuck me."

They passed a turnoff to a lake campground, and farther down the hill the road began to flatten out and another, smaller road branched off to the left. The trailing car turned on its left-turn signal and made the turn.

Cartwright said, "Huh."

They could see the lights of Santa Ynez ahead when the caravan of cars, following Sovern, took a left turn, onto what seemed more like an uphill driveway than a public street. As Baxter slowed to follow, Kaiser said, "Look."

Cartwright turned her head. They couldn't see the actual car. They could see it was coming slowly and that the headlights were super-white.

Baxter was already into the turn, said, "Shit. Too late to turn back."

And it *was* a driveway. At the top was a U-shaped motel with a half-dozen scraggly palm trees spaced along the edge of the approach. Parking was all along the motel's U-shaped perimeter, both front and back. Sovern led the caravan past the building and around to the back parking lot.

Before they could follow, Kaiser said, "Rod, stop. Stop."

"What?"

"I want to see if anyone follows us up." They waited a few minutes, looking for bright-whites, but no other cars came up the hill.

Kaiser said, "Okay," and Baxter took the truck around the motel to the back, where the hackers were pulling their suitcases and computer gear out of their cars.

Letty got out on the tarmac and asked Kaiser, "What do you think?"

"I don't know." The motel was not at the top of the slope but had been built into it. The slope continued up from the back of the motel and was heavily treed, as was the downslope in front of it. "You put a guy up there with a rifle, you'd have a hell of a hard time digging him out of all that brush."

"They'd have to know where we are."

"My gut tells me they do know," Kaiser said. "I believe that car was following us. But I'm not sure. If it was, and if they come in with a team, at least part of it will be up on that hill."

"Then we oughta get up there first," Letty said.

TWENTY-SIX

As the hackers began spreading through one wing of the motel, Letty, Kaiser, and Cartwright walked all the way around the outside. The building was a single-story squared-off U shape, the bottom four feet built solidly of red brick with a white wooden superstructure above the brick.

A flickering "Ynez Crest Motel" sign stood in front, above a flickering "Vacancy" sign. The building was old—perhaps fifty years old. Each room had a window facing a parking lot, with curtains that were stiff and hard to close, and a window with venetian blinds that looked out to a corridor that ran down the center of the wings. The wings had rooms on both sides, with hollow wooden doors facing the corridor; Letty suspected Kaiser could punch his fist through the doors. No protection there.

A short center wing connected the two arms of the building, and contained the office, a vending machine room, a little-used lounge with a sofa, a few easy chairs and a television, and a yoga room. The owners, two trust-fund hippies, were friends of Sovern, and had hoped the yoga room would attract more customers, but it hadn't. That room, with its polished wood-strip floor, was empty, except for twenty rolled-up and slowly disintegrating rubber-like yoga mats and a small brass bell of the kind used to signal the end of meditation.

"The brick is good," Kaiser said. "The interior corridor is good, too. We can move people around without them being seen. If we're hit when people are asleep in their rooms . . . These guys had grenades and a couple grenades through each window would wipe us out."

"Fire," Cartwright said, pointing at the ceiling. "It looks like the whole thing above the brick is old, dry wood . . . Fire would push us out in the open."

"Can't let that happen, can't let them get close enough," Letty said. "Sovern says they need more time, at least a day."

"If they're coming for us, that could be tough," Cartwright said.

"We don't want the hacks to hear that, not after the hotel," Kaiser said. "If they heard you, they'd be out of here in a heartbeat."

"So we keep our mouths shut. I don't think the Russians will hit us in daylight—they'd be too visible and we'd see them coming," Letty said. She pulled her phone and checked the time. "We've got about four hours until sunrise. If that car with the European lights was following us and calling back to LA, I can't see that they could get a whole crew up here and do recon and hit us while it's still dark."

"I agree. We've probably got twenty-four hours," Cartwright said. "They'd come after midnight when most cops are in bed."

Kaiser nodded: "That doesn't mean we won't want to have a few guns awake during the day."

THE MOTEL'S FRONT DESK was manned by a retiree who stayed up nightly until one o'clock, then locked the front door and went to sleep on a rollaway cot in the back office. He'd stayed up to greet the hacking group, but as soon as they'd signed in and Letty had paid for the rooms with the NSA credit card, he grumpily disappeared into his makeshift bedroom.

A little later, Letty knocked on his door and when he cracked it open, she asked, "Do you have a landline telephone?"

"Not for about ten years," he said. "Now let me sleep." He shut the door again.

Sovern found them while they were doing their survey, and said, "We can move chairs and tables out of the individual rooms and take them to the yoga center . . . use it as a workspace. I already checked with Manny and he said okay. We might want to throw him some extra dollars when we leave." Manny was one of the owners.

"Do that first thing tomorrow," Letty said.

"How's the wi-fi?" Cartwright asked.

"Good," Sovern said. "The cable comes right down the highway and we're hooked into it."

"You guys need to make your own work schedule. John and Barbara and I will be up overnight," Letty told Sovern. "Jane and Patty can take the watch tomorrow while we sleep. That'll have the three of us up and alert tomorrow night. Barb thinks that if the Russians come after us, that's the most likely time. They'll be under time pressure, too. If they're coming, they could do some recon tomorrow afternoon. And listen: we need to finish this thing. As soon as we can. You've got to be awake and directing traffic. I've got some speed if you need it."

Sovern shook his head: "I'm good for now. Ask me tomorrow."

Cartwright looked up at the drop ceiling, of warped and discolored polystyrene tiles. "Fire. I can't help thinking . . ."

"I saw a fire extinguisher somewhere," Sovern said. "But only one."

THEY DECIDED THAT CARTWRIGHT would climb the slope above the back of the motel, taking her M4 with her. Letty would go out to the highway at the end of the motel driveway, move back into the brush and watch the passing traffic for people who might be scouting the place. Kaiser would stay at the motel as the backstop.

Kaiser: "We've got those two Minis we took from the Russians at the SkyPort. We give one to Letty and one to either Jane or Patty, whoever is most familiar with them. Probably Jane—we'll want Patty to stay with her cameras. That'd give us some heavy firepower all the way around."

Letty: "Yes. If they walk in, if they try to sneak in, we'll hear them. If they try to crash in, with vehicles, we'll have automatic weapons on them from all sides. It'd be like a car wash, but with bullets."

They all looked at her and Kaiser shook his head. "Sometimes . . ."

Cartwright: "Don't say it. It'll just piss her off."

Letty: "What?"

FOR THE FIRST NIGHT'S WATCH, Letty, Cartwright, and Kaiser would carry three of the radios with their earbuds. Letty suggested they hit the vending machines for something to eat until the shift change, which they decided should be at nine o'clock in the morning, giving Longstreet and Bunker a chance to get some decent sleep.

Cartwright and Kaiser were okay with the vending machines, but vetoed anything in crinkly bags, like potato chips: they wound up emptying Oreos into Ziploc bags, which could be opened silently.

After more talk about tactics, Cartwright left to climb the slope in back. "Letty, listen," Kaiser said. "You don't want to move, you don't want to make any kind of artificial noise. Make sure the radio only feeds through the earbuds . . ."

"When I was a hunter, I had rabbits and deer walk up to me," Letty said, interrupting. "You take care of yourself, I'll take care of myself."

Kaiser stopped, then said, "Sorry. Sometimes, that whole Stanford California-girl personality makes me forget where you come from."

LETTY LEFT HIM at the motel and walked downhill along the edge of the driveway, until she got to the street. She found a sunken place between two slender trees, which gave her cover, but from which she could see down to the highway without moving her head.

The night wasn't exactly silent; it was calm, a barely perceptible wind filtering through the trees, ruffling fallen leaves. Cars and pickups went by at irregular intervals, fewer and fewer as the night deepened. None seemed to be doing recon, as far as she could tell. At four o'clock, she had to stretch her legs; at five, she ate three Oreos, twisted the lid off a bottle of orange soda, and took a sip, wrinkling her nose at the sweetness. Would have gone for a root beer, but the machine didn't have any.

At six, light was seeping into the woods. Usually, the hour before dawn was the time when you'd see small animals and deer up and moving around. She saw nothing, heard nothing out of place.

At six-thirty, dawn, more vehicles began passing by her hideout, almost all going east, apparently headed for jobs in Santa Barbara. That continued until nine o'clock; she hadn't heard or seen anything worrisome on the roads. The radio buzzed, and Cartwright said, "Heading in. I think the hillside is good for now. We need to get Jane up here and Patty out where Letty is."

Kaiser came up: "I'm not too bad, I could take either spot, for a while . . ."

"You need to sleep just like we do," Letty said. "We need to be wide-awake all night."

"All right. I know Jane's up. I haven't seen Patty. I'll get them started out there," Kaiser said.

BUNKER SHOWED UP twenty minutes later, carrying her handbag; Letty gave her the Mini Uzi and asked if she could handle it.

"I've seen them before, never shot one—but yeah, I can handle it. If worse comes to worst, it'll scare the heck out of anybody who it's pointed at. Get their heads down, give me a chance to run."

"My exact thought," Letty said.

With Bunker settled into the spot between the trees, Letty walked up the driveway to the motel. She was tired from the stress and motion of the past three days, and ready for bed. She met Kaiser and Cartwright in the motel lounge; they were talking to Sovern, who said, "We need food. Lots of it. I gotta work, but if we could get a couple people to run down there, hit a supermarket . . . we still got that microwave Paul bought."

"Sooner the better," Letty said. "We might still be good for a while."

"I'll go," Kaiser said.

"I'll ride shotgun," Cartwright said. "Maybe check with the rest of the crew and see who wants what. Get a list going."

They all went down to the yoga room, got a list; Baxter claimed to have lost eight pounds, said he was starving to death, and somebody else said Baxter had broken into the vending machine and free candy, cookies, and chips were pouring out. "It's like the revolution is here."

Baxter volunteered to go shopping with Kaiser and Cartwright. They left, and Letty went down to the room she shared with Cartwright; she'd just opened the door when she heard somebody shouting, "Yes! Yes! Woo-hoo!" in the yoga room. She thought about investigating, but similar explosions happened every couple of hours. When the tumult died away, she went to bed instead.

She was nearly asleep when there was a knock at her door. Sovern was in the hallway, and he said, "We got a break. Emmy located a train guy in Belarus, in Gomel, the town of Gomel, which is north of Kyiv. Big rail center. He apparently knows she was spear phishing, but it looks like he's pro-Ukraine. He's letting Jack download the guts of his whole system."

"How soon will you be able to actually . . . you know, mess with trains?" Letty asked.

Sovern turned over his wrist to look at it, pretending to look at a watch that wasn't actually there, and said, "According to moles on my wrist, maybe tonight. We gotta get a little lucky. There's a lot of military material heading down toward Kyiv, and a lot already there. We know, though, that the Gomel computer can talk to the computer in Voronezh, in Russia, which is east of Kharkiv, which is in Ukraine on the border with Russia. Voronezh is another big train center feeding military material toward Ukraine. So that's good: we should be able to screw up both of them."

"Push it, stop fucking around," Letty said. "The war is on and it's not looking good. Let's take the fuckers down."

"Not fucking around, we're busting our balls," Sovern said. He started to turn away, and then frowning, turned back and said, "Something strange is going on with the Russians. We're talking to people in the train stations, and they say the Russian troops in Belarus don't seem to know they're heading into combat. They don't seem to have much . . . stuff. You know. Ammo and food. Fuel. It all seems really disorganized, thrown together."

"Good. Let's disorganize them some more," Letty said.

She went back to bed, only to wake up again when Cartwright came in an hour later. "Sorry about the noise," Cartwright said, as she sat on the second bed and started pulling off her shoes. "The war is nuts. We were watching it on TV in the supermarket. It's everywhere. Craig says we're making good progress toward screwing up the Russian trains."

"I heard," Letty said, sleepily. "You get all the food?"

"We cleaned out the store's microwave section. We got so much food that Kaiser made me stop at an appliance place and buy another microwave."

"Gotta eat," Letty said.

"Emmy's boyfriend up in Belarus downloaded the whole hard drive on his computer. Their master program wasn't designed by rocket scientists; Craig says it's actually based on an old program used by Union Pacific," Cartwright said. "One of the guys recognized it. It's thirty years old and it's full of security holes. We'll own these guys by tonight."

"Faster the better," Letty said. "Ninety percent is better than one hundred percent, if it gets us out of here before dark. After that . . ." She shrugged.

Cartwright crawled into her bed. "Sleep as long as you can," she said. "If we can't push the button today, until after dark, and if they really do know where we are . . ."

"See you tonight," Letty said.

Bad dreams.

Flashbacks to her childhood, to the disaster she'd witnessed and fought through in Pershing, Texas, the year before, to another gunfight, as a teenager, with out-of-control drug dealers . . . All colorful, the color being blood red.

For three or four hours at midday, she was restless, kicking around the bed, before finally falling into a deeper sleep. When she woke up, she sensed something different about the room. Momentarily disoriented, she rolled on her side, toward the window that looked toward the front parking lot. She reached over and pushed a curtain aside, and immediately recognized what was different: it was dark outside.

She looked at her phone: it was almost seven o'clock. She muttered, "Holy cats," and rolled out of bed; she'd been more or less asleep for nine hours and felt reasonably sharp, but with the sense of running late.

Cartwright had already snuck out: her bed was empty and her shoes were gone. Moderately embarrassed, Letty limited herself to a one-minute shower, brushed her teeth, put on the same set of clothes that she'd been wearing that morning, and hurried down the hall to the yoga room.

She could hear a lot of talk; Kaiser and Cartwright were standing just inside the door, and Kaiser said, "We decided to let you sleep," and Cartwright added, "Craig says we're about there. We're ready to put our code into the central computers."

"Then we're done?"

"Not quite. They want to watch it work for a while. But, we're close."

"No big alarms during the day?"

Cartwright looked at Kaiser, who tilted his head to one side, and said, "Patty says we've been cruised. Starting around three o'clock, she thinks we were cruised a half-dozen times, three different cars. Jane's still up on the hill, Patty's still down on the road. You need to get a bite to eat, and then you and Barbara really ought to get back outside, relieve Patty and Jane."

"Microwave burritos," Cartwright said. "Mmm, mmm."

"Burritos are good," Letty said. "Listen. Let's turn on every light in the motel that we can. Outside and inside. There are some guests who aren't with us, but let's get the lights on in all of our rooms and all the empty rooms."

Cartwright frowned: "Why?"

"So that people moving in on the motel will stand out against the light, if we're behind them. We should let them go by us, unless they're coming down right on top of us. Once they're by us, they'll be better targets—and if they're looking into the lights and then turn to look for us, in the woods, they'll be night-blind."

Cartwright nodded: "What you said."

LETTY ATE HER BURRITO in the yoga room. The hacker combine was leaning on Sovern and the man Letty knew only as Jack.

Jan and Michele had determined that some of the codes on the sides of the railcars indicated military priority shipments. Working with the central computers, they thought it likely that they could scatter those boxcars across western Russia. They could even send some of them across Belarus to Latvia, Estonia, and Lithuania, all of which were opposed to the war, but had the same rail gauge as Russia, and Russian trains crossed those borders without detailed checks.

"Gotta get it done, gotta get it done," Letty told William, who was working his way through a pack of Twinkies as he stared at a computer screen. "C'mon, you guys. Push the button. Any button."

William smiled and said, "Not quite yet. Soon."

Behind him, the television showed Russian trucks on the highway to Kyiv, and a voice-over suggested the Ukrainian capital would probably fall within a day or two.

"Better hurry, or there won't be any point," Letty said.

TWENTY-SEVEN

When Letty finished the burrito, Cartwright came by and said, "Time to gun up."

"I want to look at the Net for one minute," Letty said.

"No woman on earth ever looked at the Net for one minute," Cartwright said.

"I need to see if there's anything from Delores," Letty said, as they walked toward their room. "I'm starting to feel like we're out on a limb, and there might be a bureaucrat behind us with a saw."

"Yeah? I always feel like that," Cartwright said. "I thought that was what people felt like."

Cartwright changed into jeans with a black long-sleeved shirt as Letty brought her laptop up, found nothing new from Delores Nowak. She detoured to the *Washington Post* to see what they had to say about the war. They had a lot to say, but not much more than what Letty had known two days earlier.

Cartwright said to Letty, "C'mon, reading the papers won't help us. Let's go."

After checking out with Kaiser, Letty and Cartwright hustled to their spots in the trees. Bunker told Letty that she was sure they'd been cruised. "They weren't great at it. They'd slow down when they got close and speed up when they were past. Of course, they didn't know I was up here watching them."

Letty got the radio from her, wiped the earbud on her blouse, plugged it into her ear and checked in with Cartwright, who was back in her spot. When Bunker had gone up the driveway, Letty settled back into her hole and looked at her phone. A little after eight: and Kaiser and Cartwright both thought the Russians would come in after midnight, if they came at all.

Letty forced herself to relax. She'd found, as a hunter, that if she relaxed, she was not only physically quieter, but also eliminated a psychological buzz. Almost all nonhunters, including smart ones, scientists, thought the buzz was purely mythical; or bullshit.

Letty disagreed. She believed in it, as did her father. People trained in stakeouts, cops who were friends of her father, had told her that they'd not look directly at a target, either a person or a location, because the people being stalked could pick up on it. An empty mind was worth cultivating, and she had done that.

Letty was watching the road and Cartwright was quiet in the woods behind the motel when Kaiser called at nine o'clock. "Wanted to let you know. Sovern pushed the button on all of it—they tell me the Russian military stuff will start to scatter. Might be too late to do any good, the Russians are pushing hard toward Kyiv, but . . . they tell me we've done everything we can. Ain't no more, according to the big brains."

Letty: "John, could you come down and take my spot? I have to phone . . . home. Like E.T."

"Give me five minutes: you haven't heard anything?"

"Not a thing. There's nobody out here but me."

Kaiser came down, moving silently along the edge of the driveway; he was almost on top of her before she saw him. Ten minutes later, closed in her room by herself, Letty called Delores Nowak.

Letty said, "It's done. The hacks substituted some operating systems in the Russian rail's central sorting computers and we're scattering military priority boxcars all over Russia. There are some that will probably turn up in Latvia, Estonia, and Lithuania, so the security people in those countries should check all the incoming boxcars from Russia. Some of them may contain military material that they'll want to impound."

"Wonderful! I will pass that along," Nowak said. "We're all still at work here—we've brought in cots. There's also some concern about a couple of dead bodies at the SkyPort."

"Who's concerned?"

"LAPD and the FBI. We're talking to them. One of the dead men has been identified as a consular officer at the Russian embassy in Washington and is suspected of being GRU. The state department is talking to the embassy. The other man hasn't been identified. He could be, probably is, a Russian NOC . . . an operator with non-official cover. The FBI is backtracking him now. They were both armed . . ."

"Does the FBI understand the reason that they're dead?" Letty asked.

"They know some of it—they've been grilling the hotel employees. Digging bullets out of the hallway's walls, and their crime scene people are pulling prints out of the rooms you guys were in. You know the FBI: they want the I's dotted and the T's crossed."

"I'm a little worried about our legal liability . . ."

"Stop worrying. You are thoroughly covered, even if the FBI doesn't know it yet," Nowak said. "We're about to have an intense interagency discussion of the situation."

"A clusterfuck."

"That's an unkind characterization," Nowak said. "So what's next, now that you're done out there?"

"We'll tell the hackers to scatter, at least for now. To hide out. We figure the Russians will be pissed for a while."

"If you collect the names, we'll give them NSA cover. We'll watch over them twenty-four hours a day. If we see Russians trying to trace them, the FBI will be all over them."

"Good, I guess. Some of the hacks might not like the NSA watching over them . . . might not think it'd be a good thing. Anyway, I'll send the names along," Letty said. "But: we think the Russians may know where we're at, right now, so we don't want our people to scatter until daylight. Overnight, if there's trouble . . . there could be more bodies."

"Try your best to avoid that. We'd hesitate to send in police protection or the FBI, since the incident at the SkyPort. They get all fussy," Nowak said. "It would be best to handle it informally, as you've been doing."

"All right, but tomorrow . . . the survivors are coming back to Washington."

"We'll give you a parade," Nowak said. "Seriously, this is going to be a feather in some caps, including Senator Colles and you and me. We thank you. And really, try not to shoot anyone else."

Before going back down the driveway, Letty stopped at the candy machine to see if anything was left that she could eat quietly. She got the last pack of Peanut M&M's, emptied the pack into a pocket, and threw the package into a trash can. Sovern came down the hall and asked, "Any chips left?"

"Corn chips," Letty said. "Barbeque."

"Ah, man, that barbeque grease fucks up a keyboard."

Letty asked about signs that the rail attack had been effective, and Sovern gave her a quick summary: the answer was *yes*. Military logistics cars, Sovern said, were beginning to stray away from the front. As they walked together toward the door, Melody burst out of the yoga room and shouted, "Cell phones just went down. All of them. Nobody can call out."

Letty looked at her phone: no service. She called Cartwright and Kaiser on the radio and with Sovern listening in, said, "Cell phones are down."

Cartwright came back, speaking in a near whisper: "We're being jammed. Maybe. Or a crow just shit on the Verizon antenna. How's the Internet?"

"It was fine, the last time I looked," Letty told her. "Craig says we're monitoring the attack on Gomel and it's looking good, and so is Voronezh. They've scrambled the manifests in both places and turned around a lot of cars that were carrying army rations and diesel, so . . ." '

Jack stuck his head into the hallway and called, "Hey: The Net just went down. Everywhere."

Letty passed that along.

Kaiser, quietly: "They're here and they'll be coming in. We've got to get the computer people ready to move. Probably want to put them in the hallways . . . mattresses on the floor. Tables people can get under and stay lower than the brick walls. We need to find all available fire extinguishers."

"You better get up here and organize that," Letty said. "I'll be coming down the driveway right now."

Letty went back down the driveway, trying to sneak up on Kaiser, who said, "I saw you coming when you stepped out of the motel door."

"Liar."

"It was like watching a dump truck back over empty soda cans," Kaiser said.

"We'll discuss this at a later time," Letty said. "Along with your other misrepresentations, deceptions, and distortions."

"We'll need to reserve a good block of time, then," Kaiser said. "Listen, my little *Fucking Fabulous* turtle dove . . . They're not here yet, but they're coming. Keep your head down. And your ass."

And he disappeared up the dark driveway.

THEY WEREN'T THERE YET, but they were close.

Volkov was in a sandy turnoff that went a few car lengths back into the brush along the highway into Santa Ynez. Why the turnoff was there, he didn't know. The site had been spotted that afternoon by the scouts and selected and marked on satellite photos as a good place for a command post, out of sight of the highway, but very close to it.

He'd backed the car into the turnoff to make it easier to get out in a hurry; Step was with him, worried by the planned night attack on the motel. He'd shared his view with Volkov that killing was almost always bad for business. Volkov had dismissed the suggestion with an impolite fart noise.

"We are at war and not only with the stupid Ukrainians. With the stupid Americans, also. And the Balts and the Poles and the Hungarians. There will be a lot more dead than two or three here."

"Maybe . . . maybe," Step said. Still bad for business. Not just his business. He'd been reading the *Wall Street Journal*, which was reporting that with the Western boycotts, Russian businesses, all of them, were about to go down the toilet.

After two of his three men had been killed at the SkyPort, Volkov, enraged, had asked for, and had gotten, six more operators. Four of them had flown in from New York and Washington on a private jet, so that weapons and other eyebrow-raising gear, like combat night-vision goggles, were not a problem. Two more had come from San Diego, by car, also with guns and gear. With the surviving man of Volkov's original three, the lucky driver at the SkyPort, they had a force of seven, not counting Volkov or Step.

Volkov had reluctantly agreed that Step's men, who'd been employed as loaders and drivers of contraband merchandise, were not gunmen; they were, however, perfectly good drivers who would drop the gunmen along the highway and pick them up at a prearranged rendezvous after the attacks. The drop-offs included spots a half mile up and down the hill on either side of the motel driveway, from where the operators would walk in. They were all linked to each other, and to Volkov, by radio, with earbuds.

Volkov and Step had driven in first, so they'd be in place when the personnel drops began, at eleven o'clock.

LETTY WAS SITTING in her hole at midnight, chilly and bored, when her radio vibrated twice, the vibrations three seconds apart. Cartwright.

Cartwright said nothing, but Letty and Kaiser knew what the two vibrations meant: somebody was moving in the woods near her. At that instant, Letty heard one piece of brush separated from another, a very quiet, but still audible, ripping sound; a moment later, a leaf was crushed.

Somebody was coming down the hill above her, traversing at the same time, so he would pass above her, headed toward the motel. The stalker was probably wearing night-vision goggles, she thought, because he was moving so confidently; she prayed they weren't thermals, or he'd see her heat signature. Against that possibility, she slowly, slowly brought the Uzi around her body until the barrel was pointed in the direction of the sounds she'd heard.

Then, moving slowly as paste, she took her radio out of a pocket and squeezed the transmit button twice, as Cartwright had: another person in the woods. She got a single vibration back from Cartwright, in acknowledgment.

There were more light disturbances, all moving above and past her. Not like a squirrel, or a small animal; those tended to be noisy as they scavenged through ground litter for hidden food. This was careful, but larger and heavier. When the noisemaker had moved away, twenty yards, thirty yards, forty, Letty risked moving, slowly rolling over on one hip, then standing, keeping one of her trees between herself and the intruder.

She dipped back in her pocket, to the radio, and squeezed it three times, the signal that she was moving herself, so Cartwright and Kaiser would know.

The man in the dark stopped moving for a moment, and she froze. Then he started again, and she took a step from behind the trees, toward him. As long as he moved, she did, not trying to close the distance, waiting until he was approaching the motel, where he'd be silhouetted against the light.

She made three moves, tracking him. She was ultracautious,

aware that there might be a third man in the woods, a spotter, looking for anyone who might interfere with the attack. She was behind a screen of saplings and underbrush when she caught a glimpse of the man in front of her, or his head, against the glow of the motel lights.

His head seemed almost round, and too large—a helmet, she thought—which meant that he'd also be wearing body armor. She waited a minute, motionless, then another minute, and he began to move again.

His head, or helmet, seemed to be floating; she couldn't see his body, which meant that he was dressed all in black, or in dark forest camo. She moved again, hanging back, watching as he closed in on the motel.

A HUNDRED YARDS up the hillside, another man was moving more quickly, and less silently, down the hill. He loomed out of the darkness like some mythical golem, wearing black body armor, a helmet, and probably night-vision goggles, Cartwright thought.

Depending on the sophistication of the goggles, and their reaction to the lights of the motel, he might have taken them off, in which case he would be as blind as she was.

He moved in fits and starts, pushing brush out of the way with what probably was a longer weapon than the Minis that the hotel gunmen had carried. She was unmoving, low to the ground, behind the jumble of the trunk and branches of a fallen tree. The golem would cross the line of her weapon with a few more steps, and she reached into a pocket and found the radio and pushed the transmit button and held it down for a full five seconds.

She was signaling that she was preparing to take a shot. If the golem was wearing typical body armor, he would be vulnerable around the neck, the armpits, and the lower body. He began moving, became more visible as he got close to the motel lights.

She waited, took a breath, adjusted her sight line, and when he stepped into it, fired a burst of three shots *bapbapbap* into his legs, knocking him down. He screamed involuntarily and collapsed, but she could still make out his helmeted head and she fired another burst at a point she believed would be below the rim of the helmet, then bounded toward him, and when ten feet away, fired another burst below the helmet.

"One down," she blurted into the radio, and then ducked back under the cover of a two-trunked tree, sat and froze.

When the gunshots blew out through the trees, three bursts in measured succession, the man Letty was tracking first did a crouch, and then he actually stood up, as if to see better to his left. Letty couldn't see the front sights on her Mini as well as she might have wished, but with what she could see and what she could guess, leveled the weapon and fired a burst.

The man dropped—dropped, he wasn't simply ducking—and almost certainly had been hit. She moved closer, using trees as cover, until she could see his body as a dark shape. She fired another short burst into his pelvic area, and a third into his neckline.

She dropped into the nearest cover and said into the radio, "Another one down here."

The hackers freaked out when they heard the bursts of gunfire. Some rolled onto the floor, from their beds, some crawled to the hallway doors and looked out, to see if anyone knew what was happening.

Kaiser was in the hall with his M4 and he shouted, "Everybody out of bed, into the hallway, stay below the level of the brick walls." He shouted it three times, and in a few minutes, all the hackers and their friends and families were in the hallway, on the floor.

Catrin's German shepherd took cover under a table, her tail curled tightly around her, and Catrin said, "She thinks they're fireworks. She hates fireworks."

Kaiser had awakened Bunker when Cartwright's first alert came in, and she was sitting on the end of her bed, looking at the camera feeds, when she saw a man in SWAT-team black, with a black mask and a helmet, come out of the trees below the motel, moving carefully toward it between guest cars.

She shouted down the hall, "John, there's a guy in the parking lot coming up to the guest wing, not the hack wing, the guest wing. He came up the hill from the front. He's using cars for cover."

Jane Longstreet stepped into Bunker's room: "I heard that. We're sure he's a Russian?"

"He's carrying a suppressed Mini," Bunker said. "It's down by his side, but it's there. He has night-vision goggles up on his forehead. He must have pushed them up when he got close to the motel."

The caretaker, awaked by the gunfire, came running down the hallway dressed in a white tee-shirt and boxer shorts, saw hacks moving into the hall on hands and knees, and shouted, "Hey! Hey! What's the hell's going on out there?"

Kaiser waved his weapon at the man: "Get down. Get down below the bricks."

The man didn't; he turned and ran the other way, disappearing into the center entry area. Longstreet ran after him, got to the corner and looked down the center wing, saw guests moving out of the far wing and toward the front desk. She shouted at them, "Go back! Go back! There's an active shooter. Stay below the bricks . . ."

Bunker called, her voice cool: "The bogie is across from the end of the guest wing . . . John, can you take him from where you are?"

Kaiser on the radio, said, "I got a bad angle and got cars in the way, I'll have to come down there."

Longstreet overheard and shouted back, "Stay where you are, cover our folks. I'll take this guy."

Kaiser: "Are you sure about that, Jane? I might be able to take him when he clears the cars . . ."

"I'm not sure he's going to do that. He might try to kick the service door at the end of the guest wing," Longstreet shouted. "I'll take a look."

"Careful."

"Always." She stepped over to a wastebasket and pulled out the plastic bag inside of it. There wasn't much inside of it, but what there was weighed it down. She wrapped the top around her left hand and trotted through the entry wing, moving fast past the glass door, around the corner into the guest wing, where some of the very few guests were in the hallway, barefoot in jeans and sleepwear, and she shouted, "Get down, get down, active shooter."

They saw the Beretta in her hand and most went to the floor, while one couple dodged back into their room. Somebody was screaming like a child might, high-pitched and spasmodic, but it wasn't a child; Longstreet thought it might be a man.

Another man was moving up behind her, and when she turned, she realized it was Baxter. "Probably ought to stay back," she said.

"Don't worry, I will, but just in case you need something . . ."

She nodded. "Okay. Don't come through the door, though."

"I thought you had one of those Uzis," Baxter said.

"I do, but I like my Beretta," she said.

At the end of the hall, the door under a red exit sign was closed and locked from outside, but not inside. Longstreet had her Beretta in her right hand, next to her side, safety off, cocked, ready to fire. Taking a breath, she turned the doorknob with her bag hand, whispered to Baxter, "Steady, now, stay back . . ." then bumped the door open with her hip.

THE RUSSIAN WAS down to her left, moving toward the door. She pushed out, carrying the bag, turned toward the Russian, who'd frozen when the door began to open. His right hand carried the Mini pointed at the door, and then in Longstreet's direction, but not exactly at her.

She was a black woman, carrying a garbage bag, who'd stopped, open-mouthed, when she saw him. She registered his face, dark eyebrows, and he registered the garbage bag, and might have mistaken her for a member of the oppressed proletariat. He lifted his left hand and put a finger across his lips, signaling that she should be quiet.

LONGSTREET SAID TO HIM, "Quiet, my ass," snapped the Beretta up to hip height and as he began to react to the gun, shot him through the nose, directly below the lenses of the night-vision goggles he'd pushed up on his forehead. Not quite fast enough, because he'd been fast as well, pulling the trigger at the same instant that she had. A single nine-millimeter slug hit her at the side of her butt, two more in her midsection, and she went down.

Baxter, in the doorway, screamed, "No," and reached out and grabbed her by her shirt and at the same time looked left at the Russian, who was on his back, not moving. Baxter dragged Longstreet into the motel and she groaned and said, "Sonofabitch hit me in the butt. Get Kaiser . . ."

Baxter ran to the end of the hall, where it turned to the office, and shouted, "Kaiser! John!"

Kaiser shouted back, "You okay?"

"Jane's been hit. Bring your med kit."

Kaiser disappeared for a minute, then came running down the hall with a medical bag. When they got back to Longstreet, they found her lying on the floor, wide-awake, looking more angry than hurt.

Kaiser helped her unhook her jeans, and armored vest, and then he and Baxter rolled her up on her uninjured hip. Kaiser pulled her underpants down to look at the wound, as a stream of blood ran down her hip. He said, "It's through-and-through. You're bleeding, but you're not gonna die. You're not even gonna limp, but we need to get you to the hospital in the next few days . . ."

"I . . . felt like I got hit in the gut," Longstreet gasped.

Kaiser nodded. "You did. Right in the armor. You got two nine-millimeter holes in the front of your armor, but nothing coming out the back of it. You're gonna have bruises, you're gonna look like some asshole jabbed you with a pool cue a couple of times."

Made her half laugh, but then she gasped and said, "It's starting to hurt."

"I got something for that." Kaiser dug in the med kit and said to Baxter, "Go get some guys. Bring that old man's, the night manager's, cot down here, we'll use it as a stretcher and move her over to the other wing, next to me."

Baxter ran to do that, was back in a minute with Able and the cot. As they came up, Kaiser was putting an auto-inject syringe back in the med kit and said, "I'm killing the pain, she'll be sleepy in a bit. Let's move her."

As he and Able did that, Baxter went to the outer door, opened it, and stuck his head outside. The Russian hadn't moved; he was ten feet to the left. Kaiser called, "What are you doing?"

"Be right back," Baxter said. He ran to the Russian, picked up the Mini Uzi by his side, yanked off the night-vision goggles, turned, saw a couple of Mini magazines poking out of pouches on the dead man's vest, grabbed them, and ran back into the motel.

"That was stupid," Kaiser snapped.

"Yeah, but I got a gun, and some night-vision goggles for you, if you want them."

"I'll take them," Kaiser said. "Let's move Jane."

Kaiser and Able picked up the cot and Kaiser said to Baxter, "See if you can find some furniture to block the doors. Anything that would slow down an entry."

"Got it," Baxter said. "I'll do it now." He held up the Mini and the magazines. "I think I know how to use this, but . . . maybe you can give me some tips."

"Yeah, right," Kaiser said, and he and Able carried Longstreet down the hall and around the corner.

When Longstreet was in the yoga room, in a corner next to the brick wall, Kaiser called Letty and Cartwright on the handset and told them what had happened. "I stopped the bleeding and we got another one. That's three down. But Jane needs a hospital as soon as we can get her to one."

Neither Letty nor Cartwright risked a vocal answer. Both gave the transmit button a single squeeze, in acknowledgment.

Baxter got one of the guests to help him carry a couch to the door at the end of the hallway, and they wedged it between the hall walls and against the door. "Nobody coming through there," Baxter said. He'd slung the Mini over his shoulder and the man kept looking at it. "Mini Uzi," Baxter said. "Took it off a dead Russian."

VOLKOV WAS TAKING REPORTS from his men, and he didn't like what he was hearing, and not hearing. He could get no response from three of them, and they'd heard three different bursts of gunfire; he suspected that was not a coincidence.

He had two men still in the trees, approaching the motel from the far side, another hiking up the hill to a point where he could cover the main doors of the hotel, and a fourth moving down the highway toward the driveway that led to the hotel.

One of them called in: there was no door on the far side, only at the ends of the wings of the U-shaped structure, and another in the middle of the back side, opposite the front door. "Our best chance is to approach the side and to go through a window. Once we're inside, we will be among them."

"Do what you can," Volkov said. "We are taking casualties."

"We know," the man had replied, dryly. "We can hear machine guns."

Volkov had no answer for that, so he didn't answer.

BUNKER, WATCHING HER CAMERAS, saw the two men break from the trees and run to the side of the motel, and she shouted down the hall at Kaiser, "We've got two bogies on the side of the guest wing. Right in the middle. Looks like they might try to go through a window."

Kaiser shouted, "I'm coming."

A moment later, he ran past her, and past the lobby with its glass door in a fraction of a second; there was no response from the Russians outside, and he continued running to the far wing, where Baxter was sitting behind a couch, the Mini propped atop it. A half-dozen chairs and couches scattered down the hallway in what amounted to an obstacle course that would slow anyone running down it but wouldn't provide any protection from a gun.

"Good idea. But we've got . . ."

"I heard," Baxter said. He picked up the Mini and said, "I figured out the gun. Pretty simple. And there's nobody in those outer rooms, so if somebody comes out . . . it's them."

Kaiser stared at him for just a second or two, then said, "When you pull the trigger, the barrel will try to ride up. Push down at the top of it. Don't block the ejection gate, that's . . ."

"I know where it is," Baxter said. "Like I said, it's a simple machine."

A dozen guests were spread along the hallway, lying on the floor, and Kaiser called, as quietly as he could, and still be heard, "Listen, folks, you all crawl down to the far end. Do it now, crawl. Stay low."

They started scrambling down the hall and Baxter said, "Ten rooms down the outside. If they're in the middle, we should probably hear them breaking in."

"I'll go," Kaiser said. "You wait here."

"Nah," Baxter said. "I'm coming."

Kaiser didn't argue. They went down the hall, to the middle of the hallway, and stopped there, between doors, and listened. From the other end of the motel, Bunker called, "Incoming."

And they heard the window glass break, and then more breakage: apparently there was no way to do it silently. The noise stopped, and Kaiser whispered, "They're probably inside."

"Yes."

"They'll open the door to peek out. When they do it, I'm going to unload on them," Kaiser said. "You don't shoot unless you see me go down. And for Christ's sakes, don't shoot me. Be ready if one of them comes out through the door and I'm down or reloading."

Baxter said, "Yes."

They waited.

VOLKOV TOOK A REPORT from the two men: "We're inside the motel room. Nobody in here. There's a connecting door, so we have two rooms. We're going to move out into the hallway."

"Let me know when you command that wing," Volkov said.

"Moving now."

A moment later, Volkov and Step heard the roar of an automatic weapon, and not one of theirs. That was followed by another burst that Volkov was sure was a Mini. The exchange was brief, but at the rate of fire of modern weapons, a lot of lead had been blown downrange.

Volkov, urgently: "Six, report. Report. Six, report."

Long silence.

Step, slouched in the passenger seat, said, "I don't think Vanya and Dima will be reporting. I think they're dead."

IN THE MOTEL, Kaiser had been waiting for the door to open and when it did, he pulled the trigger on his M4, hosing down the door and the thin walls on both sides of it. When he stopped firing, there was a gap of absolute silence, deepened by the fact that both he and Baxter had been semi-deafened by the gunfire. Nothing was coming back at them and Kaiser punched out the magazine and slapped another one in place, dropped to his stomach and poked at the shattered door with his gun barrel. A man lay on the other side, thoroughly chopped up, a gun by his outspread arm.

As Kaiser moved his barrel to cover the rest of the room, looking for the second body, the next door down the hall began to open and Baxter saw it and said, "John, there's . . ." But then he saw the gun barrel leading a man through the doorway and he pointed the Uzi and squeezed the trigger, aiming it like he would a Super Soaker, and squirted out the full magazine into the door and wall beside it.

He was accurate enough; Kaiser had rolled and turned, his gun aimed down the hall, and he blurted, "What?"

Baxter said, "Gun . . ."

Kaiser crawled down to the door, did a quick peek inside, then turned and stood. "Got him," he said. He stepped back to look in the first room, slapped Baxter on the back and said, "Good job, buddy. Saved both our lives. Get that guy's gun, his goggles, and his magazines. I'll strip my guy. Block the door with a couch when you're back out."

He went back to the first man. Baxter stood in the doorway looking at the man he'd killed, and said aloud, "Oh, my God."

The man he was looking at had been alive and vital one minute earlier, and now he was dead, and Baxter had killed him. Standing there, looking at the body, he had a moment of clarity about Letty and Cartwright: "Better you than me," he said.

He fiddled with his Mini for a moment, dropped the magazine, and snapped another one in place, pulled the charging handle and let it snap forward to get another round in place.

"Better you . . ."

AND STEP HAD SAID, "I don't think Vanya and Dima will be reporting. I think they're dead."

"Silence. One more word . . ." Volkov went back on the radio. "Two, where are you now?"

"In the trees, thirty meters above the driveway entrance."

"I'm coming down the hill to join you," Volkov said. "We've taken casualties."

"I will watch for you. Come quietly."

Volkov had another Mini on the floor behind the passenger seat, along with a pair of night-vision goggles. He checked the Mini's magazine, put another magazine in his jacket pocket, switched on the night-vision goggles and pulled them over his head. He said to Step, "You will wait here. I'm going to meet Ilya, to assess the situation."

"You don't need to go anywhere to assess it," Step said. "You have only two men left. One is in a terrible position at the front of the hotel; you should pull him out. The other . . . I don't think you should join him. There has already been shooting near the end of the driveway."

"This is necessary," Volkov said. "You will wait here, but move over to the driver's seat in case we have to go quickly. If we call you, come fast."

"I will listen for your call," Step said.

Volkov wasn't often directly involved in what spy novelists called "wet work"; he was a supervisor and an executive, not a blue-collar worker. But he was desperate to stop the hacking. The top authorities at the GRU knew what the threat was, and he'd been sent to stop it.

If it wasn't stopped . . . he would just as desperately need the money he'd stashed in case of such a failure. He was thinking Costa Rica, or possibly Chile. He'd been stationed at the Russian embassies in Venezuela and Guatemala and spoke decent Spanish.

Still, he'd prefer not to run, so here he was, walking down a dark highway with a gun in his hand, above an obscure motel in Santa Ynez, California.

Ilya hissed at him as he approached, and Volkov moved into the trees. The other man, dressed all in black, put his face close to Volkov's ear and said, "There may be a shooter at the far end of the motel, in the woods."

"Will she have goggles?"

"I don't know. She could—her own or taken from us. I ask you, what is the goal now? They are barricaded inside the hotel and they may have operators out here in the trees."

Volkov whispered back: "The goal is to see if there is anything more to be done. We'll approach the hotel, assess the defenses, and decide then."

LETTY HEARD THEM coming before she could see them. She was wearing the night-vision goggles taken from the man she'd killed. They were not the latest or best model and everything was outlined in a brilliant acid green. She'd trained with more modern goggles, which translated everything into white light; still, she could see in the dark.

When she heard the footsteps above her and toward the highway, she signaled to Cartwright, Kaiser, and Bunker. Kaiser swore once, then pressed the transmit button and said, "Letty, Barbara, whoever just pressed the transmit button: we've knocked down five of them and I doubt there'll be many more. Don't take any unnecessary risks; I think they'll be pulling back."

He got back a single vibration as an acknowledgment.

VOLKOV AND ILYA moved as soundlessly as they could down the hill toward the motel, which was the one source of light in the post-midnight darkness of the valley. Sometimes, stepping out from behind a tree, they'd catch too much light, and the night-vision lenses would overload and flare before the autogating could reduce the sensitivity.

Ilya was carrying a Mini Uzi, and their movement wasn't soundless. The brush constantly dragged at them, snagging their clothes and hats and ski masks. Volkov's involvement in the attack had genuine tactical aspects—he'd shoot somebody if he had to, and if he could—but also, and more importantly, it had display aspects. He was displaying his bravery and selflessness should they be reviewed at the Aquarium, as GRU headquarters was called.

He was, actually, fairly brave; not enough for a medal, but he was prepared to take reasonable risks. The risks in attacking a group of computer hackers were less, in his opinion, than the risks of fucking with his bosses.

As he and Ilya moved down the hill toward the motel, they came up to a tree that had perhaps been blown over by a storm. At the base of the tree, there existed a hole, invisible in the dark, even with the night-vision goggles, and Volkov fell into it.

Stunned by the fall, he thrashed about, cursing, not understanding quite what had happened; his night-vision goggles got pushed cockeyed, and Ilya whispered, harshly, "What are you doing?"

"Get me . . ." Volkov lifted one hand that he might be helped back to his feet, from the awkward position in the hole, and used the other hand to push the night-vision goggles back in front of his eyes. He did that just in time to see Ilya's head explode, followed instantly by the sound of a shot.

The no-longer-living Ilya fell on top of him and Volkov pressed deeper into the hole and let Ilya bleed on him. Moving, he thought, would not be a good idea; he was prepared to remain in his hole all night, if need be. While he really was somewhat brave, he was not imprudent, and one thing he knew for sure: he was not alone in the woods.

AFTER FIRING AT THE MAN coming down the hill, and seeing him drop, Letty sank back into her hole. Kaiser, speaking through her earbud, asked, "If you can, pull back to the motel. Staying out is too risky: I believe we've won this thing, no point in dying now."

She squeezed the transmit button to acknowledge the call. Thinking it over, she decided that Kaiser was probably right. And with the night-vision goggles, she could probably see somebody coming through the trees after her, if there was anyone else out there.

Moving an inch at a time, she crawled out of her hole, and staying on her hands and knees, began crawling crabwise across the hillside, parallel to the driveway.

VOLKOV HEARD HER GO. If he could hear her, she could hear him. So he let her go, the sound of her departure dwindling as she moved farther away through the trees. When he could no longer hear her, he risked a move on his own, pushing Ilya's body away and beginning to crawl through the trees to the highway.

No one interfered. He hunkered by the highway, listening, then scurried across it and into the trees on the far side, waited for a minute, then two, listening again, then began trudging uphill toward the car. He'd lost six men; he'd recall the one remaining and warn Washington of a possible disaster coming their way, although the identities of the men, he'd been told, had been scrubbed clean.

As he withdrew, he warned himself to move slowly, to use his night vision to scan the far side of the highway for any sign of movement. There was none, and twenty minutes later he arrived at the car and found Step sitting in the passenger seat with the side window down.

"We have . . ." he said.

STEP WAS A very good businessman, and like experienced businessmen everywhere, he knew when to cut his losses. Volkov would be deflecting blame for what now looked like a disaster, and there weren't many survivors left to blame.

Step was one.

Volkov didn't get to finish the sentence because Step shot him three times, rapidly and accurately, twice in the throat and once in the head and Volkov dropped in the weeds at the side of the turnoff.

Step got out of the car, sat by a wheel, and waited for any movement. After five minutes, looking the whole time at the lump that was Volkov, he stood, grabbed Volkov by the jacket collar, and, after checking both ways, dragged the body across the highway and into the woods, and left it there, another victim of the firefight, of the psycho women, or so he would claim.

That accomplished, he ran back to the car, got on the radio and called, "Pickup. Pickup. Operation canceled, drivers and operators, go to designated pickups."

He got back one acknowledgment and he sighed. Bad business, he thought. Bad business, and bad *for* business.

THAT WAS THE END OF IT. Letty, Cartwright, Kaiser, Bunker, and now Baxter stayed on guard the rest of the night, and in the morning, almost certain that the Russians had retreated, put the coders in their cars and told them to scatter before the cops and the FBI arrived.

Able collected the boxes of computer chips, and the coders headed back to Los Angeles. They would move on from there, as soon as Able delivered the cash. Letty told them not to tell anyone where they'd be; to tell not even her, so she couldn't be forced to tell the cops or the FBI or the NSA. She gave all of them the number of her NSA phone so they could call if there was trouble.

She told Sovern that as soon as they had phone service, to call the FBI and report the shootout, and its location, and to tell them that they needed an ambulance at the motel.

Then they waited. But not for long.

As clusterfucks went, this one was epic; bureaucrats would be telling the story to their grandchildren.

TWENTY-EIGHT

Two months later:

A slate-colored rain slashed down sideways, obscuring the shrines of empire arrayed around her. Back down Constitution Avenue, the Washington Monument had been a humble white stump, its peak invisible in the lowering gray clouds.

The air smelled good and clean, except for the sidewalk worms: not bad for late April, a sign that spring had arrived.

The rain had been coming down, more or less steadily, for two days, and on the Virginia side of the Potomac, a sodden pro-Ukraine protest, drenched marchers with their blue-and-yellow flags, stomped resolutely toward the bridge over the river, where a platoon of wet cops waited.

Letty was wearing a red-and-white rainsuit designed for sailing, over jeans and a cable-knit sweater, and was dry from her chin to her ankles and from her eyebrows up, and warm. She'd walked across the Potomac from Arlington, which had seemed like a good idea at the time, but now she was tired of hearing the storm beat against her hood, the spray droplets trickling across her face.

THE SHOOTOUTS IN CALIFORNIA had created a monthlong bureaucratic bun fight, with ramifications still rattling around the intelligence and law-enforcement agencies. The essential problem was that a top secret operation, which was still top secret, had gone public. The FBI, the DHS, the CIA, the NSA, and the California Bureau of Investigation all had fingers in the pie.

The feds were trying to elbow the local authorities out of the case, and it looked as though they would succeed. With the eyes on the federal investigation going all the way to the top, Colles had suggested to Letty, Baxter, Cartwright, and the Ladies that they no longer had to worry about the outcome.

Letty wasn't sure she believed that, because even one poorly placed bureaucrat could cause trouble. On the other hand, the people who you *never, ever* wanted to cross seemed to be on her side.

And it was all classified top secret.

Arseny Stepashin was nowhere to be found. Listening devices both inside and outside a Russian spy center in San Diego picked up the name, and a hint that he'd flown out of Los Angeles and was now in Moscow.

The report was incorrect; he and Victoria, now with new names and passports, were relaxing in the sunshine of the Sunshine State: Miami, to be precise, where they fit right in. Step was in talks with Wesley Bunne (Bob) and Sharon Pecker (Sue) about the possibility of funding a new software enterprise. They all agreed it looked promising.

Boyadjian, Lawrence, and Martin had been turned upside down by the FBI, but there'd be no prosecution, for lack of cooperating witnesses, and because the government really didn't want to deal with defense attorneys' demands for disclosure. Besides, it was all top secret.

LONGSTREET, A MONTH after the shooting, was still in physical therapy, but didn't think she needed it anymore. She was sanguine about her scar and pleased with her kill-shot outside the motel. She didn't talk about it with the Ladies, but they all knew about it, because Letty and Cartwright told them, despite the fact that her wounds, and the source of them, were classified. A little extra cachet for the Lady.

Baxter had driven his truck back to Maryland. He hadn't flown, because they wouldn't have let him fly with a Mini and six magazines, which he wanted to keep. Back home, he also bought a Beretta 92 and started working out at a gun range. He'd never be in a class with Letty, Cartwright, Longstreet, or Kaiser, but he wasn't bad at it. He knew machines and geometry, and shooting was machines and geometry.

His NSA career had gotten a boost—word about the motel shooting had gotten around, and he was looked upon with the kind of respect that only gunfighters get. Although he was doing well, he was also talking to Cartwright about her security service concept. If it got off the ground, she could use a competent hacker with government connections . . .

So he was happy, though he hadn't lost any weight, and occasionally, in the night, saw in his mind's eye a blood-soaked, bullet-riddled body in a motel doorway.

George Hewitt sold his six boxes of stolen Intel chips to a dealer in Austin, Texas, for a price that was way too low, but enough to realize his dream of starting a horse motel, catering to horse transport trailers, off I-40 near Elk City, Oklahoma. The business would thrive from the start, and he would later be welcomed into the Elk City Golf and Country Club.

Daniel Delph's body, buried in the Mojave, would never be found.

So LETTY WAS CRUISING through the rain on a cool spring morning, heading for work, not thinking about much except that the rain had become increasingly annoying. Acting on impulse, she ducked into the Smithsonian Institution to get out of the downpour. No plans to go to the Smithsonian, no plans to look at anything in particular. The Smithsonian was the closest open door and that was good enough.

The metal detector at the Smithsonian's door beeped as she went through. Letty already had her credentials case in her hand with the federal carry permit and Senate ID. She handed it to the door guard as she folded down her hood. The guard looked at both documents, then at her, and at the documents again, and asked, "Are you sure you're old enough for this?"

"I'm sure," Letty said.

A supervisor had come over. He looked at the docs, raised his eyebrows, took a closer look at her and said, "Letty Davenport. You're the young woman on the bridge."

"Yes. If we're talking about the Pershing Bridge."

"She's good," the supervisor said to the guard.

A thoroughly soaked man, folding an inadequate umbrella, was standing past the guards, looking at her, as he shook himself like a dog.

He had unkempt reddish-brown hair, a three-day beard, wore khaki-colored canvas shorts and hiking boots with the top of the socks turned down. Steel-rimmed glasses spattered with drizzle. A long-sleeved overshirt, sleeves rolled to his elbows, was worn open to reveal a John Lee Hooker tee-shirt. Tiny beads of water clung to his forearm and lower-leg hair. He was square, rather than lanky, like SpongeBob SquarePants, and not unlike Able in form.

He sort of looked, Letty thought, like Theodore Roosevelt.

Letty had always been attracted to lanky men, tall, thin, V-shaped, third basemen and shooting guards and wide receivers. This guy looked like he did squats for entertainment and could roll a Prius if he could get a grip on it. Square face, heavy shoulders, thick neck. He wasn't quite scowling but had managed to make himself totally unattractive.

As she went past him, he ran a hand through his wet hair and asked, "The Pershing Bridge. You still carrying a gun?"

"Maybe," she said, and kept walking. She turned right toward Fossils. When she glanced back, she saw that he'd kept going straight toward Human Origins. She was used to having men pay attention to her, at least for a while; this guy was paying no attention at all.

Which was the beginning of an improbable sequence of events that found her, three weeks later, naked, flat on her back on his bed, a vanilla-scented candle burning in the corner, while Jackson Nyberg slowly stroked her with his tongue.

This was inappropriate for an initial sexual episode, she thought—or rather, she later *thought* she thought—and she later thought she tried to say, "Let's not go there yet," but remembered herself, dimly, saying instead, "Ark, ark, ark," like Sunny the Seal. Then she'd stopped thinking about anything in particular, although she was aware of her heels drumming on his lank white bachelor sheets . . .

Variations of which happened more than once that night. The

next morning, perhaps the tiniest bit dazed, she arrived at the Senate Office Building carrying her briefcase and a gallon jug of margarita mix for an upcoming office party.

A freckled, redheaded female friend glanced at her, then looked again, and said, "Wow."

Letty stopped, turned: "What?"

"You look," the redhead said, "like the most thoroughly fucked woman in Washington, DC. That takes some *serious* butter-churning."

Letty blushed, an automatic but unfamiliar reaction. "Janet! Jesus!"

"Hey, it's not a bad thing," Janet said. "But you rarely see somebody who breaks into the top ten, much less hits number one."

"Shut up," Letty said as she unlocked her office door, smiling down at the key.

Janet: "Am I hearing a denial? I think not."

JACKSON NYBERG WAS an archaeologist who specialized in the preservation, and occasionally the excavation, of ancient Native American sites. He was half North Dakota Swede and half North Dakota Sioux—or, as he said, North Dakota Dakota—enrolled as a member of the Spirit Lake band.

One reason they got along, Letty thought, was that they'd grown up only a couple of road hours apart, in a cold, bleak, sparsely populated part of the country, and in equally tough circumstances. Simple survival had made them equally stubborn and equally independent.

A week after they began dating, Nyberg had met Kaiser, who later said, "I like him. I believe he's a good guy. Doesn't know shit about guns, though. Interesting that he doesn't drink at all."

"He told me two of his grandparents were alcoholics," Letty said.

"That's a problem for a lot of Indians . . ."

"Actually, it was his Swedish grandparents," Letty said. "He told me that in the old days, out there on the prairie, in the winter, there was nothing to do but drink and screw, and you could only screw so much. He said at the end, his grandfather committed suicide by chugging three bottles of homemade rye whisky. He died on the living room floor of acute alcohol poisoning while his drunk wife sat there on the couch, looking at him."

"Nice story," Kaiser said. "Different times."

Then Kaiser tried to hit her with a stick. Letty parried with her cane, which she'd kept when she got home from California. Kaiser was ready for that, deflected the parry, and whacked her on the ass. She said, "Ouch!" and "Cheater! We were talking!"

"Making sure you're alert," Kaiser said. "America needs more lerts."

He was joking, but he was serious about improvised weapons: she'd have a bruise. When they'd finished the stick-fighting drills, they changed into street clothes and walked out to a Starbucks.

Their street clothes included guns, of course. They didn't even have to think about that.

LETTY AND NYBERG were in Nyberg's bed at nine o'clock one night, Letty's head in the crook of his shoulder. He'd been in Colorado, looking at a roadside cut that might have uncovered an ancient burial ground, and had gotten back in town at six o'clock.

They'd smoked a little weed, were bathed in the odors of marijuana and melting vanilla candle wax—Nyberg only had one candle, so vanilla was what you got—and were talking about nothing, when her cell phone buzzed on a bedside stand. She picked it up and looked at the screen.

"Girlfriend," she said. Cartwright. "You back home?"

"For the time being," Cartwright said.

"How's Sovern?"

"Sovern is Sovern. In his own terms, he's just fine."

"Oh-oh. The good looks wear off?"

"Not really. I'll be going back out, time and again. You know, for a refresher. As a matter of fact, the intermittent thing is his preference and that's fine with me, too. What are you up to?"

"Relaxing with a friend."

"Nyberg?"

"Yes. Is this conversation going anywhere? If not . . . I would like to get back to relaxing. We could talk tomorrow."

"I wanted to tell you that the Justice Department has assigned the overall investigation of . . . what happened in California . . . to a lawyer named Jason Goff," Cartwright said. "Goff is regarded as the laziest, dumbest, least effective lawyer in the department and is treasured for those qualities. Assign a case to Goff and it's as good as dead, but nobody can say that Justice didn't look into it."

"He does sound useful."

"Yes. He's widely known in the bar association as Jerk Goff. He's already been disciplined twice for inexcusable error. Anyway, I thought you'd like to know. You can go back to relaxing."

"I will. Want to go up to the Ladies next week?" Letty asked.

"Sure. Let's do rifles," Cartwright said. "I know where I can get my hands on a sneak version of what's gonna be the Army's new infantry rifle, a 6.8 millimeter XM-5 from Sig, and you're a Sig girl. The military version of the cartridge will crack Level 4 armor, as I hear it. I'll give you a call."

She clicked off and Nyberg asked, "What was that all about?"

"Oh, the usual," Letty said. "Guns and men."

"Yeah?"

"Yeah . . . And you know." She picked up her 938 from the bed-stand, cocked and locked, ready to go. "Mostly guns."